Praise for Mary Sullivan

"Brilliant…Mary Sullivan pens a heart-warming
story about the healing power of love…
that will tug at the heart and leave us smiling."
—*CataRomance* on *A Cowboy's Plan*

"The addition of a secondary romance
adds depth and complexity to this story."
—*RT Book Reviews* on *This Cowboy's Son*

"Sullivan has written an exciting, first-rate tale
that will have you holding your breath one
moment and reaching for a tissue the next."
—*USATODAY.com*'s *Happy Ever After* blog
on *No Ordinary Sheriff*

"Sullivan has woven a web of deceit, excitement
and thrills while still managing to find
the lighter side of love and emotion."
—*Fresh Fiction* on *No Ordinary Sheriff*

"A poignant tale of two wounded souls who
find comfort, love and ultimately happiness."
—*The Romance Reader* on *No Ordinary Cowboy*

"*Because of Audrey* by Mary Sullivan
is a wonderfully written story with great characters,
side characters and wonderfully merging
different storylines."
—*HarlequinJunkie.com*

MARY SULLIVAN

grew up a daydreamer amid the pop and fizz of Toronto's multicultural community, wondering why those around her didn't have stories rattling around in their brains, too. New ideas continue to pop into her head, often at the strangest moments. Snatches of conversations or newspaper articles or song lyrics—everything is fodder for her imagination. Be careful what you say around her. It might end up in a novel! She loves to hear from readers. To learn more about Mary or to contact her, please visit her at www.marysullivanbooks.com.

MARY SULLIVAN

Home on the Ranch: Montana

♦HARLEQUIN® THE COWBOY COLLECTION

Recycling programs
for this product may
not exist in your area.

ISBN-13: 978-0-373-60657-3

HOME ON THE RANCH: MONTANA

Copyright © 2014 by Harlequin Books S.A.

The publisher acknowledges the copyright holder
of the individual works as follows:

A COWBOY'S PLAN
Copyright © 2010 by Mary Sullivan

THIS COWBOY'S SON
Copyright © 2010 by Mary Sullivan

This edition published by arrangement with Harlequin Books S.A.

For questions and comments about the quality of this book,
please contact us at CustomerService@Harlequin.com.

® and TM are trademarks of the publisher. Trademarks indicated with ® are registered in the United States Patent and Trademark Office, the Canadian Intellectual Property Office and in other countries.

Printed in U.S.A.

CONTENTS

A COWBOY'S PLAN   7

THIS COWBOY'S SON   269

A COWBOY'S PLAN

To my wonderful agent, Pamela Hopkins;
thank you for having faith in my writing.

To my editor, Wanda Ottewell;
thank you for your amazing editing skills,
but even more for your love of a good story.

CHAPTER ONE

C. J. WRIGHT STARED at the stubborn jut of his son's jaw and prayed for patience.

"I want Gramps." The request in Liam's whisper-soft voice hurt more than C.J. could say.

Liam sat at the far side of the table, his nimbus of white-gold hair lit by sun streaming through the kitchen window, turning him into an angel. The kitchen smelled of coffee and bacon and eggs, all of the old familiar scents that should have brought comfort.

C.J. placed the box of breakfast cereal and a spoon on the table in front of Liam, carefully, then stepped away.

"Gramps," he called, "you got a minute?"

"Yep." Gramps's voice drifted from the living room followed by the sounds of him folding the newspaper, then shuffling down the hall. All for the sake of one little boy.

C.J.'s grandfather entered the kitchen, stooped and leaning on his cane. When had his shoulders started to roll forward so much?

Gramps glanced at Liam's mulish expression and said, "Someone else used to look like that when he didn't get his way."

C.J. couldn't smile at Gramps's attempt to lighten the mood, to pretend that Liam's actions were normal for his age. C.J. had never been so stubborn that he wouldn't let his own father take care of him.

Gramps, stalled by the hurt C.J. knew showed on his face, gestured with his head toward the living room. "Take your coffee and go read the paper."

While Gramps poured Liam a bowl of oversweetened cereal, then poured milk on it—doing the things that C.J. wanted to do himself—C.J. passed behind Liam to refill his mug.

Mug full, he reached a hand to the back of his son's head, to stroke it, but thought better of it. Liam would shrug it off anyway.

C.J. set his jaw and strode to the living room. He stopped in front of the window and stared out at the fields lying fallow. Waste of good land. He needed to get the store sold and out of the way so he could ranch full-time.

Always so much damn waiting.

His grandmother's old lace curtains smelled dry and dusty. No wonder. She'd been gone ten years. He noticed something white tangled in the lace. Dental floss. Gramps had used it to mend a tear.

C.J. wouldn't have done any better himself. Weren't they the pair? Now, his young son had entered the house and the job of turning him into a grown man was all on C.J.'s shoulders.

Damn, what a load. C.J. exhaled roughly.

Gramps's two-step limp sounded behind C.J.

"He's eating." Gramps placed one arthritic hand on C.J.'s shoulder. The affection and heat of the touch eased some. "He's still young."

"Am I spoiling him by giving in?"

"With any other kid I'd say yes, but not with Liam. He lived a hard couple of first years."

"What did Vicki tell Liam that makes him dislike me so much?" C.J. cursed her to hell and back. It was bad enough that she was bleeding him dry. Why did she also have to turn his son against him?

"Some kind of poison that made sense in her own mind, I guess." Gramps settled onto the sofa with a huff of pain.

"The drugs changed her," C.J. said. "She wasn't always like that, Gramps. Not at the beginning."

"I know." The newspaper rustled behind C.J.

"Has Liam ever mentioned what his mother said about me?"

"Nope. Not a word."

C.J. stared at his coffee mug on the windowsill. The stains of old coffee, where he'd set his mug on this same windowsill and stared at these same fields, stood testament to the countless mornings he'd done this. Lord, how much longer before Liam began to accept and trust him?

"Keep being kind and patient with the boy," Gramps said. "He'll come around in time."

C.J. paced the length of the room. "It's been eleven months." Eleven long months of bashing his head against Liam's resistance.

He ran his hand over the bristle on his scalp. When he'd brought Liam home to live with him, he'd shaved his hair military short and had traded in cowboy shirts and jeans for more conservative clothing, so damn afraid that Child and Family Services would find some crazy excuse to take the boy away from him. He missed his hair.

Oh, grow up.

C.J. headed for the hallway. He couldn't believe he'd just thought something so stupid. Every change he'd made was worth it if it kept his son safe with him on the ranch.

"You two have a good day." With one hand on the front doorknob, he called, "Liam, you have fun with Gramps today."

No answer. The ring of a spoon against cheap china followed C.J. out the door.

JANEY WILSON CROUCHED in the shade of the weeping willow on the lawn of the Sheltering Arms Ranch. Its branches soughed in the hot breeze scuttling across the Montana landscape.

She stared at the delicate child in front of her whose gaze was as wide-open as the prairie surrounding them.

"Katie," she said, "I can't play with you right now." *Liar.* "I need to go do something." *Coward.* "It's something important I have to do right away. Okay?"

Katie stared with solemn brown doe eyes, silent and wise before her time and so much like Cheryl Janey couldn't breathe.

Sunlight, filtered by the leaves of the tree, dappled Katie's face, underlining the dark circles beneath her eyes and highlighting her sallow skin.

Cancer did terrible things to children.

Unforgivable things.

Janey touched Katie's small shoulders, the thin cotton of her old T-shirt worn soft. She nudged Katie toward the field across the driveway where the ranch's latest batch of inner-city kids played a game of touch football.

"Hey, you little hoodlums," the ranch foreman, Willie, yelled, "this ain't *tackle* football."

Willie lay on the ground under a wriggling pile of giggling children—all of them cancer survivors.

Janey closed her eyes. She couldn't take much more of handling these children daily while her heart bled.

"How long are you going to keep this up?" Startled by the rasp of a bark-dry voice behind her, Janey spun around. Hank Shelter stood on the veranda of his house watching her, his big body relaxed and leaning against a post, but his eyes too perceptive. She tried to hide her pain, but wasn't fast enough.

"How much longer can you do this?" he asked.

Before she answered, he raised a hand. "Don't insult my intelligence by claiming you don't know what I'm talking about."

She exhaled a breath of frustration. "Hank, I'm okay, really. I'm dealing."

"No, you aren't *dealing,* Janey." The regret on Hank's face broke her heart. "You haven't been able to in the year you've lived here."

"I can try harder," she insisted.

Even in the shade, a drop of sweat meandered down Hank's cheek. "Being this close to the kids is killing you."

He left the veranda, his cowboy boots hitting each step with a solid clunk, and approached. Janey tilted her head back to look at him.

"You haven't gotten rid of any of your demons." He gestured toward her clothes. "You're still wearing your armor, but it doesn't seem to be doing you much good."

Janey flushed. True. Here on the ranch her attire wasn't helping her to deal with the children. But on the few times she'd joined Amy to run errands in town, it had sure come in handy.

"I've watched you turn yourself inside out with sorrow," Hank said. "It isn't getting better. It's getting worse.

"*You're* getting worse." He touched her shoulder. She flinched. He dropped his hand. "Sorry."

Hank was a good man, an affectionate one. He liked hugging and touching people. Janey didn't.

Hank gestured to the children in the field. "Working with the kids is wearing you down, and it's killing Amy and me to watch it. Something's got to give."

Janey's heart sank. Her pain was affecting Hank and Amy. She'd thought she'd hidden her grief so well. She couldn't justify harming them. She had to do something, go somewhere. Now.

"As much as we love you," Hank said, "Amy and I can't watch you like this, darlin'. We brought you here to heal, not to cause you more pain."

Janey pressed her hand against her stomach. How could she stand to lose the ranch? If not for the pain the children caused her, it would have been perfect.

Janey caught a glimpse of Amy in the front window, with baby Michael in her arms. Just looking at mother and son started an ache in Janey's chest.

She wanted her own little girl back.

She stilled, willing the ache to pass quickly.

Hank must have detected something in her face, because he glanced over his shoulder and saw his wife and son.

He turned back to her and raised one eyebrow, as if to say, *Get my point?*

"There's too much hardship for you here," he said.

The decision she'd been avoiding for too many months loomed. "Yeah," she whispered. "You're right."

"I'll help you in any way I can. Do you want to go to school? Take some college courses?"

"Hank, I dropped out of high school to have Cheryl." She'd been fifteen and terrified.

Hank cursed. "Sorry, Janey, I should have figured that out already."

"I was working on my diploma when she died, taking correspondence courses."

"You can stay here while you finish getting it."

A shout from the children in the field served as an exclamation mark. *You'll still have to deal with us!*

"Maybe not such a good idea." Hank cracked the knuckles of his right hand. "I'll pay for you to rent a room in town while you return to high school."

"That's okay, Hank, I still have all the checks you gave me."

"What?" Hank's eyebrows shot toward his hairline. His dusty white Stetson followed the motion. "You haven't cashed *any* of them?"

Janey shrugged and shook her head.

Hank sighed. "Amy's gonna have your guts for garters."

Janey glanced over his shoulder, but Amy had disappeared.

"Didn't I hear her tell you months ago to cash those?" Hank took off his hat, ran his fingers through his hair, then slammed it back onto his head. "They'll be stale-dated and the bank won't cash them. Tear them up and throw them out."

Janey toed a small branch that had fallen from the willow. She hated disappointing Hank.

"Why didn't you cash them?" he asked.

She shrugged. "I haven't had to. You and Amy give me everything I need here."

Out in the real world, she would need that money.

Hank pointed a finger at her. "I'm going to write you a check and you're going to cash it today, young lady."

The check she'd received in the mail last week from Maria Fantucci's lawyer burned a hole in her right pocket. She knew she still had to deal with it. Now Hank, too, was going to give her money.

"Hank, I don't want to take anything from you. You and Amy have done so much for me."

"You've earned your paychecks. Do you think anyone else here works for free?" He frowned. "We'll miss you. You do great work with the children, 'specially considering how hard it is for you."

Hank turned when he heard the screen door close. Amy had brought out a checkbook and a pen. Hank joined her.

"I heard," Amy said.

Janey stood still, clamping her throat around a scream trying to erupt, *I don't want to leave.*

"I'm sorry, honey," Janey heard Amy say. "Between having the baby and planning the rodeo, I haven't been keeping up with the books."

"You know I'd do them if I could."

The love between Hank and Amy was so palpable, Janey felt like an eavesdropper.

"You okay?" Hank approached with a check in his hand, but Janey didn't reach for it.

Holding Michael, Amy watched, her face unlined except for the worried frown that Janey knew she'd put there.

"Yeah, I'm fine," Janey finally answered, but the rough croak of her voice gave her away.

"Aw, hell, no, you aren't," Hank said. "It'll get easier in time."

"Did it get easier for you?" Janey asked. "After your little boy died?"

Hank stared hard at the grass near his feet and nodded. "Took a long time to get over Jamie's death, but it did get better, eventually."

His son had died of leukemia when he was two. At least Janey had had six years with Cheryl.

"About a year after Jamie died—" Hank placed a hand high on the trunk of the willow "—I started bringing young cancer survivors here. He's why I do this." He looked at Janey with sympathy in his hazel eyes. "It helped. A lot. You'll find something for you that will help."

Janey doubted it.

"Cheryl died a whole year ago," she said, "but it still hurts so bad."

"Losing a child," Hank murmured, "is a tough thing to get over."

Janey sighed. "Yeah, it sure is."

"Take your time figuring out what you want to do," Hank said. "Visit the library to research careers and schools. You got a place to live here as long as you need. But give yourself a break and stay away from the children."

He handed her the check, the paper crisp and clean on her palm. "Take this. Amy said you're going to deposit it today if she has to drag you there."

Janey's laugh felt good. "It's okay. I'll go by myself."

"You want a ride?" Hank asked.

"No. I feel like walking." She glanced at the check. "Twenty thousand dollars?" she exclaimed. "Are you guys nuts?"

"That's a year's salary."

"It's way too much. You gave me free room and board."

"Naw, it isn't enough." Hank rubbed a hand across the back of his neck. "Honest, Janey, I wish I could give you more."

Janey closed her eyes for a minute, gathering strength, pulling the butterflies roiling in her stomach under control.

"Okay," she said, "I'll open an account in town and try to figure out what I'll do next."

She turned toward the driveway and started the walk into town.

"Good luck, darlin'," Hank called. "See you at din-nertime, okay?"

Her step faltered. She'd felt safer here on this ranch than anywhere else on earth.

Cripes, Janey, pull yourself together. This isn't the end of your life with them.

No, it wasn't, but after the first step she took toward town, things would be different.

Suck it up. Do it.

She continued down the driveway toward the small highway that would take her to Ordinary, Montana.

Maybe now she could start work on the dream she hadn't thought about since Cheryl's death. Maybe now she could let herself consider her future.

Yeah, now was the time to finish her education—she could afford college!—to become one of those women who dress up for work, who wear beautiful clothes and expensive shoes and red and pink lipsticks. For sure not black.

She could become one of those women she used to envy on the streets of Billings who worked for busi-nesses and owned businesses and who were important. No one would dare to hurt them.

One thing she was sure of—she'd never live in poverty again.

She couldn't go back to Billings, though. Just couldn't. Maybe she could live in Ordinary and do college long-distance.

While she walked, she skirted the edges of that dream, considering some possible actions, discarding others. Forty-five minutes later, still without a firm plan, she pushed open the bank's heavy door and stepped in.

"Can I help you?" an older woman asked from behind one of the wickets. Her nametag read Donna. Looking down a long sharp nose at Janey, she studied her from head to toe. Judging by the sour pout of Donna's mouth, Janey had been found lacking.

Tough. The old prune could kiss her butt.

She frowned and approached the window, then reached into her pocket to pull out the checks. The woman shifted and slyly put one hand below the counter. *What the heck?*

"I'm not here to rob the bank," Janey said. Cripes. Why would the woman think she was?

Donna blushed.

Janey set the checks on the counter. "I want to open an account." She also passed over the envelope that Mrs. Fantucci's check had come in, to prove she lived at the Sheltering Arms, that she had a permanent address.

When Donna picked up Hank's check, her eyes widened. The other one was smaller.

Mrs. Fantucci had died and left all of the money in her savings account to Janey. Eleven thousand dollars and change. Janey's eyes stung. She missed her old neighbor.

Mrs. Fantucci hadn't judged her too hard.

Janey had done odd jobs for Maria, some shopping, laundry, cleaning, but it must have been more than anyone else had done for her.

Janey filled out the bank's application form and handed her ID to Donna, who took it to the manager.

Donna returned, her expression polite now, and told her she had a new account.

Janey asked for a hundred dollars cash and for the rest to be deposited. When Donna handed her the receipt with her balance on it, Janey's breathing stuttered. Almost thirty-one thousand dollars. She'd never known having money would feel so liberating.

She had to figure out her next step. Where would she live?

Her hands shook. *I'm not ready.*

You have to be.

She offered Donna a reluctant "Thanks," and headed for the door.

The heat outside hit her like the slap of a wet facecloth and she lifted her heavy hair away from her neck.

What now? She had to get a job to make enough for rent.

The past year of security on the Sheltering Arms hadn't been reality. Real life was dark and gritty and unfair. She knew that. It was time to step out of that safe cocoon and get on with life. It was time to stand on her own two feet.

She'd done it before and she could do it again.

Janey Wilson didn't do helpless.

CHAPTER TWO

JANEY'S FIRST STEP in her job search took her to the hair salon. She could do the simple stuff. Wash hair. Sweep the floor. The owner, Bernice Whitlow, had visited Amy's mother, Gladys, at the ranch, and had treated Janey well. Yeah, she wouldn't mind working for her.

When Janey stepped inside the shop, Bernice looked up from her customer, an older woman with white hair. The woman looked Janey up and down and stared at her feet.

"Aren't those boots hot?" Her voice came out high-pitched.

They were the only boots Janey owned and she liked them.

"Hiya, sweetie," Bernice said, her voice warm enough to melt honey. Janey tried not to show how much she liked that Bernice called her *sweetie.* It was a lot better than the things she'd grown up with on the streets of Billings.

"You here for a cut?" Bernice asked.

"I'm looking for a job."

The old woman snorted. "You're not going to get one dressed like that."

Bernice touched her shoulder and said, "Norma, hush."

Janey ignored Norma and forced her chin up a notch.

"Oh, sweetie," Bernice said, "I don't have a position available."

Janey swallowed her pride. "I can wash hair. I can sweep the floor."

"Economy's slow." Bernice's regret sounded sincere. "I can't afford to hire anyone right now. Honest, honey."

Damn.

"Try over at the diner." Bernice sprayed Norma's white hair with about half a can of spray.

Janey coughed.

"They're always busy," Bernice said.

The diner. As in being a waitress?

"Okay, thanks."

Janey left the store, heard Bernice say, "Good luck." Norma said something, too, but it didn't sound flattering. Janey was glad she hadn't caught it.

She trudged across the street to the diner, the sun on her back branding her through the black cotton of her dress.

She pulled the fabric of her bodice away from her skin for a minute, then stepped into the diner, a noisy, buzzing hive of activity and conversation.

A cook at the grill behind the long counter yelled, "Order up."

People filled every stool at the counter and every red fake-leather booth.

Wow. Bernice was right. The place was hopping.

A waitress rushed by without looking at her. "Sit wherever you can find a seat, hon."

That brought the attention of the people in the nearest booths to her. They stopped talking and studied her clothes.

She curled her fingers into her palms.

More people stopped talking. A hush fell over the crowd.

They watched her, some with interest, some with plain old curiosity. She couldn't tell if there was disapproval.

No. She couldn't do this. She couldn't work under the microscope like this, in front of so many people. Not every day. The attention stifled her. She couldn't breathe.

Crap.

She stepped back outside.

An ache danced inside her skull.

She walked down the street, studying the businesses as she went. Barbershop. Nope.

Across the street was a hardware store, Scotty's Hardware. How hard could it be to sell nails?

She crossed the street and stepped inside.

A middle-aged man stopped what he was doing and turned to her. Must be Scotty.

"Can I help you?"

"I'm looking for work."

The old guy's eyes bugged out. "Here?" he said, his voice coming out in a thin squeak.

"Yeah." Nuts, she didn't know a thing about job-hunting. What was she supposed to say?

The owner stepped a little closer. He smelled like cough drops. "You ever worked in a hardware store before? You know anything about power tools and home renovations and paint and lumber?"

She shook her head.

The guy straightened a pile of brochures beside the register, all the while checking her out from the corner of his eye.

"'Fraid I can't help you."

Her pride caught in her throat again. "I can sweep floors." Man, she had trouble saying that, but she'd lived through worse in her life. She could do this.

The guy looked up at her and there was maybe sympathy in his eyes. "I just don't have work right now. Times are slow."

"Yeah." She turned to walk away. Where to now? It wasn't as though the town was a hotbed of opportunities.

She opened the door but his voice stopped her.

"Listen," he said. "C. J. Wright's been advertising for a store clerk for a month now. Try there."

Janey looked at him. She wasn't imagining it. The guy really did seem sympathetic.

"Who is he?" she asked.

The guy stepped up to his window and pointed to the other side of the street and down a bit. "Sweet Talk. The candy store."

"Thanks. I appreciate it," Janey said, meaning it, and left.

She studied the shop while she crossed the road. *Sweet Talk*. Two bright lime-green signs stood out in the window.

One sign said they needed a full-time employee and one said the store was for sale.

A full-time employee. To do what? Working in a candy store wouldn't be rocket science, right? She could count money, could pack things into bags.

She remembered coming in here on her first day in town a year ago, with Amy, passing through on her way to the Sheltering Arms for the first time. Cheryl had been dead for a month. Janey didn't remember a whole lot from that time, other than feeling cold and dead. Or wishing she were dead.

A sign on the door told her to watch her step. Glancing down to make sure she didn't catch one of her big boot heels, she opened the door. She'd fallen once before in a store in the city and had earned herself a goose egg on her forehead that had hurt for days.

Sweet scents of chocolate and peppermint drifted toward her and tugged at something wonderful in her memory, but Janey knew there had been nothing in her life with her parents that had felt as warm as whatever was hovering in the far reaches of her mind.

Footprints painted on the worn wooden floor caught her attention. Or paw prints, she should say. Of rabbits and kittens and deer, in pastels, all leading to different parts of the store.

She looked up and gasped.

Warm dark wood covered the walls and candy cases, contrasting against white porcelain countertops. Jewel-bright candies shone behind the spotless glass of those cases.

Three long stained-glass lamps hung from thick chains attached to the ceiling and lit the candy displays.

Big chocolate animals stood on shelves that lined the walls, each one of them decorated with icing in every conceivable color.

She smiled.

This is a happy place.

One rabbit had been "dressed" with icing in an intricately detailed, multihued vest. A deer wore a saddle of gold and silver, as if a wee elf might hop on for a ride any minute. An owl wore a finely decorated house robe and carried an icing book tucked under one arm and a chocolate candle in the other, as if he were preparing to sit for a cozy read before he headed to bed for the night.

Cellophane, gleaming and crisp, covered the animals. A huge polka-dot bow gathered the plastic above each animal's head.

Why would anyone want to sell this store? Was he nuts?

If she owned Sweet Talk, she'd polish the wood every day, and dust the cellophane on the animals, and smile when she sold them to customers. To children.

She covered her mouth with her hands, awed by this big, whimsical treasure box of a shop.

Around and through all of it drifted sugar and spice, scents so yummy her mouth watered.

Oooooh, Cheryl would have loved it here. Her girl would have *adored* it. Had she ever come in with Hank and Amy? Janey hoped so.

The wonderful feeling that was haunting her, that was calling from the darkness of vague memories, burst full-blown into her consciousness.

Grandma.

She hadn't thought about her grandmother in years. This memory came from when Janey had been even younger than Cheryl's six years. Grandma had visited a few times and, every time, had doled out in equal portion hugs and candy, the only times Janey had ever tasted it.

Janey gazed at the wonder of the shop, that it should, after all of these years, call a long-lost part of herself into the light.

Those visits had thrilled the solemn child Janey had been, had represented the few happy memories in her poverty-challenged life, the *only* good memories from her childhood.

Then Grandma had died and Janey had rarely had candy again.

She'd give anything to feel that euphoria, that joy even if only for a day. The only other time she'd felt anything better had been at Cheryl's birth.

Man, she could definitely work here.

Children would come into this store, but Janey would deal with their parents. She could make children happy without handling them.

She felt like laughing and whispered, "Who made this store? Whose idea was it?"

"My mother's."

Janey startled at the sound of the voice. On the other side of the counter stood a young man, taller than her, maybe six feet, his brown hair cropped soldier-short.

She'd only met him the one time a year ago, and she'd forgotten how good-looking he was, what an impact that chiseled face made.

Perhaps five years older than her, shadows painted his brown eyes. Janey knew all about shadows. Dark lashes too thick and pretty to be masculine ringed those eyes, but the square jaw framing the deep cleft in his chin was purely male.

He didn't smile, just wiped his hands on a towel and watched her without blinking. How long had he been watching her?

Janey sensed a kindred spirit in the woman who'd started this shop. "Can I meet your mother?"

"No," he answered and Janey's spirits plummeted. "She's dead."

"Oh," Janey breathed, "I'm sorry."

He smoothed a long-fingered hand down the apron he wore over a short-sleeved, blue-and-white-striped shirt with a button-down collar. She didn't know men still wore those. Not young men, anyway.

His dark brown eyes did a perusal of her and the easy warmth of the last few minutes dissolved. She waited for the criticism she knew was about to come. She stood out too much in this small town.

Well, he could kiss her butt. She wanted this job and she was going to get it.

For a split second, his features hardened, his lips flattened, before he apparently remembered that she was a customer.

"I'm C. J. Wright. I own this place," he said, his voice almost as rich as the chocolate she smelled melting in a pot somewhere. "Can I help you?"

C.J. HAD SEEN this woman before, when she'd stood in his store with Amy Shelter, when Amy had returned from Billings to marry Hank.

C.J.'s memory hadn't exaggerated. She looked like a punker. Or a Goth woman.

That day the young woman with Amy had looked real sad—like she'd been crying day and night for weeks.

She didn't look sad today, though. She looked tough and determined.

The unrelenting black of her dress echoed the big platform boots, the black lipstick and nail polish, and the half inch of mascara coating her lashes. Looked like she'd applied it with a trowel.

Her plain dress, black cotton hemmed at the knee, should have been conservative, but it hugged every curve like it was made of burned butter and hit him like a sucker punch to the gut. He'd never seen anything like her in Ordinary. With her piercings and the tiny tattoo on the inside of her left elbow, she looked too much like Vicki for comfort.

Damn.

In her defiant stance, one hip shot forward and one black-nailed hand resting on it, her head cocked to one side, tough and cynical, he saw himself as a teenager. She was no longer an adolescent, but not by much.

No way did he want her here reminding him of his younger days, of times and troubles best buried.

He threw down the towel he'd dried his hands with. He had his life under control. He'd sown all of the wild oats he ever intended to. These days he had the best reason on earth to behave well.

Something about her tough beauty called to him, but he resisted. God, how he resisted.

She wasn't beautiful. She was trouble.

Pure, cleansing anger rushed through him—anger at himself. The days when he found a woman like this attractive were long gone. He hadn't spent the past year reinventing himself to be drawn back into the wildness a woman like this inspired in him.

Get your shit together, buddy.

With an effort that left him shaking, he pulled himself under control.

"Can I help you?" he asked, cordially, as if she was any other customer.

She pointed out the window and said, "I want that."

He looked out to see BizzyBelle wandering down the middle of the road. Nuts, she'd gotten out of her pen around back, again. Bizzy had to be the wiliest cow in Montana.

He turned to the woman on the other side of the counter. She still pointed out the window.

"You want my cow?" he asked. Wow, crazy.

"Your cow?" She turned a stunned face toward the window, saw Bizzy and blinked. "No, not the cow. *That.*"

His gaze shifted to the two bright green papers in his window and his hope soared.

"You want to buy my store?" he asked. "Really?" In four months, he hadn't had one single nibble and time was running out.

"No," she said. "I want the job."

"Oh, I see." The job. No. No, he didn't want her here every day. Just his luck, he needed an employee and the only candidate was this Goth creature who would probably scare most of his customers away. Nuts.

"What are your qualifications?" he asked.

She shrugged, as if she didn't care whether or not she got the job. "I can count money. I can put stuff in a bag." She'd obviously never gone job-hunting before. She showed neither deference nor humility, nor, come to think of it, any eagerness to please.

"That's it?" Nervy chick, coming in here with no experience.

"I've been working on Hank Shelter's ranch for a year. He'll tell you I'm a hard worker."

She flicked her hair over her shoulder. Maybe he could get her to leave if he appealed to her vanity.

"You'd have to wear a hairnet to cover all of that." Her shiny hair ran over her shoulders like blackstrap molasses and disappeared down her back.

How long was it? To her waist?

"Whatever," she said.

Whatever? Rotten attitude for a job candidate.

"You want the job or not?" he asked, impatient now.

"Yeah," she said, thinning her plump lips. "I want the job. I just told you that."

He frowned. "You don't sound like you want it. You're making it real easy for me to say no."

Panic washed over her face, quickly hidden. "I want the job. Okay?"

"You'd have to cut your nails. You can't knead candy with those."

Her eyes widened. "I'd be making candies?"

"Yeah, what did you think you'd be doing?"

"Selling them. You make them here?" She was suddenly pretty excited. Over making candy?

He nodded. "A lot of them."

"Can I see where you do it?" she asked.

"Okay." He directed her to the doorway to the back room. "I can't let you back there without an apron and a hairnet and heavy shoes, but you can look from here."

She glanced down at her boots and back up at him. A smile hovered at the corners of her mouth. "These aren't heavy enough?" Her smile turned that upper lip into a pretty cupid's bow framed by a heart-shaped jaw. Too attractive.

He reined himself in. "Those're okay." He sounded more like a peevish child than a twenty-six-year-old businessman.

With a puzzled frown, she turned away from him and studied the back room and the big machines that filled it, silent sentinels in a gray concrete-block room.

He'd grown up with this and had no idea how a stranger would see it.

Nodding toward the machines, she asked, "You'll teach me how to use those?"

Presumptuous chick. She thought she already had the job.

"*If* I hired you, I would teach you."

She turned around to look at the candies in the cases and the chocolate animals throughout the store. She pointed to a bunny.

"You make those, too?"

He nodded.

"Can you teach me how?"

He nodded again. "We'd have to see whether you have talent for it."

Her face turned hard. Those full lips thinned again. "Okay, listen, I want this job. What do I have to do to get it?"

Man, she was serious.

"Who else is applying for it?" she asked, aggressively.

That was the problem, wasn't it? No one else had. Nat had left over a month ago and C.J. hadn't found a soul to replace him. He was losing money on the apartment upstairs that sat empty now that Nat worked in the city.

How was C.J. supposed to rodeo if he could never leave the shop? He worked too many hours, six days a week.

With the Jamie Shelter Charity Rodeo only a month away, he had to practice. He needed the prize money and dammit, he'd get it. Those back taxes on Gramps's ranch weren't shrinking while C.J. struggled to find a way to pay them.

"No one else wants the job," he said.

Triumph glittered in her eyes.

Man, he wanted to say no, didn't know what the townspeople would think of her. What if they stopped shopping here because of her? But the desperation he'd been feeling for weeks rushed through him tenfold, urging him to take a chance on her. He could handle any attraction or call of the wild her appearance sparked—her rotten attitude and prickly personality would help. With a little discipline and keeping his eye on the end goal, he'd get over his impulses.

"Okay. You've got the job." If the townspeople didn't like her, he could always fire her.

She perked up.

"Can you start tomorrow?" C.J. asked. The sooner he could put in more rodeo hours the better. "9:00 a.m.?"

She nodded.

"Okay, see you then." He spun away as if dismissing her, but she didn't leave.

She stepped back around to the customer side of the counter. "I want to buy candy."

"Sure. What'll you have?"

TOUCHING THE COOL WINDOW of the display case, Janey stared at the assortment of commercial candies available—SweeTarts, candy buttons, licorice pipes, Pixy Stix, Mike and Ikes, marshmallow cones—and secretly rejoiced. She'd gotten the job.

She needed to celebrate. She'd get candy for the kids on the ranch, even if it would kill her to spend enough time with them to pass the candy around. Just because it was hard for her to be with them didn't mean she didn't want to see them happy.

They were poor, inner-city kids who'd survived cancer. They deserved a lot of happy.

C.J. filled bags with the candies she pointed to.

Another case held the homemade candies.

She asked for a scoop each of saltwater taffy and humbugs.

C.J. added the total. "Twenty dollars and five cents."

She handed him two of her twenties.

"Do you have any change?" he asked.

She shook her head. Donna had given her only twenties.

"Okay." He handed her back one of the twenties.

"I don't have the nickel."

"Doesn't matter. I'm not gonna change a twenty for five cents. I won't go broke if I lose a nickel."

Nope, she couldn't let him do that. It went against the grain to take anything for free from a man, especially a stranger.

"Take some candies out of the bag," she said.

"What? Get real." He waved her away.

"Take some candies out," she ordered, unyielding.

He frowned, took a couple of Tootsie Rolls out of a bag and threw them back into the case. Then he handed her the three bags.

"Okay?" he asked in a tone that said *are you satisfied?*

"O-*kay*," she replied, and meant it. *Now,* it felt all right. "Thank you."

She turned and walked to the door. If she had her way, that guy wouldn't be here, and she could sit among all these beautiful animals and drink in the atmosphere of the shop for the rest of the afternoon.

Just as she stepped through the door, C.J. called, "Hey. I don't know your name."

"Janey Wilson." She closed the door behind her and, through the oval window decorated with the store's name in black-and-gold letters, watched him walk into the back room.

She took a couple of steps, then decided she wanted a candy.

Just as she reached into the bag of humbugs, someone hit her from behind, a massive man who shoved her against Sweet Talk's window. The scream that should have roared from her died in her throat.

CHAPTER THREE

POUNDING HEART, trembling fists, throat aching with screams she couldn't release—terror immobilized her.

An odd smell floated around her. The foul aroma deepened and she realized it came from the man behind her, along with a wall of heat.

She turned her head a fraction, caught a glimpse of someone brown, huge. Wearing a fur coat? In September?

He shoved her in the middle of her back, slamming her against the plate glass. Her head hit hard. Pinpricks of light floated against her eyelids.

This can't be happening. Not again. Not in broad daylight. Not in Ordinary. The town disappeared. Darkness fell and she was on her way home from school after a basketball game. Someone shoved her into the bushes, someone strong who bruised and scratched her. She smelled sweat and garbage and city dirt and cigarette breath. And the pain. Too much pain.

She couldn't breathe.

The man grunted and she was back in Ordinary in the middle of the day. She got mad. She was supposed to be *safe* in Ordinary, the safest place on earth, Hank said.

"Nooooooo." Her voice croaked out of her.

The man's hold on her was so strong and massive she

couldn't get free. No hands to grab, no wrists to break. He was behind her and she couldn't turn.

Why were men such cowards?

This time she was going to see the face of her attacker.

She pushed against him, but he shoved her harder, knocking her head again.

More starbursts of pain.

He smelled of hay and dirt and, oh, God, the stench. What had he been eating?

She waited for the pain to start, down there, but he wasn't doing anything, just leaning into her with what felt like hundreds of pounds of weight. What did he *want?*

"Help," she tried to yell. It came out a little stronger. He didn't stop her with a hand across her mouth the way the other man had.

Her blood boiled and she pushed until her arms shook with the strain. He didn't budge.

She opened her mouth to scream again and the man behind her let out an enormous, ungodly…*moo?* She covered her ears. The bags in her hands slammed against her cheeks. The sound roared on, deafening her, stunning her.

She took advantage of an easing of pressure and spun around. A huge hairy nose chucked her chin. Enormous brown bovine eyes stared her down. Oh, lord, a cow. C.J.'s cow. The one he'd thought she'd wanted.

She couldn't relax. Couldn't laugh about this. That dirty street, that darkness, that pain still lingered in her mind, floated out of her and played across the blue sky like film noir.

Forcing herself to recognize that she was in Ordinary, on Main Street, she breathed in the heat of the September sun to banish the chill she felt in her bones.

The nose mashed her back against the store window. The animal sniffed her bags, tried to take one from her. She closed her eyes and held on.

The door of the shop opened and she heard C.J.'s voice. "Hey, Bizzy, back off."

Then the pressure eased. She opened her eyes. C.J. stood beside her, holding the cow at arm's length, a frown between his eyebrows.

"You okay?" he asked.

She shook her head. Her tongue wouldn't work, wouldn't form words. The bags of candies fell from her nerveless fingers. The cow grabbed one of the bags and started chewing on it, paper and all. C.J. snatched the other two from the ground.

"I ran out when I heard something hit my window," he said.

At that moment, an even stronger odor emanated from the cow's rear end. Janey gagged.

C.J. shrugged. "Candy makes her pass gas." He shoved the cow. "Take a hike, BizzyBelle."

When the cow tried to lick his hands, he pushed her harder. "Buzz off."

The cow ambled away, running her enormous tongue over her big hairy lips.

"You have to show them who's boss," he said. "Just like any animal."

Janey remembered that lesson from Hank, from when he'd taught her how to deal with horses. Her nerves skittered too badly and those memories were too devastating for her to feel like the boss right now.

"Come here," C.J. said, reaching for her arm.

She flinched away. Her teeth ground together.

C.J. raised his hands, palms out. "Okay. C'mon into the store. We need to get something cold on that bump." He pointed to her forehead.

He gestured for her to precede him through the door.

She stood just inside the shop and felt lost. She needed her equilibrium back, needed to get away from those old images. A terrible urgency raced through her.

"I need to wash my hands," she said.

She felt C.J.'s warmth behind her. "Head through the workroom to the washroom at the back."

She ran past the candy machines to the bathroom and found a sliver of soap beside the faucet. She carefully set down the remaining bags then turned on the water as hot as she could stand it, then washed her hands. She rinsed, then washed her hands two more times, until she felt the stain of those memories flow down the drain.

She couldn't find a towel. With her hands still wet, she fell onto the closed toilet lid and rested her forearms on her knees. Droplets of water fell from her hands onto the worn black-and-white linoleum floor. She saw C.J.'s boots enter her line of sight.

He ran the water, washed his hands, then handed something to her. She sensed him holding himself back. Probably afraid to touch her after she flinched away from him out front. How embarrassing. She could imagine how stupid he must think her.

"Your forehead is swelling." He pointed to her face and handed her a wet cloth. "You're going to have a bump."

She pressed it to her forehead, weakly. The memories exhausted her. Always.

"I can show you how to make friends with Bizzy-Belle for next time," C.J. said.

She stared at him, heard the words but had trouble understanding their meaning.

Her head buzzed and she breathed hard as if she'd run a marathon.

"Are you all right?" he asked.

"Give me a minute," she answered but her voice sounded thin. She hated her weakness for showing.

HER FACE WAS IN DANGER of being swallowed whole by her eyes, two enormous brown-black windows to a terrified soul.

She didn't look like the tough-edged woman who'd practically demanded the job. She looked like a scared little girl.

"You want a glass of water?" he asked.

She nodded, sort of looked as though she couldn't form words. Man, who would think a cow could scare a person so much?

She looked young up close, her face chalk-white against the jet-black hair.

The red collar of her dress had tiny skulls embroidered in black. The short sleeves revealed arms with the least blemished skin he'd ever seen. No freckles. No scars. Just that tiny tattoo on the inside of her left elbow, but he couldn't make out what it was.

She closed her eyes and took a deep breath. He could see her breasts swell against her dress. Her scent, tropical fruit and coconut, wrapped around him like a silk scarf.

He dumped his toothbrush out of the glass that sat

beside the faucet and ran cold water into it, then handed it to her.

She drank half of it in one go.

She sucked in another great big breath. A second later, all of that air whooshed out of her. The tough woman was back in full force.

Handing him the half-full glass of water, she rose. She was short compared to his six feet.

"I have to go," she said, unsmiling and cold again.

Hugging the wall, she inched around him and left the room.

JANEY STEPPED OUT of the shop. How was she supposed to get over the past when the slightest thing set her off? Well, maybe not the slightest. Up close, Bizzy-Belle was huge.

For a minute, she stood still, allowing the sun to warm her, until she felt under control again.

No way would she let this defeat her.

She'd just gotten a job. She would finally return to her studies.

She looked to the sky and imagined Cheryl watching over her. *Oh, baby girl, I wish you could be here with me.*

On the sidewalk up ahead, a dirty rag heap of a man sat on a concrete step leaning against the closed door of a shop, holding a torn paper coffee cup in his hand.

So even in small towns there were homeless people? She thought that only happened in the city, around cheap apartment buildings like hers that had smelled of mildew and cabbage. She was never going back to urban poverty. *Never.*

She reached into her pocket for a five to give to the

guy, and then remembered that all she had were twenties. Man, it was hard for her to give away so much of her precious store of money.

His head, his shoulders, his chest all bowed forward, as though he was closing in on himself.

Aw, buddy, I know how you feel. I know that kind of emptiness.

Maybe she should get him a burger from the diner. That way she'd know for sure he wouldn't buy booze instead of food. Who was she to judge, though?

Whatever gets you through the night, pal.

She took one of her twenties and dropped it into the paper cup.

Startled, the man glanced up and studied her with bloodshot eyes, watery and gray and unfocused. Broken veins dappled his nose. Janey would be surprised if he were half as old as he looked.

"Th-th-thanks." He took in her clothes and her hair. "Are you rich?" he asked doubtfully.

"No. I just got a job at the candy store, though."

"That's good." He nodded. "Jobs are good."

He had no gift for conversation, had probably burned half his brain cells with hard liquor.

"Don't you spend that all in one place," she said. On impulse, she opened the bag of humbugs and dropped a few into his cup on top of the twenty.

Janey continued on her way down Main Street to walk the few miles home to the ranch.

"Wait." The order from the deep voice stopped her cold.

Janey turned around.

A tall, thin man loomed over her with his hands

clasped behind his back and his thick dark eyebrows arched above his big nose.

His suit of unrelieved black looked hot as hell for a day like today. Janey wore black as a statement. What was this guy's excuse? Then she realized what he looked like—some kind of holy man. A reverend or a priest?

The deep vertical line between his eyebrows, below his massive forehead, made him appear as though he chewed on the world's problems every night for dinner.

He looked really, really smart.

Janey lifted her chin.

"Yeah?" she asked, giving her voice the edge that protected her from people like the preacher, from the look on his judgmental prudish old face.

The Reverend rocked back on his heels. "You like Sweet Talk, do you?"

Janey nodded. Why the heck did it matter to this guy whether she liked the candy store?

"Did I just hear you tell Kurt that you were going to work there?"

Kurt must be the homeless man's name. "Yes," she answered. "That's right. The owner hired me."

The Reverend rocked forward onto the soles of his feet and nodded. "Did he?"

"Yes." She cocked her head to one side. What did the old goat want with her?

"Really?" he said, his voice silky, a hard glint in his eye. "I would advise you not to take the job."

"What?" she asked. "You're kidding, right?"

"No, I'm not. Don't take the job my son gave you."

His *son?* This was C.J.'s father? Wow, he didn't look anything like him. "Why shouldn't I take the job?"

"I raised a good boy. He doesn't need trouble from someone like you."

"Someone like me?" Rage almost blinded her. "Who do you think you are?"

"I'm protecting my son," Reverend Wright said. "Why does your type always latch onto him?"

Her *type?* Huh? What the—

"You're way off base." She propped her hands on her hips and stood on her tiptoes to get into his face. "I don't want your buttoned-up prude of a son," she said. "I want a job."

"Leave him alone. Get a job somewhere else. I'll even put in a good word for you. Try the diner."

Janey couldn't be sure, but it seemed as though the guy was desperate.

"No one else will give me a job," she said glumly.

"If you're going to work in the candy shop, you have to clean yourself up, look respectable, not like a hooker."

"A *hooker?*" She was the farthest thing from a prostitute that a woman could be. "What, only *virgins* can work in Ordinary?"

His face hardened. "Get away from here. Go to another town. You can't work here."

Janey reeled. "Who died and made you God?"

The Reverend's cheeks flared red. "Don't ever, *ever,* use the Lord's name in vain in front of me again."

For a moment, she was afraid.

He turned his back on her. Leaning down toward Kurt, he said, voice tight, "You don't have to beg for handouts. You don't have to sit in the heat. Come to the rectory and we'll feed you."

Kurt rose and followed the Rev down the street. The good Samaritan had charity in his heart for a member of his flock, but none for a stranger. Not very reverend-like behavior.

He walked with his hands behind his back, his shoulders slightly stooped, a big black cricket with long thin limbs.

Because of that split second of fear she'd felt, she shouted at his back, "Drop in tomorrow for some candy. I'll serve you myself. Maybe it'll sweeten your disposition."

She turned and stomped out of town.

No way was someone as priggish and uptight as that Looney Tune holding her back.

"Just you try and stop me." After what she'd lived through in her twenty-two years, the preacher man didn't intimidate her one bit.

Halfway home, a cloud passed across the sun, like a dark harbinger of bad tidings. *Harbinger.* Great word. She needed to bring it home to Hank. He loved words.

The cloud turned the Technicolor scenery into black and white. No, not all of the landscape. Only the tiny portion she walked through, like a cartoon character with a rain cloud hovering over her.

Unsure why that made her feel afraid, she shivered.

C.J. STEPPED OUT of the store onto sun-drenched Main Street to hunt down BizzyBelle and put her back in her pen. His father and Kurt walked up the street toward him.

"Kurt," his dad said, patting the man's shoulder, "I need to talk to my son. Head on over to the rectory. I'll only be a minute."

He turned to C.J. and said, "Un-hire that girl." No preamble. Just an order.

"What?" Since when did Dad interfere with how C.J. ran the candy store?

"I said, don't hire her." The Reverend clasped his hands behind his back. "She's a bad influence. A Satanist."

"For Go— For Pete's sake, Dad. She isn't a Satanist."

"She most assuredly is. Have you seen the way she dresses?"

"Of course I have. It's just her style." His own doubts about hiring Janey bothered him. He didn't need to hear them echoed by his father.

"I have a mission in life," the Reverend intoned, "to keep my son safe and on the right path."

Not that old argument again. "Dad, I'm twenty-six." Sometimes the frustration threatened to explode out of him. "I make my own decisions in life."

His father looked at him with that reproach that said C.J. had disappointed him. But the man in front of C.J. wasn't his father. He was the Reverend Wright.

"You know," C.J. said, "I'd like you to slip off your holy mantle once in a while and just be my father." An ordinary man talking to his ordinary son.

The Reverend frowned, obviously lost. Dad didn't have a clue what C.J. was talking about.

"I'm not in the mood for one of your fire-and-brimstone lectures this afternoon."

"Son," the reverend said—C.J. hated when he called him *son* in that sonorous voice he used on the pulpit— "your life is finally on the right track. Keep it that way."

"Dad, I am. I only hired the woman. I'm not dating her."

"Get rid of her," Reverend Wright said.

"Mom left the store to me. I assume she thought I

could handle the responsibility." C.J. shoved his hands into his pockets. "Besides, there aren't a whole lot of people in town who want to work in a candy store."

He started toward Bizzy, who was eating something at the curb on the far side of the street. Scotty waved to him on his way from the hardware store to the bank.

"What about the rodeo?" Dad asked, shooting the conversation off in another direction.

C.J. stopped. So. Dad had heard about that. "What about it?" he snapped.

"I heard you signed up for Hank's rodeo. Why are you involved in it again? Have you no respect for David's memory?"

"How dare you accuse me of such a thing?" With his back to his father, C.J. squeezed his lips together. Yeah, he had a lot of respect for Davey, but he also had no choice.

C.J. turned to face down his father. "I knew Davey better than anyone and I'll bet he'll root for me when I finally get back up on a bronc." Which he planned to do tonight.

As usual, Dad's mouth did that lemon-sucking trick that occurred whenever they talked about the rodeo.

"You don't want to go down that road again. Look how it ended last time." With a final look of reproach, Reverend Wright walked toward the church, tall, sure of himself, and implacable.

C.J. scrubbed his hand across his short hair. Yeah, he remembered. It had ended with Davey's death. C.J. needed that prize money, though.

It's not just about the money, his conscience whispered. *Not by a long shot.*

"Oh, shut up."

C.J. shook his head. His return to the rodeo was all about the prize money. That was it. He would rodeo and win. He had someone to cover for him in the shop now. No way was C.J. getting rid of Janey.

No matter what Dad said, C.J. wasn't returning to his wild ways. He'd grown up and worked himself over into a mature man. Couldn't Dad see that?

C.J. was in no danger of falling backward. He could control any superficial attraction to Janey and he would rodeo for the money, then get out of it again. No worries, no danger.

Reverend Walter Wright strode down Main Street toward the rectory.

He'd thought things were finally okay.

C.J. had settled down, had grown up and taken responsibility for the boy he'd sired with that trollop from the city.

Now, along came the young Gothic girl to tempt him. What if he again became that wild man he'd been throughout his teenage years? Walter couldn't live through that again. Was the Gothic woman nurturing C.J.'s dangerous dreams of the rodeo? Had they been seeing each other for a while and Walter hadn't known?

His hands grew damp. Someone said "Hello," and the Reverend nodded. He had no idea who had just walked past him.

He couldn't go through the nightmare of C.J.'s adolescence again. He couldn't watch C.J. fall into temptation, turn his back on everything Walter had taught him, sire another child out of wedlock. C.J. had survived that dark day four years ago when a bull had gored David Franck, but what if this time it was C.J. who died?

Reverend Wright craved the solace of his church and stepped into its cool interior. It immediately brought him a measure of peace.

Someone had left an arrangement of yellow asters and pussy willows and Chinese lanterns in a large vase on the altar. Most likely Gladys Graves, Amy Shelter's mother. Bless her. Walter thought about her too often.

Last weekend, the ladies had polished the wooden pews until they gleamed and smelled of Murphy Oil Soap. He ran his hand across the back of one of them. How many hands had touched this over the years? How many souls had he saved? Or was it all an illusion?

He backed away from that thought. Of *course* his work was good. Of value.

He continued up the aisle, toward the altar and the small stained-glass windows that framed it.

Walter shivered and stepped to the side of the altar, lit a votive candle, knelt on a hard bench and prayed for the repose of Davey's soul. He also prayed for forgiveness for the bull that had gored Davey four years ago. He asked God's forgiveness for himself, for the gratitude he harbored in his soul that the young man gored had not been his own son.

As he stood and limped toward the back of the church with pins and needles bedeviling his feet, and as he closed the church door, as he walked around the outside of the church to the rectory, he still worried about his son and resented that woman.

He stepped into the cool foyer.

When he picked up the day's mail, his hands shook. He stared unseeing at the letters, then dropped them on the table and rested his fists on top of them. He hung his head.

"Rev?" The voice from the living room sounded hesitant. Reverend Wright looked up. He'd forgotten about Kurt.

"You okay?" Kurt asked.

The Reverend pulled himself together and straightened. "Did Maisie feed you?"

Kurt nodded and stood. "I heard what you said to that young woman about not working in the candy store." He shuffled toward the door. "She got a job. Jobs are good."

Kurt opened the door of the rectory. "She gave me twenty dollars, Reverend. Nobody gives me twenty dollars."

He stepped outside, leaving the door to close behind him with a solid thud.

So the Goth girl wasn't all bad.

Walter tried to smile, but it felt sickly. Kurt didn't understand why he had to keep C.J. safe. The Reverend couldn't lose him the way he'd lost his wife.

Elaine had died on the road, speeding, as was her wont. He'd warned her so many times to slow down, but she'd been a hard woman to tame.

Truly his mother's headstrong son, C.J. was tempting fate again by entering that damned rodeo. How could the Reverend survive his death or disfigurement? He was all he had left.

He had to find a way to stop C.J.'s involvement in the rodeo and with that woman.

CHAPTER FOUR

AFTER AN EARLY SUPPER, Janey stepped out of Hank's house, drawn by the hubbub in the yard. A bunch of people were coming over to practice for the rodeo. Only four more weeks.

It seemed every night was busy in one way or another. There was so much to do to get the second annual event off the ground.

Their neighbor, Angus Kinsey, was dropping off a couple of broncs for practice riding tonight. He jumped out of his pickup and walked around to the back of the horse trailer to open the door. A couple of ranch hands came to help out.

Janey stared at the children sitting on a blanket in the middle of the lawn. Ten children waited, some as young as six, some as old as eleven. All of them waiting for her.

She clenched her fingers on the bag of candies she'd brought home for them.

The children shifted restlessly. One of them spotted her and cried, "There she is." Some rose to run to her, but she lifted a staying hand and they sat back down.

No use putting it off any longer. She walked down the stairs and approached them. Katie patted the empty spot beside her on the red plaid blanket. Janey hesitated, then sat.

Leaning forward, she dumped the candies in the middle of the children who squealed and grabbed for them.

Some grabbed for her. Such physical creatures, always touching or waiting to be touched. Every pat on her hands, every glancing elbow or brush of sweaty little fingers left an invisible bruise. For a moment, she folded in on herself. When would this damn pain end? How much was she supposed to bear?

Stop feeling sorry for yourself.

She shoved her backbone into a rigid line.

"Hey!" Janey said, forcing their attention to her. "Only eat the candies if you're sitting still. The minute any one of you starts to run or jump around while you're eating, I'm putting them away. Got it?"

They nodded.

"One candy at a time, right?"

They nodded again.

Katie picked up one SweeTart with her fingers and held it up to Janey. "What does it say?"

A blush of sweat rose on Janey's forehead and upper lip.

"Love you," she croaked.

Katie crawled onto her lap and Janey shrank from her, but Katie just leaned closer, forcing Janey to hold her or fall over backward. There was no way to get away from the child without hurting her feelings.

Janey straightened and rested one shaky hand on Katie's knee.

Katie picked up a pastel green heart and pointed to it. "Number 4! What do the letters say?"

"Love U 4ever."

"You, too." Katie rested her head against Janey's chest and put her thumb into her mouth. Bad habit, especially for a six-year-old. Cheryl never sucked her thumb. Cheryl was a good girl.

Janey gave herself a proverbial tongue-lashing after that uncharitable thought. As if Katie wasn't a good child. The girl had lived with too much in her short life. She was allowed her weaknesses, allowed to take comfort wherever she could find it.

Janey rested her head on Katie's peach-fuzz scalp for a second, then shoved her spine into a ramrod post again.

She felt an adult hunker down beside her in Katie's abandoned spot and released a ragged sigh. Probably Hank coming to give her hell for being with the children.

"What are you doing?" Nope, not Hank. Amy.

Janey looked into her pretty unlined face and asked, "What do you mean?"

Amy nudged Janey's shoulder with her own. "You know what I mean. Why are you here with all of the children?" she whispered close to Janey, her breath scented by her after-dinner coffee. "You should be avoiding them."

"I know." Janey smiled bleakly. "I can't seem to help myself. I saw the candies in the store and wanted to bring some home for the children. It makes them happy."

"While it makes you miserable."

Janey lifted one shoulder. "Yeah."

Amy tapped her knee with one finger. "You're too generous for your own good."

Not possible. She felt too much resentment against these children. Why had they survived while her Cheryl hadn't?

Kyle jumped up from the blanket with a lollipop in his mouth. "Watch this," he shouted and began to jump.

"Sit!" Amy and Janey ordered at the same time.

Kyle sat and poked John in the ribs. "Knock it off, buster," Johnny yelled, as loudly as usual.

Janey picked up a ladybug near Katie's sandal and put her in the grass away from harm. "I got a job today, Amy."

"That's great. Where?"

"In the candy store."

"With C.J.? You'll like working with him. He's a great guy."

Janey didn't answer, didn't know how to chart a course through the ocean of feelings that had troubled her today, not the least of which was her reaction to the good-looking owner of the store.

A roar went up from the crowd gathering at the fence. Someone had fallen off a bronc.

More pickup trucks pulled into the yard, parking where they could and lining the lane. The crowd along the fence grew.

One cowboy parked close to the road. Janey watched him walk up the laneway. C.J.

She stared. He walked with a long stride, his thigh muscles flexing with each step.

He wore a pair of old jeans and a plain white T-shirt and the different clothes changed him. This was how C. J. Wright was supposed to dress, like a cowboy or a rancher. Like a normal guy from a small town in Montana. Not in button-down collars and gray trousers. Who the heck wore that stuff anymore? What on earth was the guy thinking when he put those clothes on in the morning?

She wished she hadn't seen him like *this,* though. He looked strong and fit and younger and so, so masculine in his cowboy hat.

Katie turned in her arms, drawing Janey's attention away from C.J. "Are you going on a horse?"

"Nope, not a chance." Janey's smile felt fake. She truly hoped Katie didn't sense that fakeness, or her discomfort in holding Katie on her lap.

When C.J. entered the yard, Angus noticed him and gave him a hard slap on the back.

C.J. grinned and returned the greeting. Janey's breath caught. Men. So physical, so big, so attractive and so dangerous.

Why was C.J. here? He hadn't joined the rodeo participants before. Was he going to ride a bronc?

She must have leaned forward because Katie protested.

"Give Katie to me," Amy said, "and go have some fun."

Janey didn't have to be told twice. She all but dumped Katie into Amy's lap, and then immediately missed the girl's weight in her arms.

She was a bona fide screwball. No doubt about it. She couldn't live with children and couldn't live without them.

She trudged toward the far end of the fence, away from C.J. and jumped up onto the bottom rail, throwing herself into the cheering, anything to keep her mind away from fragile Katie, or loud Johnny, or attention-starved Kyle.

AT SIX O'CLOCK, C.J. had rushed through closing the shop, then had gone to the grocery store and picked up an apple, a banana, three bags of chips and two chocolate bars. So much great chocolate at work, yet sometimes he craved the cheap stuff.

At the cash he'd grabbed an energy bar and had run into the alley behind Sweet Talk and jumped into his old Jeep.

By the time he'd reached the Sheltering Arms, the food had been history and he was licking chocolate and salt from his fingers, still hungry, but there was nothing he could do about it.

He parked behind a row of pickup trucks lining Hank Shelter's driveway.

His nerves jittered.

Before he got out of the Jeep, he put on his beige cowboy hat, settled it firmly onto his head. It changed him, made him feel stronger, as if he could handle anything.

People milled in the yard, near one of the fenced-off corrals. A cloud of dust rose from it. Everyone let out a huge cheer. Someone had fallen off a bronc, no doubt.

Despite the anxiety gnawing at his gut, C.J. remembered this much about the rodeo. The testosterone and the competition.

He stared around the Sheltering Arms. The buildings and grounds looked tended and clean.

A couple of ranch hands coaxed a bronc out of a horse trailer.

Someone slapped him on the back. Angus Kinsey.

"Hey, Angus," C.J. said. Angus was a great guy. Like Hank, he was generous with his property, his horses and his broncs, and had let C.J. practice on his ranch as much as he'd wanted when C.J. had worked there part-time as a teenager.

"How're things?" Angus asked. "You sold that candy store yet?"

The way Angus said *candy store* left no doubt what he thought of C.J. owning one. C.J. shook his head and laughed. Raging cowboy testosterone. "Not yet."

"You need to get rid of it and start ranching, boy."

"Amen," C.J. answered.

This was what he wanted. A life of hard labor on a ranch with other cowboys. With camaraderie and sharing the highs and the lows of cattle ranching, with earning a living with his hands and body then falling into bed at night exhausted from a day of good solid work, and teaching his son how to ranch. His greatest desire? To give his son a future.

His own future did *not* include candy-making.

When he glanced along the bodies lining the white fence, arms and elbows resting along the top of it, his sights zoomed in on Janey before any other individual, and that bothered him.

She stood on a lower rung watching someone in the corral. When she leaned forward, her dress hiked up the backs of her legs, well above her knees.

Lord, for a petite woman, she had great thighs.

He inserted himself among the spectators. He felt Janey watching him and looked her way. The black lipstick she'd had on earlier was gone. Her own natural pink shone on her full lips. They looked soft and moist and pretty. Damn.

"Hey, C.J.!" Hank picked himself up from the dusty ground inside the corral, where the bronc had just dropped him, and grinned. "You want to go a round on Dusty here?"

"Sure," C.J. called, but his pulse suddenly raced. *Do it. Just get in there and do it.*

He felt her eyes on him when he climbed over the fence.

He hadn't done this in four years, since the day Davey died.

"Davey," he whispered beneath his breath as he approached Dusty, "help me."

The bronc shied away from him.

Kelly Cooper caught Dusty and held him still. C.J. climbed on and settled himself in the saddle, grinning at Kelly as though there weren't ten devils dancing in his chest. God.

The second Kelly let the bronc loose, the animal bucked.

The bronc's first buck slammed through C.J., made his teeth snap together, nearly threw him out of the saddle. He curled his fist around the rope, ignored that it cut off circulation.

He tightened his knees against the horse, used his uncanny sense of balance to stay astride.

Each kick and landing thudded through his back, his arms, legs and butt. His blood pounded. Dust flew into his eyes.

Yelling and cheering swirled around him.

His right arm ached, his fist wrapped in the rigging burned, and every particle of his spine felt as if it was being permanently twisted. But he hung on, breathed hard and felt the buzz, the high that had always trumped everything else. Common sense had never, ever stood a chance.

He jumped from the bronc, ran away from those dangerous hooves and laughed. And laughed. Taking off his cowboy hat, he waved it in the air and shouted, "Whooooohooooo."

The applause of the audience coursed through his body like the beat of his blood. He jumped over the fence and accepted the handshakes and slaps on his shoulders.

"It's good to have you back," Angus said, and C.J. knew what he meant. It had been too long since his last rodeo. Four long years filled with bitterness and anger.

He banged his hat against his leg and a puff of dust rose from his jeans. He laughed again for the pure pleasure of it.

C.J. got up on a bronc three times during the evening, each time more thrilling than the last and, at the end, headed to his truck in the hush of dusk, willing his heart rate to slow and his body to relax, to come down from the high he hadn't experienced in so long.

From behind him, Shane MacGraw tapped C.J.'s hat forward over his face. "Hey, glad you got over whatever kept you away from rodeo, man."

C.J. caught his hat, shoved it back onto his head and grinned. "Thanks, Shane."

He slipped into the driver's side of his Jeep and sat still for a moment. He knew what Shane had assumed, what they had all thought—that after Davey's death he'd been afraid to get back on a bronc or a bull. That he was afraid he, too, would get killed. That he hadn't overcome his fear tonight to ride again.

Let them think that. The truth was far worse for him. It was eating him alive. He hadn't feared the broncs or the bulls or that he might not like riding anymore, or performing.

He feared that he'd like those seductive sensations

too much—of his blood whipping through his body, of excitement buzzing in his head, and of the adoration of the crowd. That he'd crave it even more than he used to in the old days, like a demon that had sunk in its claws and C.J. couldn't shake free. He didn't want that demon dogging him again. What if he couldn't control it this time?

Who would take care of Liam then? Liam deserved someone whole and responsible.

C.J. had hoped he was over that wildness that reminded him too much of his pretty impetuous mother and of his own crazy period after Davey died, of his life in the city and a dangerous flirtation with drugs and booze. He had to *force* himself to be done with all of that shit.

By the time he pulled into the driveway of the Hanging W and stopped in the yard, he had himself under control and the demons of his past put to bed for the night. He could control them.

One arm resting on the open window, he drummed his fingers on the door and studied the small house. The place was dark. Gramps must be in the back room watching TV, as usual.

There hadn't been a female in the Wright family in too many years. And it showed in the details—the house was clean, but didn't sparkle. No flowers graced the dirt around the foundation. The furniture was only serviceable, the decorations nonexistent.

C.J. stepped out of the car and up onto the veranda, avoiding the third step that looked to fall apart any day now.

He walked into the house and called, "Gramps?"

"Back here," came the muffled response.

Gramps sat in the closed-in back porch, watching a small TV propped on a rickety table. *Dancing with the Stars* blared. He slurped tea from a heavy china mug.

Moths beat against the screens of the open windows.

Liam sprawled on the sofa beside Gramps asleep, one leg hanging over the edge, his small hands curled into fists.

C.J. bent over and kissed his sweaty head. How come kid sweat smelled so much better than man sweat?

"How long has he been asleep?" C.J. asked.

"'Bout an hour." Gramps patted the boy's leg with one gnarled hand.

C.J. picked up his son. Liam rested boneless in his arms, as trusting as a newborn kitten. C.J. would do anything to have Liam trust him half as much when he was awake.

Instead of carrying him straight up to bed, he sat on the sofa with his boy on his lap. These opportunities were so rare.

He picked up one of Liam's hands. It covered a fraction of C.J.'s callused palm. Every nail on every finger of the tiny hand was perfect. Dirty, but perfect. He kissed the pale smattering of freckles on Liam's nose.

He should wake him to wash and brush his teeth, but C.J. didn't have the heart. He should get him settled into bed.

In a minute.

Gramps bent his head in the direction of the TV. "In the next couple of minutes, they'll announce which pair's being booted off the show. I think it's gonna be Cloris Leachman. She's a hell of a gal, but she can't dance worth shit."

C.J. laughed. "Gramps, how did you raise a daughter who ended up marrying a minister?"

"Don't know." Gramps looked at C.J. with brown eyes so like his own. C.J. definitely took after his mother's side of the family. "He's a good man, though. Does real good work with his church."

Yeah, he knew that.

"I'm going to put Liam to bed." He headed for the stairs, staring at the child limp in his arms.

"How did you happen?" he whispered. "How did something so good come out of the craziness that was me and Vicki?"

C.J. had missed the first two and a half years of his son's life. If he had to fight with his last cent, he was never missing any again.

He settled him into bed wearing his T-shirt and superhero underwear, then got a damp facecloth from the bathroom and wiped Liam's face. A smear of something that looked like dried mustard and ketchup mixed together came off after scrubbing.

Liam squirmed. Even in his sleep, he hated getting washed.

Looked as if Gramps had made hot dogs for dinner again. The kid needed more variety in his diet than hot dogs every night. So did Gramps.

In the next second, C.J. reminded himself that Liam had probably eaten better in the last eleven months with him and Gramps than he'd eaten in the prior two and a half years with his mother in Billings.

C.J. trudged downstairs.

Grabbing a bowl of cereal, he poured milk on it, wandered to the front of the house and stepped outside.

A faint breeze drifted toward the veranda, carrying with it the chirp of crickets.

Thinking of Liam, he leaned against the railing and ate his cereal. Now that he'd tasted fatherhood, he wanted more—a wife to share his burdens and his bed and to give Liam brothers and sisters.

Seemed like all C.J. did these days was wait. Wait to sell the store to become a full-time rancher. Wait for Liam to finally accept him. Wait for the right woman to come along to start a family. Wait for that family, so Liam could have little brothers and sisters.

Moonlight ran like pale butter over the land. In his imagination, C.J. caught a flash of little girls running in the fields with midnight dark hair and big black boots.

Wacky. Weird.

He shook his head to clear it of that crazy image.

His cereal gone, he returned to the kitchen, rinsed his bowl and spoon then wandered to the back porch.

"I hired Janey Wilson today. The girl who lives at the Sheltering Arms."

"The weird dresser?"

"Yup."

"Hank mentioned her." Gramps looked up at him. "You had any interest in the store? Any nibbles?"

"Nope." C.J. rubbed the back of his neck. "The sale sign's up in the window. Has been all summer. All the tourists saw it. I've advertised in papers across the state. Haven't had a single bite."

"Why not?" Gramps said.

C.J. had wondered the same thing. "Don't know."

Gramps shifted the leg resting on an old footstool.

"How's your leg?" C.J. asked.

"Knee hurts like a bugger. Can't wait for the operation."

"Anything new from the hospital?"

"Nope. Still waiting for a spot."

C.J. grabbed a cushion from the sofa and put it under Gramps's foot on the stool.

"How'd the rodeo practice go tonight?" Gramps asked. "You do okay?"

"Better than I expected." Gramps was the only soul on earth who knew how terrified C.J. was of entering the rodeo and of being sucked into that vortex of wildness in his soul. "My back feels like it's been rearranged into a pretzel."

Gramps huffed a laugh. "You riding broncs or bulls at the Sheltering Arms?"

"Broncs," C.J. answered. "Won't get on a bull until the day of competition."

Gramps nodded, as if he already suspected that. "You'll do good, son." He swallowed the last of his tea. "You'll win. Now that Amy won't let Hank ride the bulls anymore, you've got no competition out there. You always were the best after Hank."

C.J. stood. If only Dad had that much faith in him. "You heading up now, Gramps?"

"Naw, I'll watch one more show and then drag my old bones to bed. You go on. Don't worry about me."

C.J. headed for the door.

"Son?"

C.J. turned at the soft word.

Gramps watched him with kinder, wiser brown eyes than the ones C.J. saw in his own mirror. "Glad to see you having fun again."

C.J. shrugged. "I just need the money."

"Sure." Gramps's voice was quiet, but there was an undercurrent in the softly spoken word that C.J. refused to heed.

He climbed the stairs to the second floor, passing through the moonbeams cast through the small round window on the landing. Where else other than on this land could he find the security he needed for his son? No way was he dragging him back to the city to live in an apartment that smelled of rotting food and dirty clothes.

His son would live a clean, healthy life if C.J. had to turn himself inside out to make it happen.

He needed this land. Provided they didn't lose it to the government for back taxes first.

CHAPTER FIVE

JANEY SHOWED UP at his door at nine the following morning and said "Hi," with a wave of her fingers. Instead of her I-don't-care-what-the-world-thinks-of-me belligerence of the day before, she seemed reserved. Self-possessed.

She stood in front of him wearing a knee-length black skirt and a bright blue tank top she'd covered with a top made out of fish net, like she'd sewn a bunch of sexy lady's stockings together into one top and had thrown it over herself. She didn't seem to notice that it fell off one really white shoulder. All he could wonder was whether that skin felt as soft as it looked.

Man, he didn't need this today. He shouldn't be thinking of her that way.

He had to cover that peekaboo top. Even with a tank top underneath it was too tempting. Grabbing a clean apron from a hook, he thrust it into her hands.

"Here, put this on."

She did and it swamped her. She tied the strings around herself twice and made her waist look small above her generous hips. He curled his fingers and stuffed them into his pant pockets.

She'd piled her hair into some kind of neat bun on the back of her head. Good.

He took her to the candy-making room and gave her a tour. His voice echoed in the large room, bounced off the open ductwork in the high ceiling above as well as off all of the metal machines that didn't quite fill the space—the pulling machine, the hot table, the batch roller, the rope sizer, the revolving die, the carousel cooler and the wrapping machine.

He explained what each machine did. He patiently answered all of her questions, and there were a lot of them. Her interest seemed genuine.

Behind him, a huge gas range waited for the first pot of syrup to be put on to boil.

They stepped into the generous walk-in pantry and he showed her the candy-making supplies.

He took her through using the cash and weighing the candies and where to find their individual prices.

When Scotty came in for his weekly stash of menthol cough drops, C.J. guided Janey through dealing with a customer and giving out change.

Scotty thanked Janey and added, "Glad you got a job."

Janey returned his smile.

She seemed to have left her attitude at home today. Maybe she'd be okay in this job after all. C.J. covered a lot of the candy-making process, told her which candies were made on the premises and which were commercial.

Coop Yates came in with supplies C.J. had ordered from Billings at the end of last week. Coop smiled at Janey.

"Hi," he said.

She smiled shyly in return.

For some reason that bothered C.J. She hadn't smiled at him like that yesterday when she'd come in looking for a job. He took a case of sugar from Yates and shoved it into Janey's arms. "Take this to the back room and unpack it. It all goes into the pantry I showed you earlier."

Janey did as she was told but not before shooting him a puzzled frown.

Coop gave him an odd look.

"What?"

Coop shrugged and said, "Nothing." He handed C.J. the paperwork for the goods, C.J. signed receipt of them and Coop left.

C.J. carried a couple of more boxes to the pantry.

"Unpack and shelve this stuff, too."

He took a dolly out front and carted back the rest of the boxes.

They wiped the shelves then unpacked everything.

The telephone rang. C.J. strode to the front of the store to answer it.

"C.J.?" Mona's voice on the other end of the line sounded frazzled. Diner must be busy. He checked his watch. Lunchtime. Where had the morning gone?

"What's up, Mona?"

"We're all out of mints here. Roscoe Hunter is bugging me about it. Says he's not leaving without his daily mint. Can you believe it? Old coot." Her voice sounded as if she had pulled away from the phone a bit. "Yeah, I'm talking about you, Roscoe. Is it your personal aim in life to make me miserable?"

C.J. laughed. "You want me to bring some over?"

Mona released a huge sigh. "Would you? You're a doll, C.J. I don't want Roscoe's murder on my conscience."

"Be right there." He hung up.

He heard a noise behind him.

Janey took a large paper candy bag from the stack and dropped a leaking bag of sugar into it.

"Do you want to return this?" she asked.

"How much do you think we lost?"

"A couple of teaspoons."

"Not enough to worry about. I'll find a jar to put it in."

He realized he was hungry.

"Did you bring a lunch today?" He'd been so distracted by her peekaboo top first thing this morning he hadn't noticed whether she'd been carrying a bag.

"No," she said.

"Listen, I have this thing I do. I take new employees out to lunch on the first day. I have to run some mints over to the diner anyway."

She made a noncommittal sound.

"Lunch is my treat."

She nodded. "Okay."

C.J. grabbed a box of commercial wrapped mints from the back room then headed out of the shop.

Janey followed him onto the street.

"Aren't you going to lock the door?" she asked.

"Naw. The tourists are gone for the season and it's mainly just local folk around now."

She looked at him like he had a screw loose, and muttered, "Naive."

That bugged him. "This is Ordinary. These are my people."

She turned away and stalked down Main Street. "It's your funeral."

It reminded him that she was a stranger here and that she didn't know the town the way he did, and it showed how different they were.

"WHAT SHOULD I DO?" Walter asked, leaning forward in the diner booth toward his lunch partner, Gladys Graves.

Gladys had come to town a year ago to visit her daughter, Amy, at the Sheltering Arms and had never left. Walter had been watching her ever since, hoping they could move a little closer together.

Gladys folded her hands on top of the table between them. "You've already talked to C.J.?" she asked.

"Yes. The boy won't listen to me. He's still trying to sell the store." Walter watched the ghost of a sad smile play around Gladys's lips, her mouth small in her face, her cheekbones high. Fine lines radiated from the corners of her eyes. She didn't color her hair. It curled around her face in a soft white cloud.

As he always did, Walter marveled at how beautifully she was aging for a sixty-something. Amy had inherited her beauty from her mother.

"How much interest does C.J. have in the store?" Gladys asked.

Walter shook his head. "None. It's a good business, though, and brings in a steady income. He wants to liquidate, though, so he can pay taxes on the ranch and get that deadbeat Vicki off his back."

Gladys raised her narrow white eyebrows. Walter knew why. Because he rarely used terms like *deadbeat*. He didn't call people names. "That woman deserves that and more for what she's put C.J. through."

"Maybe," Gladys said, reasonably. "Drugs do awful things to people, though. You know that."

"Gladys, I know you think I'm being unreasonable, but C.J. is my only child." Walter covered his mouth with his hand. "I want him safe and happy."

"C.J.'s no longer a boy," Gladys said. "He's doing a good job of turning his life around. Have faith in him."

"I try to. I really do. It's hard when he's becoming involved in the rodeo again and hiring the likes of that Gothic girl who'll invite him into her bed and—" Realizing his mistake, he cut himself off, but too late. Gladys was fond of that girl, lived with her on the Sheltering Arms.

The smile fell from her face. She picked up her purse and started to slide out of the booth.

"Gladys, stop." A rush of panic sent his head spinning. He reached for her hand and held her still, wouldn't let her leave. "I'm sorry. We won't talk about her. We'll discuss something else."

"I'm loyal to my friends, Walter," she said. "Janey is a good woman."

"I know—"

"No, Walter, you don't." She stood and watched him with pity in her eyes. "You are wonderful in your care of your flock and a good, good man, but sometimes you can be as dumb as a stump."

She turned and left, barely missing Mona, who carried their lunches to the table.

Walter stared after her. What had he done?

He stared at the bowl of soup in front of the spot Gladys had vacated, then at the sandwich he no longer wanted.

AWESOME! *Awe. Some.* Janey walked down the street beside C.J.

So far, she loved everything about the candy store. Even working with C.J. had been okay. She craved his knowledge. Too bad she couldn't split his skull open and take everything he knew so she wouldn't have to deal with the reality of the man.

Just as Janey and C.J. passed the barbershop, raucous laughter flowed through the open doorway onto the street. Janey glanced in. A bunch of old men sat around while the barber worked on a man in one of the chairs in front of a wall of mirrors.

"Hey," C.J. called and they waved.

Janey lifted her hand in a tentative wave, then kept walking, not waiting to see whether anyone returned it.

They passed Kurt, asleep in the same doorway he'd been in yesterday. C.J. reached into his pocket and tossed some change into the paper coffee cup, but with such an air of distraction, Janey wasn't certain he was even aware that he'd done it.

They approached the New American Diner. *New* forty years ago, maybe.

C.J. opened the door and stepped back to allow her to enter ahead of him. A lot of people here seemed to have manners.

She nearly collided with a woman running out.

"Gladys!" she blurted.

Gladys looked preoccupied. A frown marred her usually smooth forehead.

"Janey," Gladys said. "Just going in for lunch?"

Janey could tell Gladys was trying to sound cheerful, but she wasn't pulling it off.

"What's wrong?" Janey asked.

Gladys took a deep breath and visibly calmed herself. "I'm fine. I'll see you at the ranch for dinner."

Then she whirled back and said, "You're a lovely young woman. Don't take any shit in there." She gestured with her head toward the diner, then stomped away.

Gladys never stomped, and she never, ever swore. Janey got goose bumps.

She stepped into the restaurant and halted inside the door, wishing that C.J. had entered first. The place was packed. Conversations swirled around her. She recognized no one.

The noise level reduced when people spotted her. Not another bug-under-glass moment.

With her makeup and hair and weird clothes, she attracted attention, but it was all part of her strategy called hiding in plain sight. Sometimes, though, she wished she could be normal and walk out into the world as herself, but that was never going to happen, was it?

The world was a tough place and a girl did what a girl had to do.

The chatter of conversations picked up again.

Then C.J. stepped in behind her, unaware of the problem.

He looked around the diner and frowned. A second later, Janey realized why.

Every booth was taken.

C.J. started forward, slowly, his steps heavy. He approached a booth across from the grill.

No. No, I do not *want to sit with C.J.'s father. Absolutely not.*

When he motioned her to precede him into the booth opposite the Rev, she hesitated, realized she couldn't do a thing, couldn't walk out of here without embarrassing all of them.

She slid onto the bench seat and folded her hands in her lap. The Reverend watched her from beneath bushy dark eyebrows, shooting twin daggers of animosity her way.

Right back atcha, Rev. I'm not any happier about being here with you than you are with me.

"C.J., can you eat that soup?" The Rev pointed to a bowl sitting on their side of the table. "My guest had to run."

Janey's stomach rumbled. "Was it Gladys?"

The Rev sent her a keen look. "That's none of your business, young lady."

"Dad—"

"Gladys is my friend," Janey said.

"Janey—"

"She's my friend, too," the Reverend replied.

"Then why did you make her cry?" Janey leaned forward on the bench.

Reverend Wright pulled away. "She was crying?"

If Janey didn't already know him as an uptight prig, she'd swear he felt bad for Gladys.

"What did you say to her?"

The Rev's face turned bright red. "Nothing," he mumbled.

If Janey didn't know better, she would think his flush was shame.

"Liar," she said. "I got your number the minute I met you, Rev."

He scowled. "Don't call me that. It's disrespectful."

"So is your attitude toward me." Janey opened her mouth to say more, to let loose her hostility and put this self-righteous man in his place.

"Stop it. Both of you." C.J.'s tone was sharp.

Chastised, Janey sat back.

He pushed the bowl of soup toward her. "If you want it, eat it."

She glared at the Reverend one last time. "Okay, but only because I don't want it to go to waste." She started in on the soup.

A waitress approached with a pot of coffee in her hand.

"Hey, Mona," C.J. said, sliding the box toward her. "Here are your mints."

"Thanks, C.J. Bill the diner, okay?" She picked up the box of mints, turned and slammed it onto the counter. "Knock yourself out, Roscoe."

Janey turned in her seat to watch over C.J.'s shoulder. An older man wearing a plaid shirt and a frown that looked permanent reached in for a mint. "Only wanted one," he grumbled.

Mona winked at C.J. "Grumpy old man," she whispered.

"I heard that." Roscoe turned and walked out of the diner.

"Today's specials," Mona said, "are cream of potato soup and meat loaf surprise. Be back in a minute for your orders." She ran on her way.

Janey's stomach growled. She hoped she was getting a whole lot more than a bowl of soup for lunch. "Wonder what the surprise in the meat loaf is?"

"Spinach and boiled eggs," C.J. said. "They have it here once a week. It's good."

C.J. straightened his cutlery. The Rev ate his sandwich staring down at his plate. The pair of them looked everywhere but at each other. Weird. She didn't think she was imagining the tension between them.

She finished the soup and pushed the bowl away from her.

Mona hustled to the table and pulled an order pad out of her pocket. "What do you want?" She stared at Janey. Janey didn't think she saw rudeness there. It sort of looked like curiosity and maybe, admiration?

C.J. looked down at Janey. "What'll you have?"

Yes! She could have more food.

"Turkey club on brown, please, toasted," Janey said. "Can you make the bacon well-done, please?"

A slow smile spread across Mona's face. She obviously hadn't expected Janey to have manners. Sometimes, it was good to turn people's expectations upside down.

"What kind of potatoes do you want?"

Janey perked up. "Fries." Her stomach grumbled again. "Can I have them with gravy?"

"Sure. You want a coffee?"

Janey nodded.

"I'll have to get another pot."

"Take your time if you have to. You're real busy."

Mona grinned. "Thanks."

C.J. ordered the same thing, without the gravy.

The Rev watched her while he ate, a puzzled frown on his face.

"What?" she said, jutting her chin forward.

The Rev opened his mouth to respond, but C.J. shot him a look and he closed his mouth.

A couple of people called for refills on their coffee. Mona returned with a fresh pot straight to Janey's table. "Since you were willing to be patient, you get the first cup of the fresh stuff."

She winked at Janey.

Janey shrugged, raised her shoulders to her ears, and smiled, a tiny one. Warm blood rushed up her neck and cheeks. Someone actually liked her.

The Reverend finished his meal. "Tell Roy lunch was excellent, as usual. What do I owe you?"

"I'll get it, Dad."

Reverend Wright looked at C.J. "Thanks," he said, then stood and left with a backward glance at Janey, that puzzled frown still firmly in place.

Mona took the Rev's dirty dishes and put them on the counter behind her, reaching between a couple of big men, then raced to fill more coffee cups.

C.J. moved to the other side of the table, facing Janey.

The hot coffee smelled almost as good as the scents from the grill.

She pulled a small bowl of packets of sugar toward herself and took out three of them, pinching one corner from each packet.

Mona placed a small pot of cream onto the table.

C.J. drizzled a little into his coffee. "You made a friend in Mona. She doesn't usually take to strangers."

"I respect working women." *I want to be one.*

Janey dumped all three packets of sugar into her coffee at once. She stirred then added cream to the brim.

She sipped it. Good. She sipped again, then topped up the cup with more cream, replacing the liquid she'd swallowed with more cream, sipped another couple of times and added more cream. It cooled down the coffee fast, but she didn't mind. She took another sip. Warm and sweet and rich.

She looked up to find C.J. watching her and flushed under his heavy stare.

"What?" she asked, belligerence a weight in her voice.

"You sure do like your coffee doctored," C.J. said.

Defiance stiffened her spine. "The cream and sugar are free."

C.J. looked puzzled and said, "Okay."

Mona brought their meals.

Janey squirted lots of ketchup on her fries because, like cream and sugar, it was free. C.J. could think she was as weird as he wanted to.

She bit into her sandwich and chewed. Oh, man, heaven. She bit off more. Before she knew it, she'd finished all but one quarter, forgetting that C.J. sat across the booth from her.

All of Hannah's amazing food that Janey had eaten in the last year, three meals a day plus snacks, hadn't managed to fill the gaping hole inside of her that growing up in poverty had carved out.

C.J. continued to eat his sandwich and fries. Janey touched a dot of ketchup on her plate with her forefinger and licked it.

She wanted to eat that last quarter of her sandwich, but wrapped it in her paper napkin instead.

"You saving that for later?" C.J. stood.

Janey shrugged and slid from the booth.

C.J. paid for the food and they left the restaurant.

Kurt still sat on the sidewalk just past the diner, awake now.

Janey handed him her piece of leftover sandwich.

"You again," Kurt breathed. "Thanks."

She nodded and walked away, felt C.J. watching her but refused to meet his eye. If he didn't like that she gave part of the food he'd paid for to Kurt, he could kiss her butt.

CHAPTER SIX

THE FOLLOWING MORNING, right before C.J. was about to open the store, he asked Janey to grab a box of Tootsie Rolls from the back to top up the bin.

While in the pantry, she heard the door chime ring. A customer. When she swiped a cloth across the top of the box to remove a faint layer of dust, it rang again. She rushed to the front and found the store *flooded* with people. She'd had no idea the place could get so busy.

"Janey, come over here and help me serve customers." C.J. scooped candy into a bag.

She set the box of Tootsie Rolls down and ran to stand beside him.

"Find out what Bernice wants," he said.

"Hi, honey," Bernice said. "Glad to see you got a job."

Janey offered Bernice a tentative smile. "Can I help you?"

"Give me a small bag of after-dinner mints. Real small." She patted a generous hip. "Wish I could eat more, but I have to watch my waistline." Bernice's husky laugh filled the room.

A man wearing a greasy hairpiece and a greasier smile said, "Bernice, come over to my place tonight. I'll be happy to show you what I think of your waistline."

"Mason, if you were half the lady killer you think you are, I'd have dated you long ago. Dream on."

Chuckles filtered around the room.

Janey scooped a handful of pastel mints into a bag.

Bernice handed her a five-dollar bill and she made change.

"How much did the candy weigh?" C.J. asked.

"Three ounces."

"Good, you got the price right."

She handed Bernice her change.

Janey turned to the next customer. A short, wiry man asked for two chocolates with mint filling. Janey served him.

She turned her back to the customers and whispered to C.J., "Wow, the people in this town like their candy in small bits."

His answering grunt didn't tell her much.

When Janey turned to serve the next person, the hairs on her neck stood up and she got the eeriest feeling that everyone waiting to be served was staring at her. She glanced around. They were.

She shut down, went into automatic pilot mode.

She fumbled the bags, dropped two of them on the floor.

"Throw those out," C.J. said.

She tossed them into the garbage can then served two more people. She'd never met them before, had no idea what their names were. She tried to smile but couldn't, her discomfort freezing the muscles of her face.

She dropped half a scoopful of humbugs into the neighboring caramel bin.

"What's wrong with you?" C.J. asked.

"Nothing. I'll clean it up later."

The thinning crowd still focused attention on her.
Stop staring at me.

She wished she could say it out loud.

"I gotta run to the back for a special order for Howard," C.J. said. "Finish up with the others, okay?"

Janey looked around. Her breath came a little more easily now that there were fewer people in the shop watching her.

Ten minutes later, every customer had been served. The empty room felt hollow with just the two of them left in it. She picked humbugs out of the caramels and returned them to their own bin.

C.J. opened the drawer of the antique cash register with the big brass keys. "Haven't had that many people in here at one time since Labor Day weekend brought the tourists out."

Janey felt him watching her. "They came to see me, didn't they?" she asked, her voice low.

"Yeah. Word that you were in the diner with me yesterday probably spread after we left."

"Did you know they'd do that?"

"I figured they might come to gawk at the Goth woman I hired."

"Why?" She couldn't help the defensiveness in her tone.

"You stand out here."

"Don't you people get TV? Don't you know that that—" she poked a finger in the direction of his chest "—isn't the way normal people dress? You all need to move into the twenty-first century."

C.J.'s jaw tightened. "Get real. If you don't want people to stare, then dress normal."

She picked up a towel that lay on the end of the counter and stomped to the back room. Trying to control her temper, she took her time hanging the towel just so on the rod in the bathroom.

In the city, her clothes hadn't mattered, but here? In this dinky little town? They mattered too much. They didn't see enough oddballs. She guessed that Kurt was about as odd as they got.

She gripped the towel rod for a minute. What if she dressed like a normal person? Who would she be then? How would she protect herself?

C.J. appeared in the doorway. She straightened and stared at him, forcing her chin up.

"It won't last," he said. "They'll get used to you and stop staring. In a day or two, you'll be one of us."

She glanced around the back room at the gray cinder-block walls and the high ceilings and the big steel machines that spun sugar and water into children's dreams and swallowed hard.

"What do you think they thought of me?"

"You fishing for compliments?"

She stared at him. "What do you mean?"

"I mean you want me to tell you they all probably thought you were pretty?"

She shook her head, confused. "They weren't coming in to criticize me?"

"You think they were here to condemn you? Man, you have a low opinion of humanity. They were just curious, that's all."

She wanted to be here. Liked the work.

"It's better than what I'd been afraid of," C.J. said. "That they'd stop shopping here. We made a tidy little sum for only forty-five minutes' worth of work."

Janey knew C.J. was trying to make her feel better and she appreciated it.

He leaned against the doorjamb and gestured toward her with his chin. "So why *do* you dress like that?"

How could she explain it to him? "Life isn't always kind to people. I've been through a lot. I put these clothes on to keep people away from me. So I won't get hurt."

Why was she confessing so much to this guy?

"It's your shell?"

"Yeah. It keeps people away."

"That might work in the city, but it won't work here. The townspeople are just too friendly."

This time he gestured toward the store with his chin. "No one said anything bad, did they?"

She shook her head no.

"They didn't look like they thought anything bad, did they?"

"No."

"Same thing happened a couple of months ago when a rock singer came sniffing around looking to buy a ranch. Everyone went a little nuts over him for a while until they got used to him."

"Yeah?"

"Yeah. This will calm down in a day or two."

He turned toward the pantry. "I need to check something with the supplies."

The door chime rang.

"I'll get that," she said, already feeling better after C.J.'s pep talk.

She walked to the front of the building.

Just inside the store, she stopped. Two people stood

in front of the counter, an older man, in his seventies maybe, and a young boy, about three at a guess.

They had to be relatives of C.J. The boy looked an awful lot like C.J. His son, maybe? Did he have other kids? Was he married?

She hoped the kid didn't come into the store very often.

The old man, a toughened, sun-dried version of C.J. in maybe forty years, had a smile as pretty as C.J.'s, wide and white.

"Can I help you?" she asked.

"Sure." The older man stepped forward. The child grabbed his hand and followed. "Is C.J. around?"

Janey called for him.

C.J. smiled when he saw them and walked around to the front of the counter.

Janey must have made a noise because three generations of men with brown eyes flickering with hazel highlights, and deep clefts in their chins, stared at her. She had the dizzying sensation that in some strange fateful way she was looking at her future. Holy moly. The skittering of spider feet up her neck creeped her out.

This was too weird. Why would she think she'd ever be part of C.J.'s family? No way was she ever having a conventional life with a husband and kids. No freaking way.

REVEREND WRIGHT STEPPED into the church and stopped.

Gladys stood by the altar arranging flowers in an oversize vase.

He started down the aisle toward the front of the church, studying her.

A small trim woman, her effect on him was anything *but* small. He liked her slim waist and her soft hips.

Gladys. Look at me. See me for who I really am and care for me anyway.

He stepped up to the altar, the three marble stairs muted by a gold runner.

She smelled like tangerines, like a crisp fall day.

"Gladys," he whispered.

Gladys turned and smiled. So. She'd forgiven him. Thank you, dear God.

"Gladys," he said. Sometimes that was enough, just to say her name, to know that she was near, to acknowledge to himself how much he cared for her.

Perhaps it was time to do something about that. His hands felt too big. He was clumsy. Awkward.

"Would you care to join me in the rectory for tea?" he asked. The voice that rolled to the rafters every Sunday sounded thin.

What if she said no?

Her eyebrows lifted in mild surprise and she smiled, her white teeth framed by soft pink lips.

He adored her smile. "Thank you, Walter. I'd like that."

As he led her through the side door to the rectory, she walked beside him silently.

"You are always calm," he blurted.

"I'm happy these days, Walter." Her flowered skirt swirled around her legs when she stepped into the rectory ahead of him, then moved aside to allow him to lead her to the kitchen. "I live with my daughter and her wonderful husband, and I'm surrounded by children most days."

"So life with Hank and Amy agrees with you?"

He filled the kettle.

"Yes, life on the Sheltering Arms is more than I had hoped to have at this stage in my life."

Gladys sat in a captain's chair at the round oak table a parishioner had donated years ago.

Reverend Wright sat opposite her, his slightly unsteady hands folded in his lap.

"And you, Walter?" Gladys asked. "Are you happy?"

His name sounded good in her gentle voice.

"Not as happy as I'd like." He leaned forward. "Gladys, may I speak openly?"

"Of course. What's troubling you?" Walter had the eerie feeling that their roles were reversed, that Gladys was the minister and he the penitent.

"It's C.J." He rested his knobby elbows on the table and covered his mouth with his hands. "I'm worried about him."

She leaned forward, too, ready to do battle, this woman with soft eyes and a soft heart and a backbone of steel. "Yes, I know. About Janey."

"No. About the rodeo."

"Hank's rodeo?" Gladys asked.

"Yes. C.J.'s involvement worries me. Four years ago, his best friend was gored by a bull in the ring. C.J. was there and saw the whole thing. He'd been rebellious since his mother's death in a car crash, but after Davey's death he went really wild."

He hesitated. "I didn't know how to comfort him. All of these years I've offered comfort to everyone in town, but I didn't have a clue how to make this all right for my son. He left for the city and plowed his way through alcohol and women."

Could he tell her the rest? When the kettle whistled,

he stood, absurdly relieved. He filled the teapot and set it on a trivet on the table.

While she waited patiently for him to finish, he sat again. He needed to get things off his chest. "I was—" He coughed and began again. "To my shame, I was glad that it hadn't been C.J. who was killed that day."

"Of course you were."

His gaze flew to hers. "It wasn't wrong of me to secretly rejoice that the young man killed wasn't my son?" The bitterness in his voice shocked him.

"It was a very human response." She laid her hand on his on the tabletop and he was humbled by her generosity. Who was the better person here? Certainly not him, although he was a man of God.

He poured their tea and gave thanks for this lovely woman.

A quiet half hour later, during which time they spoke of nothing and everything, he escorted her out of the rectory. She climbed into her car and opened her window.

"Gladys," he said, leaning his forearms on the window well of the driver's door. "I haven't dated a woman since my wife died six years ago."

He stared at his long fingers, gangly like the rest of him. He was no prize. "I don't know how to date."

"Of course you do, Walter. We just had a very lovely date, didn't we?"

"Did we?" he asked quietly, praying it was true, hoping he had finally started something with Gladys.

When she put the car into gear and pulled away slowly, her Mona Lisa smile spoke of things he hadn't dared to wish for.

He'd only ever lain with one woman. How odd to

think that, at this late stage in his life, he might have another chance at love.

At the sound of the phone ringing inside, he ran to answer it.

"Walter, how are you?"

"Max, I'm okay." Max Golden was his closest friend.

"Listen, I heard C.J. hired that girl from Hank's place. You okay with that?"

Max knew him so well. "No. I'm worried. I really wish he wouldn't have anything to do with her."

"I thought so. I'll put on my thinking cap and see if I can come up with some ideas to help you out."

"Thanks, Max. You're a good friend."

"You coming to the powwow on Saturday?"

"I wouldn't miss it for the world."

Between Gladys and Max, he might be okay.

"JANEY, THIS IS my grandfather and my son, Liam," C.J. said, confirming her guesses about their connections.

After nodding to her, the older man turned to C.J. "Hospital called. Some poor old bugger died the day before his knee-replacement surgery. They're taking me in his place. I'm heading over now. Operation's tomorrow morning at ten."

"Gramps, that's great. I'll drive you over."

"Naw, don't worry. You stay here with Liam."

"Right. Yeah. He'll have to stay here with me." C.J. approached the boy. "What do you think? Want to watch me teach Janey how to make candies?"

"Every day?" Janey asked and, at the urgent tone underlying the question, C.J. raised his eyebrows.

"Yeah," he answered, "for a month or so."

Janey's stomach lurched. Every day for a month. No,

she didn't want that. Hadn't she gone out of her way to escape the children on the ranch?

Don't worry about it. You can survive one month.

Surely one kid without cancer would be easier to handle than a ranch full of cancer survivors. This kid had a full head of hair and a healthy glow. She could do it. Really, she could. Too bad not a lot of conviction bolstered the thought.

C.J. escorted his grandfather to the door.

"Gramps, I'm so happy for you. Liam and I will come visit in the hospital tomorrow night. See how the operation went."

"Looking forward to it." With that last remark, the old man left and Janey stood alone in the store with C.J. and his son, wondering whether she could go home sick. It would be the truth. She sure felt sick, emotionally, mentally.

And then what? Call in sick every day for the next month? She needed this job and she needed this store and she couldn't avoid this little boy.

Suck it up, Janey.

She'd been doing that all of her life and was so damned tired of always having to pretend to be strong.

The child didn't answer his father's question about helping to make candies. Nor did he take his eyes off Janey. He walked over to her and pointed to her face. Janey didn't know what he wanted. She looked at C.J. From his puzzled frown, she gathered that he didn't know either.

Liam still stretched his hand toward her face. He wanted to touch her. No. She didn't want to do this, but she did, because the child was…a child. Kids deserved what they needed.

She bent forward and the boy put one finger on her mascara-coated eyelashes. He touched her eyebrow ring and nodded, and Janey jerked away from him. Being touched by a child hurt, even one who wasn't recovering from cancer, or fighting it, or dying from it.

He touched the tattoo on the inside of her left elbow with one finger and left it there, staring. His hand, his incredibly tiny soft finger, sent a dagger shooting through her. Oh, yes, *any* child's touch could hurt her these days.

"What's this?" he asked, his voice barely audible.

The shock on C.J.'s face quickly turned to anger. She hadn't done anything wrong, so she knew it wasn't about her. So what was he angry about?

She returned her attention to Liam. "It says *joy.*" She'd gotten it a week after Cheryl was born when Janey realized what a blessing in disguise her baby was.

"Spell it like that?" He scratched it lightly with his nail.

Janey shivered and nodded. "In Japanese."

"Japanese?" Janey nodded to the boy. "'Kay."

He curled his small fingers into the palm of her hand and she grasped them, couldn't help herself, but it hurt. They were even smaller than Cheryl's had been when she'd died.

Resting his head on her arm, he leaned against her and put the middle fingers of his other hand into his mouth.

MAN, LIFE WAS UNFAIR.

C.J. had learned that lesson the day his mother had died and he'd been left with only the harder parent, the prickly and uptight and severe one, the less adored one who had not one sliver of Mom's zest for life. But why did life have to continually kick C.J. in the teeth with its unfairness?

A swollen, unreasonable anger flooded his chest, but darn, Janey had done in six minutes what he hadn't been able to do in close to a year—crack the crust of Liam's outer shell.

It wasn't fair.

Liam hadn't looked content, or stable, or trustful since C.J. had rescued him from Vicki.

All it had taken from Janey was a shovel load of mascara, piercings and a tattoo—shades of Vicki that Liam no doubt recognized on another woman.

Had C.J. done the right thing taking Liam away from his mother? He remembered the dirt in the apartment, and Liam in a filthy diaper and hungry and crying. Yes, he'd been right to do it, but it seemed that Liam missed his mother nonetheless. Or a reasonable facsimile. What a mother represented.

Janey tried to wriggle her hand out of his son's tiny fist, but he wouldn't let go. She turned and headed into the candy-making room and he followed like a little lamb.

A look of such pain crossed Janey's face that C.J. wondered about its source.

He phoned his dad and told him about Gramps going to the hospital.

"Can you come out with Liam and me to the hospital tomorrow night and drive Gramps's car home for him? I don't want it to sit in the parking lot for the next week."

"Of course. Glad to hear Randal's having the operation. I'd like to visit with him for a while. Has he read the latest John Grisham?"

"I don't think so."

"I'll pick it up for him."

"Great. Liam and I will have an early dinner, then I'll pick you up. Is seven okay?"

"See you then."

C.J. dropped the receiver back into the cradle. About time Gramps got his knees fixed.

He followed Liam and Janey into the back room to check on what they were doing. They had the back door open and sat on the one concrete step that led outside.

BizzyBelle lay in a patch of sun, her big mouth chewing her cud slowly and lazily.

"BizzyBelle is my friend," Liam told Janey. The words about broke C.J.'s heart. Was there anyone on this earth with whom Liam wasn't friendly besides his own father?

"She's big, isn't she?" Janey asked.

Liam leaned his head on her arm. "Yeah."

Janey looked down at the top of his head. Even in profile, her face couldn't disguise her pain. What was that about?

Then he remembered that she'd had a daughter who'd visited the Sheltering Arms for a few weeks and then had died later. It knocked the wind out of him.

Oh, God. No wonder it was hard for her to touch Liam, or have him touch her.

What a mess they were all stuck in.

He craved Liam's attention and love. Liam deserved a good mother and latched onto a woman who reminded him of his own. Janey probably wanted her own child back rather than having to deal with someone else's.

C.J. needed an employee. Janey had to have a job.

Gramps was having long overdue surgery. His recovery would take a month, at least.

So, the three of them would be here with each other for that month. The only person he could think of to take care of Liam for that time was his dad. C.J.'s pride wouldn't let him ask, though. Dad had disapproved of his having had a baby out of wedlock. He'd disapproved of his hiring of Janey and Janey was the problem here right now.

What a mess.

The store's doorbell chimed.

"Be with you in a minute," he called.

"Don't take too long," a female voice said. "I'm on a tight schedule."

C.J. stilled. Damn. Marjorie Bates. The Children and Family Services worker on his case.

CHAPTER SEVEN

C.J. STARED at Liam and panicked. If Marjorie knew he was here for the next month, close to those big machines, hanging around while C.J. boiled huge pots of syrup, she'd flip.

Was there a law against having kids in the back room of a place like this?

He didn't want to take a chance on finding that out from Marjorie.

"Take Liam out into the backyard and stay there until I tell you to come in."

Janey looked alarmed by C.J.'s tone. "What? Why?"

"Just do it," he ordered, none too gently.

She did as she was told, but frowned before she left.

C.J. closed the back door then headed out front.

"Hey, Marjorie," he said, trying to sound as casual as possible.

Short and wide, Marjorie reminded C.J. of Gramps's John Deere tractor, strong and dependable, but plain.

Her perennial frown seemed deeper than usual. Bad news? She wasn't unkind, but she took her responsibilities seriously.

"Where's Liam?" she asked without preamble.

"What do you mean?" C.J. scooped salt-water taffy into a bag. He knew she liked it. He wasn't above bribery.

"I went out to the ranch first. There was no one there."

"Gramps must have taken him somewhere. If you'd given me notice, I could have arranged for Liam to be there."

Marjorie set one hand on the candy display case. "I've received a complaint about you."

C.J. stilled. "About what?"

"It doesn't matter. I have to check them all out."

"A complaint from whom?" He knew the belligerence in his voice wouldn't earn him points with Marjorie, but who the hell had filed a complaint against him with Children and Family Services? And why? Even before he finished the thought, he knew. Vicki's parents.

"It was the Fishers, wasn't it?"

Marjorie nodded. "They're worried about the company you're keeping." Damn. Janey? He wasn't keeping company with her. He was only employing her.

"I'm not keeping company with anyone," he said. "I don't date."

Marjorie didn't respond to that. "They're only trying to make sure their grandson is okay."

C.J. doubted that. They were playing dirty. Probably someone in town had called them yesterday to tell them about Janey. Who had they grown that close to in town? Who was their spy? Why was this person spying, calling the Fishers in Billings? Stirring up trouble for him?

"You're sure everything is okay with Liam?" Marjorie asked.

"Yes." Damn. He shouldn't have shouted. He moderated his tone. "He likes the ranch, he likes his grandfather. He likes visiting the store."

Marjorie still looked troubled, but said, "I really do have a tight schedule today. I'd better go."

She took the bag of candy he proffered and headed out of the shop.

C.J. sagged against the counter. His breath whooshed out of him. What the *hell* was going on? Who was talking to Vicki's parents? Who did they know in town?

He stalked to the back door, but stopped when he saw Janey and Liam through the small window, in the yard with Bizzy, their heads together while Liam talked to her. Talked to *her,* said more in a few minutes than he'd said to C.J. in a year.

He had people spying on him to jeopardize his custody of Liam when C.J. loved the daylights out of his son, and his son would rather spend time with a stranger than with him.

His pulse quieted, but only after he hauled himself under control with a crazy effort. Why was life so hard and complicated? Why couldn't a man have a simple, straightforward relationship with his own son?

Opening the door, he stepped out.

Just then, Liam squealed, "*Peeeyouuuu,* stinky," and squeezed his little nostrils shut between the thumb and forefinger of his right hand.

Whoo. BizzyBelle had farted—a real doozy. C.J. closed the door so the smell wouldn't drift inside.

Janey waved her hands in front of her nose and dragged Liam to the far corner of the backyard. She laughed, a light airy sound so foreign to her clothing and ugly boots and piercings, and to her big tough attitude, that C.J. did a double take to make sure that beautiful sound was really coming from her.

C.J., arrested by the look on her face, watched for the pure pleasure of seeing Janey light up.

Could anything be less conducive to appreciating a woman than standing in a bubble of BizzyBelle's gross methane gas? And yet, he couldn't stop watching Janey. She sparkled.

Liam joined in with a tiny high-pitched giggle, the first time C.J. had heard his son so happy. Liam threw himself against Janey's legs and her back hit the fence at the end of the yard.

As if the sappiest violins played their sympathetic strains through his head, C.J.'s sinuses tingled.

Someday Liam would laugh like that for him, without big stinky cow farts or a pretty woman making it happen. Just C.J. himself, a vow he intended to keep.

Liam lifted his arms for Janey to pick him up. She did and turned her face to the sun and closed her eyes.

Liam settled his head on her shoulder and tucked his thumb into his mouth. C.J. knew what that meant. Liam could be asleep in no time. He looked as though he was nearly there already.

Janey looked down at him and C.J. watched the oddest emotion cross her face, not anger nor resentment, but something achy like regret.

How old was her daughter when she died? Older than Liam, for sure.

That begged another question. Janey was barely into her twenties, so how young had she started having sex? How old was she when her daughter was born?

Was it one guy or had she been promiscuous? He had a right to be cautious around her and to curb his attraction.

He approached and said, "You had a little girl."

Janey jumped. He'd startled her. She slammed the shutters on her feelings so fast he felt a cold breeze.

"Yes. Her name was Cheryl."

"I heard she died. I'm real sorry about that."

She touched Liam's baby-fine hair, took a small tuft of it and rubbed it between her fingers. "Thanks."

"How old was she?"

"Six."

Man, life was harsh.

If Cheryl had been six, at her birth what had Janey been? Still a child?

"How old were you when you had Cheryl?"

Janey looked at C.J., defiance and attitude in her expression. "Not that it's any business of yours, but I'd just turned fifteen."

"Fifteen?" Cripes, she'd been screwing around when she was only fourteen? Maybe she was as wild as she looked. "How old was the baby's father?"

She shrugged.

What the hell did that mean?

"Were you married to him?"

"No."

A pulse beat in his neck. "Do you still see the father?"

She shook her head.

"Does he know about his daughter?"

Again, she shook her head, but her cheeks got red.

So, she'd kept her daughter a secret from the child's father, just as Vicki had done to him. Rotten thing to do. He'd been thinking lately that maybe she was a better person than Vicki. So wrong. "Did he ever pay support?"

Again, she shook her head.

He took Liam from her, too roughly, but Liam didn't stir. "I'm going to put him down for a nap." As much as her decisions pissed him off, her situation wasn't for him to judge. Her daughter was dead, so what did it matter? The thought turned down the volume on his anger.

"A nap?" she asked. "Does he have a cot here somewhere?"

"There's a vacant apartment above the store, partially furnished."

"An apartment?" Janey perked up.

"You interested?" As long as she wasn't blatantly promiscuous—and come to think of it, he'd heard no rumors indicating she was—while she lived there, it could work. The rent would certainly help.

"I might be."

"C'mon. I'll show it to you."

Through a door from the candy-making room and up a flight of stairs, C.J. led her to the apartment.

He stepped inside and Janey followed through the sparsely decorated living room into the spacious bedroom at the far end of the apartment.

"Can you close the blinds?" he asked Janey.

She did while he set Liam on the bed and removed the child's sneakers, each one so tiny he could hold it in the palm of his hand. He put them on the rag rug on the floor beside the bed.

Pulling back a faded well-worn quilt his grandmother had made years ago, he settled Liam in, covering him with the soft fabric.

When he removed his hand from the boy's shoulder, Liam woke up, cranky, as he always did when his nap was interrupted. He looked around, wild-eyed, then saw Janey.

"I want you," he said. He patted the bed beside him. "Here."

Janey took off her big boots and climbed up onto the bed, lying on top of the quilt in the warm room. One short black sock had a hole in the toe.

Below shapely calves, her ankles were small, like her wrists.

Her hip curved up from the bed, inviting touch.

Liam curled onto his side toward Janey and dropped off to sleep again.

Her dark eyes watchful, Janey stared at C.J., wary and aware.

Why did women look their most feminine when lying down? Why did Janey have to look so womanly and motherly beside his son?

That sense of waiting flooded him again, but what did it have to do with Janey?

He stepped away from the bed and cleared his throat.

Janey blinked, slowly. She curled one arm on the pillow and rested her head on it. Something like a low-simmering…hope?…passed over her face. "This is a nice apartment," she said. "Is it expensive?"

"No. I give a bit of a break if the renter works for me."

He named a sum and she nodded. "I want it."

"Okay. When do you want to move in?"

"I'll get Hank to drive my stuff over. When can I get a key?"

"Today if you want. It's for the front door of the shop."

Liam snuffled and rolled over. Janey laid her hand on his back and he settled. C.J. backed out of the room.

wax out of her right ear. "It sounded like you said not to come."

"That's right. It's on my land," he said, pointing a finger her way. "You aren't invited. Got it?"

"The sign says everyone is welcome."

"Everyone but you."

She felt Mona step forward. "Hey—"

Janey grabbed her arm. She didn't need Mona fighting her battles. "Who do you think you are?"

"Max Golden. A good friend of Reverend Wright."

Janey recognized his name. He was one of the rich ranchers, had a snotty daughter named Marnie who'd visited the Sheltering Arms once and hadn't given Janey the time of day.

He pointed at her. "He's worried about his son."

Janey put her hands on her hips and leaned forward. No way would she let this a-hole know how much he was hurting her. "Has the Reverend been talking behind my back?" she asked, standing on her toes to get into his face.

"Just to his friends. He's concerned. His son means a lot to him. He doesn't want you messing him up."

"I'm not," she said, spreading her hands. "I'm just working at the store. What's wrong with you people?"

"Nothing. We're protecting our own."

"What'd I ever do to you?" She'd done nothing, *nothing,* to C.J. or the Rev or Max Golden.

"You got my friend real worried. I take care of my friends."

Mona stepped forward. "Max, sometimes you can be a real douche bag."

Janey liked Mona more and more by the minute.

Max ignored Mona and leaned close to Janey. He'd

used too much aftershave. She barely restrained herself from stepping away from him. She didn't back away from idiots.

"Don't. Come." With that, Max turned and left the store.

"Hey," Mona said, taking her arm. "Don't let him get you down. There are lots of good people in this town."

Janey nodded. "Thanks for sticking up for me."

"Anytime." Mona grinned. "Gotta go."

She hurried to the cash register.

Janey shook her head. "Just forget about him."

She bypassed both the cereal and the rice aisles. She and Cheryl had lived on enormous bags of oatmeal and rice, one of the cheapest things she could buy and still hope to put a little meat on Cheryl's bones. If she never saw another bag of either, it would still be too soon.

Picking up a big block of cheese that was marked down because it was near the due date, she checked it out. No mold. Looked fine. She grabbed a huge box of cheap saltines along with a big jar of peanut butter and one of raspberry jam, the cheapest on the shelf, along with a loaf of whole-wheat bread. A round loaf of bread studded with seeds and nuts and cranberries tempted her, but it cost too much. Someday, when she felt secure in her job, she'd try something like that, toasted, with expensive jam that had maybe pears or apricots in it.

At the smallest deli she'd ever seen, she splurged on a small plastic container packed with sliced strawberries, blueberries, small melon chunks and pineapple. Liam would like it. She grabbed a plastic spoon.

After paying, she left the store and returned to Sweet Talk.

Liam still sat where C.J. had left him in the corner of the store, picking candy dots from paper.

Janey took them from him. When he protested, Janey pulled the fruit salad out of the bag and walked to the small cast-iron table in the front window. Intrigued, Liam followed her. When Janey reached into the bag to unpack it, he pushed her hand away and shoved his head into the bag to see what else she'd bought. God, he was cute. The tiniest blush of a smile played around the corners of her mouth.

He pulled out the cheese and said, "Want some."

"Okay. Just a minute." Janey walked to the back, to the one shelf on the far wall that C.J. charitably called a kitchen. She got out a pot and poured in some of the milk that she'd bought.

C.J. stood at the back of the room filling orders for a number of long-distance clients. He barely registered her presence.

"I'm making hot chocolate for Liam," she said.

"Great. Put some on for us, too."

Janey did that and returned to the front with a small cup for Liam. She opened the fruit salad and gave Liam a spoon. He picked up one single blueberry and put it into his mouth.

Janey sat across from him on the second chair and laid out the rest of the food.

Liam got up to return to his candy and Janey picked him up and put him back at the table.

"Sit. You need healthy food."

He let out a wail. C.J. came running.

"What's going on? What are you doing to Liam?"

C.J. COULDN'T HELP but stare at Janey. She sat on one of the chairs in the front window with sun shining on her hair, turning it into a glossy blue-black river running down her back.

"I'm being real mean," Janey said. "I'm making him eat food that won't rot his teeth."

Janey's sass set him off. He deserved it. She was feeding *his* son. He should have been on top of that.

Liam sat opposite her, pouting.

The table was covered with food. Janey had bought all of this? He should have thought of it himself. Damn. Of course, Liam needed more than candy and the box of crackers C.J., frazzled and frustrated, had grabbed from the cupboard that morning. Liam had been giving him a hard time because Gramps wasn't there. C.J. needed patience. Why wasn't he a better father when he tried so damn hard?

What would happen if Marjorie found out that the major part of Liam's diet these days was candy? It would prove to her exactly what he feared—that he had no right to try to be a father.

"I want candy," Liam whimpered.

"No, Janey's right." It was tough to admit it when he wanted to tear a strip off her hide for making him look bad.

He came close to Janey and whispered. "What are you doing?"

"Making lunch?" She looked confused.

"You trying to make me feel like a bad father?"

"What do you mean?"

Man, he hated when she got that wide-eyed look of puzzlement and innocence. It made her look too young and pretty. His attraction to her bothered him.

"C.J.'s *my* son. What are you doing with him?"

A frown formed between her eyebrows. "I'm just giving him lunch."

"That's my job." He felt aggressive and volatile and like such a damned failure as a parent.

"He's been eating too much candy," she said, building up some steam of her own.

"Who are you to criticize me?"

"Now you're being stu—" Her gaze shot to Liam. "Silly."

She ignored C.J. and sliced a banana for Liam, cutting away bruises, the way a good mother would.

When Liam realized he wasn't getting candy he settled down, the way an obedient kid would.

They were a great pair—Janey and Liam. And then there was C.J.

The banana smelled overly ripe. For no good reason, that bothered him, too.

"How much did the groceries cost?" He might not have thought about lunch, but he could pay for his own kid's food.

"It's okay. I didn't mind buying it."

"How much was the food?" He enunciated like he was talking to a child.

"Fifteen bucks and change."

The ring of the drawer of his big old cash register opening sounded loud.

He grabbed a ten and a five and slammed the drawer closed.

"Here."

She must have sensed he wasn't fooling around and took it.

"From now on, I'll feed my own son."

"Fine."

C.J. studied the groceries on the table. "You got all of that for fifteen bucks?"

"Yeah. I'm a good shopper."

Liam sipped hot chocolate, leaving a chocolate moustache on his upper lip.

"You want lunch?" Janey asked C.J. She sounded reluctant, but good manners trumped peevishness.

"Yeah, okay," he said, trying not to sound as childish as she did. "I'm going to get a mug of hot chocolate. Want some?"

Janey nodded.

C.J. returned to the store just as Calvin Hooks stepped in from outside.

He'd left his fly half undone. His cardigan had a hole in one sleeve. Calvin was getting shabbier with age.

"Hey, Calvin," C.J. said. "What can I do for you?"

"Sorry. Bad timing. 'Fraid I caught you at lunchtime." Calvin looked over the spread of food on the small table. "Looks good."

Janey stood and motioned to her chair. "Would you like to join us?"

"Don't mind if I do." Calvin sat in her chair.

C.J. shot a glance at Janey, willing her to tell him what she was doing, but she ignored him. He stared at Calvin. The guy was staying for lunch?

"We're just having peanut butter and jelly on brown," Janey said. "That okay with you?"

"Sounds good."

She took a mug of chocolate from C.J. and placed it in front of Calvin.

"C.J., you want one or two sandwiches?" She pulled a stack of bread out of the wrapper and started building sandwiches.

"Two to start."

"Can you get that old chair from the back room?" she asked. "And a couple more plates?"

C.J. did so, bemused. Janey was pretty well acting as though the store was hers. Why had she invited Hooks to stay? Calvin could have been served and on his way by now. Janey was…too generous.

Still, the scene looked warm and inviting, and C.J. wanted to be part of it. He'd had no hand in making it, though, and maybe he didn't deserve to sit at that table. He wasn't winning any medals for father—or employer—of the year, was he?

He rubbed his chest and joined them.

Liam handed Calvin a strawberry from fingers coated with peanut butter and jam.

He handed a square of melon to Janey. She ate it.

C.J. squeezed his chair in between Janey and his son.

Liam stared at the peanut butter on his fingers and stuck them into his mouth and sucked on them, then picked up a blueberry and handed it to C.J. C.J. didn't remember Liam ever offering anything to him before now.

He tried to take it from Liam with his fingers, but Liam said, "No. Me."

C.J. bent forward and opened his mouth. Liam slipped the berry into C.J.'s mouth, his tiny index finger touching C.J.'s bottom lip. C.J. chewed and swallowed while Liam watched his Adam's apple move.

So insanely sweet.

His throat ached. *Do it again.* But Liam returned to drinking his chocolate.

"Liam," Janey said, her voice soft, "wipe your hands

on your towel before you handle your daddy's food. Okay?"

Liam nodded.

"I don't mind," C.J. whispered, because his throat threatened to close up on him.

His determination to become a good father hardened into shellac in his chest. Someday, in some way, he'd finally get it right and Liam would treat him this way always, and the Janeys and Marjories of the world would never find another fault in him.

Someday, Liam would be a true son to C.J.

Janey put two sandwiches on his plate and he bit into one, but found it hard to swallow with all of the emotion of the moment clogging his throat.

This was all so…strange. He didn't know what to think of it.

Calvin finished eating and stood. "Where should I put the dirty dishes?"

"I'll take care of them," Janey answered. "Thank you for joining us."

"That was real good. See you, C.J."

He left the shop.

"He didn't buy any candies," C.J. said.

"I don't think he came in for candy. I think he wanted to share our lunch."

"How do you know?"

Janey smiled, sweetly. "He passed by the window four times."

C.J. stared at Janey. Who was she? A saint who gave to anyone in need? Or a touchy, sharp-mouthed Goth woman who'd started having sex too young?

Man, he felt weird, itchy, unsettled. As though his

world was changing but he didn't know how, or how to make it stop so he could feel stable again.

He needed stability for his son, too.

The woman sitting on the other side of the table was the source of these weird feelings. That troubled him.

Maybe it was time to get his dad to play match-maker between C.J. and someone in his congregation, time to ask him to find C.J. a sober, mature, conserva-tive woman who would make a good wife and full-time mother for Liam.

That thought made him even itchier, made his future look like a life sentence of carrying a ball and chain around, without excitement or highs. *Well, that's what you want for Liam, isn't it? Someone stable?* Yeah, but what did that do for him?

Suck it up, C.J. We've been through this before. Do whatever you have to do to see Liam settled and safe. To hell with your needs.

He shot to his feet and picked up dishes from the table and carried them to the washroom, where he rinsed them in the sink, slamming them against each other too hard. He left them there to drip-dry because he couldn't find the towel.

He remembered that Liam had it wrapped around his neck. He stepped out front again to get it. Janey and his son still sat in the front window limned by sunbeams and looked too, too good together and all he could see were his own inadequacies. If he sat with them again, that sunlight would shine on the missing pieces of his life.

"Janey," he barked, startling them both. "Lunch-time's over."

CHAPTER EIGHT

AFTER DINNER, Janey wandered out of the house, where she found that cowboys and ranchers from surrounding properties had shown up and were milling in the yard. She stood on the veranda and watched as another couple of pickup trucks circled in the driveway and parked. The excitement building in the yard infected her. Maybe she'd watch for a bit. It might make a change from the mood she'd picked up at work. TGIF.

Man, she was tired.

C.J. had been so weird all afternoon, short and brittle with her, as though she'd done something wrong, but all she'd done was feed his kid, as he should have been doing himself. Then she'd also fed a poor old guy who needed it. It's not as if she broke the bank buying that food. She'd been as cheap as she could.

"You can almost feel the leaves starting to turn, can't you?" Amy stepped out of the house and stood beside her with Michael in her arms.

"Yeah, the evenings are starting to cool down." Janey leaned against the veranda post.

"I'm going to see whether my foolish husband is riding broncs tonight."

C.J. drove into the yard and parked, then stepped out of the Jeep just as he shoved the last of a chocolate bar

into his mouth. His square chin flexed while he chewed.
Janey liked his strong jawline.

*Stop. Don't go thinking about things you like about
this guy. He's been nothing but trouble for you anyway.
Half the town thinks you want to bonk him or corrupt
him somehow.*

Looking away, Janey walked to an empty spot at the
corral fence. She tried to ignore C.J., but found that she
heard every word he said, that he hovered on the edges
of her vision like a guilty conscience.

He lifted Liam out of the Jeep, who squealed when
he saw Janey and wriggled to get out of his father's
arms, then made a beeline for her and threw his arms
around her legs.

How was she supposed to deal with this? The father
didn't want to have anything to do with her while the
son was all over her.

Looking up, she found Amy watching her. Amy
handed baby Michael to Hank, then approached. She
leaned in close to Janey.

"Are you okay? You look pale."

Janey gestured toward Liam, leaning against her with
his head pressed against her thigh.

"It's just hard. He likes me."

"No wonder," Amy murmured.

Janey smiled.

"Those clothes and those boots will only protect you
so much," Amy said.

"What do you mean?" Janey asked.

Amy folded her arms on the top rail of the corral,
facing a couple of broncs and a few men on the other
side of the fence. "Someday you are going to have to

put your fears and your grief to rest and participate in the world around you."

Janey shook her head, not wanting to understand, but fearing that she did.

Amy turned to her. "A wise woman once taught me that with children it is today that matters. As adults, it is our job to rise above our own problems to nurture the children around us, to give them the fullest, richest experience of life, every day, no matter what the past held for us." She rested one hand on Janey's shoulder. "Or what the future might hold for them."

Janey stared across the corral, unseeing. "Whoever taught you that sounds really smart. Who was she?"

"You. After Cheryl died." With a sad smile, Amy squeezed her shoulder and walked away.

Amy was right. Children deserved so much. Liam deserved more than she'd been giving him. Everything she'd done for him she'd done halfheartedly.

Janey picked up Liam and sat him on the top rail facing her. He laughed and clapped his hands. Such a sunny boy. No matter what his mother had done to him, today, at this moment, he was happy to be here. How could she turn her back on that?

She'd been planning to ignore C.J., but he approached her holding his beige cowboy hat, passing the brim from hand to hand. He was nervous?

"Listen," he said, "I'm sorry about being surly today. I shouldn't have gotten mad at you for feeding Liam."

"Yeah," she said, her tone hard. She wasn't letting him off the hook too easily. "You weren't very nice."

"I just—" He took his time settling the hat on his head, then watched her from under the brim, the shadow of it cloaking his eyes. "Sometimes I worry that I'm not up to the job of fatherhood. I haven't known Liam for long. It was a shock to find out about him."

"You didn't know him as a baby?"

C.J. shook his head, obviously not wanting to share more than that.

They stared at each other until Janey grew nervous. "Are you scared today?" she blurted. "Of the broncs?" Dumb, dumb questions.

C.J.'s face flattened and she wished she could swallow back her words.

He looked as though he was trying to figure out whether to give her a piece of his mind or to walk away. Then he sighed, "Yeah. A bit. Not in the way you think, though."

He rubbed a hand across the back of his neck. "Is it that obvious?"

She shook her head. "I don't think so. I just saw a little the other night."

She pretended a nonchalance she didn't feel. There were so many questions she wanted to ask, starting with, "Why do you rodeo if it scares you?"

"It doesn't scare me." He twisted the hat in his hands. "It excites me like it used to. Too much."

"Why is that a problem?"

"I need to settle down, for Liam's sake."

She understood it all now, the clothes, the crazy short hair, the forced…conservatism she felt in him sometimes. He thought these things would make him a good father. Poor guy was so far off base.

"Why are you trying bronc busting again?"

"I want to compete in Hank's rodeo. I want to win."

"Why?"

He opened his mouth to answer, but one of the ranch

hands yelled, "Hey, C.J., get in here and try out this bronc."

He shrugged and said, "Gotta go."

As C.J. entered the corral, Janey turned Liam toward the inside of the corral so he could watch.

"Your daddy's going to ride a bronc."

"Bronc?"

Janey had been wondering about Liam's speech. He sounded so young. Cheryl had been a real chatterbox when she was Liam's age. That is, before the cancer hit.

Hank approached them. "Hey, kid," Hank said, elbowing in beside her.

One of the cowboys got up on a bronc named Twister. C.J. stood inside the corral watching. Janey watched him.

Stop it. Think about something else besides C.J.

"Hank, can I ask you something?" Janey said. "Even if it sounds stupid?"

"Sure. Shoot." He watched the bronc kicking in the corral.

"Why don't the broncs eventually give up fighting all of these riders and get tame like other horses?"

Hank glanced at her. "These horses like to buck."

"Buck," Liam whispered.

Hank smiled. "It's what they live for. Every so often, a horse is born who can't be ridden, who just loves to buck."

Janey pointed to the bronc when he threw the cowboy. "Twister *wants* to buck?"

"Uh-huh," Hank responded.

"Weird."

"Weird," Liam murmured.

"Rodeo gives Twister a chance to do it all he wants."

"Cool," Janey said.

"Cool," Liam mumbled.

She couldn't drag her gaze away from C.J. He approached the center of the corral, his jaw square-cut with tension, his eyes trained on a bronc one of the ranch hands led out of the stable.

"What horse is that?" she asked Hank.

"Double Trouble."

Tall and lean, C.J. strode toward where the cowboy held Double's reins. C.J. mounted, the cowboy let go, and all hell broke loose.

In the year she'd lived here, Janey had never seen another horse that bucked so high and so hard. Unlike C.J.'s performance of the other night, there was no grace in this ride.

C.J. flew from the bronc's back, landing hard. Puffs of dirt flew up around him. Double Trouble ran to the other side of the corral. C.J. lay on the ground for a minute rubbing his hip.

"He's okay," Hank leaned toward her and said.

"Huh?" she asked.

He stared at her hand on his arm, where her fist clutched a handful of his shirt.

"Oh. Sorry." She smoothed the fabric, then wrapped that arm around Liam.

C.J. jumped up with a gleam in his eye and called out to another cowboy. "Hip, bring out another one."

He looked mad enough to spit, but Janey saw beneath the anger to a simmering excitement, to a determination to rise to the challenge.

Why did she have to read this man so easily?

"C.J.'s doing pretty well," Hank said. "Considering."

"Considering what?"

"I guess you wouldn't know, would you? Four years ago, a bull gored C.J.'s best friend with one of his horns."

Janey's mouth fell open. "Did the man die?"

"The animal pierced Davey's heart. He was dead by the time the medics carried him out of the arena."

"Oh," Janey said, staring at C.J. preparing to ride another bronc. "Did C.J. stop riding then?"

"C.J. never returned to the rodeo until now." Hank lifted one boot onto the bottom rail of the fence. "He's registered for the charity rodeo."

Had C.J. been there when the bull gored his friend? Had he watched the life drain out of him? It was horrific to think about. So what was so important to him that he had to return to it?

C.J. mounted a horse called Blue and rode him out. He had to be the best rider here, except for Hank. He jumped off the bronc and strode to the fence.

Janey peered around Hank and the cowboys leaning over the fence, slapping C.J. on the back and shoulders. C.J. looked happy. Another practice, another day C.J. survived. She should tell him how proud she was of him. Then she remembered how edgy and cantankerous he'd been with her all afternoon and decided, no. Not a chance.

He'd probably snap at her again when she was only trying to be nice.

She felt Hank watching her and looked up at him.

Shoot.

Hank bumped her hip with his own.

Shoot.

Janey sighed. How could Hank see feelings in her for C.J. that she barely recognized herself?

ON SATURDAY MORNING, Janey lay in bed and stared at the ceiling, cradling the tiny stuffed bear she'd bought for Cheryl just after her birth. Max Golden's warning rang through her memory.

Through the small window, the day looked bright and clear, perfect for a powwow.

Footsteps mounted the stairs to the third floor, shuffled down the hallway and stopped in front of her bedroom. Someone pounded on the door.

"Come in," she called.

Hank opened the door and peeked around it. "You coming down for breakfast, sleepyhead? Hannah's porridge will be hard as cement if you don't hurry."

A streak of caramel wove its way from his widow's peak through his thick dark hair. Amy was such a lucky woman to love an awesome guy like Hank. Oh, great. First, she envies the woman for her baby and now for her husband.

"I'm not coming down for breakfast," she said. "I'll get some toast later."

Hank frowned. "You okay?" he asked. "I've never known you to pass on a meal."

This was just the excuse she needed to get out of going today.

"I don't feel so good. I'm not going to the powwow today."

Janey wanted to wipe the worry from his face, but she just couldn't go today. As much as she'd like to spit in Max's face, she couldn't bring trouble to Hank and Amy, especially not with a neighbor. She didn't want to force them to take sides. Best to not go.

"What's wrong?" Hank asked. "You have a fever?"

"No. It's my stomach. It hurts."

"You want an Alka Seltzer or something? Some Tums?"

"No. That won't fix what's wrong with me today." She hoped he would believe it was a womanly problem. She knew that would embarrass Hank and he'd let it go.

"Oh," he said, and sure enough, blushed. He backed through the doorway. "Okay. You take care of yourself."

He turned to leave, then looked over his shoulder. "You want me to come back later to check on you?"

Janey smiled. *Oh, Hank, you're too old and like a father to me, but I wish there were more men in the world like you.* "No. Just have fun."

He smiled and left the room, closing the door behind him with a quiet click.

There. It was done. She'd lied to her best friend. An hour later, after she heard the cars and school buses leave with the family, Hannah, the ranch hands and this month's batch of kids, she crawled out of bed and got dressed in ancient sweatpants and one of Hank's old plaid shirts.

She washed up and applied her makeup, but when she turned to leave the room, she stopped and turned back to the mirror.

No one was around. So why put on makeup? Good question.

Why *did* she put it on?

Not only couldn't she stand to have other people see who she really was, she couldn't even face herself and accept who she was.

The makeup and clothes were more than armor to protect her vulnerability from the crap life dealt, from people hurting her; they also hid her shame, that emotion she refused to look at because she didn't have a clue how to get over it.

As always, like acid, the feeling burned a hole in her stomach. Her hands shook. Why hadn't she recognized before how much of her still lived in shame over something that had never been her fault or her choice?

She turned away, abruptly. *Get your shit together. Don't get sucked into all of that psychological type of stuff. Forget about it.*

Walking down the stairs to the first floor in the rare quiet of the house, she missed the children's chatter and their distraction. She stood still, suddenly realizing that she had never been in this house when not one other soul was present. She'd be alone for the day. She'd become too used to all of the people on Hank's ranch, to being surrounded by children.

Can't live with them and can't live without them.

She'd never have another child because she couldn't have sex, didn't want touching, and would never get married. So...she would live alone.

Oh, man, oh, man, that hurt.

She'd better get used to it. Soon she'd be settled into the apartment in town, where she'd spend her non-working hours by herself.

She could be crazy about a guy like C.J., but the relationship would never go anywhere. She was damaged goods and no decent man deserved that.

The town was right. She shouldn't be anywhere near C.J. So, it was a good thing she wasn't going to the powwow.

On that thought, she entered the empty kitchen and made herself toast and a coffee. Wandering out to the veranda, she sat on a wicker chair and ate, contemplating the beauty of Hank's ranch. Golden fields stretched to the horizon, where the gray and mauve of distant hills merged with a blue sky dotted with white cotton-candy puffs of clouds.

Perfect day for a powwow.

A horse whinnied in the stable. She supposed all of the chores had been done. She set her empty plate and coffee cup onto a wicker table.

Nothing to do. Too bad the store was closed.

She rose and wandered to the two Adirondack chairs under the huge weeping willow on Hank's front lawn. She sat on one, rested her head on the high back and watched sunlight play hide and seek with the wind-shimmered leaves.

Green and supple and clean, those dancing leaves calmed a corner of her soul. She wished she could grab a bunch of them with her always and that they stayed alive forever, like a small bundle of hope, so that everywhere she went their promise of renewal would stay with her.

Her eyes closing, she wondered what C.J. and Liam were doing at the powwow and if they missed her.

HOLDING LIAM'S HAND—it'd been a struggle to get Liam to let him—C.J. wove through the crowds milling on Max's land. The dull roar of dozens of conversations drifted around him.

Max had outdone himself this year. His best pow-wow yet.

Huge teepees stood erect and exotic on the trimmed lawns.

Dancers in Native American ceremonial dress performed to the beat of drums, their soft leather and beaded clothing and long feathered headdresses stunning in the Montana sunlight.

Rows of barbecues held bison burgers and steaks, and the scent of charred meat drifted on the breeze.

Huge buckets of water and corn cobs boiled atop propane stoves.

"You hungry?" he asked Liam.

No answer. Story of their life together.

C.J. passed a table of condiments. He remembered Janey's appetite at lunch this week, her generous use of the free cream and ketchup. She was going to love this.

That thought stopped him cold. Why did he care what she felt about anything? But he kept looking around and realized he was watching for her.

He wandered the grounds until he saw Hank and Amy and their baby.

"Hey," he said. "Is that little Michael?"

"Yes." Amy pulled the blanket away from the baby who snuggled in some kind of harness that Amy wore on her front. C.J. saw a tiny head and two miniature, closed eyes. Kid was asleep.

"Cute little guy." He wished he'd seen Liam when he was that young.

Amy beamed. He didn't think he'd ever seen a prouder mother.

"Where's Janey?" He tried to make the question sound nonchalant.

"She's at home," Hank said. "Sick."

"Sick?" Alarm shot through him.

Hank raised a placating hand. "Nothing serious. She'll probably be fine tomorrow."

Damn. He nodded to Hank and Amy and went on his way. Too bad Janey was missing this.

Dad stood with Max beside the drinks table. C.J. sauntered over and greeted them.

Max clapped him on the shoulder, full of bluff good cheer. "You having a good time?" C.J. suspected he'd probably already had more than a couple of beers.

"Max, this is your best powwow yet. Great job." He shook Max's hand. When he tried to pull it away, Max held on.

"Listen, C.J.," he said, sliding close and bathing C.J. with beer breath. "I hope you appreciate the favor I did for you."

C.J. smiled. "Favor? What favor?"

"You know." Max jabbed him in the ribs. Dad grabbed Max by his other arm, but Max shook him off. "With that young woman. You know, getting her off your case."

C.J. got a sick feeling in his gut.

"What do you mean, getting her off my case?"

Dad said, "Max, maybe you shouldn't—" but Max was too far gone to realize what he was doing wrong.

"Told her she couldn't come today. Told her she wasn't welcome on my land."

A terrible cold seized C.J. "You told her not to come?" He felt deep anger, but sounded deadly calm. He flung an arm out to encompass their surroundings. "To an event that everyone else in town is invited to?"

Max must have sensed he'd been indiscreet. He pulled away from C.J.

"Every single person from three or four counties is welcome," C.J. said, "but you told Janey she couldn't come?"

The hottest lava flooded his body, surged into his

veins. He clenched his fists for fear he might truly hurt the man.

"Of all the petty, narrow-minded stunts—" He couldn't go on with the lava filling his throat.

Max looked bewildered, turned to Dad, who stared at the ground, his mouth a thin line of disappointment.

Dad reached for C.J., but C.J. flinched away. "Did you ask him to do this?"

Dad shook his head, but C.J. didn't know what to believe.

"I only told him about my concerns." The Reverend looked ashamed, but was it true?

"C.J., I'm sorry, I—" Max stretched a hand toward C.J., then dropped it.

C.J. *should* be happy that she wasn't here today. She made him crazy when she was near. Or rather, his feelings did. He hated that she'd kept her daughter away from the child's father and yet, day after day she seemed so decent, calm and patient with Liam and even with C.J., despite the countless ways he behaved like a bear.

"This is too unfair," he said. "Too mean-spirited." He should leave it alone, but couldn't. "I'm going to get Janey and bring her back here. Got it?"

"I really wish you wouldn't," Dad said. "For your own sake."

"I'm getting her for *her* own sake. If she was looking forward to this, she deserves to be involved as much as anyone else here."

Max's answering nod looked sheepish, the high cheekbones of his Native American heritage turning darker.

"Go," he said. "Get her. Bring her here."

"Damn right I will. Dad, watch Liam for me." He didn't give his father a chance to say no.

C.J. stalked away, past the barbecues and the teepees and the dancers, plowing a single-minded path through the crowds, not stopping when someone called to him.

In the field that served as a parking lot, he jumped into his Jeep and left the Golden ranch, spinning his wheels in gravel when he turned onto the highway and sped to the Sheltering Arms Ranch.

CHAPTER NINE

C.J. FOUND JANEY in a chair on the lawn under the weeping willow.

Asleep.

She looked so young in sleep. No sharp edges or belligerence or attitude. What made her tick? Why wasn't she this pretty, soft woman all of the time?

"What happened to you?" he whispered.

The high ponytail she'd pulled her long hair into made her look younger still. Her body, though, was a woman's body, ripe and full.

He touched her forearm, found her skin every bit as soft as he'd imagined, and whispered, "Janey."

JANEY FLOATED in a lovely, lovely dream. C.J. was there and his chocolate velvet voice whispered her name. They walked through a grassy field toward a windrow of trees and shrubs. C.J. showed her a way through to the other side, where a pond surrounded by weeping willow trees baked in the lazy sun of a summer afternoon. Pale slim leaves dotted the shore of the pond, circled idly on the water.

Sunlight glinted from the surface.

A cicada called in a silence colored only by the soft shush of a small waterfall at the far end. The scent of the sweetest flowers drifted by.

She'd never seen such a beautiful spot.

They took off their clothes—she her Goth and C.J. his button-down starchiness—and stepped into the water, just two naked people free of fear or pretence, C.J. tall and strong and tanned, her own body round and white, soft in some areas, strong in others.

Only themselves.

They slipped underwater holding hands. C.J. moved like a sleek otter, pulling her through water warm on the surface and cool in its depths.

They came up for air.

C.J. ran his fingers through his long hair, sluicing water off and back into the pond. She did the same with her own long hair.

She lifted her weightless legs and floated on the surface, letting the sun heat her pale body.

"Janey," C.J. whispered beside her.

She reached for his face. It hovered into view, blocking out the sun.

"Janey," he whispered again, his face mere inches from her own. Maybe he would kiss her. Please, yes. She formed her lips into a soft pucker and waited for him.

When he did nothing, she grasped the back of his head and pulled him close.

"Janey!" His voice sounded loud and…desperate.

She opened her eyes. C.J.'s face blocked the light of the sky, his brown eyes gazed into her own with an intensity she'd never seen before. She'd never noticed the small lines of darker brown in his irises.

He smelled like fresh air and one of his mints. She smiled.

"Hey, sweetheart," she whispered and laid the palm

of her hand against his face. As corny as it sounded, she'd always wanted to have a sweetheart of her own.

A rough hand on her shoulder shook her to awareness.

"C.J.?" she asked, trying to look past him. She was sitting in full sun, the shade of the willow tree yards behind her now that the sun had changed position with the advancing afternoon.

As if his skin scalded her, she jerked her hand away from his cheek.

Seized by the horror of what she'd done—she'd called him sweetheart *out loud*—she slammed her hand across her mouth.

He flew away from her, turned his back and stood in the unrelenting sun. Air hissed between his teeth.

"Oh," she moaned. "I'm so sorry."

"Don't be," he said, and he sounded breathless, as if he'd run a great distance. "You were dreaming and I surprised you."

He was being kind, understanding, but she couldn't shake off the mood of the dream, or the fact that *he'd* caught her dreaming of *him.* Maybe he didn't know that, though. Maybe he thought she'd been dreaming of someone else. Please, please, please think that.

"I'm here to take you to the powwow," he said, his breathing under control now.

"I can't go."

He came to her, bent forward and rested his hands on the wide arms of the chair.

"Listen, I talked to Max and he's real sorry for saying you weren't welcome. He said it's okay for you to be there."

She shook her head. Awake now, her spirit raised

its figurative head. *Figurative.* She had to save that word for Hank.

"Max Golden can kiss my butt. I'm not going where I haven't been welcome."

C.J. hung his head, then straightened away from her. She knew he heard the implacability in her tone. *Implacability.* Another good word for Hank.

"So you're going to miss everything?" he asked. "The dance, too?"

Dance? Oh, she would love to go to a dance. She'd missed all of that in high school. Damn Max Golden.

"I guess," she muttered.

"But why?" C.J. spread his arms wide. "It's not even on Max's property."

Janey sat forward. "It isn't?"

"No, it's at the Legion Hall. Beside the church."

"Oh, it's your father's place." She sat back, deflated.

"*Not* my father's place." C.J. looked as though he wanted to give her a good shake. "It belongs to the whole town. *Everyone* is allowed to attend the town dances."

When she didn't answer, he forged on, "Dad said he didn't know that Max had talked to you. I believe him."

"Should I trust him?"

"I think so." C.J. nodded. "Yeah. You should."

He folded one hand into a fist and wrapped his other hand around it.

"So, will you come?" Why did he look so hopeful? Maybe he felt really bad about what Max had done to her.

A dance. Oh, she would love that. She'd never gone to one single dance in her life.

"Okay," she said, perking up. "I'll go."

C.J. smiled. "Great. I'll pick you up at seven." He strode to his Jeep.

"Whoa, wait." Janey jumped out of the chair and ran after him. No way should she spend time alone with him, especially not after that dream.

"I'm not going with you." She couldn't possibly sit at home waiting for him to pick her up, like they were on a date or something. Uh-uh. No way. "I'll walk in."

"What? C'mon, I don't mind picking you up."

The thought of sharing his small vehicle for the drive into town unnerved her. No. She didn't want that.

"That's really great of you, but no, thanks. I'll walk into town." She turned to head inside, not giving him another chance to argue.

"See you at the dance," she called over her shoulder and mounted the steps of the veranda. By the time she opened the front door of the house, she heard his Jeep start and spray gravel on its way down the driveway.

Warm fuzzies lingered from that beautiful dream, as well as thoughts of C.J.'s beautiful body. She'd rather die than swim naked with a man, but, oh, that didn't mean she couldn't dream.

He'd stood up for her, against the Rev and Max Golden. Not only that, he'd driven all the way out here to tell her so and then had invited her to the dance.

She touched her cheek with its layer of liquid foundation, then her eyelashes with their thick coating of mascara.

Stop it. Stop thinking all these warm fuzzies. Nothing's going to happen with C.J., not when you are too ashamed to let yourself *accept who you really are, let alone him, let alone anyone, not even Hank and Amy.*

She needed to get her shit together and *keep* it together.

AT THE POWWOW, Walter watched his son storm away, his stride long and angry.

"Max," he said. "I wish you hadn't told that woman she couldn't attend."

Max hung his head and scuffed the toe of his boot in the dirt. "Sorry, Walter. I thought I was helping you."

Walter rested his hand on Max's shoulder. Max had a heart of gold, but his impulses were so often misguided.

"Thank you, Max, but I think we'd better set those kinds of machinations aside."

Max nodded, suddenly sober. "You want a beer?" he mumbled.

"No." Walter spotted Gladys on the other side of the field. "Max, you've done a good job. Enjoy yourself."

He walked away, edging his way around the outside of the field until he stood behind Gladys.

"Hello," he said.

She turned around, already smiling. "Walter."

He forgot about Max, about the Goth girl, about C.J. He stared at the dignified woman in front of him wearing a flowered summer dress, low-heeled sandals and an oversize sunhat, and wondered how he could be so fortunate as to have her smiling at him so sweetly.

"Gladys," he said and, with her permission, tucked her arm inside his elbow and wrapped his long fingers over hers. They strolled around the grounds.

Walter remembered seeing a local jeweler's stand and steered them in his direction.

Would Gladys allow him to buy her something? Was that too bold? He didn't know. He'd been too long without a female companion.

Gladys picked up a small jade heart on a thin gold chain.

"It's the same color as your eyes," he said.

"Is it?" She stared up at him, perhaps hoping for more, but he didn't know how to say romantic things.

"Gladys, would you let me get it for you?" He wanted to give it to her, to have her happy with him, and to wear the necklace and think of him.

"Walter, you don't have to buy me things."

"I want to."

"If you're not careful, I'll begin to think you're trying to buy my affections, that you'll expect something in return."

He felt his eyes goggle. She thought that of him? That he would try to— "No. Never. How could you... my goodness, Gladys. I wouldn't—"

She laughed. "Oh, Walter, you are priceless. I'm pulling your leg."

She fingered the necklace in her hand and looked up at him. "I would love to own this necklace. I will think of you when I wear it."

Yes!

Walter paid for the necklace and fumbled with the clasp when he tried to put it on her.

"Let me," she said, fastening it around her neck. It looked pretty against her pale skin. Walter felt good, proud.

She took his hand in hers and led him away from the vendors and the crowds, toward the far end of the field.

"Walter, I like you."

"Gladys, what on earth do you see in a sober old beanstalk like me?" Judging by her raised eyebrows, he'd startled her with the question. He'd startled himself, had no idea where it had come from.

"I see many things, Walter." She toyed with the

sleeve of his dark jacket. "Integrity. Caring. High morals. Solid ethics."

She stopped and stared up at him. Way up. She was such a tiny thing.

Beyond all reason and propriety, he wanted to kiss her, here in the middle of a sunlit lawn with all of Ordinary's citizens strolling nearby, talking, laughing, leading perfectly normal lives while he stared at Gladys's lips and thought the most improper things.

She dragged him toward Max's house and around to the back. In the shadows, she took off her hat and laid it on a lawn chair. Away from the sun and prying eyes, he set his hands on her shoulders, leaned toward her, and released that tension that stiffened his spine every hour. He let go of that pretension to superiority he'd carried for too many years, touched Gladys's soft pink lips with his own and breathed in her talcum-scented peace.

He simply rested his mouth on hers and it was enough for now.

"Gladys," he whispered and rested his forehead on hers.

"I've waited a whole year for this," she said.

She had? While he'd been bumbling around in the dark, trying to figure out how to get close to her, she'd been thinking about *him?*

She wrapped her small hands around his wrists, stood on her tiptoes and whispered, "More, Walter."

He pressed his lips to hers and felt her tongue touch his mouth. He jumped back.

She smiled as if she had a secret that she might share with him, but only if he was very, very good. He imagined Eve smiling just so when inviting Adam to share in her love play.

"Gladys, we shouldn't—"

"It's been a long time for me, Walter," she said. "At my age, I don't want to waste time."

She stood on her tiptoes again and ran the tip of her tiny tongue along his lips.

"Gladys, my dear," he breathed before he opened his mouth and let her in.

She tasted like coffee rich with cream, and endless uncounted lonely nights finally put to rest. She tasted like salvation.

Oh, you. You sweet woman.

She leaned against him, so he felt the shapes of her breasts and released her, too quickly. She stumbled and he had to catch her arms so she wouldn't fall.

She placed her hand on his chest, where her fingers branded his skin through his shirt, reminding him where unbridled impulse led—to trouble.

He exhaled roughly. "Gladys, I can't."

"Oh, Walter." Disappointment weighted her voice. "We're too old to waste time. Think about it, dear. Do you really want only your fear and your narrow morals for company at night?"

She walked away, and it felt like losing Elaine again. He'd paid a high price the first time around with Elaine. He couldn't do that with Gladys.

JANEY DRESSED CAREFULLY, not that she had much to choose from. She handled her clothes with a soft touch, trying to decide what she wanted against her skin tonight.

She opted for a black velvet dress she'd found in a secondhand shop. Pretty sure it wasn't real velvet— she'd paid next to nothing for it—she liked it anyway.

The fabric moved under her hands as though it had a life of its own.

Stepping into it, she pulled it up over her hips and threaded her arms through the lacy sleeves, careful that she didn't catch the lace with her nails. Boning in the bodice supported her breasts. A wide hood hung down the back. This was by far her favorite dress.

She ran her hands down the skirt. Probably someone's old Halloween costume, but she loved it anyway.

A fresh coat of black polish sparkled on her nails. She looked at herself in the mirror. Everything in its place. Everything just right.

She pulled on her platform boots. She'd rummaged in the kitchen drawers until she'd found some black shoe polish. Her boots shone almost as brightly as her nails.

The skirt of her dress fell to just above her ankles and floated around her boots and knees as she hurried downstairs.

She pulled the door closed behind her and made sure it was secure. She didn't have a key so she couldn't lock it.

By the time she reached town, a layer of dust coated her boots and the hem of her dress.

On Main Street she ran into Mona, who wore a brightly patterned short dress and red on her lips to match. She looked so much younger in street clothes than in that plain blue waitress's uniform. Maybe only twenty-six, twenty-seven.

"Hey," Janey said, "I like your lipstick."

Mona smiled. "Thanks. Let's go."

They walked down Main Street side by side. The street was bare, but Janey could hear music in the distance.

"Fiddles?" she asked.

"Yeah," Mona answered. "Only dances they have here are country dances. You want something different, you have to head out of town."

The music got louder as they approached the Legion hall.

"I don't remember you coming to any of the town's dances before. Why not?"

"I don't know. I guess I thought I might not be welcome."

Mona turned a surprised look Janey's way. "Why on earth not?"

"I guess 'cause of the way I look. The way I dress."

"Hey, only a handful of people in this town are that narrow-minded."

"Yeah, I'm beginning to think you're right."

Mona smiled. "You'll like the dancing, even if it isn't twenty-first century. It's fun." She led the way into a hall swollen to the rafters with music.

C.J. grabbed Janey's hand the second she got there. He must have been waiting for her.

"Let's dance," he said. No *hello,* just an order.

"But—" Did she really want to argue or did she want to dance? No-brainer. Dance won out.

The music stopped and people changed partners.

"C'mon." C.J. dragged her to a group of people nearby.

"This is country, sort of like square dancing," he said. "The caller will tell you what steps to make, but just follow whatever I do."

A couple of people stared at her. She couldn't tell what they were thinking. She wanted to slink back out the door, but instead straightened her shoulders.

The music started again. Fiddles. Banjos. Accordions. She'd never heard anything like it. C.J. twirled her, then handed her off to someone else in the square. Hands pushed and pulled her in the direction she was supposed to go.

The room, faces, colors whirled around her.

Everything happened so quickly, she didn't have time to worry about being touched.

She laughed.

By the end of the song, she was breathless.

"Whew! I need a drink."

"This way." C.J. dragged her to the refreshment table. A few people stepped out of the way when they reached it.

"C.J., why're you hanging around with that girl?" Some guy with a big white handlebar moustache glared at her.

C.J. turned his way, slowly, as if measuring his response. "Has Dad been talking to you?"

"He doesn't have to. We're good, God-fearing people. We don't need a Satanist in our midst."

"I'm not a Satanist," Janey said, her jaw tight. "I don't worship the devil."

"Why do you dress like that?"

She looked down at herself. "I like this dress."

This was so bogus. That she would even have to defend herself, her pretty dress against someone with such a closed mind...

"Screw you," she said, and the man flushed. Good.

She stomped away, heard C.J. say, "Where is your spirit of tolerance Dad preaches so much about, Harold?"

"Don't waste your breath, C.J.," she said over her shoulder.

"Janey is a good person," she barely heard C.J. say.

He was defending her again. Why? Because she worked for him?

At that moment, she wanted to hate the whole world, to keep all of them at arm's length, especially C.J. for causing such crazy feelings in her.

She found an unoccupied piece of wall and leaned against it. Most people were being so nice to her except the very few over whom the Rev had influence. So why did what this guy just said bother her so much?

First, because she'd been having such a good time and second, she'd seen that glimpse of shame in herself earlier today. People like Harold made it flare up and reminded her that it sat hot and hard in her gut like a burden, and she was so tired of carrying it around.

CHAPTER TEN

C.J. HAD TO DO SOMETHING. Most folks in town weren't bad, but Janey seemed to attract the worst of them. Still, C.J. couldn't let the narrow-minded few define his home, nor could he let them treat Janey so badly, no matter how itchy and unsettled she made him feel.

And he couldn't let someone like old Harold Hardisty ruin her evening.

Just because she dressed weirdly didn't mean she deserved this treatment.

"C.J., stop. Don't get involved." His father stepped up beside him, but instead of looking angry, he looked sad, regretful.

"Did you hear what Harold said to her?" C.J. asked.

His father nodded.

"Dad, you're the minister here. What is our responsibility as good Christians. Huh?"

"With that tongue of hers, she can take care of herself." C.J. noticed that he'd dodged the question.

"She shouldn't have to put up with this stuff just because she dresses differently."

"Last thing you need is trouble." Dad was right about that.

"I know, but still…"

"You're so close." C.J. understood what he meant, so close to the perfect life.

C.J. barked out a laugh that sounded bitter. "Am I, Dad? My son, my own flesh and blood, won't talk to me. I don't have a good mother to offer him. I might not even be able to save the ranch if I can't win the rodeo or sell the store."

He watched Janey cross the room to lean on the far wall, where she crossed her arms and slammed the sole of one foot against the wall, unladylike for a woman in a long velvet dress.

A nation unto herself. Alone. Separate.

He couldn't leave her alone. Damned if he knew why. Maybe he was too decent.

Or maybe you want more from her.

In spite of his common sense, in spite of Janey's crustacean-tough shell, despite her past history, C.J. knew he would help her.

"Dad, what some of the people of this town are doing is wrong."

The Reverend hissed out a breath. "C.J.—"

"Dad, you should have seen her learning how to make candy. She was like a kid. She isn't mean-spirited."

As far as he could tell, her main problem was that she was overly defensive. Was there a crime against that?

"I'm introducing her to my friends."

He searched the room for buddies who would hang out with her, who would appreciate the quirky woman she was.

Spotting a few of them in a corner of the room, he strode toward Janey and took her hand, pulling her away from the wall.

"Hey, what—"

"You're meeting some of my friends."

She surprised him by hanging back.

"What's wrong?" he asked.

"I don't want to meet anyone. I'm going home."

Her cheeks blazed sumac red. Her eyelids hid her eyes, but he thought he detected moisture at the corner of one of them.

He spun her around and stood in front of her, to hide her until she got herself together.

"I hate these people. All of them." Her tone was caustic, but her fingers worried the soft fabric of her dress as though it was a lifeline to a better place. He'd noticed this about her—that when she was upset, she touched things.

"Listen," C.J. said, "Harold Hardisty's nothing but an unhappy old man." He held her arm, leaning forward to try to get her to look at him. He needed to see her eyes, to find out whether this evening could be salvaged for her.

Someone bumped them and she glanced up. He saw what he needed to know—that she was hurt, yes, but also angry. He needed to fix that. She thrust her chin forward. Good, he'd use that defiance she cloaked herself in to his advantage.

"Hardisty lost his wife to cancer. He owns a piece of land that God himself couldn't raise cattle on. He blames everyone else for his misery. Don't judge the whole town by him."

She didn't respond and he shook the arm he was holding. "He's a miserable old guy. The problem is him, not you. Get it?"

Janey nodded and looked better, but there was a sullenness to her now that hadn't been there when she'd arrived.

"Why are you doing this?" she asked.

He wondered that himself, thought to tell her it was out of the goodness of his heart, that it was strictly charity, but he knew she wouldn't like that one bit and would probably construe it as pity. Besides, that wasn't the whole truth, was it? He liked her, genuinely liked her. He refused to acknowledge that something stronger than liking was brewing inside of him. As long as he didn't recognize it…

So, he told her a small bit of that truth. "I think you're a good person who shouldn't be treated badly by narrow-minded people."

She watched him, assessed him, and nodded, her eyes clearing of some of the hurt. "Thanks," she said.

"You're going to stay and we're going to spend time with my friends."

The signs were subtle, but C.J. could see the fight and backbone rise in her again. "Okay," she said, "let's go."

Ha! The little fighter was back in business.

He led her across the hall until they joined a group of young men.

"Guys, this is Janey. You've seen her around town."

They nodded and stared at her curiously.

"Janey, this is Timm Franck." Timm nodded.

C.J. pointed to scruffy Allen Hall, who shoved a crust of pizza into his mouth then put his hand out to shake Janey's. "Whatever you do," C.J. said, "don't leave your food lying around or he'll scarf it."

Everyone laughed, and the corner of Janey's mouth curved up infinitesimally.

Pointing to a stunningly handsome man, C.J. said, "This is Remington Caldwell. Heard you'd come back to town, Rem. How're you doin', man?"

C.J. introduced two more young men, Jason Miller and Réal Gomez.

C.J. turned to include all of them. "Janey works for me."

"When did you start?" Timm asked.

"This week."

"How do you like working for this slave driver?" Réal grinned and jerked a thumb in C.J.'s direction.

"Has he been giving you any free samples?" Allen asked and everyone laughed.

C.J. could see Janey starting to relax and felt good about it.

JANEY COULDN'T BELIEVE what was happening around her. It seemed she'd lost control of her own life. She should be fighting harder to leave, but C.J. wouldn't let go of her hand. She gave it a good tug, but he held on tight.

She refused to look at why she didn't flinch away from his touch as she did with everyone else.

The light-haired guy with the shirt buttoned to his chin stepped forward. Timm.

"Let's get in on this dance."

C.J. relinquished her hand to Timm, whose palm was slimmer, his fingers longer, and cool.

Timm was younger than she. He seemed shy and sweet. Nerdy.

They turned toward the dance floor and found the dancers breaking down into couples. A slow dance? No, too weird.

Timm seemed to hold back, too, once he realized the floor wasn't breaking down into squares. She peeked up at him. His face looked as red as hers felt.

Timm put one hand on her waist and held her other hand.

They touched each other with the timidity of a pair of deer.

He could barely keep to the beat of the music. After the third time he stepped on one of her feet, he looked even more embarrassed than she felt.

In fact, he looked so uncomfortable that she had to make him feel better. "Good thing I'm wearing my heavy boots tonight." She grinned at him.

"Sorry," he said.

"I'm not. This is my first slow dance ever. I like it."

She felt his shoulder relax under her left hand. How odd for her to be putting someone else at his ease and trying to make him comfortable with being so close to her. "Your first one ever?"

"Yeah." She shrugged as if it didn't matter, but Timm smiled at her so sweetly that she added, "I never had much chance to go to dances when I was a teenager."

"Neither have I," he said, though he looked as though he was still a teenager—eighteen or nineteen.

"I guess the whole town knows why I couldn't. I mean, having a baby so young. I guess everyone knows about Cheryl?"

"Yes. We were all sad that she died."

Janey nodded, couldn't speak for a minute. When she had her emotions under control, she asked, "You're a good-looking guy. I bet all the girls want to go out with you. Why haven't you gone to many dances?"

If possible, his cheeks flared even more red, and Janey felt herself blush. "Was that a dumb question?"

"No, I guess you haven't heard."

"Heard what?" she asked, but Timm looked so distressed that a lump formed in her throat.

"When I was eleven, I caught on fire by accident. My chest was burned really badly."

Janey's eyes drifted to the top button of his shirt.

"Yeah," he said. "That's why I keep it buttoned up. I have scars."

"So, you couldn't go to dances because…"

"Because I was always either in the hospital having surgery, or at home recovering."

Janey grimaced. "And now?"

"Now, I'm finished. Doctors have done as much as they can."

Too, too sad. Why was there so much hardship in life? Janey said, "You haven't stepped on my toes in five minutes."

He grinned as if there was a load eased inside of him.

Taken with a thought, she stopped moving. "Wait a minute. Franck. Your brother died in the rodeo. And you got burned."

"Yeah," he said, smiling sadly. "It was hard on my mom."

"No frigging fooling. It must've been awful," she answered.

He twirled her gently and she noticed C.J. watching from the sidelines. Why wasn't he dancing?

"Timm, I'm really sorry about what happened to you." She knew how heartbreak felt.

"You're a nice person to talk to," he said.

"I am?" No one had ever said that to her before. Something warmed deep in her chest and she smiled. She liked this guy. Too bad he was too young for her. Too bad she could never have a boyfriend.

C.J. appeared and cut in. He was frowning and took her hand and led her out through the side doorway.

"Where are we going?" she asked.

He continued walking away from the people hanging around outside of the Legion Hall, puffing on the cigarettes they couldn't smoke inside, the smoke dissipating on the cool September breeze.

As soon as they reached a spot she assumed he chose because they were a safe distance from people, he let go of her hand like it was a hot potato.

"What were you thinking flirting with Timm like that?"

"What are you talking about?" This was coming out of left field. "No way was I flirting."

"Way," he shouted, sounding like a sullen little boy. "I saw you smiling at Timm. A lot."

"Of course I did. He's a nice guy."

"He's too young for you and he's been through enough in his life. He doesn't need you messing him up."

"I wasn't messing him up," she yelled. "I was dancing with him. What is *wrong* with you people? I'm not looking for a boyfriend. Got it?"

"Yeah, I got it." Now he *looked* sullen as well as sounding it. In the gathering gloom of dusk, he looked darker than usual, older, but his facial expression was pure little boy, as if someone had taken his toy away and he couldn't get it back.

Was he jealous? *Whoa, slow down,* she ordered that strange thought floating through her. Was she the toy C.J. thought Timm was taking away from him? Did C.J. even know he was acting jealously?

In spite of all of her screwed-up-ness around boys

and men, and despite the fact that nothing would ever happen with C.J., man, oh, man, did his jealousy ever feel good. It flattered her, and she'd had too little of that in her life.

"Listen, thanks for introducing me to your friends," she said, softer now.

"No problem."

They both stood there, as if neither of them knew what their next step should be.

C.J. took her hand again, lightly this time, and said, "Let's go back inside."

Janey hadn't needed anyone to take care of her in years, but it felt good to make friends. They entered the hall and headed toward Mona and the girls hanging out with her.

Max Golden's daughter, Marnie, a tall, cool blonde, sauntered by. She nodded to C.J. and ignored Janey.

"That was rude," C.J. said. "I would have introduced you if she'd given me half a chance."

"Hey, it's nothing new. I never was popular in school."

"No?"

Janey shook her head. "You?"

"Yeah. I was good at sports, until—"

"Until what?" she asked.

"Until I started to rebel and stopped hanging out after school."

Janey bumped into someone and apologized.

The young guy, a redhead dressed all in denim, turned to her, smiled and said, "Hey, no problem. Want to dance?"

She started to say yes, but C.J. steered her toward the far end of the hall.

"She's busy, Jim," he said.

Jim laughed. "I'll let it go this time, but I'm getting a chance at the next dance." He winked at Janey.

Wow, that guy was flirting with her. How cool was that?

She turned her attention back to C.J. "What did you do instead?"

"Instead of what?"

"Hanging out at school and doing sports?"

"I hung out with my friend, Davey. We smoked up when my dad wasn't around. Hung out with girls. Drank. Busted broncs. Got involved in the rodeo."

"Do you miss him?" Janey asked.

"Who?" C.J. stared hard at a poster on the wall for a performer coming to town next month.

"You know who," Janey said.

"Yeah, I miss him." His jaw had a mulish jut, and Janey knew she wasn't going to get anything else from him about Davey.

A slow song started. The fiddlers morphed their instruments into the sweetest violins.

"Come on," C.J. said. "Let's dance."

Why not? She'd survived a slow dance with Timm. The second C.J. touched her, though, she knew it wasn't going to work.

Where she'd felt safe with Timm, she felt anything but with C.J.

His big hand engulfed her right hand.

His palm on her back burned through her dress.

Warm breath misted the air near her ear. He smelled like soap and citron.

His hand painted slow circles on her spine.

"Soft," he whispered.

The dress or her?

Her nerves skittered, danced as fast as any jig or reel, or whatever those fast songs were called the band had already played.

Calm down.

His cheek brushed her hair and she nearly moaned. She longed to touch him more, to lift her cheek and rub it against his. She wanted to curl against him like a kitten and lap at his neck.

He stepped closer.

One of his thighs touched hers and she jumped away. The hand on her back steadied her.

She couldn't do any of the things she wanted. All of it led to shame.

A wail started in her chest, pressed against her ribs and her heart with an insistence that became sharp. *Why can't I be normal?*

She started to shake and knew C.J. could feel it. She refused to look at him, knowing what she would see on his face, in his eyes. Disgust.

Her cheeks burned. *Please,* she begged the floor, *just open up right now and suck me down.*

He's only a man.

Her breathing came in huffs, so she held her breath. *That's the problem. He's a man.*

Dizziness washed through her.

Stay.

Can't.

She jerked away from C.J., tried to say something, couldn't. Vision blurring, she ran from the room, through the front door of the hall and down the street.

She swiped tears from her cheeks.

"Janey?" someone called. Amy.

Janey stopped and turned. Oh, Amy.

Amy stood beside her car. "Are you okay?"

Amy was the perfect choice—safe. Janey flew into Amy's arms, knocking her against the car door.

"Janey," Amy breathed. "What's wrong?"

Janey sobbed on Amy's shoulder. She wanted to spill her guts so badly.

"Shh, tell me what's wrong so I can help."

"Amy, why?" Janey cried. "Why can't I be normal?"

"You mean in the way you dress? Was someone rude about it?"

Janey could feel her stiffen, like a mother cat preparing to defend her litter.

"No, I mean me, the inside of me that's broken."

Amy pushed her away with a gentle shove. "Get in the car. Michael and I are heading home. You're coming with us."

Janey sighed. This was exactly what she needed, for Amy to take care of her for a while.

She settled into the passenger seat and closed her eyes. While Amy drove, Janey concentrated on bringing herself under control, on breathing, on mending her tattered nerves.

On organizing her muddy thoughts to share with Amy.

After Amy settled Michael into bed and returned downstairs, she poured them both two small glasses of something.

One lamp banned the darkness from Janey's small corner of the room.

Amy sat on the far end of the long sofa and handed her a liqueur glass.

"I don't like alcohol," Janey said.

"I know, but it's only Baileys. Right now you need something."

Janey sipped the drink and it burned going down. "That's strong."

Amy smiled. "Have more."

The second sip tasted better and warmed her throat.

"Now talk," Amy ordered. "What's going on?"

Janey rubbed the velvet of her dress between her fingers. So soft. "It's hard to talk about."

"The rape?"

Amy was the first person outside of Janey's own family she'd ever told about it.

"How did you know?"

"I noticed you were with C.J. a lot this evening. I wondered what was going on." That statement ended with a question mark in Amy's voice.

"I don't know. I feel so many weird things when I'm with him."

"Like what?"

"I like him," she said, staring into the café-au-lait tint of her drink. "Well, not always. Sometimes. He can be pretty stubborn."

"Aren't they all?" Amy softened that with a smile.

"I guess. C.J. makes me feel too much. I—" She leaned forward. "I love it *and* I hate it when he touches me."

She took Amy's hand. "I'm so afraid."

Amy squeezed her fingers. "Of what?"

"I'm so afraid I'm permanently damaged," Janey said, touching her chest. "Here. Inside."

She drank more Baileys. It slid down her throat.

"Of being with a man. Of sex. I'm better with a little

bit of touching now, but I feel like I want to do more with C.J. and that scares the crap out of me."

She finished off her drink and slammed the glass onto a side table. "I got so scared I couldn't slow dance with him. I ran away. He's going to think I'm crazy."

"I saw you slow dancing with Timm Franck earlier. It looked like you didn't mind."

"But Timm is harmless. He's like one of my younger brothers."

"Yes, I see the difference. How does C.J. feel about you?"

"I don't know. Sometimes, he looks at me like he wants to eat me and other times like he can't stand me."

"Oh-kay, so we know he's attracted to you."

"Really?"

"Yes, but he doesn't want to be."

"Amy, I say the worst things to him sometimes."

"Of course you do. You're protecting yourself against getting hurt."

"Yes, exactly!"

"That's okay."

Janey continued on as if Amy hadn't spoken. "How can I like a guy who's so uptight he shaves off most of his hair and wears button-down collars, for Pete's sake?"

"He wasn't always like that," Amy said. "He's dressing out of character these days because of Liam. He doesn't want to give anyone any excuse to take the boy away from him." Amy patted Janey's hand. "You're seeing through the starchy clothes to the man underneath."

Janey blushed. "Sometimes I wish I really could see under his clothes, but what good would that do? I can't *do* anything about the way I'm attracted physically to C.J."

"Not yet."

"Not ever."

"Never say never." Amy stood and headed for the stairs. "Let's go to bed. You look exhausted. This will work out one way or another."

Janey doubted it. Her feet were heavy on the stairs.

Her arms were heavy when she cleaned herself for the night. She stared at her pale face in the mirror.

How was she going to face C.J. the next time she saw him?

Her body felt even heavier when she lay on the bed, like someone had loaded it with too many feelings, all of them conflicting with each other.

Damn you, C.J.

How could she possibly go to work on Monday?

She turned her hot face into the pillow.

CHAPTER ELEVEN

ON SUNDAY MORNING, C.J. drove to the Sheltering Arms and pulled into a yard that was quiet, eerily so.

Where were the ranch hands? The kids?

He thought he'd heard someone mention last night they were bronc busting here today. He must have been mistaken.

He parked the Jeep and jumped out into the neat and tidy yard. Flowers in the window boxes of Willie's apartment above the garage shone red and white in the sun.

Still day. No hint of a breeze rustled the leaves of the willow tree or the grain in the fields.

He didn't know how he felt about maybe seeing Janey today after last night.

C.J. stepped up onto the veranda and knocked on the front door.

Janey answered. Her eyes widened when she saw him.

She stared, couldn't seem to say anything any more than he could.

Her cheeks turned pink.

I'm thinking about last night, too, about you in my arms, about the surprise of you, not as an employee, but as a woman.

He shoved his hands into his jean pockets.

Stop thinking that way.

Holding her had done something strange to his insides. He'd held her before when he taught her to knead the candies and had felt the sharp, adolescent lust that she'd provoked.

But last night? Last night had been different, deeper, more disturbing. Dancing face-to-face with her breasts against his chest quickly became too intimate and scared him to his toes.

Something had changed between them last night and he didn't know what it was, was afraid to look at it too closely. If he didn't acknowledge how much he'd liked holding her and wanted to hold her again, it wouldn't be real.

She looked different.

She wore old faded overalls with holes in the knees. The red plaid of her flannel shirt looked great against her pitch-black hair. God, she was cute, sweet, despite the dark cloud of her makeup.

He couldn't think of a thing to say.

"Hi." Lame.

"Hi," she answered and seemed to have a brain as mushy as his. The shape of a paperback book showed in a hip pocket. The top of a chocolate bar peeked out of one of the breast pockets of her overalls.

She sure does like her sweets.

She folded her arms across herself as if for protection. From him?

Then he realized she must have thought he was staring at her breasts.

His gaze shot to her face.

Her cheeks turned a darker red, the way his own

cheeks felt, burning hot, as if someone had stretched the skin on his face too tightly.

The skin on his entire body felt too tight. Damn.

He didn't want to want the Goth girl, but he'd seen too much kindness and compassion in her beneath the hard-edged exterior to believe she was truly bad.

But was she truly good? How about having a kid when she was still a kid herself? And how about not telling the father he had a kid?

With a start, he realized he worried for more than just Liam's sake. He worried for himself. Vicki had put him through the wringer. He couldn't go through that again.

But she only looks like Vicki.

Yeah, but why those clothes and the piercings everywhere and the tattoo? What was she hiding? What if it called to that part of himself he thought he'd buried, the side that led to bad decisions and poor choices? He had to protect himself.

"I thought there was bronc busting here today," he said, his tone all business.

"It's at the Hungry Hollow."

Hungry Hollow was the neighboring working ranch that Hank's mother, Leila, owned.

"Everyone went over a while ago," she said.

"Why didn't you go?"

She shrugged with only one shoulder, as if even that was an effort. She looked stunned in a deer-in-the-headlights kind of way.

He was intelligent. She was sharp-tongued, quick. Why the hell couldn't either of them think of a thing to say?

Muttering "Thanks," he turned toward the Jeep, but spun back with an abruptness that startled her.

"What happened last—"

Panic swept across her face and she held up a staying hand, as if to say, "Don't ask."

He nodded.

Just as well. Did he really want to know the answer?

He headed to the Jeep and rode out to the Hungry Hollow.

When he got there, he stared at the teeming pack of men and women surrounding the corral and, to his surprise, didn't feel like hanging out with them today.

He wanted to be with Janey. That thought puzzled him and scared him and unsettled him, and he needed to explore it.

Without stepping foot outside of his truck, he spun it around and headed into town.

He stopped at the grocery store and bought the fixings for a picnic. Not that he knew much about picnicking, but he put in an honest effort.

He ran over to the rectory to pick up Liam.

"Where are you taking him?" Dad asked.

"On a picnic." He looked his dad in the eye. "Once I got to the bronc busting, I just didn't feel like doing it. Thanks for being willing to take care of Liam so I could do that."

It had been a real concession on Dad's part to watch Liam so he could rodeo. Guilt, perhaps, after yesterday's fiasco with Max and the powwow, or maybe the trouble Hardisty had caused Janey last night, had motivated Walter.

C.J. buckled Liam into his car seat in the Jeep, then headed down the highway again.

This time when he drove into the Sheltering Arms,

Janey was reading under the willow on the front lawn. She seemed to like that spot a lot.

She stood when she saw the Jeep, her mouth hanging open, her half-eaten chocolate bar in her hand.

He got out and approached her, his heart doing a funny little dance.

"Hey," he said, tongue-tied again.

"Hey, yourself." He watched her swallow.

C.J. nodded his head toward the bar. "That all you're planning to eat for lunch?"

She looked at the chocolate as if she'd forgotten it was there. She shrugged. "I didn't feel like cooking anything."

"You want to go on a picnic?"

"With you?"

"With Liam and me."

She nodded and placed her book on the lawn chair.

"You need anything from the house?"

"No," she whispered.

"Okay, let's go."

She walked beside him to the truck and climbed into the passenger seat. She greeted Liam and he cried, "Janey!" and giggled.

C.J. noticed the candy bar in her hand, forgotten. He took it from her and bit a huge chunk out of it. Sweet. Good. Great. He wished he could taste her on it.

She watched him, stared at his lips while he chewed. He stared at her pretty mouth and wanted to trade spit with her. Dumb idea.

"Me!" Liam yelled from the backseat. He pointed at the candy bar.

"What do you say?" Janey asked, half turning in her seat to look at Liam.

"Please." He clapped his hands.

While looking Janey in the eye, C.J. tossed the end of the candy bar into the backseat where it landed on Liam's chest. Bull's-eye.

She laughed.

Liam giggled.

C.J.'s heart swelled.

He drove them to his ranch but continued down the lane past the house to a clearing near a small pond. He used to love this spot as a kid.

He stepped out of the Jeep and handed a threadbare quilt of his grandmother's to Janey.

"Pick a flat spot and spread that out."

Liam raced across the clearing and threw himself onto the quilt Janey was trying to straighten out.

"Hey, buster," she said. "How am I supposed to get this straight so we can eat?"

Liam rolled on the quilt and giggled.

Before taking the food out of the vehicle, C.J. strode over and picked up two corners of the quilt. He cocked one eyebrow at Janey and she caught on right away. She grabbed the other two corners and they lifted the quilt off the ground.

Liam rolled toward the middle. At a nod from C.J., they threw him up into the air and caught him when he fell back to the quilt. He laughed the deep belly laugh of a child.

Something inside of C.J. warmed. How could he ever get enough of that sound?

They did it again and again until Janey had to stop.

"My arms are burning," she said, her cheeks pink, her smile wide.

They lowered the quilt to the ground. Liam scrambled off and ran after a butterfly. C.J. watched Janey spread out the quilt.

What was happening here? What was he doing?

Hell if he knew.

He retrieved the food he'd bought earlier.

Liam had run out of interest in butterflies and was pulling the blossoms from the stalks of wildflowers.

Janey knelt on the far edge of the quilt and helped C.J. unload the bags.

"Why did you come back to get me?" she asked.

C.J. stopped what he was doing and stared at the pattern of the quilt, at the muted greens and blues and yellows.

"I don't know."

He looked up at her and she watched him, expression solemn.

"I just felt like being with you today." He shrugged. That was the best he could do. He hadn't looked at his motivation too closely. "Why did you come?"

"I don't know," she said and looked around at Liam running in the field, at the trees overhead, at the small pool of water, as if she'd come for the scenery. As if it was any prettier here than on Hank Shelter's ranch.

So. She wasn't looking too closely at her own feelings either. Fine. They could keep it light, maybe the best course of action today.

Liam made a beeline for the water and C.J. jumped to his feet and caught him before he fell in.

"Lunch first, buddy, then we'll talk about swimming."

Liam squirmed in his arms and cried. He broke away from C.J. and threw himself on Janey. She barely managed to keep them both upright.

"Wanna go in the water," he yelled.

"Later," she said. "Daddy wants to have lunch first."

"I don't like Daddy."

"Kids say things like that all the time," she whispered while Liam dived for the grocery bags. "They don't mean them."

"Yeah, I think this one does," C.J. answered. He knew he sounded low, but his skin was still itchy with Janey so close and his heart was still breaking every time his own flesh and blood turned away from him.

Janey helped him make lunch.

A cantaloupe rolled out of one of the bags. Liam hit it with his hand and said, "Want some, please."

Janey picked it up and looked around, lifted bags and looked into them. Looked at C.J.

"What?" he asked.

"Did you bring a knife?"

A knife. Crap. "No." His face burned. He was a hell of a picnic packer.

A smile kicked up one corner of Janey's mouth.

Liam smacked the melon. "Please, I want some!"

"Liam, your daddy forgot to bring a knife. The only thing you're going to be doing with this is using it as a drum."

Liam grinned and squatted on his haunches. He pounded on the cantaloupe until his palms were red.

C.J. handed him a sandwich that Liam left lying on a paper napkin. Janey handed it to Liam and he ate it. C.J. looked away.

After lunch, he rolled his pant legs up to his knees.

He reached for Liam but the boy scooted toward Janey.

"What do you want?" she asked.

"Just thought I'd strip him to his drawers and take him into the water."

Janey pulled Liam's T-shirt over his head then pulled off his pants until he stood in only his underwear.

When C.J. stuck out his hand to walk to the water, Liam dived into Janey's arms.

"You!" he shouted.

"Liam, say, 'Will you take me, please?'" Janey said.

He cocked his head to one side. "Will you take me, please?"

"Your daddy would like to take you in the water."

"No. Daddy leave."

C.J.'s head shot up. He stared at his son. God, the pain. What more could he possibly do for his son? Why wasn't it ever enough?

"You want him to leave?" Janey asked. "Liam, that's not nice."

"No, Daddy won't leave *now*. Daddy *will* leave."

Janey frowned at C.J. "What does he mean?"

"I haven't a clue."

"Okay, listen," Janey said, getting on her attitude again. "Daddy isn't leaving now. We're all going into the water together. Got it?"

"'Kay," Liam said and waited while Janey rolled up the legs of her overalls.

They walked to the pond together, Janey holding one of Liam's hands and C.J. holding his other, but only because Janey put her foot down and forced him to.

The water was cool in the shade, so C.J. directed them toward a sunny spot. His boy laughed and splashed his feet.

Despite the gloom and pure frustration he felt that

Liam still didn't accept him, C.J. smiled. There was something so sweet about doing fatherly things.

"You like this?" Janey asked.

"Yeah. Now that I've had a taste of fatherhood, I want to do more of it. I want a passel of kids running free on my land, coming home to the suppers I provide for them and to sleep in their beds under my roof."

A look of such longing crossed Janey's face that C.J. asked, "What's wrong?"

He watched her mind work, watched her pull herself together until she said, "Nothing."

Liar.

"That's a really nice image," she said and stepped away to wander through the bulrushes at the far end of the pond.

Liam moved to follow her but slipped. His head went under the water. C.J. grabbed him under the arms and pulled him out.

Liam came up sputtering and wailed. A soggy, muddy superhero drooped down Liam's bum.

"Easy," C.J. said, patting him on the back. "You're all right."

"Janey," Liam screamed and Janey strode back through the water and took him from C.J.

"You're tired," she said. "Time for a nap."

She carried him to the blanket where she took off his underwear and dried him with a corner of the quilt. She pulled his clothes on, then settled him in the middle of the quilt and lay down beside him.

C.J. felt the frustration of his own not doing for his son.

He stepped out of the water and lay down on the other side of Liam. Janey was pulling her beautiful Madonna routine again lying beside Liam, all soft curves and gentle touches on the child's hair.

A shot of lust raged through C.J.'s body and with it, anger. He didn't want to desire this Goth beauty with the sometimes angelic face and black fall of hair caressing her shoulder, her heavenly body lying only a couple of feet away and tempting him.

He needed a woman of whom the state of Montana would approve, one who didn't look and dress like Liam's mother—the woman the social workers had taken Liam from and put into his, C.J.'s, safekeeping.

He rose on his elbow, lunged across his sleeping son and grabbed Janey's chin, met her mouth with his wide-open and seeking, with his tongue demanding *let me in.*

She didn't. She sagged against him for a moment then pulled back. Tried to break away.

He held her chin hard, trying to bite into her, to feed from her essence on the desperate answers he needed to questions he couldn't frame.

Her palm landed hard on the side of his head. Stunned by the pain, he pulled away.

"What—"

She stared at him, wide-eyed and terrified, and he shook himself.

"Sorry." His breath whooshed out of him like steam from a locomotive. "Sorry."

He hung his head and scraped his nails across his scalp. "I don't know why I did that." He reached a hand to comfort her, but she scooted toward the edge of the quilt and onto the grass.

"Stop. I won't hurt you." He sucked in a deep breath and held it, then let it blow out of him in a calming arc. "I won't hurt you. I promise."

Janey edged back onto the blanket, but watched him warily. "Why did you kiss me?" Her voice sounded thin.

"I don't know."

"Did you bring me out here to do that?"

"No," he shouted. Liam stirred and C.J. lowered his voice. "I just wanted to be with you, and Liam. I don't know exactly why I kissed you."

"Don't do it again."

He turned and stared at her. "I won't." With his gaze, he willed her to believe him. She seemed to.

"I'm living with a lot of stress these days," he said. "That's not a great excuse, I know, but I can't seem to keep myself on an even keel."

She made a sound that might have been agreement.

"I need money," he said. "I might lose the ranch and I might lose Liam and I can't stand the thought of either thing happening."

"Why is it so important to raise him on the ranch? You can raise a kid anywhere as long as you give him a lot of love."

"I know, but…" How could he explain? "I grew up with my mom and dad in the rectory beside the church. It was dark and cramped and confining. Dad's many rules suffocated me. The ranch, though, symbolized freedom for as far back as I can remember. It was all about fun and fresh air and hard work, too, and I loved it. I want the same for Liam."

He cut his hand through the air. "I don't want him in a crowded apartment or a small house. I want him running free on the land."

They lapsed into silence and left soon after Liam woke up.

Liam cried when C.J. dropped Janey off at the Sheltering Arms, setting C.J.'s already ragged nerves on edge.

CHAPTER TWELVE

"HANK, CAN YOU DRIVE ME to Sweet Talk?" Janey asked after Sunday night's supper.

Hank looked up from the book he was reading to a child sitting on his lap. "You're going in to work tonight? At this time? Does C.J. have a big order or something?"

"No, I'm moving into the apartment over the store."

Hank's eyebrows shot up. "You are?"

"Yeah, I guess I forgot to tell you. I don't have a lot of stuff. If you're too tired, I can probably carry my clothes over in two trips, but it might be dark by the time I walk into town the second time."

"No way are you walking into town tonight. Of course I'll drive you." He handed Justin to Willie, who picked up in the story where Hank had left off.

Janey ran upstairs to get the bags she'd packed. She didn't have much and it was mostly secondhand, but it was hers.

Just as she left her washroom with her toiletries in her arms, Amy showed up.

"You're leaving?"

"Yeah. I'm renting the apartment above the store."

Amy watched her dump her makeup and shampoo into a plastic shopping bag and said, "Stop. I'll be right back."

She returned a minute later with a black satin cosmetic bag.

"Here," she said. "Put all that in here."

It was beautiful and so feminine—so much like Amy herself. Janey had never owned anything like it and vowed that one day when she'd made her dream come true, when she worked at a business and wore pink lipstick, she'd buy herself a bag as pretty as this one.

"Thanks, I'll get it back to you later in the week."

"No. It's yours."

The gesture nearly knocked her to her knees. They were so good to her. Amy and Hank had done so much for her. Janey could never repay their kindness. She ran her fingers over the fabric and whispered, "Thank you, Amy. I'll take very good care of it."

Amy gave Janey's hand a squeeze. "I know you will."

They carried Janey's bags downstairs where Gladys and Hannah waited.

"News travels fast in this house," Janey said.

Hannah gave her a bag chock-full of food and groceries. Gladys wrapped Janey in her arms and whispered, "I'll miss you."

Amy did the same. "If it doesn't work out, come straight back home, okay?"

Home. Oh, Amy, I love you, too.

Janey tried not to show it but she felt teary-eyed. These people were her friends and she felt so blessed to have found them in the last year.

Hank helped her load her stuff in the truck.

They were quiet on the drive, until they reached the town limits.

"Sorry to drag you out so late," Janey said. "You've

been busy lately, though, and I really wanted to get moved in."

"It's okay. You know I don't mind."

Hank waited while she unlocked the door and flicked the switch that turned on one of the store lights. He hauled her things upstairs and checked out her apartment.

"This is nice. It just might work out for you. I have a little old TV you can have. Do you want it?"

Janey nodded. "That would be good."

Hank placed his fingers on her shoulder in a fleeting touch. "You take care. If this doesn't work out for you, give me a call and I'll come get you, okay?"

"Thanks, Hank."

She walked him out and he waited to make sure the front door was locked before driving off.

Janey headed upstairs, turning off lights as she went, until she was in her *own* apartment with just a table lamp on. The room felt cozy.

She put away the groceries and food from Hannah, including a huge slice of homemade lasagna left over from dinner.

After wiping out the small medicine cabinet in the bathroom, she filled it with makeup and toiletries.

She checked out the bed. After she said she would rent the place, C.J. had promised to wash the bed sheets. She sniffed the pillowcase. Fabric softener. He had cleaned them.

The miniature white Stetson that Hank had given to Cheryl at the end of her visit at the Sheltering Arms took pride of place on the knob at the outside corner of the metal headboard.

Like the street outside late on a Sunday evening,

the apartment was quiet. It would be perfect when she started her studying.

She tucked her clothes into the dresser and the closet. Then, with nothing else to do, she sat in the living room.

Thinking hard, she couldn't remember when she'd last felt this alone. Except for yesterday with the pow-wow, the ranch was always hopping and alive with people.

Her mind wandered to thoughts of her family, of Dad and Tom and the twins, Grace and Janet, and the youngest, Shannon.

In the dead quiet of the apartment, with no distractions, she realized how much she'd missed them. She'd forgotten how Shannon used to call her every day after school. No way would they want to hear from her now, though. She hadn't contacted them once in the past year. She hadn't been able to. Couldn't talk about Cheryl.

She wondered if she could work up the nerve to contact them again, or if she had lost them for good.

THE FOLLOWING WEEK BROUGHT with it more of the same in the candy business, learning to make more candies—saltwater taffy on Tuesday and filling chocolate moulds on Wednesday.

Throughout, Janey felt something shift for her. She started to love the little store and the work involved and almost all of the customers.

Calvin stopped in for lunch again on Wednesday and didn't complain about the repeated menu of peanut-butter-and-jelly sandwiches. Neither did C.J. say a thing about Janey feeding Calvin.

On Thursday, C.J. taught her how to make icing and

paint the animals. She started with a small rabbit and did a *great* job.

On Friday morning, Janey ran downstairs at ten to nine to open the front door for C.J. and Liam. They'd been a few minutes late every morning this week. When they arrived each morning, Janey could tell they were frustrated with each other.

She set out some crayons and a coloring book she'd picked up.

The bell rang and she turned to greet them, but it was a woman Janey didn't recognize. She wasn't from town.

"Can I help you?" she asked.

She studied Janey with a puzzled frown. "Have we met? Are you one of Vicki's friends?"

"No, I'm not. Who are you?"

"Is C.J. here?"

"He'll be in any minute."

"I'll wait for him in my car."

Who on earth was that and how did she know about Liam's mother?

Ten minutes later, C.J. showed up with Liam, who was crying.

"What's going on?" Janey picked up Liam and rocked him in her arms.

"He wouldn't eat breakfast."

"How about if I go to the diner and get him some fried eggs?"

"That's okay. I'll go."

C.J. left the store and Janey sat at the table in the window with Liam on her lap, waiting for C.J. to return. At the sound of raised voices a while later, she looked out the window.

C.J. stood arguing with the woman who'd come into

the store. Janey had witnessed a lot of C.J.'s moods, but she'd never seen this particular blend of anger and...desperation? Suddenly she wished she'd lied to the woman and sent her on her way rather than having C.J. deal with her when he was obviously having a bad morning.

The woman got into her car and drove off. C.J. stood on the sidewalk staring after the car until it was history.

When he entered the store with a foam container holding Liam's breakfast, his step was heavy.

"Are you okay?" she asked.

"No."

"What's happening? Who was that?"

"Marjorie Bates. The social worker who handles Liam's file."

"What did she want?"

"She wanted to know why you were working here. She said she recognized you from when you used to go into the Child and Family Welfare Services office in Billings. Why?"

"Because of Cheryl. I was only fifteen when she was born and living on my own. Welfare was the only way we could survive."

"Did you know Marjorie?"

"I don't remember ever seeing her there."

"She wants me to take Liam into Billings next Thursday for an interview. She didn't like that I was bringing him into work today. She thinks it is only for today, so don't say anything other than that. Okay?"

"Why would I say anything? I'll probably never see her again."

"Well…" C.J. rubbed the back of his neck. "She wants you to come into the office with me and Liam next week."

"Me? Why? I only work here."

"I know, but I think she guessed that Liam is in here more often than just today and that you work here full-time."

"It's because of the way I look, isn't it?"

"I think so. Yeah."

She hated this. Before moving to this town, her appearance had protected her, kept her safe hiding in plain sight. But now people judged her harshly and unfairly. Couldn't anyone see her? The real her?

And she so did not want to return to the services office. Despite how nice her social workers had been, every visit had stripped away a little of her pride and added to her shame. She'd wanted so much more for Cheryl and herself. Still did. But this wasn't about her, she thought as she looked at C.J. It was about him keeping his son, as he deserved.

"All right. I'll come. Can I visit some people and run some errands while we're there?" Maybe she'd have the courage to phone her family, to rebuild the bridge she'd let crumble with her grief.

"Yeah. I'll close the shop for the full day. I'll pick you up here at nine."

"Okay."

On Saturday, Janey was operating the store on her own. C.J. was at Angus Kinsey's ranch with most of the local ranchers, busting broncs.

The Rev was babysitting Liam.

When she served her first two customers, a ripple of excitement ran through her. It was like being a shop-owner, like being a businesswoman.

Bernice had just left after picking up some dinner

mints when the door chime rang. Janey came back into the store.

Two young guys, strangers, stood looking around. They wore black clothes heavily laden with silver chains and studs. Their dyed black hair was either really dirty or coated with product to keep it superstraight and covering most of their eyes.

They wore black nail polish.

Their piercings outnumbered Janey's by two to one.

One of them wore a black-leather dog collar studded with silver spikes.

Punks.

They looked tough and strung-out on something. Dangerous.

Was that what some people saw when they looked at her?

Danger?

"What can I do for you?" she asked.

"I need money," one of them said.

Great. Her first day alone on the job and she was about to be robbed. Not if she could help it.

"The bank's across the street."

"I don't have an account there," the guy wearing the collar said.

"You don't have a bank account anywhere," his buddy added.

"So what do you want me to do about it? That's not my problem."

"Give me money, bitch." Dog collar ran around the counter and shoved her out of the way. She fell against the cash register and banged her ribs. She sucked in a breath.

"No. Get out of here." She was nobody's victim. Never again.

"Out of my way," he yelled and slammed her against the counter. Red-hot pain exploded through her back.

He opened the cash and pulled out all of the large bills.

Scooting around the candy cases he ordered, "Let's go!"

His friend ran out of the store ahead of him.

Janey rounded the candy cases and ran out of the shop after them, catching up with them on the sidewalk.

"No," she yelled.

She lunged for him and caught a fistful of hair. Her fingers slid off but not without catching something. A chain that ran from a ring on his ear lobe to another ring at the top of his ear got caught around her finger. When the guy ran forward, one of the rings tore through his skin.

"Aaargh," he screamed.

Janey came away empty-handed, the chain and ring hanging from the one ring that had held.

He turned and backhanded her across the face so hard, her head snapped back and slammed against the window. Pain flooded through her skull and she slid to the ground, her legs as useless as if they were boneless.

She heard a car starting then tires squealing. She thought vaguely that the car needed a tune-up.

Then the old guys who hung out at the barbershop surrounded her, all helping her to her feet.

A deep voice said, "What happened here?"

One of the old gentlemen said, "I think she was robbed, Sheriff. We saw a couple of punks drive off. One of them had a bunch of bills in his hand."

She couldn't open her eyes. Everything swam when she did.

A different voice said, "The other one had one of those big chocolate animals in his arms. A rabbit, I think."

They stole a rabbit?

"Did you know those men?" the sheriff's voice asked.

"Never...saw...them before."

"She fought like a madwoman, Sheriff," another voice said. "You should have seen her. She was amazing."

The sheriff helped her to her feet and steadied her with an arm around her shoulders.

"Washroom. I need the washroom."

The sheriff helped her into the store.

"Hurry," she whispered, while bile rose into her throat.

Her feet left the floor and the sheriff carried her the rest of the way, setting her down in front of the toilet not a second too soon.

Janey lost her breakfast and probably most of last night's dinner, too.

The sheriff got her a glass of water. She rinsed and spat.

"You okay?"

"Better."

She took a second to steady herself then walked to the front with the sheriff trailing her.

Looking at the disarray of the cash register, she swallowed.

"Looks like they got about a hundred bucks." She swayed and the sheriff led her to the table in the window.

"Sit," he ordered. "Let me look at you."

An older man with gray eyes, thinning hair, broad shoulders and a stomach that stretched his shirt, he studied her eyes.

"You might have a concussion. Are you dizzy?"

"Major dizzy."

"Still nauseous?"

She nodded but that made her super dizzy again.

"Okay, let's get you to the hospital."

"I can't leave. C.J. isn't in today."

"The store can close for one day."

She locked the front door after grabbing a handful of mints for her mouth and her stomach, and climbed into the police cruiser. Sheriff Houston drove to the nearest hospital forty miles away.

Janey hadn't been in a hospital since that horrible day Cheryl had been hit by that car—easily one of the worst days of Janey's life. But before that when Cheryl was receiving treatments, they'd practically lived in medical centers. Oddly, Janey had been comforted by the experience. The nurses, doctors and specialists had cared for Cheryl with attentiveness and compassion that rivaled Janey's. The staff had made the process less scary, less daunting. Her treatment today replicated that.

After a thorough examination and a bunch of tests, the doctors had determined that she had a concussion and would need to take it easy for the next few days.

She was exhausted by the time the sheriff dropped her off at the store. She locked the front door behind her and climbed the stairs to her apartment, slowly and with a lot of effort. Man, she felt rough.

The bump on the back of her head ached, her swollen eye throbbed and her stomach remained unsettled.

She put on the kettle, made tea when it boiled, then sat on the sofa with her feet on the coffee table.

Not ten minutes later, she heard the pounding of feet on the stairs, taking them two at a time, and hoped like crazy it wasn't someone to rob her because she might have used up all of her fight earlier today.

C.J. burst through the door.

"Janey!" She'd never seen him like this. Stricken. Panicked.

When he saw her, he pulled her into his arms and held her against his chest. Her feet dangled above the floor.

"Are you okay? Were you hurt?"

She didn't like to be held, hated to be touched, but at this moment, she didn't care, just wanted it to never end. But she couldn't breathe. "Squeezing too hard," she squeaked.

"Oh, God, sorry." He set her back onto the sofa and reached over to turn on a table lamp.

"Your face." He winced. "Damn. I should have been here."

"Why? They would have beaten you up, too."

Leaning over her, his shirt stretched across his muscular shoulders, and she amended, "Or maybe not."

"Listen, I'll never leave you alone again."

"You have to. Didn't you hire me so you could practice rodeo while I took care of the store?"

"Yeah, but it shouldn't have cost you this." He caressed the corner of her swollen eye. "Damn, I'm sorry. Are you hurt anywhere else?"

She should ask him to stop touching her since she wasn't completely comfortable with it. She would.

When it stopped feeling good. "My ribs and back are bruised."

C.J. clenched his fists and swore.

More feet sounded on the stairs, more than one person.

Hank, Amy and Gladys entered the apartment, Hank with a small TV in his arms and Amy with a piece of equipment—a DVD player or a video machine. Gladys carried a bag of groceries, which she took straight to the kitchen.

Oh, boy, her eyes felt prickly. *Don't cry. Don't get sappy.*

She wanted to. They were such awesome friends.

Hank and C.J. set up the TV across the room.

Amy took one look at her face and got a cold face-cloth from the bathroom. "We should have brought ice."

"How did you all know what happened?"

"Houston came out to the Circle K and told us about the robbery." When he looked at her, C.J. swore. "Bastards."

She must be turning some pretty interesting colors.

"I think they got about a hundred dollars. They got a chocolate rabbit, too." For some reason that bothered her more than the money. "I'm really sorry about that."

He sliced a hand through the air. "I don't care about the money. I met Calvin hanging around by the front door. He said you put up a fight."

Pointing a finger at her, he ordered, "Next time, let them have whatever they want." His lips thinned. "And stay as far away from them as you can."

"Amen," Hank murmured.

"But—"

"No buts," Hank and C.J. answered in unison.

Gladys came out of the kitchen with a big mug of soup that smelled heavenly.

Amy brought the quilt from the bed, wrapped it around Janey, then rinsed the facecloth with more cold water and applied it to Janey's eye.

"I really love you guys," Janey whispered and her voice sounded shaky.

Amy kissed her cheek.

Gladys said, "We love you, too, sweetheart."

Hank cleared his throat noisily.

C.J. said, "You want *Twilight* or *Love Actually*?"

"Love Actually."

"I'll make popcorn," Gladys said.

SHE STAYED IN BED all day Sunday, and Monday as it turned out, as well. Her ribs and back were stiff and sore. Gladys and Amy came in each day and cooked and fed her.

Liam wanted to see her but C.J. wouldn't let him because of the discoloration of her face.

Still achy Tuesday and Wednesday, C.J. let her do a little around the store. Liam cried when he first saw her but, in time, grew used to the purple and green around her eye.

ON THURSDAY MORNING, Janey stared at herself in the mirror. She hadn't put on a speck of makeup for the visit with the counselor.

She couldn't help but recall those early days when Cheryl was a baby and nobody at Child and Family Services had wanted to believe that a girl as young as Janey had been could raise a child on her own and do a good job of it. Their doubt had been evident in every spoken word. Janey had proved them wrong, of course, and by the end, her counselor had been okay.

She studied herself in the mirror again. The only colors on her face were her fading bruises.

Why are you doing this? C.J. doesn't mean anything to you.

Yeah, he does.

For the first time in her life, she'd met a man who tempted her to want a normal life—the house, the kids, the pets…the husband. The whole picket fence ideal. She couldn't make that happen, but she yearned to so badly.

C.J. and Liam had become important to her.

She tried to imagine a life with C.J. and Liam, but couldn't, not as the damaged person she was now.

She was scarred and scared and full to her core with burning shame—undeserved and unearned, but her burden to carry in life nonetheless.

She'd been raped and beaten down by poverty and lost her shining girl, all before she was old enough to figure out who she really was, and what she might have been capable of given half a chance in life.

The girl in the mirror brushed a hand down her cheek. When was the last time she'd gone out without foundation?

Seven years or so ago.

Her skin felt soft, smooth, as though it could finally breathe.

Pale morning sunlight slanted in through her window making her skin look pearly.

What would C.J. think?

She plunked herself down onto the bed. *It doesn't matter what he thinks.*

She jumped up and paced to the window. *Yeah, it sure does matter.*

Why was it so hard to leave the house without makeup?

Oh, man, she'd used it for protection for so long, she didn't know how to be in the world without it.

And the shame. It wasn't like she had a black mark on her face that said this woman should be ashamed. She had that mark on her soul, though, and didn't have a clue what to do about it.

She breathed deeply, once, twice, walked across her room and opened the door.

C.J.'s and Liam's voices drifted upstairs.

She entered the store and stopped. Her hands shook. She slid a hand down the smooth fabric of the skirt she'd bought yesterday.

Look at me, C.J. Look at me.

He did, staring at her with his mouth hanging open. "Janey?"

JANEY DIDN'T HAVE ON a speck of makeup. Not one speck.

God, she was pretty, and fresh, and so clean.

She'd pulled her hair into a high ponytail, emphasizing her heart-shaped face.

Standing in the store fingering the fabric of her green skirt with one hand and straightening the collar of her pink blouse with the other, she looked younger than usual. Innocent. Soft.

Vulnerable.

Was she afraid that he wouldn't like her this way?

Oh, yeah, he liked her.

He inched forward.

She stepped closer to him.

He must have moved again, too, because she was suddenly right in front of him, close enough for him to touch her.

"Hi." Her voice sounded whispery, breathy.

"Hi," he answered and swallowed. Hard.

She stared at him with huge eyes no longer hidden by those enormous black spider legs she ladled on every day. Why did she ever think she had to hide such pretty dark eyes?

"You look good."

Her gaze skittered away from his and she flushed. "Really?"

"Why?" he blurted.

She shrugged one shoulder and stared at the candy cases. Her profile looked more refined with her pony-tail emphasizing her fine jaw and sharp little chin. "I don't want you to lose Liam because of the way I dress."

That wasn't what he'd meant. He was asking her why she hid herself from the world when she was perfect the way God had created her.

"Thanks." He smiled. "It means a lot to me."

She turned that huge gaze back to him. She'd ditched the black lipstick and her pretty bow-shaped mouth turned up at the corners in response to his smile.

She was starting to relax, to look less as though she'd spook and run.

She'd ditched her makeup and her clothing and a bunch of her piercings for him, so he wouldn't lose his son. He didn't know what to make of it, but knew that he felt more than mere gratitude. He felt too much for her.

He slammed his hat onto his head. "We gotta go."

"Janey's where?" Liam asked, peeping around Janey's legs, clearly not recognizing her.

"Here," she said and squatted in front of him.

Liam peered into her eyes. A frown creased his forehead.

Janey seemed to be holding her breath. C.J. knew she'd been uncomfortable with Liam, hadn't wanted to spend a lot of time with him at the start, but right now she looked afraid that he would reject her.

Liam nodded. "'Kay." He took her hand in his and leaned against her.

A hiss of air escaped Janey and she blinked hard.

C.J. led them out to the Jeep.

Janey settled Liam in the backseat then started to climb in beside him.

"Might as well come up here," C.J. said. "He'll fall asleep the second we hit the highway."

Janey came around the truck and climbed into the passenger seat. She had trouble with the seat belt.

"Sorry," C.J. said. "It sticks."

He took the buckle from her hand, brushed her cold-as-ice fingers, and locked it into place.

"You nervous today?" he asked.

"Yes," she whispered.

"Why?"

"A whole bunch of stuff." She didn't elaborate.

Flat fields and distant hills flew by at a brisk speed. C.J. needed to get into Billings and through the appointment so he could take his son back home again.

He must have been crazy to insist that she sit up front with him. She smelled like coconut and tropical fruits. Edible.

Janey cleared her throat. "Can I make more than one stop in Billings?"

"Sure. Where?"

She shrugged, as if she didn't really care whether she stopped wherever or saw whoever it was she wanted to visit, but her fingers betrayed her. They rubbed the hem of her skirt, smoothed it over her knee then rubbed it again.

Throughout the long drive to Billings, she said not a word, but her fingers continued to knead and smooth that skirt until he thought she'd wear a hole in it.

"What's going through your head?" he asked.

"Is it okay if we don't talk for a while?"

"Sure." What the hell was she so worried about? He'd forgotten that Marjorie had recognized her. That's why she was here. Had she been in some kind of trouble when she lived in Billings, besides giving birth way too young?

Had she ditched the makeup to hedge her bets against whatever else was going to happen with Marjorie today?

A horrid thought and the only thing more horrid was the vile taste of fear that filled C.J.'s mouth.

CHAPTER THIRTEEN

INSIDE THE CHILDREN AND Family Services offices, a pretty young woman took Liam by the hand and led him to a spacious room with large windows along the front, where colorful child-drawn posters lined the walls.

Janey remembered it as a happy room for Cheryl. Memories of her daughter walked like ghosts through these halls. Oh, it was hard to come back here without Cheryl.

Liam ran to one of the drawings and patted it with his hands. "Mine," he squealed. Then he ran to a big plastic toy box and threw open the lid. He knew everything here. How many times had he and C.J. been here? Or had Liam come with his mother?

C.J. pointed her toward Ms. Bates's office. This used to be her caseworker Helen Strachan's office where Janey and Cheryl sat through so many meetings.

Marjorie looked frazzled. Harried.

She smiled and motioned them inside, removing a stack of files from one of the chairs. Janey motioned for C.J. to take it while she perched on a stool.

Being in one of these rooms again made her nervous.

She'd survived all of those old interviews with her caseworker, but today she felt traces of the frightened young girl she used to be, visiting this office through no fault nor choice of her own.

She used to sit where C.J. was sitting now and Cheryl used to perch on the little stool Janey currently occupied before being escorted to the happy room. Janey remembered how sick with nerves she would be, so freaking afraid she would say or do something wrong that would jeopardize her custody of her daughter. If only Cheryl were here now so Janey could take comfort from her presence. She clasped her hands in her lap to still a tremor that ran through her.

Don't screw up C.J.'s chances today. Logically, she didn't know what she could possibly say or do that could hurt C.J., but she worried anyway.

Marjorie studied her and Janey forced herself not to squirm.

"You clean up well," the social worker said.

Janey felt self-conscious about being naked. Maybe she should have put on a little makeup.

"I talked to Helen Strachan," Marjorie said.

Janey felt C.J. watching her.

"She had only good things to say about you as a mother. I was sorry to hear from her that your daughter died last year."

"Thank you," Janey said, quietly.

Marjorie directed her next comment to C.J. "I don't in the least consider Janey a bad influence on your son. Helen said she was an exemplary caregiver."

A thrill ran through Janey. God, that felt good to hear.

When C.J.'s shoulders relaxed a little, Janey realized how tense he'd been, but could sense how tense he still was.

"That takes care of the issue about the company you've been keeping, C.J." Marjorie plunged into no-

nonsense, get-down-to-business social worker mode. "Let's address this issue of Liam being at the store every day. Yes, I've heard about that. Where is your grandfather?"

"In the hospital for knee-replacement surgery."

"How long will his recovery take?"

"A month."

"How are you addressing the issue of Liam's safety in the store?"

"He's only allowed in the back room when there is an adult present."

Marjorie shot her gaze to Janey. "Is that true?"

"Yes."

"Okay," Marjorie said. "C.J., do you have any concerns about Liam that you would like to address here today?"

C.J. leaned his forearms on the desk. "Has he ever told you what Vicki said about me that makes him afraid of me?"

Marjorie shook her head.

"Liam hasn't told me, either," he said. "Or Gramps."

"I wish I could help you with that."

He jumped out of his chair and appeared as though he needed to pace, but there was nowhere to go.

"I need to know. I can't keep going on in ignorance. How can I fight this without knowing what I'm fighting *against?*"

"I honestly don't know." Marjorie watched C.J. with what looked like compassion.

She caught a file as it slipped from the desk. "We don't usually interfere in a father's relationship with his son, but I have to check out every complaint from the Fishers."

"Meddling bastards."

Marjorie's lips thinned.

"Marjorie, please don't hold that against C.J." The words flew from Janey's mouth, tripped over themselves to defend C.J. "He works so hard to be good to Liam, takes care of him really well, but Liam won't respond to him. Now these people are complaining about C.J. when he hasn't done anything wrong. If it was me and my child, I'd be upset, too."

She felt C.J. snap around to stare at her. What? Did he think she wouldn't help him? She knew how hard he worked to be a good father.

"Okay," Marjorie said. She returned her attention to C.J. "As far as I'm concerned, I've seen nothing since Liam moved to live with you and your grandfather that corroborates what they said."

"I'm not hurting my son, and you don't think *she'll* hurt my son." He jabbed a finger in Janey's direction. "So why are we here?"

"C.J., as far as I can tell, Vicki's parents don't have a case against you, but I'm compelled by the state to interview Liam to make sure. Why don't you leave him with me for a couple of hours then come back?"

"This is bogus." C.J. rapped his hat against his thigh. "Okay. Sure," he said and left the room.

At the Jeep, C.J. hesitated before getting in. Janey had opened her door to climb in when he said, "Thanks."

They stared at each other across the top of the vehicle.

"For defending me," he went on. "You did a good thing."

She shrugged. "That's okay." She said it as though his opinion didn't matter to her, but it did. Oh, it did.

"Where do you need to go?" C.J. asked.

Janey felt her nerves rattle. She'd had a reprieve from reality for the past year at the Sheltering Arms. Now, she wasn't so sure what kind of reception she'd receive in Billings.

"I'd like to touch base with my family. I haven't spoken to them in a year. They might be mad at me for that."

"Why haven't you contacted them?"

"I hadn't wanted to talk about Cheryl being gone." She actually hadn't been *able* to. "But I knew the family would want to, especially my little sister, Shannon."

"That's so tough," C.J. said. "Are you nervous?" He gestured toward her hands.

She looked down at her knuckles turning white on her entwined fingers.

"Do you want some support?" C.J. asked. "I can go with you."

Oh, boy, how did she feel about that? She found it so hard to open herself up, to let all of who she was out. She did want support, though. In a rare move, she decided to take him up on his offer.

"Yes." She nodded. "Please."

JANEY STARED at the scarred door of the apartment where she grew up. Where the rest of her family still lived.

Lift your hand and knock already. But she couldn't. The hallway smelled musty, made her nauseous, and made her regret coming back here where the air reeked of poverty.

She'd left it all behind.

Thank you, Amy and Hank, for taking me away from this.

"Is it hard to come back?" C.J. asked. She'd forgotten he was with her.

"Yes," she said. "It wasn't always a great place to grow up." Then she realized that C.J. might get the wrong impression and rushed on, "It wasn't my dad or my brother or sisters. I loved them. It was just so much work and responsibility taking care of them after my mom died. And I was the oldest yet still so young."

"How old?"

"When she died? Ten."

He gestured with his head toward the door and said, "Better get it over with."

She knocked. Footsteps sounded inside then the door opened.

Janey's baby sister, Shannon, stood in the doorway.

She stared at Janey blankly for a minute, then a big smile lit her face.

Her younger sister had grown up some since last year. No longer a gangly fifteen-year-old, she'd gained weight in all the right places. She was a knockout.

Always impulsive, she threw her arms around Janey's neck. Janey squeezed her back. She hadn't thought she'd missed anything in Billings besides Cheryl's grave.

"You came back," Shannon declared, pulling away from Janey and wiping stray moisture from her eyelashes.

Shannon was crying for her? Janey had expected anger, maybe even hatred. Instead, she was on the receiving end of a warm welcome. Her eyes misted over.

"I didn't think anyone would miss me," she said.

"We missed you." Shannon took her wrist and dragged her into the apartment.

"Wait! C.J., come in." Janey motioned him in.

"C.J.? Who's C.J.?" Shannon asked.

He stepped from the hallway into the apartment and Shannon grinned again.

"Hey," she said.

Oh, Shannon, don't look at men like that. You don't know how much they can hurt you.

Shannon looked as though she already knew her way around men. While Janey had been gone, her little sister had grown up.

"Shannon, this is C. J. Wright. I work for him."

C.J. grinned.

Janey looked away.

The apartment was still the same. The fake leather sofa still sagged in the middle. Cracks along the arms were still mended with duct tape. Dad's old flowered armchair still had the torn pocket hanging down the side that held his reading glasses and the folded-up papers of the *TV Guide.* Someone must be downloading copies of it from the Internet. Had someone bought a computer?

The walls wore the hideous turquoise paint Dad had bought at a discount ten years before.

Then she noticed something that was different. Down the bedroom hallway, the wall was lined with boxes.

She glanced at C.J. and felt her cheeks warm up. Everything looked so shabby.

He touched the old TV. "This still analog?"

Shannon shrugged. "Beats me." She obviously liked C.J. Judging by his lazy smile, he obviously liked her right back. Janey could easily rearrange his face for him.

She had the irrational urge to yell "He's mine," but that thought was so stupid it didn't warrant acknowledging. C.J. was a free agent and so was she. Funny, though, suddenly she was tired of being one. She wanted more, but how was she to get it? Except for when she'd let C.J. hold her after the robbery, when her defenses had been so low that she'd *needed* to be held, she still couldn't bring herself to consider that she could let that happen on a daily basis, in a relationship with a man— the physical affection of hugs and sex.

If she hated having any man touch her in the most innocent of ways, how would she feel if one tried to touch her *there?* Even someone she liked as much as she did C.J.? She couldn't lie to a man and promise they'd live happily ever after.

But when C.J. had held her the other day, when he'd nearly squeezed the life out of her with his muscled arms, she'd felt safe and cherished. Imagine being able to do that everyday. The loss of any possibility of that happening left her stunned, grieving.

She forced those feelings into her private core.

Get on with life, Janey. No feeling sorry for yourself.

"You guys want a coffee or something?" Shannon offered.

Before C.J. could accept, Janey said, "No, we're not staying that long." Shannon looked hurt, so Janey rushed on, "We have a few stops to make. I just wanted to see how everyone was."

She felt C.J. staring, but refused to look at him.

"We're all good," Shannon said. "Dad got promoted to foreman."

"No kidding! Does he like it?"

"Yeah. He's in a better mood these days. The extra money helps a lot."

"I'll bet. Where's Tom?"

"Working full-time at the same grocery store, but

as night-shift manager. The twins are doing all right in school. They're in their last year."

She'd missed these people, her family. She wanted family around her all the time. She thought of Hank and Amy. Yeah, she liked having family.

Everyone was older. She no longer had the weight of their care. She could talk to them now as adults. As peers.

She felt lighter, felt like smiling.

"We're moving," Shannon said.

Hence the boxes stacked in the hallway. "Where to?"

Shannon mentioned an area of town that was so much nicer than this one.

"We're going to pool everyone's wages and rent a house. We're throwing all of this away—" she gestured around the living room "—and getting all new stuff."

"Oh, Shannon, that's so great."

Shannon leaned forward. "Do you remember when I was real small and I used to call you Mommy?"

"Yes," Janey whispered.

"You made me stop, kept telling me Mommy was in heaven and you were my sister. So then I called you Sissy."

Janey had forgotten Shannon's childish nickname for her.

"The thing is, you *were* my mother," Shannon said. "The only one I've ever known."

Janey's throat hurt. Her skin felt raw, as if she'd been flayed with the sharp end of a poker.

"I never realized while you were taking care of me how *young* you were. Younger than I am now."

Shannon reached across the distance between them and grabbed Janey's hands. "Thank you."

Janey swallowed. She hadn't known that anyone cared about her.

"I missed you so much. Then there was Cheryl and you didn't live with us anymore," Shannon said and sniffed. "But at least I could still visit you and pretend Cheryl was my baby sister."

Janey's vision misted. "I used to love the way you played with her."

"I loved her and then she was gone." Shannon swiped a hand across her eyes. "Then you were gone, too. We all miss you both a lot."

"Oh, Shannon, I'm so sorry. I was hurting so badly. I couldn't stay in that apartment anymore and I couldn't come back home. I've missed you, too."

Janey didn't know who moved first, but they were in each other's arms, and the grief of the past year exploded out of her.

She dimly heard C.J. clear his throat and leave the apartment. How could she have forgotten that he was there? Shame reared in her, making her more emotional. So much to cry over—her loss of innocence and her childhood and her family and her daughter.

She cried until her emotions were spent.

There were still people in this world to love, still those who loved her right back. She hadn't realized how much her family did that for her. They were her soft place to land. Her throat felt raw. They were a fundamental part of her that she didn't want to lose.

"So many times in the past year I would come home from school," Shannon confided, "and I would want to phone you about a problem I was having there or with my friends or with a boy. You were always so smart, always had all the right answers."

"I did?" Janey asked.

"Yeah, you did," Shannon emphasized. "You have always underestimated yourself."

Yeah, too true.

"Sissy," Shannon whispered, "don't stay away again."

"I won't. About a week ago I realized how empty I felt without you in my life."

Janey led her to the sofa and they sat together. She held Shannon's hand, then pulled a tissue from a box on the coffee table and wiped her cheeks.

She told Shannon about the store. "You have to come see it."

"Yeah, I want to do that."

"Shannon, I'll come back to visit. I have a regular paycheck and some money in the bank. I can buy bus tickets now."

"I want to see the place where Cheryl stayed."

"Sheltering Arms? I'd like that. I'll send you bus fare."

They smiled at each other and Janey felt a weight lift from her shoulders.

"Don't stay away so long next time. You're part of our family."

Janey's smile felt shaky and her eyes watery—she had no idea how that was possible with all she'd cried. "Tell them all that I miss them and that I—I love them." She cleared her throat. "I have to go."

Shannon wrote something down on a sheet of paper and handed it to her. Their new address and phone number.

"We're moving next weekend."

"I'll visit," Janey whispered and meant it. She wanted to see the rest of her siblings, and her dad.

C.J. waited for her in the hallway, leaning against the wall with his arms crossed.

"You okay?" he asked.

Her cheeks felt hot. "Sorry about that. I didn't realize it would get so emotional."

"No problem. I'm glad you saw your sister today." He smiled.

"Me, too." She returned his smile.

She followed him down the narrow stairs of the three-story walk-up and stepped out into sunshine. Janey blinked, aware of a different consciousness, of a brighter day.

She'd started to heal. She could finally see that, in her memory, the good times outweighed the hard times. She was less ready to rail against fate and impotence and more ready to accept the changes in her life, to accept responsibility for future change. To make her life happen.

She had more work to do, still had to return to see the rest of the family, and put more issues to rest.

At this moment, though, it was time for a far, far more difficult visit.

She gave C.J. directions to the cemetery.

"SOMEONE LEFT FLOWERS. Shannon, most likely." Janey walked ahead of C.J. He figured they were visiting her daughter's gravesite.

He watched Janey sit on the grass beside the stone and touch the petals of a yellow aster that was starting to turn brown.

Her hand shook.

The small plastic vase had tipped over. Dry as a bone.

Janey straightened it.

"I miss you," she whispered and rested her palm on the grass, about where C.J. figured Cheryl's heart would be.

"Who brought you flowers?" Janey picked dried leaves from the stems. Her voice sounded shaky and rough. No wonder. What if it was Liam buried here? It would kill C.J.

Janey had crushed the dry leaves in her fist. She brushed the remnants from her palm. "Yellow flowers always were your favorite, weren't they?"

C.J. felt like an eavesdropper, but hesitated to leave in case she needed him.

She pulled a tissue out of her pocket and polished the small flat plaque, then pulled longer grass away from it so Cheryl's name wasn't covered.

"Does that feel better, baby?"

"Are you okay?" C.J. crouched in front of her and studied the small gravestone. He did the math and shook his head. "She was only six."

"Yeah." Janey brushed her hand over the grass with such tenderness, almost as if she was brushing hair from her daughter's eyes. "She was so beautiful."

C.J. had tried hard not to judge in the last week or so, but being here in Billings where Liam was conceived, leaving his son with a social worker so she could determine whether he was a fit father, all were playing havoc with his sense of fair play.

"Why did you never tell the father about his child?"

"It's—it's not what you think." She reached a hand toward him then dropped it in her lap.

"Hey, as far as I know there's only one way to get pregnant. With two people."

"People get artificial insemination."

"Not fourteen-year-olds."

"I know!"

This wasn't getting him anywhere. She wasn't going to tell him. He looked at the grave and his anger softened. "How did she die? Did the cancer come back?"

"The cancer didn't kill her." Janey's breathing hitched. "In the end, she was hit by a car."

Damn, fate seemed to take what it wanted, one way or another. "I don't remember hearing that. When was it?"

"A year ago."

He nodded. "Yeah, that's about when my world sort of blew apart."

"What happened?" She seemed to really want to know.

"If I tell you my story, will you tell me yours?"

She seemed to fight some kind of internal war before she finally nodded.

"You first," she said.

He sat on the other side of the grave. "I told you about how Davey and I got a little wild in our late teens. I was rebelling against my father." He hesitated, didn't really want to get into that now. "That's another story for another time. Anyway, it all fell apart when Davey died. I went really wild after that. Left the rodeo. Left Ordinary. Moved to Billings and drank too much and flirted with drugs."

He'd been so young and filled with anger and frustration and full of himself. He'd thought he was indestructible.

"I met a woman. Vicki." She'd been so sweet at the

start. There were times when he still missed that part of her.

"Liam's mother, right?" Janey guessed.

"Yeah. She was fun and kind. But she had something painful going on inside of her. Something had happened to her, but she would never tell me what."

His smile felt infinitely sad.

"We got mixed up with a rough crowd, went to a party one night and tried cocaine for the first time."

"How was it?" Janey asked.

He remembered it pounding through his veins, a jittery high unlike anything he'd experienced before.

"I hated it. It made me crazy paranoid. I thought Vicki was trying to kill me and punched her." The horror of what he'd done flooded through him and all he could see was the swelling and bruising of her face the morning after. "It terrified me. Scared me straight. Vicki wasn't so lucky, though. She kept going back for more."

"Maybe she wasn't as strong as you."

That was debatable. He hadn't felt strong those days. "I guess not. Anyway, she started hanging with those people and got hooked. I tried to get her away, even took her back to Ordinary with me. She got on a bus the next day bound for Billings and cocaine."

"What happened?" Janey asked. "What about Liam?"

"About two years ago she called asking for help."

"Help with Liam?"

"She didn't tell me about Liam."

Janey gasped. A lightbulb seemed to go on inside of her. Yeah, now she understood why he was so upset about her not telling the father about their child.

"What kind of help did she need?" she asked.

"She wanted money."

"Did you give it to her?"

"I knew she'd blow it on drugs. I gave in, though, because of the old affection I'd had for her. I drove into Billings and met her at a bar."

Remembering how bad she looked, too old for her age, he swallowed hard. "She kept calling periodically and I kept bringing her money. Then about a year ago, we met at her apartment. That's when I saw Liam for the first time. He wore a dirty diaper and nothing else." He swallowed again to hold back his bile. Liam had been so small, the sheets on his crib so smelly, the look on his face sober, as if he knew that life had already failed him and it might never get better.

"The place was a pigsty," C.J. continued. "I gave her all the money I could afford and took Liam home with me that day."

He laughed bitterly. "For two years I'd had no idea I had a son."

"Did Vicki fight you about taking Liam?"

"She was real happy to have the money."

"Okay, I'm starting to really dislike this woman."

Sometimes he hated her, too. "Her parents sure hated that I'd taken Liam home with me."

"Why had they left the baby with a drug-addict mother?"

"They didn't. They had started proceedings to have Vicki deemed an unfit mother, but I showed up before they could get custody. I sometimes think Vicki called me that week and let me come to her apartment on purpose, like maybe she hadn't wanted her parents to have him."

C.J. pressed his thumb and forefinger against the

bridge of his nose where a doozy of a headache was brewing.

"Anyway, Children's Services decided that I was a good candidate to be Liam's father. They were sure that Liam was mine and that I had a right to have custody."

"How could you all be so sure that Liam was yours?"

He tapped the indentation in his chin. "I knew right away he was mine."

"Definitely a family trait."

C.J. stood. "Let's walk a bit."

"Okay." She rose to walk beside him.

"Your turn," he said. "I've told you all about Liam and me. What's your story? How was Cheryl conceived?"

Janey stopped abruptly. Something happened to her face, a kind of shutting down.

He stepped in front of her and took both of her hands in his. She squeezed. Her hands were small, her wrists fine-boned, but it felt as though she was going to crush his fingers. Something was very, very wrong.

He bent his knees, tried to put his eyes on the same level as hers. "Tell me."

When she opened her eyes, they looked bleak, desolate.

Oh, God, not—

"I was raped."

The air left his lungs, shot right out of him. He couldn't breathe. Why was the world such a cruel place?

"When you were…?"

"Fourteen."

Man, this was huge and awful and nauseating. It really, really *sucked*. It particularly sucked that at the moment he couldn't find a stronger word for it than *sucked*.

Maybe the right word hadn't been invented that described how evil rape was.

Janey had lived through it. She was relatively sane. What an amazing, amazing person. He'd been slowly understanding she was a deeper person than he'd originally thought, but her survival over this made her heroic.

"You never knew who did it?"

She shook her head. "He jumped me from behind."

"Coward." C.J. thought of a lot of things to call a rapist who would prey on a girl barely older than a child, but couldn't bring himself to say them out loud in front of Janey. She looked as though she was hurting enough already.

"I did nothing wrong," she said. "Just stayed a little late after school. It was dark, though. You know how early night falls in November."

He nodded, numbed by ugly images that no young girl should ever have to live through.

"How? Where?"

"I'll show you."

They walked a couple of blocks to a row of thick hedges at the edge of a schoolyard.

Janey stopped.

"Here?" C.J. asked. "This is where it happened?"

CHAPTER FOURTEEN

JANEY HAD BROUGHT HIM to the edge of the high-school grounds. She stared at the bushes, remembering how they'd scratched her, how her skin had burned for a week, and even so the pain had been minor compared to her torn hymen and her bone-deep shame.

What she hadn't expected was that saying it out loud, telling C.J. about her rape, would make her feel *worse*. Another betrayal. First the rape, and now, thinking she was putting the whole rat's-ass incident to bed by saying it out loud, she'd made it worse.

She'd hidden from it for years. Now she felt stripped bare and her emotions were reeling.

"You were only fourteen," C.J. said, and she heard the shock and the anger in his voice, a mere echo of the tornado ripping through her.

"He smelled like cigarettes and beer." She clenched her hands at her sides.

"I never saw his face." Her voice rose. "I never even knew who the coward was who did it." A spasm filled her throat and rage flooded her chest.

"I had a right to choose my baby's father," she screamed.

C.J. shoved her and she hit the bushes.

"What the—" Her mind seized.

C.J.?

He shoved her harder. Branches whipped her body.
Betrayal roared through her. Not again. Not C.J.

"What are you doing?" she screamed. She shoved
him back.

"Hit me," he ordered.

She pulled away from him, but he shoved his face
into hers and yelled, "Hit me."

The tornado tearing up her chest whipped out of her
and she turned her rage on this *man,* on his betrayal.
Couldn't he see her *pain,* and yet he'd inflicted *more?*

Her hand flew to his face, slamming against his
cheek, shattering her paralysis and her fear and her
shame.

Pain shot through her hand and up her arm.

The filthiest words flew from her mouth. She
pounded her fist against his chest—the sound loud and
hollow—and she hit him again. And again.

She shouted, "Yeah!"

She slapped him again. He stood still and took it.

"I hate you. I hate what you did to me."

She stopped and stared at her rapist, breathing hard.
She shook her head and her rapist's amorphous face
changed into C.J.'s. She'd been yelling at the man who'd
attacked her eight years ago and C.J. had stood and
taken it.

C.J. smiled and she suddenly got what he had done.
He'd used himself as a surrogate, offering himself as a
target for all of that toxic rage she'd turned in on herself because she couldn't take it out on her unknown as-
sailant. C.J. had tried to give her back her self-respect.

He'd baptized a small corner of her soul. She felt better. There would still be so much work left to do, but
today was a start. Baby steps.

Like a balloon sitting in too-hot sunlight, the fight seeped out of her. She breathed hard, barely able to understand what had just happened.

C.J. smiled, softly. He looked proud of her. "Nicely done. For a small woman, you pack a powerful punch."

"I'm—"

"Don't you dare apologize." He narrowed his eyes and pointed a finger at her. "You needed that."

"Yeah, I did." She touched the red imprint of her hand on his face.

"Thank you," she whispered and stood on her toes. She rested her lips against his, the move all about profound gratitude and infinite relief and deep, deep connection.

C.J. held himself still and she knew he did it so he wouldn't frighten her.

She pulled back a little and stared into his brown eyes. Her gaze dropped to his lips. Oh, she wanted to do that again.

Janey felt the vicious violence of that assault, and her utter helplessness, begin to fade.

With this wondrous gift C.J. had given her, the knowledge that the shame was never hers but her attacker's, she could learn to heal. Maybe in time, she could let it all go, could finally be with a man the way she wanted to.

C.J. GLANCED AT JANEY. They were on their way to pick up Liam. They'd done enough for one day. He felt good about what he and Janey had been through. It had been a long time since he'd shared so much of himself with a woman.

He was glad he could be there for Janey, with her sister and at the cemetery.

He wanted to teach her to touch people. To touch him.

They stopped at a red light and he reached out a hand and laid it palm up on her knee. She flinched then stilled. Slowly she placed her hand on his.

He let out a slow breath, then said, "Thank you for being here today."

They sat staring ahead, her palm soft against his callused one. The pulse in her wrist beat beneath his little finger and he felt his own hitch up a notch to match. How fast was it in the heat of lovemaking? How languid afterward?

The light turned green and C.J. returned his attention to the road, but took his time sliding his hand away from Janey's.

Out of the corner of his eye, he saw her shiver.

He knew how she felt. There'd been no crazy lust in the touch, but something deeper, something real. Something profoundly sweet. He wanted Janey's innocence to wash away the shame of all the jaded, frantic screwing around he'd done after Davey's death.

He suddenly needed her to wash him clean.

Funny that she looked so much more cynical than him when in her Goth clothes, but he felt much more jaded than she appeared to be.

C.J. pulled up in front of the building that housed the offices of Child and Family Services.

"C'mon," he said. "Let's go get my son."

What a crazy, nerve-wracking day. "Vicki's parents can go to hell. Liam is mine and I'm taking him back home, no matter what Marjorie says."

His pulse pounded in his left temple.

They entered the building and found Marjorie in her office.

She smiled when they entered.

"How did the interview go?" C.J. asked, his jaw tight.

"The interview went just fine." Marjorie stood. "Liam's grandparents have no case against you. My recommendation is that he should stay with his father."

Thank God.

"Yeah." C.J. punched the air with one fist. "Yeah!"

Whew! He blew a stream of air out of his lungs.

"What about the next time they make a complaint?" he asked, still bitter and frustrated.

"There won't be a next time. I've already spoken to them."

C.J. felt this insane urge to hug Marjorie and to throttle the Fishers.

"How did that go?"

Marjorie smiled grimly. "They weren't too happy."

She led them to the playroom. They stood outside and watched Liam pile blocks.

Liam, you're mine. C.J. had spent too much of the last year waiting for the axe to fall on his head. It was finally over. No more interference in his life with his son.

His hands shook.

"I found out something interesting in the interview." Marjorie looked up at C.J. "Vicki didn't say anything bad about you to Liam. It was his grandparents."

C.J.'s left temple throbbed hard enough to back a rock band. "What did they say?"

"Liam kept saying, 'Daddy leave.' I finally figured out what he meant and called his grandmother Fisher to verify it. Sort of forced her to admit the truth."

Marjorie touched C.J.'s arm. "She had told him that you couldn't be trusted, that Liam shouldn't get close to you because one day you would leave him."

C.J. felt like he was hyperventilating. Evil, evil people. After what they'd put him through in the last year, they'd be lucky if they ever saw their grandson again.

"You will have to figure out a way to convince him that it isn't true," Marjorie said. "Good luck."

She turned to go, then came back. "Another thing, please work on Liam's vocabulary. He is so far behind because of the neglect he suffered in his first couple of years."

Business completed, she gestured with one hand toward the door, smiled and said, "Liam's all yours."

C.J. called into the room, "Liam, let's go."

Liam came running, passed him and lunged at Janey's legs. How was C.J. going to undo the damage the Fishers had done? He didn't have a clue.

Marjorie laid a hand on C.J.'s arm. "Good luck with the relationship you're trying to forge with Liam," she told him. "He's a very satisfied little guy these days. He'll come around in time."

"Thanks," C.J. said, and placed his hand over hers for one brief moment.

C.J. led them out to the Jeep.

Janey tucked Liam into his car seat.

"Let's go get lunch," C.J. said. Someday he'd have to figure out whether Liam could ever have a normal relationship with his grandparents. Someday. Not today. Today was for celebrating.

He yanked off the tie he'd worn today, opened the top button of his shirt and pulled his shirttails out of his pants. Might as well be comfortable and himself. At last. Liam was his. No more worries.

"Woooohoooo," he sang as he drove out of Billings.

FOR THE NEXT THREE DAYS, C.J. treated Janey as if she was nothing more than a good acquaintance, as if they hadn't learned so much about each other in Billings. As if they hadn't shared in each other's healing. It almost felt like something was holding him back, so he was keeping his distance.

Janey didn't know what to think.

Finally, in a fit of frustration on Friday, she cornered him in the back room of the shop. "*What* is going on with you?"

"What do you mean?" He watched her warily.

"I mean, why are you walking on eggshells around me?"

C.J. deflated. "You noticed."

"Yeah, I noticed." Janey folded her arms across her chest. "What's happening?"

"I'm afraid to touch you. To spook you." He knocked his fist gently on the counter. "I've never had to deal with a woman who's been raped."

"C.J., you've already taught me how to be able to touch more easily than I could before I started to work here." She cocked her head to one side. "Can't we take it from there?"

C.J. smiled. "Yeah, okay. I'll try to relax."

The phone rang and C.J. ran to answer it.

Janey entered the pantry for the fixings for another batch of humbugs.

"Hey, C.J.," she called. "Where's the peppermint extract?"

He didn't answer.

Liam sat on the back doorstep in the sun, playing with three cars he'd brought in with him that morning.

"C.J.?" she called.

He still didn't answer.

He entered the back room, steps heavy, face solemn. "What's wrong?"

"It's Gramps. He's had a heart attack."

Janey's hand flew to her mouth and she spun to make sure Liam hadn't heard. He hummed a cartoon jingle.

Janey rushed to C.J. "Is he—"

He shook his head, his eyes bleak. "He's hanging on in Intensive Care. It's touch and go."

She rested her hand on his forearm, rubbed his warm hair-dusted skin. "I'm so sorry. Do you want to go see him? You can leave Liam with me. Tell me how to close up the shop."

C.J. SPENT FOUR HOURS at the hospital sitting with Gramps and making arrangements.

By the time he drove down the driveway to his house, bone weary, he felt as though he'd been run through a wringer washer. Even though the sun was inching its way toward the horizon, the house was dark.

Empty.

Where were Janey and Liam?

The house had never felt so lonely to him without both Gramps and Liam.

C.J. was starting to have this crazy weird dream of maybe working on a relationship with Janey to see where it went. To see whether someday she might fit into his world, in this house, on his ranch, into his dreams.

Walking back to the Jeep and looking over the fields, he got that vision he'd had after the day Janey had walked into the store and all but demanded a job. He saw those little girls with long black ponytails like Janey's running through his fields.

He buried those thoughts, so afraid to jinx the fragile thing developing between himself and Janey.

Just deal with one day at a time, C.J.

He headed into Ordinary. As he turned onto Main Street, he saw Janey locking up the shop for the night. Liam stood beside her with one car in each hand while Janey held the third.

"Hi," he said.

"Hi. How did it go?" Concern etched a frown into her forehead.

"He's stable. They think he's going to be okay. He'll need to slow down his recovery from the knee operation. Even when he's fully healed, Gramps won't ever be able to ranch again. Dad and I talked about our options and it's clear I need to get this store sold so I can get the ranch up and running to capacity."

"Liam and I are just heading down to the diner for supper," Janey said. "Want to come?"

"Why didn't you close at the regular time and take him back to the ranch? I picked up groceries yesterday."

"I don't have a car and it's too far to walk."

C.J. cursed.

Liam whispered. "Bad word."

C.J. flushed, "Sorry." To Janey he said, "It completely slipped my mind that you couldn't take him home."

"It's okay. Let's go to dinner. My treat. My boss paid me this morning."

In the diner, Liam climbed all over Janey, but she barely paid him attention. She was thinking hard about something. What was going through her head?

"Do you have a cell phone?" she asked. "I need to call Amy."

"Can't it wait until you get home?"

She shook her head.

C.J. jerked a thumb toward the back of the diner. "There's a pay phone beside the washrooms."

JANEY'S FINGERS TINGLED. The craziest thought was running around inside her head. She couldn't really be thinking what she was considering, could she?

If the ranch was C.J.'s future, could the candy shop be part of hers? The world was waiting for her to grab it by the balls and take off, to finish high school and college and put on that pink lipstick and those high heels and get a good job. To become a businesswoman.

But there was a crazy thought running around in her head that might work for her and for C.J.

The thought was buzzing, loudly, calling for attention. Jumping up and down and waving its hand in the air. Pick me, pick me. I know the answer.

Could it work?

She dialed the Sheltering Arms and got Hank, who passed her on to Amy when he realized the call was about money.

Five minutes later, she was beaming.

"Are you sure this is what you want? To own a candy shop?" Amy's voice betrayed her surprise.

"This would work for me, Amy. I could take my courses in the evenings after work. The income from the candy shop could pay for school. C.J. could buy his cattle and pay the back taxes and run the ranch." Janey's hands shook. Wow, she was making decisions just like a real businesswoman.

Later, when she'd finished her studies, she could sell the shop and move to Billings to open a business there.

"Okay, Hank and I will help," Amy said and Janey heard excitement in her voice. "That little shop is a going concern. You'll do well there."

She hung up and returned to the booth.

C.J. looked up from his burger and pointed to her food. "Eat. It's getting cold."

Janey grinned. "I'm going to buy the store."

C.J. choked and coughed. His face turned red and he guzzled his glass of water. "*You're* going to buy my store?"

"Yep. I have some of the down payment. Amy's going to lend me the rest. She and Hank are going to hold my mortgage."

C.J. hooted and drew everyone's attention.

"You look the way I feel, insanely happy," C.J. said a split second before she got an up-close-and-personal look at those hazel eyes and his straight nose and the dimple in his chin and those great sculpted lips as he leaned across the table. He kissed her quickly before she had a chance to close her eyes or pucker up.

All she felt was a quick whoosh of air, then his heat surrounding her and then the touch of his lips—here and gone in a flash.

So nice.

"Do you really want the store that badly?" C.J. asked.

"It's a stop on the way to my dreams. Someday, I want to work in a big city, maybe at a big company or maybe run my own. I want to be a successful businessperson. In the meantime, I'll run the store and take business courses long-distance."

A curious expression crossed C.J.'s face—almost sad, but not quite. It passed in a flash, then he joined her in making plans and celebrating this big turn of events.

After they finished eating, C.J. and Liam drove to the ranch and she walked to the shop in a haze of euphoria. Soon, Sweet Talk would be hers. Next Monday, they would start the legal proceedings.

From then on, Janey Wilson would be a shop owner, and on her way to wheeling and dealing as a savvy successful person. Happiness bubbled up in her chest, made her breathing erratic. Wow. The day that Amy and Hank had handed Janey her year's salary and she'd opened her bank account had been a turning point in her life—more than she'd even realized at the time.

She would spend the next couple of years in the candy store spinning dreams for children, and in the meantime, work toward a bigger, more important career. A *real* career.

CHAPTER FIFTEEN

THE NEXT DAY, Janey, C.J. and Liam went to the Sheltering Arms to hang out by the pool. As soon as they arrived, C.J. explained his swimming rules to her. "No going into the deep end with Liam."

"Sure." They all ran up to the bedrooms to get changed. Janey put on her bathing suit in her old room and listened to C.J. and Liam leave the second floor to go outside.

She dawdled, on purpose, thinking about a plan she'd formed, a beautiful treacherous insane plan, probably misguided, too, but she was going to see it through. She had to break the impasse between C.J. and Liam and she hoped this would do it. She was going to pretend that she and Liam were drowning so C.J. would come rescue them and Liam would see his father as a hero.

If she lost C.J.'s respect, well…that would hurt. She would just have to live with it.

A man should know his son, should be able to touch him, to hold him, to care for him.

Her life with Cheryl had been cash poor, but wealthy in so many ways. She didn't have a strong enough imagination to understand exactly what C.J. was going through, but she did know she couldn't have borne the pain if Cheryl had rejected her.

She walked toward the back of the house and ran into

Hank as he stepped out of the washroom. Luck was with her. She needed backup in case something went wrong.

Hank's mouth dropped open.

"Janey, look at you." He cleared his throat.

Janey hadn't seen Hank since she'd stopped wearing makeup, so this was his first encounter with the plain her. Even when she had gone swimming here in the past, she'd left her makeup on and kept her head above water, except for those times when she and Amy had been out here alone and Amy had taught her to swim.

Hank's eyes suddenly looked damp. "It's good to see you, darlin'." He turned away and swiped a hand down his face as he went.

Oh, Hank, I love you, too.

When he came back to her, she whispered her plan to him and explained his role.

"Are you nuts?" he cried.

"Maybe, but I need to try this." She touched Hank's arm. "There won't be any danger. I promise. Amy taught me to swim really well."

"I know she did, but—" He pulled off his Stetson, scratched his thick hair, then slapped the hat on again.

"You'll be there behind the cabana watching," Janey said. "If anything goes wrong, you would be there in a second."

Hank looked down at her hand on his arm and smiled. Laughed.

"You're touching me!"

Janey smiled. "Yeah. C.J.'s kind of been teaching me how to do that."

"You're falling for him, aren't you?"

"Yes." She meant it with all of her heart.

"You could do a lot worse than C. J. Wright. I'm happy for you."

"Then do this for me," she pleaded. "I know it will work."

Hank bowed his head for a second then said, "All right."

When they stepped out the back door, a wave of sound met them—children screaming, Willie hollering and tossing a ball across the water over the heads of those children to another ranch hand, Rob.

They jumped on him and the water churned with a mass of legs and wet bodies and splashing water and with Rob's one arm straight up in the air still clutching the ball. He came up laughing.

Lots of kids wore bathing caps, probably so their little bald or peach-fuzz scalps wouldn't burn.

A couple of ranch hands walked the perimeter of the pool, acting as lifeguards, keeping eagle eyes on the children.

She followed Hank through the gate of the wrought-iron fence that surrounded the pool and closed it behind herself.

C.J. looked up when he heard the latch catch.

He pantomimed looking at a watch on his bare wrist and mouthed, "What took so long?" Then he did a double take. Janey wore an old black one-piece that covered most of her, but from the hot look in C.J.'s eyes, he didn't mind that it was faded with age or that it felt a bit too tight for comfort.

C.J. sat at one end of a wooden bench, with Liam on the other end, Liam's jutting jaw a small replica of C.J.'s as both wore the same mulish expression. Liam obviously wouldn't let C.J. take him into the pool, exactly as she'd hoped.

When he saw her, Liam jumped down from the bench and ran over.

"No running beside the pool," she said. He slammed into her legs and nearly knocked her over. She laughed. "Are you ready to go swimming?"

He nodded and giggled.

She took his hand and led him to the shallow end.

C.J. followed and said, "No deep end. He only likes the shallow end."

"I know. You've already told me."

She bent forward to talk to Liam.

"I'll get in first and then I'll lift you in, okay?"

"'Kay."

Janey slid into the pool, then turned around and lifted Liam in. His legs folded into accordion pleats when his toes hit the cool water.

Liam wrapped his legs around her waist and she dipped him into the water. They bobbed up and down together and watched the children. His precious body nestled trustingly against her.

"Look!" Liam pointed to a little girl floating by on a big blow-up alligator.

"That's an alligator," Janey said.

"Aggle Ator," Liam repeated.

A shrill whistle rent the air, louder than the children's shouts and laughter.

Within moments the pool was empty save for Janey and Liam in the shallow end and the empty alligator meandering across the surface of the water. Janey had dawdled upstairs long enough. She and Liam would get the pool to themselves. Good.

"Roll call," Hank shouted. He read from a list of names and got answers to every one. "Time to head inside, dry off and change. We're about to light up the barbecues."

There were complaints, but also squeals of delight. The kids had worked up an appetite.

They started to run but more than one adult voice yelled, "Walk. Don't run."

They ran for towels, shoulders hunched against the air cooling the water on their skin. The ranch hands pulled pool toys out of the water and each child took at least one to lay it neatly in a row along the pool edge to dry in the sun.

Janey knew that Hank would come along later and put everything away in the shed.

C.J. came to stand beside the pool. "C'mon, Liam. Time to get changed for dinner."

Liam stared at his father and shook his head.

"Want to go in for supper?" she asked.

Liam said, "No!" just as she'd hoped. She didn't like the crushed look on C.J.'s face, but it couldn't be helped. This would be all for the good in the end.

"I can stay here with him. I'm not hungry," she said.

"I'll sit here till you're finished," C.J. answered, but little Liam stuck his hand up, palm out and waved him toward the gate.

"No. Go. I want Jane."

"Okay, Tarzan, let's play." Janey started to splash water on his shoulders and he giggled.

She stopped when C.J. turned and walked into the house. It hurt to watch him look so dejected. She had to make this right for him.

Her hands trembled. What if this all backfired somehow? It wouldn't. Hank would be nearby, watching.

Slowly, she spun in the water with Liam snug against her chest.

She peeked toward the pool shed and saw a wisp of shadow from behind it. Hank was in place. No danger.

She swirled around slowly so she could see the back door. Just as she'd thought would happen, C.J. stood and watched them through the door's window.

Janey inched toward the deep end. Her hands shook. She was nuts to even consider what she was about to do.

Certifiable.

C.J. WATCHED from the back door and fumed. Why had Janey taken so long to come down to swim? Liam hadn't wanted to go in the water with C.J.

Story of his life with the boy. C.J.'s frustration level was about to shoot through the stratosphere. The situation promised to get worse once the sale of the store was completed and Liam was forced to spend most of his time with C.J. and no Janey to act as buffer. Not something he wanted to think about now.

As it was, he was feeling impatient at Janey and Liam still being in the pool. The three of them could be inside hanging out with everyone else.

C.J. frowned. What the heck?

Janey was moving awfully close to the deep end. Closer still.

Their heads fell below the surface of the water and C.J. flew out of the house.

Dammit, he'd told her, had *ordered* her not to go near the deep end.

Just as he got to the gate, Janey screamed, "Help!" Liam cried.

C.J.'s heart pounded. "Liam!" he yelled.

Janey flailed around.

She'd told him she could swim!

C.J. ran along the edge of the pool and dove into the deep end. He swam for them and grabbed Liam from her arms.

Liam wrapped himself around his father and C.J. hugged him hard, propelling them both toward the edge, keeping Liam's head above water.

C.J. held on to the edge of the pool and hugged Liam, breathing hard. "You're safe. You're safe." As he soothed his son, he spared a glance for Janey, who seemed to have gotten her feet under her in the shallow end.

Liam's tears dripped from his face, along with a little snot, and landed on C.J.'s shoulder. He hiccuped.

C.J. couldn't move for a minute, just wanted to hold Liam in his arms. Liam hugged him as if he never wanted to let go and it warmed C.J. to the tips of his fingers and toes.

Ah, Liam, my beautiful boy.

C.J. had to get out of the water this second, away from Janey.

He tried to set Liam on the pool cement, but Liam howled, "Daddy, no."

C.J. maneuvered himself and Liam along the edge of the pool to the steps and hauled them both out of the water.

When he walked past Janey, Liam's little head popped up from C.J.'s shoulder and he pointed at her. "Bad Janey. Bad."

Janey watched them.

C.J. couldn't tell what was going on in her head, but he shot her a look of anger and she seemed to shrivel.

He carried his son inside and strode upstairs.

IT TOOK ALL OF AN HOUR for C.J. to stop shaking. Liam lay beside him on one of the lower bunk beds in the room they'd changed in earlier. C.J. had taken off Liam's bathing suit and his own and had dried them both then had dressed Liam and himself. Liam had let him do whatever he needed to, clinging to him, had even curled against C.J.'s chest while he cried.

He lay with his head on C.J.'s bicep, playing with C.J.'s shirt buttons, humming a formless tune. C.J. held himself still, afraid to break the spell of this precious, unprecedented moment.

C.J. touched Liam's baby-fine hair, smoothed it from his brow.

My boy.

He was going to kill that crazy woman. How could he have ever trusted her with something as precious as his son? He should have known better. He hadn't trusted her at the start and he should have kept it that way.

The bedroom door creaked open and a small girl entered. She wore one red sock and one green sock. She'd tucked her white T-shirt into her shorts and had pulled them up high, with the seam twisted toward one hip. Big green eyes stared at him. A mist of red hair painted her scalp.

"I want him," she said, pointing to Liam on C.J.'s other side.

C.J. said, "Pardon?"

"I want that boy," she repeated.

Liam's head popped up. He saw the girl, then threw himself across C.J. to get a closer look.

C.J. placed his hand on Liam's back. Liam didn't shrug it off as he would have done even that morning.

C.J. felt in serious danger of spilling his emotional guts in front of these two kids.

"Who are you?" Liam asked.

"Katie. Boy, come on. Let's play."

"I'm not boy. I'm Leem."

"C'mon, Leem." She gestured toward the stairs. "Let's play."

"Wiff what?" Liam asked.

"Hank gave me trucks and cars."

Liam hurtled toward the edge of the bed and, with C.J.'s help so he wouldn't land on his head, slid to the floor.

"What colors?" Liam asked as Katie led the way to the stairs.

"Red and yellow and blue."

"Red!" Liam shouted and followed her down the stairs.

C.J. stared at the underside of the top bunk. At least one good thing had come out of Janey nearly killing his son. Liam had called him *Daddy*. Just now, he'd used him as a jungle gym. Like a real father.

Dazed, bemused and insanely happy, C.J. doubted he'd ever had a better moment in his life.

But what if he hadn't stayed to watch them through the back-door window?

If only Janey had gotten down to the pool earlier so they could have been out of the pool with the other children. If only C.J. hadn't gone inside, Liam need never have been frightened half to death.

If only— C.J. stopped. That was an awful lot of *ifs*. Too many. "Son of a—"

He bolted upright. She'd done it on purpose. He didn't know how he knew that, but he did. He felt it in his bones.

But *why?*

To get his son to see him as a protector, a rescuer, a knight in shining armor, someone strong on whom he could depend.

It had worked.

But at what cost? Liam would probably be nervous around the water for a while. And had Janey lost Liam's affection? How forgiving were children? Had she deliberately sacrificed her own relationship with a child to give C.J. this amazing gift of his own son?

He thought of her kindness toward Kurt, a homeless man most of the town took for granted and largely ignored, allowing the church to take care of him rather than take personal responsibility. He remembered her feeding Calvin Hooks.

He thought about how patient she had been with Liam when every movement he made, every glancing touch, reminded her that her own daughter was dead.

She didn't have a cruel bone in her beautiful generous body.

Yeah. She was the kind of person who would give him this awesome gift.

He rubbed his chest. He could no longer deny what his heart had been trying to tell him all along. He loved her. C. J. Wright loved Janey Wilson…and planned to do something about it.

He jumped up out of the bunk bed and smacked his head on the top bunk. Cursing, he scrubbed his scalp, then headed for the stairs, taking them down two at a time.

Hank came out of the living room to make sure C.J. wasn't a child falling down the stairs. When he noted the determination on C.J.'s face, he pointed with his thumb toward the front door.

"Beside the willow tree for the past hour," Hank said.

C.J. hesitated, saw Liam playing with Katie and glanced at Hank.

"He's fine," Hank said, "I'll watch him. I'll make sure he gets fed."

C.J.'s own stomach grumbled but he ran toward the front door. To Janey. Then he stopped. For what he had planned, he'd need the whole night.

He stepped back into the living room.

"Hank, can I ask a big favour?"

Hank walked over. "Sure. Name it."

"Can you keep Liam for the night?"

Hank's gaze sharpened. "Does this have anything to do with Janey?"

C.J. nodded.

"That girl's like a daughter to me," Hank said. "You're not planning to hurt her, are you?"

"Nope. If I have my way, Janey won't ever leave Ordinary again."

Hank smiled. "In that case, sure, I'll keep Liam tonight."

Liam ran over when he heard his name. C.J. crouched in front of him and gently pulled his son into the V made by his legs. Liam, little sweetheart, let him.

"Liam," C.J. said, "how would you like to stay with Hank and your new friend tonight?" He nodded with his head toward Katie.

"Yeah, Leem," Katie piped up. "Stay."

"Okay."

"You sure?" C.J. asked. If Liam showed the least concern, C.J. would skip his plans for a celebration with Janey.

"Want to stay."

"Okay." C.J. moved to stand, but Liam shoved his head forward and puckered his lips.

C.J. set his own lips against his son's tiny mouth for a second, smelled milk, then pulled back.

Sweetness. Pure, unadulterated, shit-kicking sweetness. His son was truly and finally his. He couldn't leave him here tonight. Just couldn't do it.

He said, "I should take you home with me."

"No!" Liam shouted. "Go! Want to stay with Katie."

"Okay, then, see you tomorrow," C.J. said, his voice none too steady.

Such trust and innocence. Such an amazing gift from the woman he loved.

When the screen slammed shut behind him, Janey jumped out of the Adirondack chair in the shade of the willow.

She tucked one hand inside the other and watched him warily, probably afraid of what he might do to her.

He stepped down from the veranda and joined her.

This crazy, gut-wrenching compulsion to lay her down in the cool grass and love the daylights out of her pushed him hard.

"Do you need anything from the house?"

"What do you mean?"

"You aren't staying here tonight, are you?"

"No, I'm going back to the store." She still looked wary.

"Can I join you there?"

A frown marred her forehead. "What?"

He rested his fingers on her shoulders. "I want to come home with you tonight."

"And Liam?"

"He's great." C.J. grinned. "He's staying here with Hank."

"He is?"

He took her hands in his, turned them palms up and planted a pair of smackers on them, then flattened them on his chest.

"He is."

Her frown eased, her face relaxed. She knew he wasn't angry, and she knew what he wanted to do at her apartment.

A faint flush fanned across her cheeks. She bowed her head, bit her lip and scuffed a toe in the grass.

"Okay," she whispered.

His heart sailed above the willow tree like a yellow kite flashing in the sun. She was his.

He couldn't wait to give himself to her for the rest of his life, and his son, too, but that news could wait until he'd thanked her properly for the amazing gift she'd given him today.

Leaning forward, he rested his forehead on hers.

"I'm not sure how this is going to work, Janey. I just know we have to try. Trust me?"

"Yes." She sounded as breathless as he felt.

They climbed into the Jeep. He gunned the engine and they took off down Hank's driveway, leaving a trail of dust in their wake.

At the store, he took her upstairs, holding her trembling hand.

They'd lived a lifetime in the past few weeks and had both changed because of it.

In the bedroom, evening sunlight streamed in with cooling air.

C.J. turned to Janey, found her watching him with wide, dark eyes, a mix of hope and fear on her face.

The hope gratified him. The fear troubled him.

"Thank you from the bottom of my heart for what you did with Liam. Thank you, thank you, thank you."

The fear eased from her eyes. "You're not angry?"

He shook his head.

Taking the ends of her ponytail in one hand, he said, "I like your hair."

He brushed his fingers down her cheek, "I like your skin," then along her jawbone, "I like this sharp little chin," then down her chest and she held her breath.

CHAPTER SIXTEEN

COME ON, Janey thought, *kiss me.*

Through her shirt, he caressed her breast.

His big hand warmed her while a thrill ran from her breast to her stomach. She closed her eyes, felt his hand skimming over her other breast, then down her stomach.

Touch me more. She'd been starving. *Starving.*

He touched her there and her eyes flew open.

"Come here," he said.

She stepped toward him.

"I'm not going to hurt you," he whispered. His hands shook.

He held her face between his palms.

When he bent to kiss her, her eyelids drifted shut.

A tiny murmur sounded low in her throat. *Oh, C.J.*

Sensations flooded her, heat and need and desire and dizzyness. She reveled in it, accepted the warm moisture on his lips, his chlorine-soap scent, the heat of his body.

"You okay?" he murmured.

She leaned close.

"I can't—I wish I knew how to kiss."

Flames burned her cheeks.

"That's okay," he said with a broad smile, "I do. I can teach you."

She closed her eyes and moved closer, looking for more.

He lowered his mouth to hers again, but instead of kissing her, he licked her lips.

"Open," he ordered, and she did, and he slipped his tongue inside.

Goodness, the kisses kept getting better and better. They lulled her, eased tension, softened her fears.

With only a little hesitation, the tip of her tongue touched his. He tasted like all of the things she'd missed in her adolescent years, and had never dared to hope for as an adult. He stood still, letting her enter and explore his mouth.

She wanted to make out all night, and all day tomorrow and all of next week.

Kissing C.J. was so freaking wonderful.

The sun streaming through the window onto her back warmed her. So did C.J.'s hands. He ran his hand to the back of her waist and pulled her close, let her feel what she did to him.

She stiffened, pulled away and stared at him wide-eyed.

"It's okay," he said. "We can go as slowly as you need to." He swallowed. "We can even stop if you want to."

She shook her head. "No." Stopping was the last thing on her mind.

He let go of her and walked to the bed, sat on the edge of it and waited for her to approach.

She was in control. Not him.

She stepped close. With a tug on her hand, he pulled her down, settled her across his legs gently. She felt treasured.

Heat flared in his eyes, but he held himself in check

and she loved him for that care, that generosity. She had nothing to fear from this man. So much intimacy, and none of it frightening or painful.

When he bent to kiss her this time, she opened to him. He explored her mouth and she his.

She squirmed in his arms, wanted to get closer to him, and pressed her chest against his, hard, trying to ease an ache in her breasts.

He pulled back, touched her throat, her collarbone, the first button of her shirt. All the while, his wrist rested between her breasts, a warm heavy masculine weight.

Her chest rose and fell. Her breath came quickly. Her pulse played a frantic rhythm.

She let him slip the button through its hole.

"You okay?" he murmured.

That wariness returned. "Don't talk. Just do it. Don't talk."

He pulled her to him, held her gently in his arms. "No," he whispered into her ear. "I won't just do it."

She eased air into her lungs, slowly, to calm herself.

He kissed her neck. "I want you to be happy. To enjoy this. I won't talk if you don't want me to, but I won't rush it either."

The wariness left, replaced by tenderness, love, confidence.

"This is right," she whispered.

"This is right," he said.

When he slipped the second button through its hole, she gazed at him steadily. He undid the third button and the fourth, then parted the fabric.

He opened the front clasp of her bra and her breasts

spilled out. The cool breeze from the window washed over her skin and she shivered.

"So pretty," C.J. whispered. "So white, like alabaster."

He took one nipple into his mouth and Janey gasped. A thrill ran from her breast to her belly. Her nipple hardened beneath his tongue.

She closed her eyes. He kissed one breast then the other, kissed the tip of her nose, and her lips, her chin, her throat, her chest, licked the crevice between her breasts, leaving every inch of her skin moist and honored by his touch.

Then he took that dark nipple into his mouth again with its hard proof of her arousal.

Instead of words, his tongue and lips spread his message of love. He whispered secrets over her skin, words of love she'd never thought her body would know. Every molecule of her skin and bones and muscles responded.

When he opened her pants and nuzzled her round belly, she gasped and threaded her fingers through his hair. When he licked her, she held him still.

"Don't make me stop," he whispered and it was more plea than command. "I need to do this."

She released his hair.

He shifted her underwear and pants lower and moved his mouth on her skin.

Her stomach trembled, but she didn't stop him.

With one swift movement, he drew her pants and undies off.

When he breathed on her, she nearly jumped out of her skin.

Resting his lips there, he breathed, in and out, waiting for her signal that she was okay with this. He gave her time to stop him, but she didn't want to.

She reached a hand down to touch his cheek. Yes.

He licked her and she nearly fell from his arms. He tightened his grip, twisted on the side of the bed and put one of her legs on his other side.

She felt the cool air on her parted legs, then C.J.'s hot, hot breath. He touched her with one finger. Stars burst behind her closed eyelids.

With one finger, he found her. He looked up at her face. She watched him.

C.J. WAS HUMBLED by Janey. How much courage did it take for her to let a man touch her after what she'd lived through?

He kissed her, there, and she tasted like new growth in spring fields, and like the mild Chinooks that blew across his land during a winter thaw, and like sun-warmed water in a shallow stream.

She tasted like herself, unique, pure and loved.

He tasted sweet Janey Wilson, and tasted more, until she fell apart in his arms.

He pulled her up and held her while she trembled, caught her when she fell back to earth, cradled her in his arms until she opened her eyes and gazed at him with wonder.

"Thank you," she whispered.

"I owe you so much more for what you did today." His voice rumbled out of him onto the breast he kissed. "I love you, Janey Wilson."

She let out a long sweet sigh. "I love you, C.J."

C.J. closed his eyes, held her tightly and leaned his forehead on hers.

Finally, C.J. was going to have it all in his life, those things he'd wanted for so long—the ranch. A wife he loved. His son loving and accepting him. More children.

He was so frigging blessed.

A breeze blew the curtains into the room and raised goose bumps on Janey's dark areolas, on the perfect alabaster of her breasts.

"Cold?" he asked.

"A little."

When he moved to get up and close the window, she said, "No. I like it."

She touched his face, ran her finger along the cleft in his chin.

"I want to see you."

She unbuttoned his shirt and pushed it from his shoulders. She unzipped his jeans over the erection that hadn't abated since he'd sat on this bed with her, then pulled the tails of his shirt out and tossed it onto the floor.

With a look of awe, she touched his chest, her hands hovering over him with the lightest touch, raising hairs on his skin.

HE WAS BEAUTIFUL TO LOOK AT, his skin smooth and tanned in some areas with sun-bleached hair lightening it, and pale with darker hair dusting it where his skin saw sun less often.

She touched it all, marveled at the contours of this man who said he loved her. She loved him, too, but as her fingers drifted toward the waist of his jeans, she wondered if she could do everything.

He'd given her a gift she thought she would never

know in her lifetime. She wanted to give him so much more.

He lay back on the bed with his hands at his sides. She frowned. She didn't know what to *do*.

"Touch me everywhere and anywhere," he said. "It's up to you."

"I don't know if I can do everything."

He studied her with a measured look. "Okay. We can do only what you want."

"Really?" She touched his chest. "If I need to stop it will be okay?"

He nodded. She touched his stomach and he sucked in a breath. With one finger, she traced the bulge in his underwear. She'd hated that part of a man, and the searing pain it had caused her, for seven years, but she didn't want to hate any part of C.J.

When he bunched the quilt in his fists at his sides, but made no move to touch her, she began to believe that he would honor her, that he would respect her fears.

"Janey," he said, "I can control myself."

She believed that, too.

"I like touching you," she said, and he smiled.

He caressed her cheek, his touch as nonthreatening as a butterfly's wing. "There is no right and no wrong."

He kissed the palm of her hand. "Janey Wilson, I want you to be happy. So do as much or as little as you like. Sweetheart, we have our whole lives ahead of us."

His face blurred in her vision. She knew what he implied.

"Do you mean it?"

"Yes, every word."

Oh, a future. A real future. A chance to have a family. To have Liam, if he forgave her. To have another child with C.J.

After a moment's trepidation, she pushed aside his black underwear and touched him there. His flesh reacted, bounced ever so slightly, a living thing. She touched him again and he reacted again.

She felt a split second of anger that someone had taken this away from her for so many years, but she'd expended most of her rage that other day with C.J.

Now, she wanted to explore, to know all of this man, to experience what most other women had with men.

Moving slowly, she tugged his jeans down over his hips, then followed that with his underwear and then, there he was. Bare and erect.

She'd never seen one before. C.J. was big. At least, she thought he was. She had no standard by which to measure him.

This piece of his body stood erect, smooth and hairless along the shaft and tip. It looked almost proud, as if it had a personality.

She put her fingers around him, measured him, felt how smooth the skin was and how stiff the shaft.

C.J. made a noise and she looked at his face. His eyes were closed. A sheen of sweat coated his upper lip. She spread her palms on his chest, one of them over his heart, and felt the steady forceful beat of C. J. Wright.

She lay down beside him on the bed and said, "C.J., teach me how to make love."

He kissed her, smoothed his hands over her body, everywhere, and she did the same with him, caressed on him the parts of his body that he caressed on her.

He smelled like soap and a distinctly male scent, like nothing she'd ever smelled on herself. Like musk.

He felt like bedtime secrets shared under the covers in a dark room, where there was only feeling and sensation.

She brushed his secret with her fingers and he brushed hers and an answering response hummed low in her belly.

C.J. stared at her with a look she'd never seen in a man's eyes before. Awe.

"You are so beautiful," he whispered.

Reaching for the quilt, he lay down with her again and pulled it over them both. The soft time-worn cotton settled over her skin, whispering around them with words like *love* and *safety* and *peace*.

A breeze kicked up through the window and C.J. pulled the quilt over their heads and their lovemaking became a dim cocoon that harbored her even as it set her free on a journey of discovery and adventure.

C.J. shared more of his secrets and asked her for more of hers and she gave to him.

Everything.

When he entered her, she held her breath, while he stretched her. Her body welcomed him, recognized him.

Their bodies touched from forehead to toes, warm, damp and dark. Janey felt the strength of C.J.'s arms around her while he moved, into her, with her, through her. His strength grounded her even as she flew, as she shattered while a shower of stars rained down around her.

She was reborn.

When he turned onto his side, he took her with him, his arms still sheltering her, still joined to her very core. His breath thundered in her ear. Hers whispered over his skin when she kissed his chin, licked his neck, touched the tip of her tongue to his nipple.

Their cocoon grew tropical, smelled earthy. He moved in her again, and then again, and took her on another journey, to the equator, to the hottest place on earth, to the core of the universe where they melted together and became one.

JANEY ROLLED OVER, aware of sunlight warming her eyelids. She floated in its warm orange haze, unwilling to open her eyes yet. So many lovely memories of last night drifted through her mind.

She reached her hand across the bed and encountered warm male skin, an arm. Then again, if she opened her eyes she wouldn't have to remember. She could see the real thing, and maybe they could make more wonderful memories.

Lifting her heavy eyelids slowly, she found C.J. lying on his side, watching her, that half smile playing about his beautiful mouth. She rose on one elbow and placed a kiss on the warm vein beating in his neck.

His arms, whipcord strong, folded around her. She'd never felt so safe, so cared for, so excited.

"We should get Liam," Janey whispered. "I miss him."

"Me, too," C.J. responded. "We'll go in a little while."

C.J. took her hand and placed it on his stomach. Watching him steadily, Janey moved her hand down his body and realized he was fully aroused.

"Did I do that to you?" she asked.

"Uh-huh. That's the effect you have on me."

She smiled. C.J. smiled.

They made love again in the morning sunlight.

Afterward, Janey lay on her back and sighed.

It didn't matter that this pleasure and sensation and fulfillment had been denied to her by past violence. She was having it all now.

She brushed her hand down the dimple in C.J.'s chin. "Thank you," she whispered.

Rolling toward her, he kissed the palm of her hand.

"Let's go get breakfast." His voice rumbled deep in his chest. "I'm starving. How about you?"

Janey nodded.

C.J. kissed her nipple and then growled. "So much beautiful flesh. So little time."

He jumped up. "C'mon, woman, get out of bed. I have a question I need to ask you and I can't do it when you're naked, or I'll start kissing you all over again."

Shyly, Janey stepped out of the bed and C.J. growled again. She laughed. She'd never felt so adored.

C.J. hauled on his jeans and shirt, and ran to the kitchen. "Hot coffee coming right up."

Janey dressed more slowly, in her undies and a big old plaid shirt. She rolled up the sleeves so they wouldn't hang down over her hands.

How had so much good happened to her in such a short time? After all of the hardship she'd survived, her life was coming to some kind of fruition—a store she adored, a child she'd grown to accept, a man she loved. Life couldn't possibly get any better than this.

She crossed her arms under her breasts to hold in all of the amazing feelings that were so new to her and walked to the window. She gazed at the picture-perfect sky.

"Cheryl, baby," she whispered. "Mommy is happy. Insanely happy."

She joined C.J. in the kitchen and asked, "So what did you want to tell me?"

C.J. put two bowls of cold cereal on the table along with a carton of milk.

"Be patient," he said with a wicked gleam in his eye. "I can't tell you on an empty stomach."

His gaze traveled over her. She shivered.

Through breakfast, Janey floated on a tidal wave of euphoria.

She stood up to clear the table.

"Stay put," C.J. ordered.

He cleared their dishes and filled the sink with soapy water.

Janey watched sunlight through the window gild his hair, setting off blond highlights in among the brown. It turned his tanned skin to gold. Not only did she love a man, she loved a crazy-good-looking one.

"Are you still going to rodeo?" she asked, as much to get her mind off his body as to know his answer.

"Yeah. I still need more money." His biceps bulged and relaxed as he worked, draped in a plain white cotton T-shirt instead of plaid button-down starchiness. His jeans fit his hard behind perfectly.

Janey tried to concentrate on what he was saying.

"Ranches suck down money." He put the dried dishes away. "After I pay Gramps's hospital bills, I'll still have money left for new cattle, but there are so many repairs I need to make on the house and outbuildings. I need to upgrade equipment."

He put the last dish away, turned to her and looked serious.

"What's wrong?" she asked.

"Absolutely nothing. For once in my life everything

is going right." He approached her. "I'm going to ask you something I've never asked another living soul."

Janey cocked her head.

When he knelt in front of her, she gasped.

"Janey Wilson, will you marry me?" His voice held a thin thread of nerves.

He was nervous? When he was offering her more than she'd ever dared to hope for in her life?

Her head spun. "Are you serious?" she asked in a reedy whisper.

"I've never been more serious in my life. I love you. I want to get married. I want you to live on the ranch with Liam and me and help me raise him. I want to make babies with you. They can wear little Goth boots instead of cowboy boots if you want. We can—"

She put a finger on his lips to stop him. He was lashing her with too much good news, with so much happiness it hurt. Any more and she would shatter. Every nerve ending bled.

Her vision misted. "Do you have any idea how much you are giving me? How much I thought I'd never have, that I didn't think I deserved?"

Her lips trembled. He kissed them and ran his thumb across them to steady her. "You deserve it all and more. You are such a *good* person, Janey Wilson. Put me out of my misery and answer me soon."

She hadn't said yes? "Yes," she blurted, then screamed it again. "Yes!"

He grabbed her to him and stood, the vise grip of his arms enclosing her in his sanctuary.

"Come on," he said. "We have a rodeo to attend."

He lifted her into his arms and carried her to the bathroom.

"I can walk," she protested.

He pretended to drop her and her arms flew around his neck, pressing her breasts against his chest.

"See?" he rumbled against her ear. "Isn't this more fun than us walking separately?"

They showered and cleaned themselves and loaded C.J.'s truck with a lunch for the two of them and Liam.

Janey had a candy shop to run, okay, so no high heels and business clothes, but she would be her own boss, she would be a businesswoman. Plus, she would have a husband and a stepchild, then more children of her own.

She ran out to the Jeep with a big smile on her face.

They stopped at C.J.'s for his rodeo equipment.

When he stepped out of the house, he gave her his warmest smile and said, "Let's go tell our son."

Our son. Her heart did a back flip, one hundred and eighty degrees of pure, unadulterated joy.

At the Sheltering Arms, amid the flurry of trucks being loaded for the rodeo and ranch hands running around and Hank barking good-natured orders to everyone with baby Michael on his shoulder, Liam ran to C.J. and threw himself against his legs.

"Daddy, look," he cried. "A red fire truck! From Hank!"

"Hank's a good guy." C.J. lifted his son into his arms and settled him on his hip.

"Had sausages. They were good."

C.J. pushed a hank of blond hair back from Liam's forehead.

Liam continued to chatter about his night at the Sheltering Arms, as if he and his father had always had this free and easy and affectionate relationship.

"Michael made a funny face at breakfast and then he smelled like poop."

Janey noticed C.J.'s Adam's apple bob when he swallowed. He looked like he wanted to laugh and cry all at the same time.

"Want to go see Daddy ride a bull?" he asked after he'd pulled himself together.

"Bull?" Liam asked. "Yeah!"

An image of C.J. lying under a bull's deadly hooves flashed through Janey and she had to bite her tongue so she wouldn't ask him to skip the rodeo.

C.J. set Liam on his feet.

Janey crouched in front of Liam. "I'm sorry about the mistake I made in the swimming pool. Really, really sorry."

Liam scuffed the toe of his running shoe in the dirt. He wouldn't look at Janey.

He looked up at his father, though. "Did you spank Janey?"

He shook his head. "We shouldn't hit people."

"Still friends?" Janey asked Liam.

Liam nodded, then leaned against her. "Look what I got."

After admiring the fire truck, she turned Liam toward C.J., who buckled him into his car seat.

Janey took one step toward the Jeep when a hand on her arm stopped her.

She turned around. Hank.

His dark brown eyes with their warm whiskey highlights studied her face. "You okay?"

"Oh, Hank," she said and threw herself against his chest. "I'm *so* good."

Hank wrapped his big arms around her and sighed.

She knew he'd been waiting a long time for a hug from her, for the evidence of her happiness.

"You've overcome so much." She felt the vibrations of Hank's rough voice in her ear against his chest.

"He asked me to marry him." Her tears dampened his shirt. "I said yes, Hank."

Hank pushed her away from him to look at her. Her happiness was so intense, she felt like she was glowing.

"You deserve this, darlin'." He turned. "C.J., you take care of Janey. She's like a daughter to me."

"Will do." C.J. and Hank shook hands.

"Hank," Janey said. "I'm going to ask my dad to give me away. If he can't come, will you do it?"

For an answer, he grabbed her to him again and twirled her around until she got dizzy. When he set her down, he had to hold her to steady her. He grinned. Hank had a smile that could light airport runways.

"It would be my honor and pleasure." He stomped away toward the house and yelled over his shoulder, "I gotta tell Amy."

C.J. wrapped his arms around Janey and kissed her forehead. "You happy?"

Janey nodded. "Unreasonably happy."

"Good." C.J. turned and climbed into the Jeep.

Janey walked to the passenger side and climbed in, her heart so full she couldn't stop smiling.

"You look the way I feel," C.J. said.

He started the engine and headed out to the highway.

Liam made car noises in his throat, imitating the Jeep's engine, and ran his car up and down his leg.

"Let's go conquer a bull," C.J. said.

CHAPTER SEVENTEEN

"Do you *have to* ride a bull?" Janey asked. The thought of him on a bull made her hands sweat. She'd seen photos of the rodeo in Hank's office. It looked too, too dangerous. "Can't you just ride some broncs?"

"Bull riding's where the biggest money is."

"Be careful today, okay?"

"I will. Between you and Liam, I've got a lot to come home to."

He pulled the Jeep into the last parking spot in the shade. Taking his gear out of the back and kissing their cheeks, he left to join the other competitors.

C.J. RAN INTO HIS FATHER outside the competitors' lockers.

The Reverend looked particularly fire-and-brimstone-ish today.

"You're going to do it." He said it as a statement, as a foregone conclusion that he'd hoped against hope wouldn't come true.

"Yeah, I'm riding today." Maybe because he'd sold the store, or because he was getting married, C.J. wasn't sure which, he just knew he wanted his father to be as happy as he was. "Listen, Dad, I'm not falling back into my old ways. I'm not going to go nuts again. Don't worry."

"I saw you enter with that young woman. Liam is comfortable with her. What's going on?"

"I'm going to marry her."

"What?" His father looked shocked and lost at the same time, his mouth open and his eyes vulnerable.

"I asked and she said yes."

"I don't know what to think of this," his father whispered.

C.J. put a hand on his shoulder. "Be happy for me, Dad. Just be happy."

"Do you love her?"

"Yeah, I really do. I want your blessing, Dad, but with or without it, I'm spending the rest of my life with her."

He walked away to prepare for his event, hoping to win some big bucks then to quit for good. He wouldn't need it anymore.

WALTER NEEDED to see Gladys. C.J. had knocked the wind out of him with that news.

He wandered the stands until he found Gladys sitting beside a pretty young woman. When he saw Liam sitting on her lap, he realized it was the Goth girl. Only she wasn't Goth.

Her hair, pulled back into a ponytail, framed a lovely face clear of cosmetics. She looked young and sweet.

She noticed him and her face tightened. This no-longer Goth girl was going to be his daughter-in-law. He couldn't process it.

"Gladys," he called, "will you walk with me for a moment?"

She stood and sidled out of the row. Her fresh scent surrounded him as they walked down the steep stairs to the ground. Walter led her outside, away from the crowds and the animals and the charcoal aroma of grilled meat.

When they reached a large maple, Walter took off his jacket and laid it on the ground on the far side of the tree. Gladys sat on the jacket and he sat on the grass beside her.

"Walter, come here. There's room for both of us on the jacket."

He settled beside her, very close, and he drew comfort from her warmth.

"You look troubled," she said. "Is it about C.J. and Janey?"

"How did you know?"

"She just told me a few minutes ago. I think it's wonderful news. If you want to keep in touch with your son and be able to see any grandbabies they make in the future, you'd better learn to accept Janey."

"Yes," he said, quietly, "I'm beginning to see that."

"She's a wonderful woman. Walter, everything will be fine."

She placed a hand on his arm, where it felt light and warm through his shirtsleeve. He covered it with one hand.

"Gladys, I need to talk to someone."

"Poor Walter," she said. "All of these years as the minister of your flock you've listened to everyone else's problems, but when you need to unload, who can you turn to?"

A light breeze flowed around them, pulling a few strands of her hair out of place. She smoothed them back down.

"Will you listen to me?" he asked. "I have a confession to make."

"Of course."

"I'm not sure that I'm fit to serve as the minister of Ordinary's flock."

"Why on earth not?"

"I made a mistake years ago, a big one. Just after I had become reverend of a small church on the other side of the state of Montana."

He straightened the legs of his pants to keep the creases sharp. "My father was a minister and it was all I'd ever wanted for myself, too. Then I visited a colleague here in Ordinary and met Elaine at a dance."

He cleared his throat because he was coming to the damning part that might very well drive this lovely woman away from him. "For the next two weeks we saw each other every day. She was beautiful, mercurial and quixotic, and I was besotted."

Gladys touched his hand, lightly, urging him to go on.

"On my last night in town, I…" He blew out a breath. This was hard. "I slept with her. She was tempting and impetuous and it was wonderful, everything I'd hoped for, but meant to save for the marriage bed.

"Three months later, she called. We had conceived C.J. that night."

He rubbed his forehead, afraid to look at Gladys, to see the condemnation on her face that he felt inside. "For the first time in my life, I had disappointed my father, something I had never wanted. I loved and respected him deeply."

"But everything was okay later? You did marry her."

"Yes, I did. And I did love her, all of our years together. But I was supposed to be the moral compass of a congregation and I had let them down.

"My friend and I traded parishes. I came here to Ordinary, married Elaine and moved into the rectory. It seemed that, for most of those years, I was constantly reining in both my wife and my son."

He turned to look at Gladys and found her watching him with compassion.

"Have I shocked you?" he asked.

"Oh, Walter, this isn't Victorian England. That was only twenty-some-odd years ago. It isn't a big deal now and it wasn't as big a deal as you thought it was then."

"Gladys, I have carried that secret for years."

"Let your guilt go now, Walter. I strongly doubt it has ever been a secret from the townspeople of Ordinary and they accept you as their moral leader."

She leaned against him. "Kiss me, Walter."

He placed his lips on hers and breathed her in. *Sweet woman of mine.*

She pulled away from him, laughing. "Walter, you are delightfully old-fashioned, but I'd better warn you, this impetuous woman isn't going to wait for the marriage bed either. Come here, my dear, and kiss me like you mean it."

THROUGH ALL OF THE EVENTS, while feeding Liam lunch, and taking him to the bathroom, through a half dozen bull rides, Janey worried a hangnail until it bled.

Finally, they announced C.J.'s name. "C. J. Wright on Whirlwind."

Janey chewed on the nail of her forefinger. *Be okay. Stay safe.*

The bull exploded out of the chute with C.J. on his

back. C.J. jerked back as the bull took off. It looked like the force would tear C.J.'s arm right out of his body.

Janey squealed.

Whirlwind bucked, shooting his hind legs into the air. C.J. leaned backward and forward, counterbalancing the bull's violence.

Janey glanced at the digital clock. Only two seconds gone.

"Come on. Come on."

C.J. held on.

Janey jumped up out of her seat.

Only four seconds gone.

"Come on," she screamed. Everyone else's screams drowned out hers.

Fans pounded their boot heels on the wooden stands. Janey's heart took up the rhythm.

Even from this distance, she could see the veins of the arm that held his bullrope bulge under his skin.

She slapped her hands over her eyes then took them away so she could see.

She wanted to watch. She couldn't stand to watch.

Her heart pounded, the beat of her pulse roaring in her ears to match the roar of the crowd around her.

Liam squealed.

The damn bull bucked again, C.J. held on and then suddenly it was over. C.J. jumped from Whirlwind's back to land on his feet and run away from the bull's flailing hooves.

He laughed and wiped sweat from his face.

Janey had just survived the longest freaking eight seconds of her life and C.J. was *laughing*?

With a shaking hand, she wiped sweat from her own forehead.

"Damn bull riding," she whispered.

Liam clapped his hands and shouted. "Damn bull riding!"

Those in the neighboring seats laughed. Janey blushed.

"Come on," she said. "Let's go see Daddy."

She ran down the stairs with Liam on her shoulder, while he giggled at being jounced. When she ran into the back of the stadium, flying past hot-dog vendors and washroom doors and concrete walls, Liam shouted, "I wanna hot dog."

"Later."

How the hell did she find out where C.J. was? Where was the back of the stadium?

"Janey!"

Janey spun around. "Amy! How do I find C.J.?"

Amy turned and started back the way she'd come. "Did you see him?" she tossed over her shoulder. "He won the bull riding."

Janey ran to keep up.

"He did?" She hadn't heard that over the noise of the crowd. Oh, C.J. would be so happy.

They turned a corner and Janey saw him surrounded by cowboys and cowgirls laughing and slapping his back.

He laughed, too.

Spotting her, he pushed his way through the crowd around him.

He grabbed her and kissed her full on the lips and Janey heard the laughter and the murmuring around her. Guess the cat was out of the bag about their romance.

She'd wanted to hold it close a little longer, so it was just their news, and their family's.

C.J. came up for air and left his arm across Janey's shoulders. "Folks, this is the future Mrs. Wright."

The name was a shock. She hadn't decided yet if she wanted to keep her own.

People smiled at her, offered congratulations.

When they found a private corner to chat before the award ceremony, Janey said, "I didn't like watching the bull riding. Are you going to do it again?"

"Nope, I don't *ever* have to again. Between you and Liam, I'm living with the best natural high on earth."

They walked with his arm across her shoulders and their hips touching. C.J. smiled down at her. "I need to work on the ranch. You, too."

She smiled and nodded. Sure, when she had time around running the shop. Someday soon she'd have to share her ideas for the things she wanted to do at the store. The tiny tables and chairs for children who wanted hot chocolate. The larger cast-iron tables and chairs for the adults who wanted to stop in.

"Hey, where'd you go?" C.J. asked. "You off in dreamland?"

She opened her mouth to tell him her plans, but someone called to him.

"C.J., they need you for the awards. Get over there."

"Let's go," C.J. said, and planted a kiss on her nose and then Liam's before turning them in the direction of the awards stand.

I'll tell him tonight.

ON THE DRIVE from the fairgrounds to the supper at the Legion Hall in Ordinary, C.J. was still on that natural high. Liam slept in his car seat.

"After I've paid off Gramps's bills, I'll purchase cattle, start building the stock for next year. Wait'll you see the new calves in the spring. Wait'll Liam sees them. He'll freak, they're so cute."

Janey smiled. C.J.'s happiness oozed out of his pores.

So did her own. C.J. was safe after his ride on the bull and didn't plan to ever do that again. She would have a man and a son to love for the rest of her life, along with whatever children she and C.J. would have.

She glanced up at the darkening sky.

Cheryl, honey, I'm going to make more babies. You watch over them for me, okay?

"I'm going to grow this strain of barley that's supposed to be really good for cattle. Then I won't have to import from other states. That will save us a bundle."

He looked at Janey. In the faint light from the setting sun and the dashboard, his face glowed with health, and happiness and love.

This man was hers.

Life couldn't get much better than this.

"You'll be able to help me on the ranch. Just wait until you see a calf being born. It's a slice of magic."

"I hope I'm around for one of the births."

C.J. laughed. "Where else would you be?"

"In the shop," Janey said. "I can hire someone to help out part-time, but as the owner, I'll be there most days. Next summer, I'll re-open on Saturdays."

"But that's the biggest news of all. You don't have to worry about the shop anymore. You won't have to work ever again."

Her lungs constricted. "What are you talking about?"

"Max Golden caught up with me just before I rode. He's buying the store. You don't have to worry about it."

The bottom fell out of her world. "Max? Buying the store?"

"Yeah, isn't that great? He offered me ten thousand more than you did."

Her chest hurt and her breathing wouldn't come properly. "You sold the shop to Max? *My* shop? *How could you?*" She scooted against the passenger door to get away from him. "Why the heck does Max want a candy store?"

"For his daughter, Marnie."

C.J. pulled over onto the side of the road. In the dim light, a frown creased his brow.

He put the Jeep into Park.

"You don't need to buy the shop anymore. You don't have to work there. You'll have a home with me on the ranch."

"I wasn't buying it because I *had* to. I *wanted* the shop." A fire burned in her belly. How dare he sell the candy store behind her back?

"It was supposed to be mine," she said. "You agreed on Friday that I could buy it."

"Yeah, but you were only doing it for me. Right? So I could have the money?"

"That is so self-centered. I was buying the shop for me, because I *adore* it and I can still study for my diploma. Couldn't you *tell* just by looking at me? You know how much I love working there. It was going to work out perfectly for both of us."

She turned on him and showed him the full extent of her passion—her anger and her grief and her shock. How could he have done this to her? Another damn betrayal.

Shoving the door open, she jumped out and stumbled on the gravel of the shoulder.

C.J. did the same on his side and ran around the front of the vehicle, the stark glare of the headlights casting their shadows long on the road.

"I didn't know."

Janey pushed past him and stormed down the shoulder toward home.

"Stop," C.J. yelled.

He caught up to her and grabbed her arm. "I said stop."

She heard more panic than anger in his command and didn't care.

"I didn't know," he said, obviously trying to temper his tone, to stay calm.

Well, she couldn't stay calm. She was losing something she loved. Again.

"How could you have misjudged me so badly?" She clenched her fists. "How could you not have understood how special my dreams are to me?"

C.J. shoved his fingers through his hair.

"I just didn't realize," he said.

"I changed for you. I opened myself up so you could see who I really am. Do you know how many years it's been since I did that with anyone?"

To her horror, she felt tears run down her cheeks and batted them away with the backs of her hands.

"Do you know how hard that was? I stripped myself bare for you."

He hung his head. She'd washed away every trace of the Goth girl she'd hidden behind for eight years. Then, in spite of her terror, she'd laid herself bare, literally. Had overcome her fear to let him touch her, make love to her.

"I *trusted* you and you didn't bother to see who I really am. You saw me in terms of how I would fit into your fantasy with no thought given to mine."

"I didn't mean to hurt you. It was a mistake."

"I don't think so, C.J. Take another look. I think the money was more important to you than me."

He set his jaw. He was getting angry, too. "I'm not that shallow."

The air whooshed out of her on a frustrated sigh. "I know. But you've needed money, a lot of it, for so long, it's a part of how you think."

She reached out to touch his arm, then pulled her hand back. "But you did make a lousy ten thousand dollars more important than me."

She turned to walk away. "You really never knew who I am, what I want and where I want to go with my life."

He stopped her. "What does this mean for us?"

"I don't know, C.J." The backs of her eyes stung, like if she didn't leave right away, she'd break down and cry in front of him.

She couldn't give him another little piece of her private self to hurt.

"I need to think." She backed away from him. "Maybe Ordinary isn't the place where I can rebuild my life. Rebuild myself."

"You can't mean that."

She kept walking. "I do."

"But—"

"Leave me alone."

CHAPTER EIGHTEEN

JANEY FADED into the edge of twilight, swallowed up by the encroaching darkness and the folly of his own damned mistake.

She was right. She had stripped herself bare for him and C.J. had never truly seen her. He'd been looking only at his own dream and had thought he could drop her right into it, tab A into slot B. Settle her down cozily on the ranch then go about his business with his family and his life all settled exactly as he'd wanted them.

He'd never bothered to find out what *she* wanted and how *he* could fit into *her* life.

He'd watched her become her own woman before his very eyes, yet he hadn't truly seen her.

She'd given him so many gifts—gifts fraught with danger for her—the stunning honesty of who she really was when she'd unmasked herself, the body that had known only violence before she'd given it to him, her boundless generous love.

His son.

Despite what she'd lived through in her life, she'd given it all with the amazing courage it took to heal that which was broken inside of her so she could offer everything she was to him.

He sank to his knees and bent his head.

Janey Wilson, what have I done?

He stayed that way for what felt like an eternity then stood abruptly.

No way was he losing that woman. If she couldn't fit into his dreams as they stood, he would change his dreams.

He jumped into the Jeep just as a pickup truck pulled up behind him.

Hank got out and strode up the shoulder of the road to C.J.'s window.

"You having car trouble? Need some help?"

"Yeah," C.J. said. "I need you to pick up Janey a little farther up the road."

"What's she doing? Walking?"

"We had a fight. I have to make it up to her, but I need her away from the store tonight. Can you take her to the ranch?"

"What am I supposed to tell her? That she can't go home?"

"Get Amy to tell her she's too upset to be alone. Hell, I don't know. Tell her anything, just keep her away from the store."

Hank strode back to his truck and sped off down the road.

C.J. waited while Hank's brake lights flared down the road, then the interior light came on as Janey opened the door and got in.

When Hank's taillights disappeared in the distance, C.J. sped off into Ordinary.

Once there, he carried his still-sleeping son inside and ran upstairs. From the double bed in the apartment, he grabbed a pair of quilts, ran back downstairs and fashioned a bed for Liam in one corner of the back room.

Throughout this process, Liam stayed asleep. C.J. left him swaddled in the quilts and went to the front.

He called Max, who answered on the second ring.

"The deal is off," C.J. said. "I'm selling the store to Janey Wilson."

"What? You can't—"

C.J. slammed the receiver into its cradle and ran to the back.

In the candy-making room, he checked out all of his chocolate molds. Which one would work best? He settled on a rabbit.

He pulled his best melting chocolate out of the pantry.

He was devising a way to get his girl back, through her stomach and her taste buds and her sentimentality. His hard-edged Goth girl was a softie at heart. He was banking on that to save him.

If this didn't work, he'd do something else. He'd travel to Billings and live with her there while she went to school. He would do *anything,* because they belonged together.

Throughout the night he worked while his son slept peacefully.

In the morning, he bundled Liam and Janey's surprise into the Jeep and, with a brief stop at home for food and showers, headed for the Sheltering Arms.

As soon as C.J. drove into the yard, he noticed Janey sitting in the roomy Adirondack under the weeping willow, with young Katie on her lap. She sure did love that tree. He was going to plant one for her, beside their house, whether in the city or on the ranch. Wherever she would have him.

The second C.J. lifted Liam out of his car seat, he

ran to join Janey and the girl on the lawn. Katie and
Liam squealed and ran across the driveway to where
the other children played in the field.

C.J. approached Janey with a big chocolate female
bunny rabbit wrapped in cellophane and tied with a big
pink polka dot bow.

"You okay with children now?" he asked. Seeing the
cool look on her face hurt.

She looked pale and her eyes were bloodshot, her
nose red. She'd been crying.

*Ah, Janey, I wish I could take back what I've done
to you.*

Her gaze flickered to the chocolate animal in his
arms and he noted a flicker of interest and a hint of
longing. Good.

Please, God, let that work in my favor.

He crouched in front of her and handed her the
bunny. She didn't take it.

"Please," he said, "open it. There's something you
should see inside."

She reached for it, her manner reluctant, but still with
that longing in her eyes that became more pronounced
as she touched the big bow.

A cheer arose from the group of children in the field,
but Janey's concentration never wavered from the chocolate she unwrapped.

When the cellophane fell to the grass and the bunny
lay bare in her hands, a breathy little "Oh," escaped her.

He wanted to kiss that gasp of surprise, to lick it, to
inhale it, to put it into his breast pocket to carry next
to his heart forever.

The girl bunny had big pink lips and wore a pink-
and white-striped icing sugar apron with Sweet Talk

written in chocolate across the chest. C.J. had colored icing with the natural carbon he used to make the black stripes on his humbugs and had spread it over the chocolate bunny's hair and pert ponytail.

One chubby chocolate hand held a roll of white paper. C.J. gently pulled it out of the hole he'd made in the hand to slip it through.

He handed it to Janey.

She took it, but C.J. didn't think she could really see it for the sheen of tears swimming in her eyes.

"Do you know what it is?" he asked.

She shrugged and raised her gaze to his and he saw hope.

"It's the deed to the store. I told Max I was selling it to you."

He leaned forward and whispered in her ear, "Is that okay?"

She smelled like tropical flowers and coconut and hope and burgeoning love. She smelled like his future. He traced his lips down her neck and she shivered.

She craved touch so much, and had known so little.

His breath whispered over her skin and she shivered. "I'm going to spend the rest of our lives together touching you to make up for how little touch you've had in your life until now."

He wrapped his hand around her bicep and his fingers grazed the side of her full breast.

"A real hardship."

She shivered again and he smiled to himself.

He wrapped his other hand around her nape and urged her forward so he could kiss her.

When he drew the soft fullness of her lower lip between his teeth, she launched herself into his arms, knocking him to the ground.

He ended up on his back on the grass, with Janey in his arms, lying between his spread legs, her tongue in his mouth and her hands roaming his chest, hidden from the children across the way by his Jeep.

Laughing, he broke the kiss and held her away from him. "Business first. Will you marry me?"

"I can keep the store and work there forever?"

"Forever, my darling Goth."

She giggled, said, "Yes," and fell on him again, her sweet tongue in his mouth and his hands roaming her delectable body.

She wiggled her body against him and he tossed her onto her back in the grass, discreetly adjusting his pants.

"Have a heart, Janey." He laughed. "Not in front of the children."

"C.J.," she said, laying her hand on his heart. "I want children. Lots of them."

C.J. pulled her head to his shoulder and whispered, "We can start tonight."

CHAPTER NINETEEN

C.J. ENTERED THE HOUSE late in the afternoon. Gramps had taken Liam to his soccer game and Janey should have arrived home from work before he left. Yep, she was. He heard the shower running upstairs.

Sweaty and dirty from his day's work on the ranch, he headed to the kitchen for a tall cool beer, but was arrested by the sound of voices quarreling.

He swerved back into the hallway and to the back porch, listening and smiling as he went.

"Let go of my toe."

"You let go of my ear."

"Mine!"

"No, mine!"

He found the three-year-old twins kneeling on the floor at the coffee table. Cellophane and polka dot ribbons lay strewn on the floor. Two chocolate bunnies sat on the table missing various body parts.

The girls had chocolate rings around their bow-shaped mouths set in heart-shaped faces. Little black ponytails bobbed at the backs of their heads.

"Girls," he said, for the pure pleasure of seeing their faces light up for their daddy.

They didn't disappoint. They squealed and jumped up, throwing themselves at him when he crouched with his arms wide-open.

"Daddy! Sarah ate one of my ears."

"Hannah is bad. She ate my toe."

"Didn't!"

"Did, too!"

"Hush," he said. "No fighting. Tell me what you did today with Gramps."

In a matter of seconds, his two chattering little daughters had covered his T-shirt with chocolate hand-prints. Their mouths had smeared his face with choco-late from their kisses.

He didn't mind, wished he could bronze the shirt, wished he could keep his two rebellious, active daugh-ters young forever.

"Go wash your hands and run outdoors while I clean up here and put dinner on."

"I want one more ear," Hannah squealed.

Sarah followed suit. "I want a paw."

They took their chocolate pieces outside while C.J. wrapped what was left of the cannibalized bunnies. He wiped his face with a big white hankie from his pocket, leaving it smeared with chocolate.

Janey stepped out to the back porch, looking even more beautiful now than on the day they'd married four years ago.

She wrapped her arms around his neck, stood on her tiptoes and kissed him. He bent forward to accommo-date her big belly.

"How was work today?" he asked.

"Great. We had tons of tourists. I left Annie and Jack there and left the store open late because there was a lineup out the door."

She pulled back and studied his face. "And you? How was your day?"

"Had to pull a calf today before Liam headed for school. I swear that kid loves animals so much he's going to be a vet."

"I hope so."

A rueful grin kicked up one side of C.J.'s mouth. "I thought we'd agreed that no more *chocolate* animals would come home from the store for the girls."

Janey hid her face against his shoulder. "I know, but today is a special day."

"Yeah?" C.J. bit the side of her neck just hard enough to get her attention. "What's so special about it?"

"It's Tuesday." Her delightful high laugh filled C.J. with joy.

"C.J.?"

"Hmm," he murmured, pulling away from her neck and turning her around in his arms, settling her back flush against him, so he could caress her big belly.

They watched the girls run in the backyard, chattering and happy.

Janey looked up at him over her shoulder. "Has life lived up to all those dreams you had when we met?"

"No," he said and she frowned. "It's better, Janey. So much better. And you?"

"Better. Perfect."

He felt his son kick his hand from inside his wife's womb.

Soon, he thought. *We're waiting for you, me and your mother and the twins and Liam and Gramps.*

He remembered all of his old frustration with constantly waiting for everything he wanted. His daughters romped in his fields under the sun, their tiny feet clad in small black cowboy boots eating up the wide-open spaces of his flourishing ranch.

His hand roamed Janey's belly again and a tiny foot moved to meet his touch.

Son, we're waiting for you.

His heart filled with joyful anticipation.

I'm waiting for you.

* * * * *

THIS COWBOY'S SON

CHAPTER ONE

WIND WHIPPED through the valley and howled around the old house like a widow keening.

A crack of thunder shook the earth. Rain pelted the windshield faster than the wipers could clear it away, blurring the outline of the cabin.

Matthew Long swore he could hear years-dead voices whispering things better left unsaid. Grief clung to this place like a bad dream, still breathed his father's obscenities and his mother's lunatic ravings.

He wished that Jenny Sterling could have found somewhere else to ride out this storm other than the house he'd grown up in.

Lightning flashed the midnight sky with midday brightness, exposing a still life of the land on which Matt had hoped to never again step foot. Weeds had obliterated any trace of the small garden his mother had once planted in the yard. A hole the size of a pebble marred one of the living room's windows.

The flat roof of the veranda listed like a drunken sailor.

The house looked forgotten and lonesome.

Warm light flickered in the cabin's windows and wood smoke scented the air. Jenny had started a fire.

Matt couldn't put it off any longer. He had to go in there and drag her back home to the Sheltering Arms.

Hank might be a friend, but he was also their employer. The little idiot needed to apologize for the argument she'd started with Hank's guest, Amy.

He turned off the engine and jumped out of the truck.

In the few seconds it took him to cross the muddy path between the truck and the veranda, the wind picked up, bending the trees beside the house horizontal and soaking him to the skin with driving rain.

The aged floorboards creaked beneath him with every step he took. He had to put effort into pushing the warped door while it groaned its resistance before finally opening.

The hairs on the back of his neck stood up. He hadn't been in here since his parents had died. What was that? Ten years ago? The living room hadn't changed one bit, except for the woman standing in front of the fireplace.

Jenny kept her back to him, ignoring him when he knew he'd made enough noise entering to rouse the dead.

Soft candlelight shone on her bare back, lit the threadbare blanket that was wrapped around her and hanging below the flare of her hips. When she bent to arrange her wet clothes in front of the fire, it slipped down to her smooth, round bottom, and anger forged a trail through him.

She had a lot of nerve ruining a perfectly good friendship by growing up. Matt didn't care how unreasonable that sounded.

A gust of wind through the open doorway blew his hat from his head but he caught it in one hand.

The cold air raised goose bumps on Jenny's skin. Even though the candlelight was too dim for him to be sure, he swore he could see them. But then, he'd noticed everything about her lately, like her curves and the new way she walked, swinging her hips too much.

Feminine curves and cowgirl strength. A stunning combination, never mind that she was feisty and fun, and made him feel bad to the bone.

His horsing-around-buddy was a better person than he could ever be, without even trying. She just was.

And now she was a grown woman.

Matt stepped into the room and slammed the door. The cabin seemed to get smaller, becoming too intimate. He rapped his hat against his thigh, spraying water across the wood floor, and threw it across the room to land on the kitchen table.

Jenny straightened, turned and looked at him with the eyes of a woman. Damn. No longer the kid he could toss into the pond when she got mouthy, she'd started to watch him with awareness, making his skin itch and his groin scream for attention.

Looking at her, he felt that old devil, yearning, swamp him. Yearning for what? For a warm body to sink into? Hell, any number of girls in town offered that regularly. For a comfort that would ease his soul? He could always wander into Reverend Wright's church for that. For…love? No way. No how. For a family? Not in this lifetime.

That yearning had been trailing him for too long. *Quit, already,* he ordered. But it was no use with Jenny standing in front of him looking like a cowboy's dream. Damn.

A flicker in Jenny's eyes echoed his desire.

"Matt," she said, gripping the gray blanket against her chest. It rose and fell with her shallow breaths.

He tried to say her name, but nothing came out. He

stepped toward her. His boots hit the floor too loudly in the quiet room.

He finally admitted what he'd been denying to himself. That he'd been aware of her growing up not in the last couple of months, but in the last few years. She'd been calling to him and he'd done his best to hide from her.

Jenny stared at him with heat in her eyes, with smoky knowledge and a woman's desire.

Lately, she'd been trying to reel him in like a calf at the end of a rope, but he was too smart for that. He'd resisted her. But here? Now? When she stood in front of him like a slice of heaven on earth?

"You play with fire, kid, and you're going to get burned." His throat hurt, sounded raw.

"I'm not a kid," she said. "I'm twenty-two."

She dropped the blanket and air hissed out from between his teeth. His gaze shot around the room, trying to look at anything but her, but in the end, he was only human.

Her thick braid fell over her shoulder to tease the nipple of one of her breasts. He groaned. Those breasts. Those mile-long legs.

He tried to be noble. "We're friends, Jenny. This could ruin it." He forced his lungs to expand and inhaled the scent of lilacs. God, she was beautiful. "I know about these things. You don't."

"I want to be more than friends, Matt."

A sheen of sweat broke out on his upper lip.

Itchy and unsettled and angry, he yanked her toward him. Roughly. Her breasts hit his chest, warm through the damp denim shirt.

She wanted to be a woman? Fine, he'd treat her like one.

Matt settled a hand on her hip. He'd held a lot of women in his time, but Jenny's skin was softer than any he'd ever touched.

She opened her mouth to speak, but he didn't want to talk. He brushed one eyelid with a featherlight kiss then moved on to her cheek, and the corner of her mouth. She shivered.

"No regrets, Jenny," he said, his voice husky. "This is sex. Nothing more."

"I want you, Matt," she told him. "What do you want?"

He felt the long-denied truth a split second before he said, "This," and his mouth came down on hers, heavy and demanding.

A rough exhalation escaped him. He braced his arm across her back and crushed her to him, forcing his erection against her belly.

Jenny breathed one word. "Yes."

He spread the blanket on the floor and brought her down with him. He lay on his back and pulled her to kneel above him so he could watch the firelight pour over her curves like molten caramel. While the windows rattled with the violence of the storm outside, the fire sent shadows leaping across the walls.

Jenny unbuttoned Matt's shirt while he unzipped his pants.

She smiled. He reached up to taste that smile.

Wrapping his arms around her, he gave her every particle of himself, taking as much as she had to offer. When he entered her, he felt like laughing, crying, shouting from the mountaintops.

Jenny came apart in his arms then lay against him as trustingly as a newborn kitten.

Matt followed her into a nameless bliss, found peace, and whispered, "I love you."

GET OUT OF here.

Firelight limned the ancient furniture Matt knew too well.

Run.

He couldn't breathe.

I love you?

Where the *hell* had that come from? It was a goddamn lie, just like everything else in this hole he'd grown up in.

Jenny lay sleeping beside him. Maybe she hadn't heard. She must have.

She craved a family. Damned if he'd hang around to fulfill her dreams. He couldn't do it.

He should have stopped this, should have left it at friendship. Sex *always* screwed things up.

He pulled his arm out from under her head and sat up. He looked frantically around the room. Shadows of bad memories danced in the corners, thickening the air, choking him.

Bile rose in his throat.

Get the hell out of here.

No way did Matt do the white picket fence, the vows at the altar and the "I'll love you forever" crap. No way did he do *kids*.

Marriages ended badly. With a bang.

I love you. What was he thinking?

The fire had long since died, and now the candle flickered out. Darkness pressed on his lungs.

Matt dressed in the dark, his fingers thick and clumsy. He fumbled on the table for his hat, slammed it onto his head and stepped toward the door. The floor creaked.

When Jenny rolled over, his throat constricted, and he felt that marriage noose tighten around his neck.

She sighed, still asleep.

With shaking hands, he pulled on his boots. Opening the door a crack, he squeezed out then rushed through the storm and climbed into the Jeep, the lowest of the low, a jerk.

A coward.

He'd never promised Jenny he was anything other than that, any better than his father or his grandfather before him. Long men didn't do responsibility.

He couldn't have been more honest. *This is sex. Nothing more.*

But was it only sex?

Aw, shut up.

When he roared out of the clearing and across the prairie, the Jeep sprayed rooster tails of mud and water.

Sayonara, Jenny.

Five years later

JENNY LIFTED another forkload of hay into Lacey's stall. She had mucked out too many stalls today, fed too many horses. Her muscles throbbed with the strain.

She'd been exhausted lately, doing both her jobs and Angus's.

Angus hadn't even turned out for the branding last week. Jenny had handled it all, had called in friends and local teenagers to help with the job. It had been a big one. They'd had a good crop of calves this year.

Maybe soon, he would feel up to doing more around the ranch. He'd been grieving for his dead son for a long time, a couple of years now. It was time to rejoin the land of the living.

The low rumble of a pickup truck caught her attention as the vehicle pulled into the Circle K's yard.

Jenny tossed her rake against the wall and stepped outside, happy for the break until she recognized that black truck and the horse trailer behind it.

Her heart writhed against her ribs.

Why was Matt Long in this corner of Montana five years after he'd left?

She'd hoped never to see him again.

When he stepped out of the truck, still as gorgeous as ever, Jenny's traitorous heart twitched, but she forced it to settle down. Fast.

Shallow charm and a killer grin wouldn't turn her head this time. She'd learned her lesson when he'd run out on her.

He could no longer set her on fire. The only thing that burned for him within her now was anger.

His five-year absence hadn't been anywhere near long enough for her to forgive him.

Had he heard the news? Was he here to mess it all up for her? She wouldn't put it past him.

"What are you doing here?" she asked, striding to within a couple of feet of him, not a trace of welcome in her voice.

He slammed the truck door, then saw her. His mouth dropped open then closed just as quickly. The line of his jaw hardened.

"What are *you* doing here?" he asked in return, leaning against the door of the truck, crossing his arms. "Thought you'd still be working for Hank on the Sheltering Arms. You just visiting here today?"

His mirrored sunglasses shielded his eyes.

She needed to see them, to figure whether he was a better man than he used to be. Not that it mattered to her. She should have never trusted the rat. Matt, the rat.

"I work here." She stepped closer.

"Since when?"

"Four years now."

He didn't comment, just brushed past her and opened the back doors of his horse trailer. Masterpiece let out a demanding whinny. They must have been on the road awhile.

"You have a lot of nerve coming back to Ordinary," she said. "Especially after the way you left. You couldn't have said goodbye? Or left a note?"

He shrugged.

No conscience.

Once a rat, always a rat.

Good to know. She wouldn't feel guilty about the decisions she'd made anymore. She'd been right to do what she'd done and the hell with Matt's feelings. They weren't her concern.

Matt backed Masterpiece out of the trailer.

Master nudged his chest and Matt took a caramel out of his shirt pocket, unwrapping it. The horse picked it up from Matt's palm with the delicacy of a surgeon.

Jenny still didn't know what he was doing here, and really didn't care, but she was booting him off this ranch.

"Load Master right back into that trailer," she ordered, her tone so cold her tongue got frostbite. "Get out of here."

"Nope," he said, ignoring her as if she were of no more consequence than a flea. "I take my orders from Angus, not from a ranch hand."

"What are you talking about? What orders?" Dread circled around her belly. Why would Angus be giving Matt orders? "Why are you here on the Circle K?"

"Angus hired me."

No way. She stared at Matt. No *freaking* way.

"You're kidding, right?"

"Nope." He raised his eyebrows at her tone. "What business is it of yours?"

She'd gotten over him years ago, but she sure didn't want to work with him. Never again. And what about Jesse?

Jenny leaned forward, getting into Matt's space. He smelled good. He still used the same aftershave and it brought back memories. Those memories were tainted, though. They weren't the gorgeous dreams she'd wanted with Matt when she was a teenager.

But then, adolescents weren't always the smartest creatures, were they?

Matt had forced Jenny to become a realist overnight. To start planning. She would never again be a dreamer. "Angus wouldn't have hired you without consulting me first."

"Why would he ask you who he's allowed to hire?"

"I'm ranch foreman."

Matt's jaw dropped. "You?"

"Yes, me." She smiled meanly. "He didn't tell you?"

"Why aren't you still on the Sheltering Arms?"

What could she possibly say? That they'd worked

there together for too many years? That after he'd run away it had hurt her to stay, to see him in every corner, to picture him on Master racing with her across the prairie? That she'd missed him every minute of every waking hour, and that they had all been waking hours?

She hadn't eaten or slept much for weeks until she'd discovered she had something worth living for, worth fighting for. She'd gotten over Matt pretty damn quickly after Jesse was born.

When she left Sheltering Arms, Angus had given her a job on the ranch he'd bought after her parents had gone bankrupt all those years ago.

She'd come home.

"I wanted to come back to my ranch," she said, finally answering his question. "Angus said nothing about hiring *you*."

"Well, he did. I know Angus Kinsey well enough to recognize his voice on the phone."

God, no.

Jenny turned and strode toward the house.

"Where are you going?" The deep timbre of Matt's voice, flavored with anger, washed over her.

"To talk to Angus," she called over her shoulder. "To get this straightened out."

"There's nothing to straighten out. Angus hired me and I'm staying."

"Not if I can help it."

"He owns this ranch. Even if you are foreman, why would he care what you want?"

She suddenly felt good enough to shout. Payback was so sweet. Matt had hurt her badly when he'd abandoned her. Let him hurt for a while.

Jenny paused on the top step of the veranda and

turned around slowly, savoring the moment. With enough smug satisfaction to drown a prairie dog, she said, "In two weeks' time, I'm going to marry Angus."

Matt whipped off his sunglasses. She wasn't sure what she saw in those blue eyes, but it wasn't happiness.

Good. She'd gotten to him.

As if sensing his owner's tension, Masterpiece stirred restlessly. Matt rubbed his hand down his neck and the horse settled.

"Angus is old enough to be your father," he said, his voice little more than a growl.

"So what?" Jenny frowned. "He's a good man. He'll make a great husband."

Take that and shove it up your nose.

She slammed the screen door behind her, shaken, letting everything that she'd just hidden from Matt flood through her, anger so piercing it wounded her, fear so deep it shredded her stomach.

Memories so shaming they burned.

This is sex. Nothing more. The cold-hearted bastard had been telling the truth. For him, it had never been more than sex. How could she have been so mistaken about Matt Long?

I love you. She'd heard him say it so clearly, but it had been a lie.

She stared at her trembling hands. If Matt had had to leave her after their night together, he should have had the good sense to stay away forever.

His timing couldn't be worse.

But she couldn't blame him for this, really. Angus had brought Matt here.

Standing in the hallway, Jenny forced herself to get control of her nerves or she'd rip into Angus with both barrels blazing. He didn't deserve that. He'd been good to her.

Dread balled up in her stomach like undigested steak. Matt couldn't possibly screw things up for her when she was so close to getting everything she'd always wanted in life. Could he?

She needed reassurance. She needed an Angus Kinsey hug.

She found him in the living room.

He stood in front of the lace-curtained window, one arm stretched high and braced against the wall. Obviously, he'd just witnessed the scene between her and Matt. He glanced at her over his shoulder.

Graying temples and the beginning of a soft middle betrayed his fifty-eight years.

He looked tired.

Angus owned the Circle K, but Jenny ran it. For two years, he'd been detached from the ranch. The death of a man's son could kill a lot of things in him. Even the love of his land.

She liked Angus, cared for him deeply.

What she'd felt for Matt had only been lust. With Angus, it was different. They had respect and a deep affection. If her heart sometimes whispered that she wanted more than that, she ignored it.

Angus must have seen something disturbing on her face. He came away from the window and opened his arms. She rushed into them, burrowing against his big warm chest.

Hold me. Help me. Reassure me. I'm so scared.

"Why, Angus?" The question came out muffled, but she couldn't pull away from him.

"Why what?" His voice echoed against her ear. "What's got you so upset?"

"I don't want Matt Long here."

"Why not? I thought he was a friend of yours. I thought you'd be happy."

"Why did you hire him?" she asked without answering his question.

"He owes me."

Jenny pulled away to look at him. "Owes you? Because you were good to him when he was a teenager?"

"No. That was freely given. This is for paying the taxes on his land for five years while he was away. So he wouldn't lose it."

"You mean he still owns it?" That cabin she wanted to burn to the ground? The one that had witnessed the worst humiliation of her life? Part of her whispered, *and the best night you ever had,* but she suppressed it. The pain on the morning after had far outweighed the pleasure of the night before.

Angus nodded. "I've been paying his taxes, but now that you and I are getting married, I need to get my life in order. I'm organizing my finances and adding you and Jesse to my will."

"So what if Matt owes you money? Why couldn't he pay you back from Wyoming or wherever he was?"

Angus seemed puzzled by the stridency of her tone. "Ordinary is his home. He should have stayed here all along."

He stepped away from her and led her down the hall to his office. "I'll show you the paperwork. Matt's going to work off what he owes me here on the ranch."

"Didn't you say once that he was doing well in the rodeo? Why can't he pay you from his winnings?"

"He had an accident with a bull."

What? Matt had been injured? By a bull? She'd always thought him…indestructible, but in confrontations between bulls and men, bulls always won. "How badly was he hurt?"

"Bad enough. Broken ribs. Ruptured spleen. Emergency surgery. His rodeo days are over for good. His winnings all went to pay his hospital bills."

"You've been keeping track of Matt over the years?"

"Of course. He's like a son to me."

Angus sat at the desk while Jenny took a chair across from him. He stretched his arms and clasped his fingers behind his head.

"I don't know what happened to make Matt leave Montana but he should have stayed and ranched that piece of land he owns."

Jenny chewed on her lip.

Angus cast her a glance. "Looked like you two were fighting out there." He gestured with his head toward the front of the house. "What was that about?"

She should tell him, now, while they were alone. It would take Angus only a fraction of a second to see the family resemblance when Matt and Jesse stood side by side. It was unfair to blindside him like that.

She took a deep breath and held it. Angus wouldn't like this. Could she make him understand why she'd never told Matt about his son? Well enough that Angus wouldn't hate her?

She couldn't stand to lose his respect.

"I need to tell you something," she said.

"Okay," he murmured, sitting forward and releasing his hands.

"Matt is..." *Oh, just spit it out and get it over with.* "Matt is Jesse's father."

"Matt?" Angus fell back against his chair as if someone had hit him. His eyebrows nearly met his hairline. "Jesse's father?"

"Yes," she said. "Jesse is Matt's son."

"I never invaded your privacy, never asked who the father was," he whispered, "but why didn't you ever tell me *this?*"

Oh, Angus, don't be disappointed in me. It hurts.

"Angus, I spend most days trying to forget it, forget that I ever had the poor judgment to get involved with him."

Matt's arrival on the Circle K changed so much for Jenny. Everything had been going along fine. She'd finally found the way to make her long-ago dreams of having a family and working the ranch she'd grown up on come true. She would finally have security for Jesse.

Angus scratched his head, as though he was having trouble taking it in. "I can't believe Matt moved to Wyoming. Why didn't he stay here and raise his boy?" His lips tightened. "I thought better of him."

Angus stood and she reached a hand to stop him from leaving the room to hunt Matt down.

"I didn't tell him."

"What?"

Jenny stared down at her fist on her thigh, at the knuckles turning white, and whispered, "I never told him."

Angus leaned forward to get a good look at her face. "Tell me I misheard you," he said, his tone low and harsh.

"You didn't." She couldn't meet his eyes. Sure, she'd

had her reasons for not telling Matt, good ones, but Angus might not agree.

"You didn't tell him he had a son and you don't see what's wrong with that?" The sharp edge of his voice grated on her skin. She'd never heard him so angry.

She lifted her chin defiantly. "No, I didn't. I'm not proud of it, but I had to protect my son. I didn't need Matt to be Jesse's father. I didn't want him to be."

"Why not?"

"I couldn't let him hang around for a couple of months or years and then abandon Jesse."

"Matt is a better man than that."

"No, he isn't. Remember what happened when he got Scotty's daughter pregnant? How Matt took off for a month and only returned after Elsa's miscarriage?"

"That's not a fair comparison. He was fifteen and running scared. He must have been twenty-five, twenty-six, when you got pregnant. He would have done the right thing."

Jenny slapped the arm of her chair. "He was still the kind of man to leave a young woman after a one-night stand, in the *middle* of that night, and never bother to find out if she was pregnant." Her voice rose. "He knew we hadn't used birth control."

"It was your responsibility to track him down and tell him."

"True, and I would have if he'd been a different person."

She'd heard him whisper that he loved her and it had set her heart soaring. She hadn't asked, begged or cajoled. He'd offered it freely. She'd thought they were about to get their happy ending and had fallen asleep with a smile on her lips.

What a fool she'd been.

The following morning, Matt had left Montana. Why would he treat his son any better than he'd treated her? He was a man who raised hopes and then dashed them.

"You remember what Matt was like back then—even in his twenties," she said, "fooling around with any woman who showed an interest. Lots of drinking on Friday and Saturday nights. Traveling with the rodeo whenever he could."

"Jenny," Angus said dryly, "you're describing half the single men in the state." He folded his arms across his chest and took his seat again, preparing to argue.

"Yes, but Matt seemed worse. His childhood was so unstable. He ran out on Elsa. He ran out on me. How could I trust him not to run out on Jesse one day?" She needed Angus to understand but couldn't tell him how that "I love you" had been the answer to fantasies she'd woven around Matt for as far back as she could remember, since the first time she'd found him lying under the cotoneaster bushes on the hill, spying on her family and the ranch, his heart full of envy. She knew he'd loved the house and this land us much as she had.

She stood and spread her hands on the desk. "My son means more to me than anything on this earth. I would protect him with my life. I'm protecting him now."

Angus shook his head. "Matt has a real decent streak inside him."

"I know." That was the part she'd fallen in love with as a girl. "But I don't trust him. Jesse will fall for him and then Matt will leave. That's always been his pattern. I know this in my bones, Angus."

Jenny felt a headache throbbing against the backs of her eyelids. The fight left her and she sat back down.

Angus came around the desk and settled onto his haunches in front of her. He took her hands in his.

"Your fingers are like icicles." He chafed them. "You have to tell him, sweetheart. It's the right thing to do."

She knew that and hated it.

"Angus," she whispered, "I'm so scared. What if Jesse gets hurt?"

"I'll be here. You'll be here. We'll make it all right for him."

"But—"

"Talk to Matt," he urged.

It was a losing battle and she gave in. "I'll go pick up Jesse."

"Where is he? At Hank's?"

She nodded. "Don't tell Matt anything while I'm gone. Promise?"

After Angus agreed, Jenny breathed a sigh and left the house.

Neither Matt nor Masterpiece was in the yard. The truck and trailer stood along the side of the stable. Obviously, Matt thought he was here to stay for a while.

Not if Jenny could help it.

CHAPTER TWO

JENNY JUMPED into her beater car and sped from the ranch.

Ten minutes later, she drove down the long driveway of the Sheltering Arms and pulled up in front of the house. The grounds were neat as a pin, as usual.

She walked to the nearest corral where a couple of mares chewed on the grass under the fence.

Jenny combed one horse's mane with her fingers, and took comfort from the animal's solid bulk.

She liked the simplicity of animals, of dealing with them. They had no problem offering loyalty and then sticking with it.

Children's voices in the stable rose and fell in playful cadence. She thought she heard Jesse's voice among them. He loved playing with the kids Hank brought to the ranch.

Her nerves hummed. Jesse didn't know who his father was. She'd managed to dodge that bullet for four years now. He hadn't asked yet, but he would.

When she and Angus married, she planned to tell her son that Angus was his father. Jesse would be satisfied with that. He loved Angus.

But what about when he got older, old enough to guess differently?

I'll deal with that when it happens.

Jenny blew a soft breath through her lips. She had to believe her marriage to Angus would work.

A mess of poorly dressed kids ran out of the stable. Jenny approached them. Some kids had holes in the toes of their sneakers, or knees worn out of their pants. They all wore baseball caps with Sheltering Arms written across the front. They were inner-city children recovering from cancer and Hank Shelter was giving them three weeks of pure, unadulterated fun. Hank took in a pack of kids every single month, year-round.

Knowing their father's drill by heart, Hank's two children, four-year-old Michael and three-year-old Cheryl, led the pack. When Amy first came to the Sheltering Arms, a small girl was visiting who had become precious to both Hank and Amy. They'd been devastated when she died, and later named their daughter Cheryl in her honor.

Another little boy, with a head full of beautiful blond locks and long blond eyelashes that would do a girl proud, ran with them. Jesse. Jenny's heart swelled, as it always did when she saw him.

"Jesse!" She waved and her son's smile lit up his face. He ran across the yard and threw himself full force into her arms. Jenny caught him, laughing while she stumbled to keep her balance.

Oh, you rare gem. Oh, my little sweetheart.

She hugged the bundle of energy so hard he finally complained.

"Mo-o-om. I can't breathe."

Jenny loosened her grip and carried her son in her arms with his legs wrapped around her waist, like a little monkey.

She waved to Hank and his children.

"Hey, Jenny," Hank called. Sometimes Jenny missed working for Hank. Sometimes she missed working with the children.

That morning after Jenny and Matt spent the night together, Hank had lost a good ranch hand in Matt. A year later, he'd also lost Jenny.

Most days, though, she was happy to be home, on her family's ranch, even if she didn't own it. Yet.

That would change the day she married Angus. Then half of it would be hers, and someday in the future, Jesse and any brothers and sisters Jenny and Angus made for him, would own the whole thing.

"I'm taking Jesse home now. See you later."

Hank waved back.

"Hank's got a baby horse," Jesse chattered. "He let me pet him. Hannah gave us nimistrome for lunch."

"Minestrone?"

"Uh-huh. It was good 'cept for the beans. Mikey said they make him fart."

Jenny chuffed out a laugh.

Jesse fiddled with the gold chain she wore. "I made a friend. Stacey."

Jenny's throat constricted. He was getting so big, no longer looked a toddler, but more a little boy. Too fast. She was in a weird mood today. Off balance because of Matt.

Some days it felt as if she carried the weight of the world on her shoulders. Keeping secrets could do that to a person, but she was about to unburden herself of the biggest one. She hoped she would feel better after that.

As she held her son in her arms, smelling the hot, active-kid scent of him that she loved, she thought, *What am I going to do about you and your father? You were never supposed to meet him.*

She silently cursed Angus for contacting Matt, Matt for agreeing to come back, and her parents for losing her ranch in the first place. She knew she wasn't being rational, so she forced herself to relax, then kissed the top of her son's head. There were some things well worth being thankful for.

She shouldn't be angry with her parents. They'd done their best. Dad had tried everything to save their ranch, had even started a quarry that had scarred part of the land.

She shifted Jesse a little higher on her hip and walked to the car. She should put him down. He was four years old, after all, but she wanted him close for a few minutes, though.

Matt was back.

What a cowpie-kicking mess. But this was one mess she was taking care of for good.

UNSETTLED AND TIRED, Matt threw his belongings onto a bed at the near end of the bunkhouse. Coming back to Ordinary was harder than he had reckoned it would be.

Driving in from Wyoming, he'd thought the trip was long. Then, all of a sudden, he'd arrived and had to face too much.

He hadn't wanted to see Jenny. He'd planned to steer well clear of the Sheltering Arms, but she was here on the Circle K. Worse still, she was foreman *and* she was marrying Angus. What a snafu.

He'd just seen her drive off the ranch in a small silver car. At least he'd have a few minutes of peace until she returned.

Matt wanted to forget that night, and that he'd *ever* told Jenny he loved her.

He didn't want to be reminded of how much he'd missed her in the past five years and the friendship they'd had before that night. Nor did he want to admit how much he'd missed this place and how it was all tangled up with his relationship with Jenny.

She'd been his anchor for years, since he was a kid. She'd watched over him. Then they'd had sex, he'd split, and he'd missed her and Ordinary more than he'd thought possible.

Matt wished he could turn around and beat a track out of here, to get away from his love-hate relationship with this community, but he couldn't leave.

He owed Angus too much money. No way could he let him down.

Why not? Angus let you down. He's marrying Jenny.

So what? You were never going to marry her. Jenny and Angus are free to marry each other.

Yeah, but still...

Still what?

I don't know.

He didn't want to have to deal with Jenny, had spent five years purging her from his mind.

A decrepit sofa sat at the far end of the bunkhouse, decorated with brown wagon wheels and rearing horses on graying beige.

Matt sank into its soft cushions that had accommodated too many rear ends over its life, of the men who'd made Angus's ranch their home for weeks, months or years at a time.

He turned on the small TV, flipped through the channels, then turned it off and tossed the remote onto the scratched coffee table.

An ancient olive-green fridge and stove and a deep freezer made up what might be loosely called a kitchen area.

Matt jumped up and left the bunkhouse. After a

while, these places all started to look the same, a blur of lumpy beds and cobbled-together secondhand furniture.

He walked across the yard in search of Angus, remembering when he used to come here as an adolescent, hiding on the low hill above the yard, in the stand of a dozen or so cotoneasters across the top. This ranch had come to be a magical place for him, a spot where parents knew how to make happy families.

Lilacs lined one side of the two-story house. Their scent wafted across the veranda. He stepped through the screen door and entered a foyer that was a few degrees cooler than the sunlit yard.

Maybe in some ways it was good to be back. He closed his eyes and inhaled.

It smelled clean, like lemon and potpourri.

Matt had spent time inside this house as a teenager. He'd loved it. Back then, it had smelled like cigars and fried food.

Far as he could tell, nothing much else had changed. The screen door let in a breeze that ruffled dried flowers in an arrangement on a table by the door.

He didn't remember Angus having a fondness for flowers. Jenny's influence, maybe? Naw, not likely. Jenny Sterling's name was listed under "tomboy" in the dictionary.

He walked down the hall, passing the living room on his right and the dining room on the left, both filled with oversize dark furniture.

He continued down the hall and spotted Angus sitting behind his desk in the office.

"Hey, Angus." Matt stepped into the room, a smile spreading across his face. This man had saved him, had just flat out saved him all those years ago.

Angus glanced up from the books he was working on and grinned when he saw Matt. He came around the desk and they met in a man-hug, right hands meeting in a bone-crunching handshake and left hands slapping each other's backs.

Matt was so damn glad to see Angus. The past five years had been filled with close acquaintances and a lot of strangers. But friends? No. It was good to touch a friend.

"Matt, it's great to see you." Angus's voice sounded rough, wet.

"You, too." Matt moved to pull away, but Angus hung on and Matt started to choke up. He knew why Angus wouldn't let go. Kyle. Matt understood how Angus felt. Kyle had been his friend.

Matt had called after he'd heard about Kyle's death, but this was the first time they'd seen each other since. Now, being on the Circle K, it was all too real.

Before coming back, Matt had understood in his mind that he would never see Kyle again, but here he had to face the truth. Here he knew it in his heart and missed Kyle badly.

Kyle had died a couple of years ago in a ranching accident, overcome by silo gas when the tractor venting the silo Kyle was working inside had died, no longer flushing out the nitrogen dioxide that built up in silos. The gas could kill in a matter of minutes. Kyle had never stood a chance.

Matt remembered the day Angus called with the news of Kyle's death—a Monday. He hadn't felt normal for a long time after that.

"Great to see you, Matt," Angus repeated. He released Matt and sat back down, his gaze glued to the papers on his desk.

Angus had aged in five years, with frown lines on his forehead, a slight bowing forward of his shoulders. Probably most of it had come after Kyle's death, as if he had given up on some part of life.

Matt gave Angus a minute to pull himself together then said, "I was real sorry I couldn't get back here for the funeral."

"You had your own problems." Angus rested his elbows on the desk. "How are the injuries? You all healed now?"

"Pretty much, yeah." Matt sat across from Angus, pretended a nonchalance he didn't feel and asked, "Heard you and Jenny are getting married."

"Yeah, the wedding's in two weeks."

"You mind if I ask why you're marrying her?" He forced himself to sound unconcerned. So what if there was an age difference? People did it all the time.

"I want a son." Angus raised a hand before Matt could object. "Sounds foolish, I know. I'll never get Kyle back, but I'd like to have children again."

Matt nodded. He'd never lost a child, so who was he to criticize? There was no fighting a man's desires after living through tragedy.

"Jesse reminds me of how much I've lost." Angus stilled and flushed, as though he'd said something wrong.

Who was Jesse? A ranch hand?

"C'mon outside," Angus rushed on and stood, steering Matt with a friendly hand on the shoulder. "Want to show you some of the new equipment I've invested in lately."

Matt knew he was being put off and wondered why. What was the story with Jesse? It didn't matter. Matt was glad to be distracted from more talk about Kyle. It hurt too much.

Angus showed him around the barns and stables, but seemed fidgety, as if he needed to get away. This went on for the better part of a half hour, then Angus said he had to go into town.

Matt sat on the top step of the veranda, watching the dust from Angus's car settle in the quiet yard.

The ranch hands must be out doing chores.

Strange homecoming, this, with Kyle dead and Jenny here and still angry, and Angus happy to see him, but somehow not acting like himself.

Matt didn't like feeling so alone.

It's your own damn fault. You're the one who's made a career out of leaving.

Yeah, but I don't have to like the results.

He should take a look at his parents' land. His land now. See whether the house was still standing.

No. He jerked to his feet and wiped the seat of his jeans. No way did he want to go back there.

He needed to get rid of that house and he could do it without ever seeing it again.

He strode down the hill to get his truck. He needed to take care of business.

Driving along the shimmering road toward Ordinary, Matt's stomach jumped. He hadn't been in Ordinary in five years.

Home.

He tested the word and tasted bitterness on his tongue.

What was new about that? Ordinary, Montana,

hadn't had much use for him while he grew up here, so why should he need it now?

The townspeople used to call him "that Long whelp." As if he had any choice who his parents were.

He steered his pickup down Main Street, absorbing details of the town, like the police station, whose hospitality he'd enjoyed a couple of times as a teen. The New American Diner sat placid, no longer new, but still popular, he'd bet. Did they still serve the best club sandwich in the West?

The town basked under a warm May sun and a picture-perfect sky. Matt rubbed the heel of his hand across his chest to ease a weird ache there.

Perversely, he pulled into a parking spot in front of Scotty's Hardware. There were other spots available, but sometimes he had to remind himself of his own shortcomings. It kept his head screwed on straight.

He wondered if Elsa still worked for her dad. He wouldn't be going in to find out.

When he walked past the store window, Scotty glared at him. Bad timing. Too bad the old geezer hadn't retired.

If Matt planned to stay long enough to pay off his full debt to Angus, he would have to face Scotty at some point. He didn't have it in him today, but that day would come.

Farther down the street, he found what he was looking for. A real estate office.

He stepped inside.

Paula Leger looked up from her desk when he entered. She hadn't changed much since high school, had gotten a little thicker in the middle, but not enough to deter from her perky good looks. She wore her hair short these days, frosted with different-colored streaks.

Her eyebrows rose and she smiled. "Hey, Matt, it's been a long time."

"I remember when your dad used to run this office," he said, happy to see a friendly face. Paula had always been a decent person, fair and more mature than the rest of the kids in their high school class. He didn't remember her ever calling him names or putting him down.

"He still does," she said. "We're partners now. What can I do for you?"

Matt smiled. No bad vibes here. He took a deep breath and then spit it out, trying to do the right thing before he had time to wonder whether it actually was the right thing. "I want to sell my parents' house and land."

If Paula felt any surprise, she hid it well. "Okay, sit down and we'll discuss it."

Paula explained how the process would go and how she would determine what she thought the asking price should be, depending on the condition of the house.

"Last time I saw the place, it was in terrible shape," Matt said. "Whoever buys it will just want the land."

"Okay. Do you have a copy of the key?"

"I've never had one," Matt replied. "We never locked the front door when I was a kid. As far as I know, the house is still open."

"Do I have your permission to go inside to appraise it?"

"Sure. Do what you need to do."

A few minutes later, Matt stepped out of Paula's office and breathed a sigh. He'd lifted an enormous weight off his shoulders. He felt scarred by everything that had happened in that house. Now he would never have to face it again.

That was done. At last.

He stopped when he saw the flat tire on his truck. Scotty? He spun to look in the hardware store's windows, but Scotty wasn't there.

It took him fifteen minutes to get the tire off, another ten to roll it down to the mechanic and half an hour to get it repaired, filled and back on the truck.

By the time Matt left Ordinary, he was tired and thirsty.

All in all, his first trip to town had been mixed. Some people were happy to see him and some clearly weren't. It was better than he'd hoped for.

When he reached the ranch, he pulled in behind a compact silver Ford that had turned in ahead of him from the opposite direction. He recognized Jenny at the wheel.

He parked behind his horse trailer and got out.

Jenny cut the engine and opened her door, watching him steadily.

Nothing friendly there.

She walked around the car and opened the passenger door. Someone really short got out. Jenny led whoever it was over to where Matt stood at the bottom of the hill.

She looked determined, almost combative. "This is Jesse," she said.

Ah, Jesse. Who was he? Who did he belong to?

Jenny didn't say anything else, just stood and watched him silently. What was going on? Kid seemed kind of familiar. Weird. He was too young for Matt to have met him before, though. Not here in Ordinary, anyway.

"Hey, Jesse," he said.

The kid looked up at him with bright blue eyes and said, "Who are you?"

"I'm Matt."

"Are you new?"

"Yep."

"I can show you around." He balanced on one foot. "I know lots of things."

"Yeah? Do you live here?"

"Uh-huh, with my mom."

"Oh? Who's your mom?"

The kid gave him an odd look, then glanced up at Jenny.

Matt studied Jenny and then the child. Where she was dark, with chestnut hair and deep brown eyes, Jesse was fair, with blond curls framing his face and thick light lashes ringing those blue eyes. But Jesse had a smattering of freckles across his nose.

Matt knew without looking that Jenny did, too.

"He's yours?" he croaked. Judging by the boy's age, she hadn't wasted any time jumping into bed with someone else after Matt left.

Matt got a weird feeling in his stomach. His nerves skittered. He asked a question he suddenly feared. "Who's the father?"

Jenny crouched down in front of Jesse and said, "Head inside the house. Angela made custard today."

"Custard!" he squealed and ran toward the house on sturdy little legs.

She stood slowly, turned around just as slowly, while a pink stain spread on her cheeks.

"He's yours," she said.

CHAPTER THREE

DAMN, ANGUS THOUGHT, what was wrong with him?

Did he have a death wish?

Sitting in his car on Main Street, he was deeply disturbed. It was missing Kyle so badly, and seeing Matt again, a kid who'd become his second son, but who could never replace Kyle.

And finding out that he'd invited to his ranch the man whose son Angus wanted for his own. What a mix-up. If only Jenny had told him earlier, he never would have asked Matt back to work on the ranch.

But you didn't warn her, did you?

She'd had no idea Matt was coming to the Circle K. In retrospect, Angus knew he should have told her, but his mind was too distracted these days.

As if seeing Matt again and missing Kyle and craving another man's son weren't enough to deal with, his approaching marriage weighed on him, too. Only two more weeks. He had to go into that with a clear head and a clean conscience. He had business to start and finish here today.

Angus stared at the Rose Trellis, knowing that *she* was inside. That she was truly back, had taken over her mother's dressmaker's shop and had no intention of leaving.

Moira Flanagan. Her name cut through his veins, landing like a load of asphalt in his gut.

You're insane coming here like this.

He had no response to that, no argument. His knuckles turned white on the steering wheel, his grip brutal but ineffective. He knew he was going to get out of the car and head on in there to see her.

He stepped out like a man heading to his execution.

Thirty-five years later, the thought of Moira still had the power to move him.

They needed to talk.

Dresses made from rose-printed material hung in the shop window. Lavish. Like Moira.

Since she'd come home for her mother's funeral, Angus had seen her only from a distance. She hadn't left town afterward, though, as he'd expected her to.

Yesterday, he'd heard that she'd taken over her mother's business in town.

He had to see her.

I'm not ready.

You've left it long enough. Get it done.

He exhaled until there was nothing left in his lungs but regret.

He grasped the knob of the front door. Forcing himself to push it open, he stepped inside, setting off a chime somewhere above his head.

The interior was dim after the bright sun outdoors, so he stood still to let his eyes adjust—and to give himself time to steel his heart.

Dresses lined one wall. The other wall was bare.

"I'll be right with you," a musical voice sang out from behind a curtain at the back of the store, deeper and huskier than he remembered from his youth, but still instantly recognizable.

It stirred memories. Desires.

The curtain flew aside and Moira stepped into the room, smiling.

She stopped when she saw Angus, the smile fading from her pale face. He drank in the sight of her. The wide neckline of her dress bared her white shoulders. She'd been a wisp of a girl back then, with breasts too big for her frame. She'd grown into a woman, and age had added substance to the rest of her body.

Lord, what a woman. He had it bad for her. Still.

He curled his fingers into fists.

Don't touch. You've got a good woman at home you're going to marry in two weeks.

Then what are you doing here?

Clearing the air.

He stepped toward her.

She stiffened. "What are you doing here?"

He stopped. The air around her swirled with tension and the scent of her rose perfume.

"Hel—" His voice didn't work, came out as a deep croak. He swallowed and tried again. "Hello, Moira."

"I asked you what you're doing here." Her tone was no longer musical, but thin with distress.

"I thought we should meet. Privately. Before we have to do it in public."

"At your wedding." Her mouth was flat. "I don't plan to attend."

He heard the resentment in her statement and his temper flared.

"You've got no right to be bitter. You left me."

"I know what I did." He wasn't sure what emotion

ran through her voice. Was there regret beneath the anger? He hoped so, hated like crazy to think he'd been the only one in love all those years ago.

"She's so young. Do you love her?"

He couldn't lie. "No."

Her green-eyed gaze shot to his face.

"I care for her, though," Angus continued. "A lot. She's a good woman."

Moira fingered the ribbon on a hat on a table. "But if you don't love her, why marry at all—especially someone so young?"

"Children." His voice shook with fury. "They should have been yours. *Ours.* They should be full-grown and working our ranch."

"Yes," she hissed, whirling away from him. She placed her hands on the counter and hung her head, the nape of her exposed neck unbearably vulnerable.

"Why did you come back?" he asked. *Why are you here to turn my life upside down?*

She refused to look at him, so he studied the top of her head and the once-scarlet hair that had faded to the color of a copper samovar.

"I came home for Mother's funeral last month, and decided to stay."

"Why?" he asked. "There was a time when you couldn't wait to shake the dust of Ordinary off your shoes."

Moira glanced up at that, but her gaze skittered away and she shrugged. The neckline of her dress slipped lower on one shoulder. Her porcelain skin used to fascinate him, white and flawless against the calluses of his tanned rancher's hands. Judging by the tremor running through him, she still bewitched him.

With careful movements he stepped closer to her.

"Was it only me in love all those years ago?" he asked. "Did you ever love me?"

She clasped her hands, but he could still see them trembling. "Always. I've never stopped loving you," she blurted defiantly. "Make of that what you will."

It felt as though a slab of concrete had fallen on him, crushing his chest. "But— You never wrote. Never called. I never heard from you."

Angus gently touched her arm and she pulled away from him.

"Of course I didn't write," she answered. "You married another woman."

"Did you think I'd stand around? I waited for you to come home. I waited for *three years*."

His hand struck the counter. "You could have called anytime in those years before I got married."

He was shaking. "I waited to hear from you. I waited and waited and waited. Why didn't you call?"

"You could have called me."

"*You* left *me,* Moira. It was up to you to let me know if you ever wanted to see me again."

"Oh, Angus, I was busy." When he would have spoken, would have lambasted her for such a flimsy excuse, Moira raised a hand. "New York is like a wild animal, absolutely voracious. It chews up young people and their hopes and dreams and spits them out ruined. I refused to be one of the ruined, one of the losers. I worked my butt off to succeed."

Her defiance left her and she looked fragile, tired.

"Did you succeed?" he asked softly.

"Beyond my wildest dreams."

"Was it worth it?"

"I don't know."

"What does that mean?"

The door chime rang and Angus flinched.

Go. Get the hell out, whoever you are. I'm not finished here.

He watched Moira wipe moisture from her eyes, subtly enough that he was pretty sure the customer behind him wouldn't notice.

He turned around. Norma Christie. Jesus, it only needed this. Crusty Christie, the biggest blabbermouth in town.

"Hello, Moira," she said. "Angus." She inclined her head, unbending that steel rod of a backbone enough to acknowledge him. She'd seemed old when he was young. She was downright ancient now. And judging by the spark in her eyes, just as nosy as ever.

Angus set his jaw. Moira turned around, her face composed, but he could see the strain in her eyes.

"What are you doing in here, Angus?" Norma gestured to the rose-patterned fabrics scattered around the shop. "You getting a dress made for someone? Your fiancée?"

Angus froze. What the heck was he supposed to say? That he had come in only to see Moira? When he was getting married in two weeks? Knowing Norma, she'd put an interesting spin on it and would spread it to half the town. It would crush Jenny if she heard. If there was one thing he knew about Jenny, it was that she valued loyalty above all else.

"Last time I checked," Norma said, "the groom wasn't supposed to order the dress for the bride. He wasn't even supposed to see it before the wedding day."

The dress. He'd forgotten. Moira was making Jenny's wedding dress. How did Moira feel about that?

He couldn't come up with a lie for Norma.

Not one goddamn word.

He saw Moira swallow, watched her pretty throat move and her full lips part.

"Angus came to pick up Jenny's dress, but it isn't ready yet."

She turned to Angus and smiled. It looked like a struggle. "Tell Jenny I'll get those pleats she wanted sewn in right away. It will only be a couple of days."

"Will do." Angus nodded at Norma and left the store, so frustrated his jaw hurt. He didn't feel any better now than when he'd walked into the store. One way or another, he would find out what had happened to Moira over the years and why she'd decided to stay in Ordinary now.

And why the hell she'd never stopped loving him, yet hadn't done a single thing about it in all these years.

MATT KNEW HE'D HEARD wrong. Jenny couldn't have just said that the boy who'd been standing in front of him was his son. He had to have heard her wrong.

She looked serious, though.

"What?" he asked, hoping against hope that he *had* got it wrong. He felt light-headed, as if he was at the bottom of a deep, deep well, with only a small circle of light at the top and someone leaning over and whispering strange things. He couldn't hear properly. *"No way."*

"Yes, he's yours," Jenny said from the top of that long tunnel. "Born nine months and three days after the night we spent together."

A shiver ran across the back of his neck. A wave

of dizziness left his skin clammy, as though he'd just walked a mile through a thick fog.

He had a son. A child.

Whooh. He exhaled through his dry lips.

He had a child.

Christ, what was he supposed to do about it? How on earth was he supposed to deal with a child?

Hoo-boy.

His feet started to itch, like he needed to run. But he couldn't leave. He had a son.

He was the boy's father, beyond a shadow of a doubt. Jesse looked familiar because Matt saw a more mature version of that face in his mirror every day.

He was a father.

His legs threatened to give out on him. He broke out in the kind of sweat usually caused by nightmares or rotgut alcohol.

The screen door slammed and Jesse came out with a small Tupperware container and a spoon in his hand. He sat on the top step and shoveled something into his mouth.

That little guy had sprung from his loins.

Afternoon sunlight glinted off the golden hair the boy had inherited from Matt.

Matt had inherited that from his own father—the dad who would never, not in a million years, have been voted Father of the Year.

Deserter of the Year, more like.

Or Drunk.

Or Layabout.

Or Wife Beater.

One hell of a frickin' package.

The old confusing, crushing amalgam of feelings

flooded him—love, hatred, admiration, sorrow, hero worship. Disappointment.

Matt stared at the child on the veranda.

I am a father.

His body couldn't decide what it wanted to do, whether he should run scared or cry like a baby.

"Why didn't you tell me?" he asked, his voice as cold as the water at the bottom of the well he was drowning in.

"I know you, Matt. You don't have staying power." Jenny looked stoic, heartless, so sure in her opinions of him.

"You never gave me the chance," he said.

"Sorry, Matt. My first responsibility is to Jesse. If that means protecting him from his own father, I'll do it."

Matt's chest burned. She thought so little of him. Who had ever had faith in him? So few people.

Angus. Jenny at one point, but no more.

Maybe he should leave, figure out another way to pay Angus back. But he knew he couldn't leave.

He had a son.

He shouldn't have come here. Life was too complicated here, even worse now that he knew about Jesse.

"You can't tell him," Jenny said.

"What?"

"You can't tell him you're his father."

Something inside his chest ached. Pride, he guessed, or was it something deeper? Ownership?

"If you tell him and then leave," Jenny continued, "he'll be so badly hurt."

He shouldn't have come back to Ordinary. And if he'd had any other option, he never would have.

A thought occurred to him. "Wait a minute. You're marrying Angus. Were you just going to let him become the boy's surrogate father?"

"Yes. We both know he makes a good one."

"Why wouldn't you tell me first before doing that?"

Jenny bit her bottom lip and appeared to be struggling with what she had to say. "I need a dependable man to be Jesse's father."

"And I'm not," Matt said bitterly.

Jenny clenched and unclenched her hands. "No," she said. "We both know you aren't."

That hurt.

She must have realized it because she stretched one hand toward him then let it fall. "Angus will be a better father than you. He's the better man for Jesse, Matt."

Jenny seemed regretful, but Matt couldn't stand to look at her a second longer, to stand in the same yard with her. Even if he was a coward at heart, even if she didn't respect him, she should have told him the truth.

He should have known he had a son.

She shouldn't be giving his child to another man to raise.

On one level, he barely recognized that he was angry with her for getting pregnant in the first place, for making him feel responsibility when he didn't want to, as if there hadn't been two of them having sex that night.

Matt turned his back on Jenny and strode to his truck, angry, afraid, too unsettled to know exactly what he was feeling. Shocked, definitely.

Man, oh, man, he hadn't been prepared for this kind of problem. Since that scare with Elsa, he'd been really careful with birth control. So what had happened that night with Jenny? He hadn't given it a single thought—

had only felt that he needed her, and that he had to
have her.

He'd lost control.

He started the engine, made sure the kid was still
sitting on the veranda and then took off down the driveway, not caring how much noise he made. When he hit
the highway, he revved the engine and burned rubber.

He didn't know where he was going, only knew that
he had to get away to clear his head.

I am a father.

As Matt neared the turnoff to his parents' house, he
slammed on the brakes, hitting the gravel shoulder in a
spray of fine stone and dust, and fishtailing. He missed
the dirt road that led into his property.

Breathing hard, he took off his hat and threw it onto
the seat beside him.

He didn't have a clue where he needed to go or what
he needed to do, but maybe it was no accident that he'd
braked before he'd made any firm decisions.

Putting the truck into reverse, he backed up and
turned onto the old road. Rainstorms had washed ruts
into the dirt, and the truck bounced off them as he
drove.

He approached the house and tried to dredge up a
memory, any memory, that wasn't bad. Not of Jenny
and him and their night together, though. That memory was good and bad and insane. At this moment, he
didn't want to think of her, not when he wanted to hurt
her so badly for the way she'd hurt him, for what she'd
taken from him.

His boots rang loud and hollow on the porch floor,
and he sidestepped a hole. The door groaned like an

old woman. Then he was inside the house and lost in memories of his childhood.

He closed the door behind him, to keep the bugs out and the really tough memories in. On second thought, he opened it again, hoping against hope that all the memories would fly out, leaving nothing more than a house. But they refused to leave. They buzzed around his head like mosquitoes ready to draw blood.

The stone fireplace still dominated the small living room and open kitchen.

An ancient Christmas tree, brown and desiccated, stood in the far corner. Silver balls and bits of tinsel hung on it. His mother's last attempt at making this place a home?

Matt held himself rigid, afraid of the emotions that would flood out of him if he let them. They threatened to drown him.

Keep it cool, Matt. Keep it cool.

He spotted a bunch of dust-coated mail on the Formica table by the door. Matt had left it there, unopened, after his parents had died. Other than he and Jenny that one night, no one had been here since then. He flipped through what was left of his parents' lives.

He picked up one large manila envelope, then stilled. He didn't have to guess what it was. He already knew. The autopsy. No, thanks. No, no, no. He dropped it back onto the table and stalked into what had been his bedroom. Not one clue to his personality existed in the room—no posters nor CDs nor photos. Nothing. No Matthew Long. He'd spent his adolescence avoiding the homestead.

Kyle's room had been messy, with football posters

on the wall and a computer and his own TV and *Play-boy* magazines under the bed.

Matt avoided his parents' room, couldn't possibly go in there, so headed back out to the kitchen.

He touched the stove and left his fingerprints in a layer of dust. When had it last been cleaned? More than fifteen years ago. Just before she died, Mom had been consumed by her anger and depression. The house had become more and more dirty, until Matt couldn't stand to eat there.

He opened a cupboard door and spotted a tin of beans and a loaf of bread, now green and dried out. He opened another cupboard door and froze. There on the second shelf, beside the salt and pepper and a bag of pasta, was a small, framed photo of his mother and him.

He looked younger than Jesse was—maybe four, maybe only three. Why was it in the cupboard? Did she want to look at it every time she reached for the saltshaker? Or had she put it here without realizing? Like when he used to find the milk, warm and sour, in a cupboard, and unopened tins of beans in the fridge?

His mother was holding him in her arms and smiling. She'd been so pretty when she was young.

Flashes of memory filled his head, glimpses of this and that, with no rhyme or reason, before finally settling on this one. He thought that maybe he remembered when this photo had been taken.

He remembered his shock later, after his mother had changed.

"MATTHEW, WHAT IS THIS?" Mama held up a pair of pants with holes in the knees. He'd put them in the laundry basket on the floor of his closet, with all his other dirty clothes, just the way he was supposed to.

"Well, what do you have to say for yourself?" Her voice sounded funny, like one of the bad ladies in the Cinderella movie. She sounded mean.

"Those are my jeans."

"I know that, you little moron."

His mouth dropped open. Mama called him a name. She never did that before.

"I mean, why do they have holes in the knees?"

He shrugged. "I don't know. I must have fallen down."

She hit him across the face. He fell on the floor and cried. Where was the mama he liked? Where was the mama who loved him?

MATT CAME OUT of his memory with the question he'd asked himself so many times as a child. Where was the mama who loved him?

It had started the day she'd slapped him and had gone downhill from there, with Mama becoming more and more demanding, her demands more and more unreasonable.

Then Pop started to stay out later and later, coming home only long enough to make sure his kid idolized him and then running off to another rodeo or another ranch or another bar.

To another woman, Missy Donovan from Ordinary.

When Pop did come home, he was angry and drunk and ready to leave again, but not before he and Mama tore each other apart in the bedroom. They went at it like animals.

When Matt was old enough, he got out of the house

before they started, and stayed out until long after they finished.

Matt's shell threatened to crumble now, to let the emotions free to kill him with their poison.

He set the old photo on the scarred countertop, face-down because he couldn't stand to look at him and his mother happy. What kind of weird compulsion had driven a warm, loving woman mad?

Was it inside him, too? Was there some sort of double curse in his life? He'd learned too much of the wrong things from his father. Love 'em and leave 'em. Don't let a woman get her hooks into you. When things get too tough, run scared.

Was he also eventually going to lose his mind the way his mother had?

And now he had a child to worry about.

What on earth had he ever learned here that would help him to be a parent?

JENNY HAD BEEN POSITIVE Matt would run, had known it in her marrow. Then why did she feel so disappointed that he had? It was nuts. She didn't want Matt sticking around or deciding that he should have a hand in raising her son.

She and Angus would do just fine raising Jesse. Angus knew how to be a good father.

She sat down on the top step beside her son and took the small spoonful of custard he offered her.

"Do you want to play in the backyard when you're finished?" she asked, smoothing his bangs away from his face.

"Yeah." He lapped up more of his custard.

Angus drove into the yard in his big silver Cadillac. When he got out, he looked tired. Frustrated.

As she'd done so many times lately, Jenny wondered what was going on with him. What was distracting him? He approached the veranda with heavy steps.

His face lit up for Jesse, though.

"Hey, little buddy," he said and tickled the boy.

Jesse giggled then offered him custard.

"No, thanks. You finish it." Angus turned his attention to Jenny. "How did it go?"

"About as well as I expected. He lit out of here twenty minutes ago. Barely hung around long enough to find out his name." She tipped her head toward her son.

Jesse finished his custard.

"Take the container to Angela in the kitchen and head out back," Jenny told him. "I'll be there in a minute."

The screen door slammed shut behind him. Jenny smiled. Kids made so much noise.

Angus put one foot on the bottom step. On his face, Jenny read a disappointment in Matt that ran much, much deeper than her own.

Angus had always wanted to think the best of Matt, and he hadn't had Jenny's firsthand experience with Matt's leaving.

"Angus, I hate to say 'I told you so,' but this is exactly what I expected."

"Where did he go?"

"I haven't a clue."

Angus glanced around the grounds. "I guess he'll come back for his stuff later."

Jenny smiled grimly. "Oh, yeah, he'll be back for Master."

He didn't think twice about leaving me behind, but he would never forget his horse.

"Then he'll go for good," she continued. "I'm sorry, Angus."

Angus mounted the stairs and rested a heavy hand on her shoulder. If she could ease his disappointment, she would, but the truth was the truth.

She stood and walked around to the backyard where Jesse played on the jungle gym. She helped him across one part that his arms weren't long enough for.

Jesse put his small feet on her shoulders and she held his waist. They'd played this game so many times in the past year, but they never grew tired of it.

Jesse squealed and giggled and Jenny laughed. The world felt right again.

Matt knew about his son now, but he wouldn't stay. Jenny could get on with her plans. She could marry Angus and raise her son on the ranch that was in her blood, that she'd wanted to live on her whole life.

She used to sit up by the cotoneasters as a child and look down on the ranch with such a swell of pride, knowing that someday it would all be hers.

Her dreams had started when she was little more than nine or ten. At the time, her world spun on an axis that was sure and constant.

Her parents loved her. One day, she would have a nice man like Daddy to love her. They were going to build a house on the banks of Still Creek.

Mom and Dad had shown her the piece of land they would give her. It was beautiful. She would raise her family there until the house felt too cramped.

Then they would all move to the big house and Mom

and Dad would take the smaller house in the clearing by the stream.

Jenny would live on the ranch her entire life, as her Sterling forefathers had done before her and as her children would do long after.

Then they'd lost everything.

Bankruptcy.

Her heart had broken.

She'd lost hope for many years, but things were finally, blessedly right. Everything would be fine.

Jenny heard a noise behind her. Thinking it was Angus or the housekeeper, she turned with a smile.

Matt stood by the back fence.

Her smile fell away.

The look on Matt's face terrified her.

He watched her and Jesse play with pure, unadulterated longing. He watched his son with hunger.

"I'm staying to get to know him." He turned and stalked away and Jenny's world turned to dust.

CHAPTER FOUR

MATT SAW ANGUS step out of the house, so he walked over to confront him. Why hadn't Angus ever contacted him, told him that he had a son? The betrayals kept mounting.

Maybe he hadn't known.

When he noticed Matt, Angus's expression turned grim. Matt's hope fell. Angus *had* known.

"You knew and you never called me?" Matt asked, a world of accusation in his voice.

"I found out only after you got here today. Jenny came and talked to me." He set his hand on Matt's shoulder. "How are you doing?"

Matt's teeth hurt. He struggled to relax his jaw. "I don't really know. I didn't have the greatest role model. I don't have a clue what to do with the boy."

"Give it time," Angus said. "It will come to you."

Matt wasn't sure about that, but he'd stick around to find out. After he'd paid his debt to Angus, he'd see how things were going with the kid.

In the meantime, he had to deal with his anger toward Jenny. Didn't Angus think it was wrong of her not to tell him?

"How can you still want to marry a woman who would keep a child from his father? Who would lie to a man about something that important?"

"Matt—" Angus cleared his throat. Whatever he had to say was clearly painful to him. "She wouldn't have lied to me. She wouldn't have had reason to."

That hurt, but Angus was right.

Matt had earned his reputation fair and square, and now had to face the consequences.

"Angus!"

A happy shout from the side of the house had both men turning their heads. Jesse barreled across the clearing and threw himself against Angus's knees.

Angus picked him up and tossed him into the air, catching him effortlessly on the way down. He had a great love for children. Too bad his wife had died before they'd had more than one.

Now that one was dead.

Matt watched Angus with Jesse and wondered if he was trying to replace Kyle with the boy.

"I petted a new horse today." The pipsqueak had a high voice.

Angus turned to Jenny with concern on his face and Matt could tell it was to see how she was doing after confessing to him.

For God's sake, Angus shouldn't be worried about Jenny. He should be worried about Matt. Only Matt. He was the one who'd been wronged. Not Jenny. She could have called him at any time in the past five years.

Jesse took Angus's face in both of his hands and turned Angus's attention back to himself. "Hank says I can go in the pool on the weekend if it's warm enough. Wanna come?"

"Sure." He put the boy down, but as Jesse turned away and headed for the house, Angus stared down at him with his heart in his eyes, full to overflowing with affection, but Jesse wasn't Angus's son. He was Matt's, and Matt hadn't had the same time to get to know him as Angus had had.

Had Angus bathed Jesse when he was a baby, changed his diaper, fed him? Had he done all of the things Matt could have done with his son?

Jesse babbled to Angus as if they were best friends.

On his way past Jenny, Angus wrapped his arm around her shoulders and the three of them walked into the house like a real family, leaving Matt feeling like an outsider.

Story of my life.

Matt felt his jaw tighten again as though someone was screwing it on too tightly. He loved Angus, didn't want to be jealous, didn't want to resent his relationship with Matt's son and Jenny, but he did.

Why? You don't want Jenny for yourself and you don't know if you want Jesse in your life permanently.

It didn't matter. It hurt to look at the three of them together.

Matt went to the stable to saddle Masterpiece. He had a bad case of jitters that needed burning off.

In the late-afternoon sun, he rode Master across Angus's fields until they were both worn out.

While he unsaddled his horse, the ranch hands returned. He knew them all—Hip and Will, Hal and Kelly, Jason and Brent. Apparently, there were also a couple of young kids fresh out of high school who came in from surrounding ranches every day, along with a pair from town.

After a round of handshakes and backslaps, they unsaddled and curried their horses and headed off to the bunkhouse for showers.

Just as Matt stepped out of the building, Angus approached.

"Matt, I want you to take your meals in the house with Jenny, Jesse and me."

No way. The last eight hours had been full of enough drama for one day. He'd already noticed the line of picnic tables in the backyard protected by a long canvas awning. Several of the hands were already strolling toward them.

"Do the hands eat in the yard?"

"As often as weather allows. Why? You want to sit with them?"

"Yeah."

"Because of Jesse?"

Jenny, actually, but Matt didn't want to share that with Angus, so he nodded.

Angus returned his nod and went back inside.

Matt headed out to the yard as a stout middle-aged woman came out of the house carrying a tureen of something that smelled spicy.

Angus had a housekeeper these days named Angela.

Dinner was Hungarian goulash and home-baked bread. Seemed that Matt always craved good food, a rare treat in so much of his early life. He wondered if his craving for it would ever die.

If he'd married Jenny years ago, he'd be eating sawdust and hay for dinner. She was a lousy cook. Thank God he'd left.

He looked around Angus's property. Pretty green fields stretched as far as the eye could see. Cattle grazed out there somewhere, getting fat on spring grasses and the feed the crew put out in the fields every morning.

A jungle gym and slide for Jesse made the backyard seem homey.

Angus's ranch hands admired and respected him.

A thought that had always spun around in Matt's head came whispering in again. Why were some people born into good families, good circumstances, while others like himself were born into hell?

Didn't seem fair.

Angela refilled that tureen twice. Matt reached for more.

After dinner, she brought out an enamel pot of coffee with a platter of homemade cookies.

Jenny came out of the house and poured herself a cup. She stood at the end of the table.

Matt tried not to notice her. Hard to do when he sat facing her and the setting sun turned her skin to gold.

A belt was cinched around her middle. Still slim even after the kid, Jenny's waist could probably still fit in Matt's hands. Maybe he should try it to see.

No! Stop those thoughts right there.

"Hal," she said, "how did you and Hip do hauling out that fencing today?"

Hal leaned back, tucking his long fingers into the front pockets of his jeans. "Good. We've got a little more to do in the morning, then we can go wherever you want."

"Take a four-wheeler and a truck and haul a bunch to the edge of MacCaffery's property. I drove out yesterday. A lot of it's been damaged by moose or elk trampling it through the winter."

Hal nodded. "You don't want any of MacCaffery's cattle mixing with ours."

"No telling whether one of their bulls might have

venereal disease," she replied. "Last thing we need is to have it spread to Circle K ranch."

Jenny turned to Will. "How about you and Kelly take the land running alongside Sheltering Arms land? I saw a couple of young bulls with broken dicks mixed in with the herd. Bring them in for shipping out. We'll sell those."

Bulls sometimes got too excited with their lady friends and hurt themselves. They weren't worth anything to the ranch if they couldn't impregnate cows.

"Jason and Brent," Jenny continued, "take the old Ford and load it up with salt blocks for the heifers you put out to pasture today."

Jenny gave orders naturally, without bossiness or bravado.

Once the business of the day was taken care of, Jenny raised one hip to sit on the end of the table while she kibitzed with her ranch hands. A soft smile lit her features. She petted the head of an Australian shepherd who rested his nose on her thigh. Matt stood, too quickly, surprising everyone. He had to get away from the sight of that wandering hand and the way it caressed the dog so gently.

MATT STOOD OUTSIDE the bunkhouse and stared up at the stars. Listening to the wind sough across the yard and up the small hill through the cotoneasters, Matt felt a familiar urge.

As a child, he used to run over from his home when he needed to get away and lie up there and spy on Jenny and her family, to watch how a real family should behave.

Later, after the Sterlings had lost the ranch to bankruptcy and Angus had bought it, Matt had spied on Angus and Kyle, to learn how a good father treated his son.

He trudged up the hill now and stood at the top, looking across the ranch. He couldn't see much in the darkness, but staring at the star-dusted dome above his head, he had a sensation that he'd felt up here before, that he was part of something larger than himself. Larger than that hellhole he'd grown up in. Larger than his parents.

He knew what he would see in the daytime. Green fields that spread as far as the eye could see. Shallow blue-purple hills that dotted the skyline.

Somewhere in the distance, his parents' house stood on the land his father had never worked, but it was Angus's ranch, Angus's house, that had always felt like home to Matt.

Below him, the house was dark. Everyone had gone to bed. Matt might have been the last man in the universe.

An owl's hoot drifted on a chilly breeze. Matt smiled and buttoned his denim jacket. He wasn't completely alone. Well, often in his life, he'd felt more comfortable with animals than with people.

Matt lay on his stomach and stretched out on the cool earth, the way he used to when he spied. The spring grass smelled fresh, felt soft. By August, it would be sunbaked and dried. It had always scratched his skin, but he never complained and he never stopped coming.

Matt would watch Angus and Kyle toss a baseball back and forth while something that smelled like heaven cooked on the barbecue.

The *thwap-thwap* of the ball hitting baseball gloves

Matt would die to own had hypnotized him, soothed him. Sometimes, he drifted off to sleep.

The branches and leaves chattering above him in the breeze spoke of those memories, of the first time Angus found him.

THE MAN PRODDED Matt's shin with his boot. "What are you doing up here?"

"Nothin'," Matt mumbled, rubbing sleep out of his eyes. He knew the man's name was Angus Kinsey, though they'd never met. "I ain't doing anything wrong."

"I've got sausages and burgers on the barbecue," Kinsey said. "C'mon down."

Matt's head shot up. He stared at the man. The guy was offering food?

"Why?" Matt eyed him with suspicion. He'd learned a long time ago that no one ever gave something for nothing.

"Because you look like you could use a good meal," Mr. Kinsey answered, his voice and eyes steady.

Matt was no one's charity case.

He was on his feet and heading toward his own land when Kinsey grabbed his jacket from behind and hauled him around to face him. Matt had gained thirty pounds of muscle in the months since he'd turned fifteen. He tried to pull away, but Kinsey was big and wouldn't let go.

Just then, Matt's stomach growled. He hadn't eaten anything since he'd grabbed the last three slices of cheap white bread from the kitchen that morning. He'd had to tear off the moldy corners.

"Put your pride in your back pocket where it belongs," Kinsey said, his voice gruff. "You're hungry and you're going to eat."

He wrapped his hand around the back of Matt's neck, where it felt strong and warm. Pop hadn't touched him like this in years. Kinsey urged him down the hill.

A lean, shiny border collie jumped on Matt. He touched her soft ear.

"That's Gracie," Kinsey said. "Sit and eat."

He shoved Matt onto the wooden seat running along one side of a picnic bench, then pressed down on his shoulders to make sure he stayed put.

Kyle was already sitting at the bench, his shoulders broad like his father's, his hair dark. Matt knew him vaguely from school. They were in the same science class.

Kyle would probably think Matt was a loser for spying, getting caught and coming down here to eat.

Kinsey put sausages on the table, not the skinny cheap tube steaks his mom bought. He could smell the meat in them—all meat, no filler. Then Kinsey put a paper plate covered with hamburgers, an inch thick on fat buns with sesame seeds on top, in front of him.

The food—God, the smell of the food—mesmerized him.

Kyle grabbed a sausage and slammed it onto a bun, squirted it with mustard and said, "Hey, you finished that science project yet?"

Matt shook his head. He didn't do homework.

"You want to work on it together?" Kyle asked with his mouth full.

"Kyle," his dad admonished, but Kyle just grinned, showing bits of hot-dog bun in his teeth.

Mr. Kinsey didn't yell, didn't slap his son upside the

head. Just shook his head and sat down at the table and dug into his meal.

Smoke drifted from the barbecue and smelled of charring meat and fat. Matt's mouth watered. His head felt light, like it was gonna float off his shoulders any minute.

Matt didn't know where to start, or how much to take. Kinsey shoved the burgers closer. "Eat," he ordered.

Matt swung his legs over the bench and tucked them under the table. No skin off his nose if the guy wanted to throw food away on whoever happened to trespass on his property.

Picking up a hamburger, Matt bit into it. It sent shock waves through his system. He chewed the meat too fast and swallowed. He wanted to savor it—couldn't—and took another huge bite. When was the last time he'd had a barbecued burger? He couldn't remember. They didn't own a barbecue at home or have money for the diner in town. As he wolfed the burger down, he blinked a lot. A kid would have cried.

When he finished the burger, he wiped his hands on his jeans.

"Here." Kinsey slid a paper napkin across the table.

Matt eyed the sausages. He wanted one bad. Could he just pick it up? Or did he have to stop eating now?

"Go ahead, eat." Kinsey shoved the plate at him.

Matt slathered mustard on the fat sausage, not bothering with a bun, then picked it up with his fork. He bit off one end and juice ran down his chin. He lifted his arm to wipe his face, caught Kinsey's eye and used his napkin.

When Matt stood to leave, Kinsey asked, "You play horseshoes?"

Matt shrugged. "Yeah, I guess."

The three of them threw horseshoes until the light faded so much they couldn't see the pegs.

Kyle ran into the house, shouting over his shoulder, "See you at school."

Mr. Kinsey said, "We eat at the same time every evening."

What was the guy after? Kinsey lived with his kid. Matt hadn't seen a woman around. Matt wasn't stupid, could guess what he wanted in return.

"Why don't you have a wife?" Matt blurted.

Pain flickered across the man's features and Matt knew he'd said the wrong thing.

"She's dead." Kinsey walked away a little and rubbed his neck. When he came back, he looked sad.

"Listen, kid, I don't want anything from you. You were hungry, right?"

Matt nodded.

"The food is here if you want it."

"Thanks," Matt mumbled. That was one thing his loco mother had managed to teach him—please and thank-you.

Matt turned and left, his spine straight and his shoulders square. He didn't return the next night, or the one after that, or the next. On the fourth night, though, Kinsey caught him spying again, watched him from the front veranda and waved him down. Matt had kept hidden. How did the guy know he was there?

Matt stood, dusted off his jeans—the only pair he had without holes in the knees—and ambled down the hill. He wanted to break into a run, to devour whatever smelled so good on the grill, but he forced himself to go slowly. When he reached bottom, he'd stick his pride in his back pocket and sit to eat, but until then he'd take his time, so the man would see exactly who Matthew Long was proud to be.

He ate three hamburgers that night and Kinsey smiled at him. Kyle asked him again to team up for the science project. He said okay.

Matt had realized a long time later that Angus and Kyle had known he was up there spying many months before coming up the hill to get him. That first night they invited him down, Angus had put lots of hamburgers and sausages on the grill to feed the hungry kid that Matt was.

That second evening while Matt was at Kinsey's, Pop came home with two new rodeo buckles and a bottle of whiskey—already three sheets to the wind when Matt returned home after dinner. The house smelled of booze, garbage and stale bedsheets. When Pop pushed Mom into the bedroom with a hot look in his eyes and Mom stared back with that crazy excitement she always had around Pa, Matt ran out of the house.

In the morning, Angus found Matt on the hill wearing only his thin denim jacket, fast asleep and curled around Gracie. The rancher took Matt down to breakfast with him and Kyle.

Matt ate three fried eggs and half a pound of bacon and maybe five, six slices of toast.

Kyle gave him clean clothes for school and Angus made him take a hot shower.

That evening, Kinsey showed him how to bust a bronc. Matt learned a lot from Angus. From Kyle, too.

MATT ROLLED OVER and stared at the moon through the trees. God, he'd missed them.

It was so good to see Angus again, so strange to see the place without Kyle.

Even now, the memories of all the food Angus had served him were so real he could almost taste them. All he smelled, though, was the warm earth beneath him. He picked up a handful of soil and sifted it through his fingers. It gave off a scent of renewal—or decay, depending on how you looked at it.

MORNING BROKE with a bright sun on the horizon and Jenny hummed under her breath on her walk to the stables, stepping through shimmering streaks of gold cast across the yard. She stepped around puddles that a midnight storm had left behind.

The long shadows of the outbuildings held the raw chill of the night's darkness that would soon melt away in the heat of the day.

In the distance, a couple of crew members headed out with feed for the cattle. Good, a nice early start.

The front door of the house opened behind her and she turned. Angus stood on the porch, a coffee in his hand and a distracted frown on his face. Less than half of his mind was on the ranch these days and it worried her. She knew it was leftover grief, but lately, though, just in the last month or so, he'd gotten worse.

Was it the wedding? Was he regretting their agreement?

They both had their own reasons for marrying, but what if Angus suddenly balked? She'd never get her ranch back.

With a worried frown, she stepped into the dim stable.

A rich tenor rang from inside one of the stalls—

Matt, singing an old Dwight Yoakam hit. So Matt was still a big fan. He used to whistle Dwight's songs all the time. She hadn't realized until just now how much she'd missed it.

"A Thousand Miles from Nowhere."

She remembered a line from the song about having bruises on the guy's memory.

Me, too, she thought. *I do, too.*

Thoughts of forgotten wounds got her back up. She'd come to terms with her past and had made plans to move on. She didn't need Matt here reminding her of her scars.

Straightening her spine, she walked down the center aisle and found Matt mucking out Master's stall.

When he saw her, he stopped singing. She stood in the silence, staring at the face she saw reflected in her son every day. Shadowed by his black hat, it gave nothing away.

"You going for a ride?" he asked, his voice husky.

She nodded. "I need to show you around the ranch."

His shoulders stiffened. "I already know this ranch."

"Yeah, but I have to update you on the way things are done these days. Saddle up."

Matt scowled.

"Listen, Long, I'm no happier about this than you are, but I'm ranch foreman and now you're one of my employees."

"Why can't I take my orders from Angus?" He sounded mulish.

Jenny hesitated then said, "Angus isn't too involved in the running of the ranch these days."

"Why not?"

"Kyle." She didn't have to say more.

"He doesn't care about the ranch?" Matt asked.

"Not like he used to. He's run out of steam, but he's working on getting it back. He'll be okay soon." She hoped like crazy she wasn't lying.

She crossed the aisle to Lacey's stall.

"Where's the boy?" Matt called.

Jenny stilled. "His name is Jesse." She turned her back to him and picked up her saddle. The guy couldn't even remember his son's name?

Matt was silent for a while then asked, "Where's Jesse?"

"He stays with Angela while I work. Sometimes he visits the Sheltering Arms. He likes going there."

Matt didn't respond.

"I spend a lot of time with him," she said hotly. "He doesn't spend all day with her. I take care of him well."

Still Matt didn't speak. She turned to look at him.

He was watching her. "I don't doubt it," he said quietly.

She'd gotten all defensive for nothing. His silence hadn't been any kind of judgment on her as a mother.

For God's sake, calm down. His opinion shouldn't matter to you anyway.

They rode out, Jenny ahead of Matt. She could swear she felt Matt's gaze on her and wished he'd pull up beside her so he couldn't watch her.

CHAPTER FIVE

MATT RODE behind Jenny, studying the woman she'd become.

A rich mahogany braid trailed out from under her beige cowboy hat, falling almost to the belt that was slung around her hips.

The jeans that covered her long legs had been beaten into soft submission by hours in the saddle and lovingly outlined every inch of those strong thighs and calves.

Her youthful promise had blossomed into a ripe maturity. Maybe having the baby had changed her.

They rode the perimeter of the ranch and, from a distance, waved to Will and Hip doing repairs on a fence.

Jenny halted at a point in the fence where the wire had either been trampled or worn down.

"So much of this fence is old. The men spend a lot of their days replacing wire."

Matt pointed to rolls of wire lined up like enormous steel donuts farther along the fence.

"You planning repairs on all the fences?"

"Yeah," Jenny said. "Those should probably be under lock and key."

Matt glanced at her. "Why?"

"They're worth a bit and there've been some thefts in the next county lately. Gasoline for ranch equipment.

Wire for fencing. A cow or two, either for meat or to sell."

"Any idea why?"

"Times are tough." Jenny stared out over the fields. "A lot of families are treading water these days."

"One step ahead of bankruptcy?"

"Yeah. I feel bad for them."

"Angus doesn't seem to be struggling too much." The fact that he could afford to replace a couple of hundred miles of fencing spoke volumes about the state of his finances. "That could cause a lot of envy in a man trying to feed a family. Maybe make him steal from a richer neighbor."

Jenny shook her head. "True, but I can't think of a farmer or rancher around Ordinary who'd stoop so low."

Matt shook his head. "Doesn't seem likely that anyone local would steal. I think your wire is safe."

He turned to smile at her, but she wouldn't look at him. He couldn't blame her. He wasn't any more comfortable with her than she was with him.

Suddenly, Jenny lifted her face, like a dog catching a scent on the wind.

"What is it?" he asked.

"You didn't hear that? Listen."

They sat in silence until Matt heard it, too—a cow lowing somewhere nearby.

"What of it?"

"It sounds like it's near the quarry. It shouldn't be. The cattle are well beyond that."

She took off without warning, leaving Matt in her dust. Not for long, though. He caught up to her, easily. He glanced sideways and saw her grin.

They'd done this all the time when they'd worked on

the Sheltering Arms, had broken into races out of the blue, just for the fun of it. Jenny spurred Lacey on, but Matt merely pulled forward, a smile tugging at one corner of his mouth. She was crazy to try to outrun him. Lacey was no match for Master.

She moved into the lead. Matt caught up again. She leaned forward. So did he. The wind flattened his shirt against his chest. A wild excitement built inside him.

The wind sent tears coursing down Jenny's cheeks, and roared in his ears.

Matt whistled, nudged Master's ribs and took off, this time leaving Jenny in his dust.

Near the quarry, he stopped and turned to watch Jenny ride up. His hungry gaze devoured every plane of her face and traveled the length of her body.

She halted in front of him, a smile on her face, her heavy breathing echoing in the suddenly quiet day, her breasts rising and falling.

Raw desire cramped Matt's gut. Jenny's hat had fallen from her head and hung down her back by the string that crossed her narrow throat. Jesus, did she have to look so much like a…a…a *woman?*

Locks of hair had escaped and hung down the sides of her face. When she reached up to tuck them back into her braid, her high breasts strained against her shirt. Matt was pretty sure she had no idea she was setting a lit match to his tinder-dry loins.

Don't do this to me, Jenny.

Her plaid shirt molded to her breasts and toned arms, tempting Matt to peel if off her and taste the inside of her elbow, or suck on the sensitive skin of her stomach while she squirmed beneath him.

Matt's gut clenched. He dragged his gaze away and

gripped Master's reins for all he was worth, ignoring the cramps he set burning in his fingers.

Stop it!

This was insane, ridiculous, history repeating itself, like before when they'd been friends and had ridden and laughed together and entertained the children who'd visited the Sheltering Arms.

Then she had grown up, he'd seen her as a woman instead of his friend and that had ruined everything.

Something inside him broke. It wouldn't happen again. He had to push her away. Fast. He'd work off his debt to Angus and then vamoose. Maybe head up to Canada this time.

What about Jesse?

I don't know.

Because he didn't know, he drew his lips into a mocking smile. His anger at himself found an easy target in Jenny.

"Still crazy after all these years?" he asked. "Running hell-bent over the prairie without a care for anyone else but yourself?"

Jenny's smile vanished. "You were doing it, too."

Good. Keep your distance, woman.

He saw the keen disappointment on her face, especially dark after the exhilaration of their run, but he was trying to stay alive here, trying not to betray Angus.

"Let's find that animal," Jenny said, all business.

Perfect.

She approached the quarry. Matt joined her at the fence that circled it. Sure enough, when he stopped on the rise at the edge of the pit, he spotted a steer on the far side, tangled up in the fence.

"What the heck is that animal doing away from the

herd?" Jenny stood on the stirrups and shielded her eyes with her hand.

"He'll have a few scratches on his hide from that barbed wire." Matt stared at the animal. "Good thing Angus is selling him mainly for beef."

"I'll get him out if you want to ride back to the ranch." After the joy of their ride across the prairie, Jenny's coolness hurt, but he'd put it there for a reason.

"Naw," Matt said, "I'll stay and help you get him out."

Jenny nudged Lacey and Matt followed her along the fence to the far side of the pit.

He pulled on his gloves and dismounted. "You have any wire cutters with you?"

Jenny handed him a pair from a small saddlebag.

Matt cut the animal out.

He watched while Jenny led the wild-eyed creature away, soothing the steer's skittishness with whispered words and a firm hand. She'd always had a way with animals and it seemed to have grown even better. He sensed no frustration in her, only the calm patience it took to coax the animal away from the fence.

Matt groaned.

Ah, Jenny, don't make me care for you again.

They returned to the house, slowly leading the steer home. Matt unsaddled both horses while Jenny took the steer to a barn to minister to his torn hide.

Matt finished with the horses then led Masterpiece to a corral to groom him in the sun.

He heard footsteps behind him and turned around.

Jenny was walking toward the stable with Jesse. The kid didn't look happy. Was she going to make him do chores or something? He seemed pretty young for that.

They disappeared from sight and, full of curiosity, Matt moved Master closer to the open door at the side of the building.

He heard a lot of coaxing coming from Jenny and unhappy whining from Jesse. What was she doing to him?

Matt's curiosity got the better of him and he stepped through the doorway.

Jenny was trying to put her son on a pony, but Jesse folded his legs up like an accordion, refusing to straighten them or separate them over the pony's back.

"Come on, Jesse. Just try it."

"No!" he shouted. "Don't want to."

"I can teach you. It will be fun."

"No, Mom, no!"

Jesse didn't want to learn how to ride a horse? How could a child of Jenny's not love horses? Wait a minute, he was Matt's son, too. How could a kid of *his* not want to ride?

What was Jenny doing wrong?

Jesse struggled to break free of her grasp.

"What's happening?" Matt asked.

"Jesse's going to learn how to ride a horse," she said stubbornly.

"No, I'm not!" Jesse yelled, just as determined.

"Yes, you are," Jenny said. "I mean it, Jesse. We're going to tackle this again."

Jesse wriggled out of her arms and ran from the stable.

Jenny looked as though she was holding on to her patience by the thinnest of ropes.

"Why are you forcing him?" Matt asked. "There has to be a better way to teach him."

He knew immediately that he'd said the wrong thing. A black thundercloud passed over Jenny's face.

"Don't tell me how to handle my son. I've been doing just fine by myself for the past four years."

"Yeah? It's not my fault you had to do it alone, is it?"

"Another thing," he said, pointing a finger at her. "I know you thought I'd run off as soon as I found out I had a kid. Well, I haven't."

Now she looked mad enough to spit. "Yet," she said and stormed out.

AFTER LUNCH, Matt headed to the stables.

Angus stepped out of the front door beside Jenny. "Angela needs supplies from town. Will you go?"

"Sure," she said. "Do you have a list?"

"Yup." Angus handed it to her.

Jenny scanned it. "Wow, she needs a lot. Eight bags of triple mix for the garden and a ton of groceries. This will be heavy. I'll get the dolly."

"I can go with you," Matt said. He knew he sounded reluctant, but he could kill two birds with one stone. Help Jenny with her chores and talk to Paula about taking the property off the market. Having a son changed everything, even that.

"I can go alone," Jenny answered tersely.

"There's something I have to do in town." The more he thought about it, the more he wanted to get it done. What if the land was all he had of worth to offer Jesse? What if Matt didn't have the staying power it would take to be a good father?

At least that land could be his legacy for his son. At least he would have that one thing to give him.

Matt would bulldoze the house, though.

"Okay." Jenny sounded grumpy.

"We can take my truck," he said. She didn't look too happy about riding into town with him.

Too bad.

As they pulled onto the driveway, Matt waved to Angus, but Angus didn't wave back. In fact, he didn't look any happier about Matt going into town with her than Jenny did.

What the heck was that about?

"TOWN HASN'T CHANGED much," Matt murmured as he drove into Ordinary.

Jenny pulled her gaze away from Main Street to study him. His tension was apparent in the stiff way he held himself. He tapped his fingers on the open window well.

She wished she could have left him at the ranch. His shoulders took up more than his fair share of cab space and his heat permeated the air.

Matt stirred, releasing the scent of detergent and dryer sheets from his black shirt.

"Street's busy for midweek," he said.

"How do you feel about coming back?"

"Fine."

"Not nervous? People here used to be pretty hard on you." They'd reacted to his family background, but Matt had pulled his own stunts, too. "This has to be tough."

"Naw."

Jenny glanced at Matt's stony profile. She thought he was lying, but couldn't be sure. She couldn't read him now. One night of sex had changed everything for them. There was a time, though, when she had always known what he was feeling, even when she was a kid.

How did it feel to return to the small town that had ridiculed his father and steered well clear of his crazy mother?

He'd had a lot to prove in this town. And prove it he had—that he was as tough a kid as anyone around.

Jenny had been fascinated by him.

When other kids had mocked him about his family's behavior, he'd get this tight, fake smile and a glassiness to his eyes, but Jenny had always been able to see the vulnerability underneath it.

Why had no one else seen who Matthew Long really was?

Had she seen it only because she knew how he felt about the gossip? No kid wants to be different, to stand out.

After her parents lost the house and then died, Jenny had stood out and hated it. Without warning, she became an orphan, passed for a while from foster home to foster home until she'd grown old enough to work on the Sheltering Arms.

People had been kind, but she'd hated their pity. She just wanted everything to be normal again. She'd lost who she was, and had been working ever since to get herself back.

She'd always known she belonged here, though. Did Matt?

She tried to see the town through his eyes now, but only saw what she always had—a farming and ranching community town. A bar and a church dished out booze and religion in equal doses. The Legion Hall put on regular dances that everyone attended.

Ordinary wasn't a perfect town, but it sure was a good one.

Matt pulled into a parking spot near the co-op where they'd get the soil, and cut the engine.

The interior of the cab settled into silence.

"You ready for this?" she asked.

He shrugged. "I was already here yesterday."

He was?

When he turned sideways to get out of the truck, his broad shoulders smoothed the wrinkles from the back of his shirt. Jenny hated that she noticed.

She followed him onto the sidewalk.

"We'll get groceries last since Angela wants frozen items. I just have to pick up a couple of things from Scotty's. Wait here. I'll only be a sec."

When the hardware store owner's daughter had acted on a really bad crush on Matt by sleeping with him, Scotty hadn't been impressed. That his sweet little Elsa had lost her virginity to a kid like Matt was a bit too low class for Scotty. Scotty wasn't a bad guy, he'd just had high hopes for his daughter.

When he'd found out Elsa was pregnant, he'd practically hired a lynch mob.

No way did Jenny want Matt in Scotty's store.

The hardware store smelled the same as it had for as far back as Jenny could remember—of sawdust, WD-40 and menthol, the last courtesy of Scotty's addiction to cough drops. She headed to the tools section to pick up a kid-size hammer and a pack of nails with big heads. Jesse had been pestering her for a hammer of his own.

She carried her items to the front counter. "Hey, Scotty. Got a small order today."

"How's things on the Circle K? You busy gearing up for the wedding?"

"Not really. Amy Shelter is taking care of everything for me."

"Uh-huh." Scotty shook his head in a meditative manner while he rang up Jenny's order. "You and Angus. I never would have thought—"

"What do I owe you?" Jenny preemptively handed him a twenty. She didn't want to hear one more person say a word about her marrying Angus. Sure, it seemed weird. The man was thirty-five years older than she was, but they were both good people. They would make it work.

"Is that hammer for Jesse?" Matt's voice behind her startled her. She spun around. Her heartbeat faltered. He was supposed to stay outside.

"For Jesse," she said, keeping her voice even.

"Matt Long, what are you doing back in town?" Scotty asked, his voice as cold as an Alaskan fjord.

"I've got as much right as anyone else to be here."

"Matt, why didn't you wait outside?" Jenny touched his arm. The muscles beneath her fingers were rock hard. She glanced down. His hands were clenched tightly enough to turn the knuckles white.

"I'll be here for a while. I wanted to get this over with."

"You've got a lot of nerve showing up around here after what you did." Scotty's face was red. He raised his fists.

"Whoa, Scotty, calm down," Jenny said. "That was fifteen years ago."

Cripes, were they going to kill each other?

"I haven't forgotten what this animal did to my daughter." Scotty's hostile gaze never left Matt's face.

Matt hadn't defended himself back then and he didn't now.

For God's sake, why not? As angry as Jenny was with Matt, she couldn't let this pass.

"Scotty," she said, building a head of steam, "Elsa was a year older than Matt and ran after him. She was just as responsible as he was."

Scotty stared at her. "What's gotten into you, Jenny? How dare you talk about my daughter like that?"

"It's the truth, Scotty. Elsa is no angel. The whole town knows it. Stop blaming Matt for something that she started."

"Yeah? Well, how about him running away like a yellow dog when he found out she was pregnant? How about leaving her to deal with it all alone?"

There was no defending that.

She risked a glance at Matt.

Matt, facing down a man with a long memory and a deep grudge, kept his expression flat.

"She wasn't alone, Scotty," Jenny said quietly. "She had you and her mother."

Matt, on the other hand, had truly had no one. His parents had never been the kind to rely on.

"Get out of my store. Both of you." The veins in Scotty's neck stood out.

"Oh, Scotty," she said, so disappointed.

She picked up the hammer and nails.

"C'mon, Matt."

She strode to the front door and heard Matt follow her then stop.

Jenny heard him say, "Stay away from my truck."

The bell jangled discordantly over the gentle click Matt closed it with.

"Thanks," he said.

"Yeah." She knew she sounded ungracious, but he'd put her in an awkward spot. She'd made an enemy of Scotty for telling him the truth that no one else had wanted to. As well, she'd just defended a man she didn't want in town either. A man toward whom she wanted no kind thoughts.

"Why did you go in there? You could have easily avoided him until you finished working for Angus."

"Where to now?" Matt asked, closing the subject.

"No. I want answers. After defending you to Scotty, I deserve them."

"I guess I wanted to see if his opinion of me had changed while I was gone." He stared off down the street, hip cocked, one hand in his pocket. "If he'd mellowed."

Not likely.

"What was that about your truck?"

"Scotty stuck a knife or a screwdriver into my tire yesterday."

Jenny sighed. "We need to go to the co-op. For soil for Angela's garden."

They walked along the sidewalk in silence. Matt began whistling softly, a tune she thought she recognized. Disjointed words and phrases ran through her mind until she recognized the song. Dwight Yoakam. "Lonesome Me." Worse still, she remembered a line from the song about the guy thinking himself worthless. Matt had so much going for him—solid, dependable ranch hand and rodeo star—but what did the people able in hometown remember? His sins.

ny's mind shot away from the sympathy for him boded through her. *You remember his sins, too.*

She threw the hammer and nails through the open window onto the bench seat of the pickup and headed for the co-op.

She hated this confusion, this feeling of not knowing what to think. Shades of gray bothered her. She liked everything in black and white.

"Come on," she said peevishly. "Let's pick up the rest and go home."

ANGUS NEEDED MOIRA. Worse, his body ached for her. He sped into town, driven to her by all that he'd once had in his life and everything that he now missed. She was key to some of the things he'd lost.

He needed to finish his talk with her.

He had questions and she'd better have answers.

In town, he counted fifty-two steps from his car to the side door of her shop. He wasn't entering through the front door, didn't want to get sidetracked by another encounter with Crusty Christie or any other customers.

Nor did he want to run into Matt and Jenny while they shopped.

Three knocks. Moira. Moira. Moira.

Fifty heartbeats before she answered the door and smiled, before she realized who stood in front of her. The greeting died on her parted lips.

"Angus?" Her wide eyes regarded him steadily, but there was something like excitement underneath the wariness.

It was only the second time he'd seen her this closely since she'd been back in town and she took his breath away.

Three long seconds later, he started to breathe again.

"We need to talk," he said.

She nodded, slowly. "All right. Not here."

He glanced up the stairs behind her, to her apartment above the shop. On the landing at the top of the stairs, a small octagonal window lit a vase of roses sitting on a tiny table.

Curiosity ate at him. Where did she cook? Where did she sit to read a book?

Where did she sleep? No, they couldn't go upstairs. Lord, no. "C'mon. I'm parked in the lane."

Moira hesitated then said, "Just a minute."

He heard her walk down the hall to her store, he assumed to lock the front door and turn the Closed sign around.

She lifted a broad-brimmed straw sun hat and a purse from a hanger on the wall. She stood beside him to lock her door, and he breathed deeply. When she stepped out into the sunlight, he filled his lungs to bursting.

Moira and roses.

He didn't move, letting her back brush his chest and her hair tease his chin. She stared over her shoulder at him, and breathed cinnamon and coffee warmth onto his skin.

If he shifted a fraction of an inch, he could set his lips on the tiny blue vein throbbing at her temple. He held himself rigid.

"Where are we going?" she asked.

"For a drive. I have questions that need answering." He took her hand in his. She startled, but didn't pull away. It was small and soft in his. His calluses must feel rough to her. He didn't care and held on tight.

With her other hand, she took a pair of sunglasses out of her bag and covered her eyes. Take them off, he wanted to say. It's a crime to hide those gems.

"We shouldn't be meeting," she said, but left her hand in his.

"No. We shouldn't." *I have to.* He opened the passenger door. When she sat, she pulled her skirt around her and drew her bare white legs inside.

Angus sat in the driver's seat and closed the door, turning the car into a one-room asylum for the terminally in love, drenched by the scent of Moira's roses and his own desire. He rolled his window down and started the engine.

Spinning the wheel, he cut through another alley to avoid Main Street and the Crusty Christies of the world.

"Where are you taking me?" Moira asked, her voice soft.

"To a meadow on the back end of my land," he said. "Where we can be private."

She stiffened beside him. "Why do we need privacy?"

He glanced across at her. She held herself still. "I mean to get answers today, Moira."

He rode in silence out of town and along the highway.

At the north end of his property, he turned onto a dirt road and closed his window against the dust. They hit a bump and Angus grabbed Moira's elbow to steady her. On even ground again, he slid his hand down the soft skin of her arm, wove his fingers through hers and held on. Refusing to participate, she kept her fingers straight. They hit another bump and her fingers clung to his.

His thumb took on a mind of its own, caressing the vulnerable stretch of skin between her thumb and forefinger. She shivered. He broadened his strokes, ran his thumb across her wrist. He felt her tremble.

Too soon they arrived in the meadow.

Angus grabbed a denim jacket from the trunk. He set it on the ground under an aspen whose leaves quivered and sparkled in the sun.

Moira stood beside him, twisting the brim of her hat between her fingers.

"Sit," he ordered.

She smiled crookedly. "Yes, master."

He huffed out a laugh. These days he didn't seem to be anybody's master, least of all his own. He barely ran his own ranch, and couldn't control the crazy emotions that plagued him.

Moira sat down beside him and tucked her legs under her skirt.

He reached for her, needed her, like his lungs would collapse if he didn't breathe her in. Now. At this very moment.

With an urgency he hadn't felt since she'd left years ago, Angus pulled her across his lap, threaded his fingers through her hair and kissed her like a man desperate for sustenance.

Yes. This.

He'd been starving. He eased his tongue into her mouth. Drank her in until the gray still life of his days burst into color.

He'd missed her. He'd missed this.

Moira moaned. Her fingers roamed his hair and shoulders with a restlessness that matched his own.

More. He needed more.

He set her back against his up-drawn thighs and found the buttons at the front of her dress.

When his fingers touched her skin, she gasped. Pulled away. Sat up.

While her glazed eyes fought for focus, he fought

for air, breathed hard, fanning Moira's disheveled hair around her pale face. Two spots of red appeared high on her cheeks.

"What are we doing?" She shook her head once. "No. I'm not the girl I used to be, Angus. I won't lie down for you so easily."

She was right. He couldn't use her like this when he was committed to someone else.

Nor could he betray Jenny.

What was wrong with him these days? He wasn't an immoral man. He jammed his fingers through his hair.

"I'm sorry." He looked at her over his shoulder.

"I won't do this," she said, her voice firm, her words relentless. "What is it you want from me? An affair?"

He stared at her. God, no.

"I don't know what I want." He held up a hand. "Wait, yeah, I know. I want us to start over. To be twenty-two years old and in love."

He brushed a strand of hair behind her ear. "I want us to have stayed together all this time."

He knew it didn't make sense, but he had to tell her the truth. "I miss Margaret. She was a good person and shouldn't have died so young."

She'd been only thirty.

"I miss my son." He stopped because he couldn't say more without breaking down and sobbing like a baby.

Moira laid a gentle hand on his arm. "I heard. I'm so sorry."

She left her hand there and wrapped her other arm around her knees.

"Tell me about him? What was his name?"

"Kyle." That said it all. Kyle. He'd been unique from the second he was born. The rest of Kyle's story he told with his heart in his throat, finishing with, "He was a great person."

"I wish I'd known him," Moira said and he believed her.

He closed his eyes and sucked in a breath. He had to ask, needed to know.

"Why did you leave if you loved me?" he asked. "No one forced you out of town. We could have had our whole lives together. You could have stayed here and had a good life with me."

"I was young and foolish." She turned to him and the regret in her eyes seared him. "Back then I wanted so much more than this town had to offer."

"I know." He exhaled roughly. "I wasn't good enough for you."

"Yes, you were. I was just afraid you wouldn't be *enough*."

"How was New York?" He couldn't disguise his bitterness. "Was it *enough* for you?"

"No. Not for a long time now." Her shoulders slumped. "A year after I left, I was ready to give up and close the store I opened there and come home. Then I got a big account. It led to other more lucrative accounts. Soon, I had almost more work than I could keep up with. But I did."

She brushed a fly from her knee. "It was good, for a long while. But lately...I—I've been lonely. When Mother died, I knew it was time to come home."

"You got here too late." Angus leaned closer, lured by Moira's beauty and her sorrow, and by his overwhelming desire to hold her.

The creases on her forehead deepened. "When I heard that you were getting married, I knew I had lost more than I could possibly understand. Why haven't you remarried before now?"

"You know why." His ragged breath stirred a lock of hair curling across her throat.

"Me?" When he nodded, she gripped her hands together in her lap. "Why are you marrying a child?"

His back stiffened. "Jenny isn't a child. She's twenty-seven."

"You're splitting hairs." Her eyes flashed. "She's obscenely young for you and you know it."

She swept her arm across the jacket, sending her hat flying. "Why?" The raw pain in her voice ate at him. "Why marry someone half your age?"

"I need children." The savage whisper torn from his throat nearly killed him. "I want my son back. I want my life back. I want children on the ranch. I need my passion for the land and the work back again."

Moira deflated like a lost balloon.

"Jenny kept the ranch going," he said. "She can give me the rest, too."

Moira dropped her arm. "You're marrying her for children? But you're—"

"Too old?" he asked, harsh and bitter in his middle age. "Yeah. I know and I don't care." He raised his voice. "I want a family again."

Moira's chest rose and fell in sync with his own. The blood had drained from her face, leaving her ashen.

The violence flooding his veins threatened to choke him.

"I have to go," he choked out and jumped to his feet before he realized where he was and that he had nowhere to go but to take this lovely, aching woman home.

He gripped her elbow and helped her to her feet, his

movements slow and steady to rein in all his passion for her and his doubts about his plans. But he was right. He had to marry Jenny. He wanted his life back.

"Angus." He heard the plea in Moira's voice. The face he turned to her was solid, implacable.

"I'm going to do this, Moira." He picked up her hat with careful movements and straightened a dent she'd made in the straw. "I'm going to marry Jenny."

He heard her cry of frustration and walked over to the car.

CHAPTER SIX

ONCE THEY'D FINISHED picking up the groceries for Angela, Matt and Jenny headed home.

They'd been driving awhile when Matt said, "What's that ahead?"

"What the—?" Jenny said.

A distance down the road, a couple of guys stood behind a pickup truck parked on the shoulder. A calf was in the bed, his mouth open like he was lowing.

"Are they— Are they stealing that calf?" Matt asked.

The rustlers saw them approaching. Not bothering to close the tailgate, they ran around the truck, jumped into the front and took off, racing down the road away from them.

"Damn thieves," Jenny cried.

Matt gunned the engine, the truck shot ahead and Jenny fell back against the passenger seat.

"You know those guys?" Matt yelled above the wind whistling through the open windows.

"I can't tell from this distance. I don't think I recognize that truck, though."

Even from this distance, it looked a hell of a lot newer than most vehicles around. Black. No license plate. Matt swerved to avoid a cow running from the field onto the road, trampling what was left of the fence.

"She's after her calf," Jenny said.

"That's Circle K land and a Circle K calf," Matt yelled. "Bastards."

He slammed his hand against the door as they sped down the highway.

At a break in the fence, the pickup spun off the road and hot-tailed it across a field. Matt followed. Jenny grabbed the door handle and held on as they hit the field after the cattle thieves.

As Matt navigated the rough untilled land, the truck bounced around like a toy. They didn't have a hope in hell of catching the jerks.

"Sons of bitches," Matt seethed. "Who are those guys?"

"I wish I knew," Jenny shouted. "I'd shoot them." She braced one hand against the roof.

The pickup truck ahead of them hit a deep hole. The calf flew into the air, bounced out of the truck and landed on the ground feetfirst, hard enough to send a plume of dust into the air.

"No," Jenny moaned.

Matt watched the calf crumple like a hot-air balloon in a windstorm. The pickup shot ahead with a burst of power.

"Stop!" Jenny cried.

"I want to get those guys."

"That calf is hurt."

He slammed on the brakes and the truck fishtailed, but he managed to avoid the calf.

He stopped just shy of the calf, who lay still on the hard-packed earth.

Matt stepped out into the hot dust, cutting a swath through it with the back of his hand. He knelt beside the still animal and stared at the mangled legs.

"Aw, jeez." He wiped his forehead with his sleeve.

"How bad is he?" Jenny stood behind him with his rifle in her hand. Matt saw the same anger on her flushed face that he felt on his own.

"What a goddamn waste." He stared at the calf and shook his head. "Broken legs."

Behind him, Jenny sucked in air. "Step out of the way, Matt."

He wrapped his fingers around the rifle barrel. "I'll do it."

She stiffened, didn't loosen her grip on the weapon. "It's my job."

"Listen, it's a real shitty thing killing an animal this young." His fingers turned white on the barrel of the gun. "Give me the gun."

She trained her serious eyes on him, unflinching, and said, "That's one of my calves. I'll do it."

The air whistled out between his teeth. He nodded and let go. She was right. It was her job. In the past, he'd never seen Jenny shirk her duties, or shy away from the hard stuff. He didn't remember ever seeing her shoot anything, though.

Jenny pulled the gun away from him.

"Call the ranch and see who can ride out here to fix that fence on the road."

While he pulled his cell phone out of his pocket and punched in the number, Matt watched her chest rise when she filled her lungs, held her breath and sighted down the barrel of the rifle.

The calf lifted his head and sent one pitiful *maa* Jenny's way.

The barrel wavered, then straightened.

The gunshot echoed in the dry sunshine. Startled

birds flew out of the trees. A rabbit charged across the field.

It took only the one shot.

Jenny lowered the rifle as if it weighed every one of that calf's three hundred pounds, her face pale.

"You want to sit down for a minute?" Matt touched her elbow.

"I'm fine." She stared at the calf. "This part never gets easy, does it?"

She turned away, hung the rifle back in its holder in the truck's cab and climbed into the driver's seat. She maneuvered the truck around until the back sat a couple of feet away from the calf. Matt jumped into the bed and spread out a blue tarpaulin.

He handed Jenny another tarp that she spread on the ground behind the young animal.

In one brief glimpse, Matt noted sadness on her face, but she got to work, grabbing the broken hind legs of the calf.

They lifted, pushed and pulled the carcass onto the tarpaulin. Jenny grunted, low in her throat. After they finally managed to wrestle it onto the back of the truck, he closed and locked the tailgate.

Jenny stood beside him, panting, sweat beading on the freckles across her nose and cheeks.

Damn, she was strong.

Damned if he didn't want to take her in his arms to comfort her. She wasn't okay, but neither was she falling apart. She was just getting the job done as well as he or Angus would have. He felt something rise in his chest, something soft, and realized it was pride. He tried to shake it off—she wasn't his—but he couldn't.

He wanted to reach for her, not for comfort now, but

for one hell of a kiss to show her how proud he was. He shoved his hands into his back pockets.

Matt stared at her, but her gaze never wavered.

"Get in." Her tone held a trace of flint.

He tapped her door, then ran around the truck and jumped in.

They found six pairs of cows and calves wandering the road, including the calf's mother. A hundred other pairs grazed contentedly in the pasture.

"This'll be hard on her," Jenny said as she stepped out of the truck. "That calf's twin died at birth. She's alone now."

She whistled and shouted, "Go on, back into the field," herding them on one side while Matt controlled the other, until the cows were back where they belonged.

Matt straightened the fence as best he could. "They can still get out, but they won't. Not as long as the fence looks sturdy." He turned to her with a grin, needing to make her feel better, but her answering smile was pained.

"Do you mind taking the groceries back to the ranch?" She looked away from him and raised a hand to shade her eyes, studying the sun-drenched field.

"Where are you going?" he asked.

"I'm going to walk across the fields. Make sure the cows are all right. I'll be okay."

"Sure. Do the Eriksons still take dead cattle?"

"Yeah. Cam pays good money. Can you get the calf there?"

"Will do. See you at the ranch."

He watched her start her walk home. In the distance, a couple of men rode four-wheelers toward her. Will and Hip, maybe. They'd take care of fixing that fence properly.

Matt drove over to the Eriksons' and left the carcass there. Cam wrote a check to Angus for the meat.

Once at the ranch, Matt backed the truck up to the door of the stable to rinse it out with the hose. He sprayed the bed and the tarpaulin until every trace of blood was gone. He washed the dirty red water away from the yard and into a field. He threw the rag he'd used into the garbage then leaned against the big utility sink inside the stable, his fingers gripping the edge.

THE SUN BEAT DOWN on Jenny's back, overheating her through her plaid shirt. Her eyes felt as if they had a sandbox full of grit in them.

Still, she trudged up the hill, trying to get emotional fallout from the incident out of her system so she wouldn't cry in front of the men. Why was she so weak?

Living in a man's world was tough. She had to work twice as hard to measure up. She knew any number of the ranch hands would have found that difficult, but none would have shed a tear. She didn't want to, she wouldn't, but her chest hurt from the strain of holding sobs in.

Give yourself a break, Jen, you just shot a calf while he stared up at you with trust in his eyes.

Oh, God, those eyes. Maybe I should have tried—

There was nothing you could do. The animal had four broken legs. You saw a lot of pain in those eyes, too.

The argument went around and around in her mind during the walk home.

When she reached the top of the rise that overlooked

the ranch house, she sat down heavily. A long shaky breath escaped her.

She plucked a blade of grass and tore it apart.

Soon, very soon, she would see all her dreams realized.

The day Dad had declared bankruptcy, she'd thought those dreams had died—of her children running across this land, of a husband she would love passionately, of annual barbecues with friends and family gathered around, of sunset rides with her husband and children and surveying the fields they'd tilled and planted themselves, watching their cattle grow big and healthy like their children, reaping the rewards of hard work.

After they'd lost the ranch, her family had gone to live in town. Six months later, her parents were in a car accident and her mother had been killed. Her dad survived his injuries but went into a decline that took his life a year later.

After that, the girl who'd known her place on earth, whose connection to her home and land had been profound, had become an unwilling nomad.

The first foster home hadn't been anywhere near Ordinary. She'd fought that first home hard and had kept fighting until subsequent homes had brought her closer and closer to town. She didn't stop until she was old enough to work on the Sheltering Arms.

A sigh so deep it seemed to start in the soles of her feet escaped her.

C'mon, Jen, time to go home. You did all right today.

She needed to see Jesse, to be with her son. His sweetness and high spirits never failed to lift her own. She hadn't planned to be a single mom, but she was doing her best to love him enough for two parents.

Angus helped. Soon, for all intents and purposes, he would be Jesse's father.

Matt wouldn't stay. Sure, she'd defended him in town, but she knew better than to expect much from him. Certainly not as a parent.

She stood to walk down the hill for dinner.

A cloud passed over the sun. Jenny saw rain on the horizon.

"WHATCHA DOIN'?"

Matt turned from brushing Master toward the small voice behind him. Jesse stood on the third rail on the outside of the corral fence, hanging from the top railing by his armpits. He banged his palms on the inside of the fence, trying to get Master's attention.

Matt watched him as though he was some kind of alien. Matt had dealt with a lot of children the years he'd worked at the Sheltering Arms and had never felt like this—tongue-tied and inadequate.

"Doesn't that hurt your underarms?" Matt pointed his chin toward the kid.

"Nope," Jesse chirped. "I do it all the time."

"What're you doing here?" Matt brought the brush down on Master's dark back. The horse preened under the rasp of bristles across his hide. "Don't you have school or something?"

"I'm too young for school." The boy looked at Matt as if he had a horseshoe for a brain. Where this kid was concerned, he probably did.

Where he'd been easy with the children on the Sheltering Arms, enjoying their antics, he was afraid of saying or doing something wrong with this one.

"What's your horse's name?" the boy asked.

"Masterpiece."

The kid bobbed on his feet, onto his toes, then down on his heels. Up. Down. Up. Down.

"You're going to ruin the heels of those boots if you're not careful." Did he just sound like a father? Weird.

"I do this all the time. My mom lets me."

"Yeah?" He couldn't help it, had to ask, "You like your mom?" Matt felt sneaky for asking, but he was curious. He'd seen signs of maturity in her. Were they real?

"Uh-huh."

"What's she like?"

"Nice. She lets me go to Hank's all the time." He climbed up to the second railing, placed his hands on the top one and lifted his feet away from the fence, balancing himself on his palms. "She let me keep a frog I found."

"That right? A frog?"

"His name's Bucket."

Matt smothered a laugh. "Where'd he get a name like Bucket?"

Jesse tilted his head. "I brought him home in a bucket."

He climbed to the top railing and sat facing Matt, hooking his boot heels onto the second railing. "I got a fish, too."

Matt turned to him and said, "Yeah? What's his name? Bowl? Tank?" but the boy wasn't listening. He was staring at Matt's belt buckle with his mouth wide open.

"What did you get that for, mister?"

"Rodeo." Matt returned to grooming his horse.

"I'm gonna rodeo when I grow up. Can you teach me how, mister?"

Matt wasn't a mister, he was a father, but Jesse wasn't allowed to know that.

Jenny probably wouldn't want him to teach the boy anything, to get that close to him. Maybe he should to spite her. She should have told him about his son.

What would you have done about it? If you're this awkward with him as a four-year-old, how would you have felt holding him as an infant?

Matt set the brush on the top railing beside Jesse. Up close, the deep blue of the boy's eyes were shot through with small flecks of golden honey, like the warm yellow flecks in Jenny's eyes. First likeness to Jenny Matt recognized in the boy aside from the freckles.

He stared, having trouble taking in that this tyke was a mixture of him and Jenny, that Jesse was the result of that one night.

"Watch!" the boy said then twisted himself onto his abdomen on the top railing, sticking his arms and legs straight out, balancing on nothing but his flat little stomach.

"Hey," Matt yelled and grabbed him under the arms, hauling him up and setting him on his feet outside the corral. "You're too old to be doing something that dumb."

His pulse was racing. Damn. The kid had the same streak of recklessness Jenny used to have. It was in the genes.

Jesse got a stubborn look and tilted his head. "What's so dumb about it?"

"You could fall off and crack your head open."

"No, I won't. I like doing it. It's fun."

"Too bad."

"I can do it if I want to."

"Not while I'm around you can't."

"You're mean." Jesse stamped his foot and ran off. "I don't like you, mister."

Wow, those words had never hurt so much. Some of the kids at Hank's had been sour and reeling from the unlucky shit life had dealt them in the form of cancer and, most times, poverty. He'd been called plenty of things before they learned to settle in and have fun.

It had never bothered him then, but it sure did now coming from Jesse.

"Yeah, well, tough," Matt called to Jesse's retreating back.

Mature, Long. Real mature.

He saw Jenny standing near the house. Crap. She'd heard him.

She stormed toward him like a mother lion with claws bared. "What did you say to Jesse?"

"I told him he couldn't balance on his stomach on top of the fence or he'd fall off and break his skull open," Matt retorted. He'd been right to stop the kid, dammit.

"Oh," Jenny said, and the starch left her spine. "Okay, thanks. That's good."

Later that day, he saw Jenny trying to force Jesse to ride and Jesse resisting. Again.

Leave it alone. It's none of your business.

Jenny had made that clear.

He's your child, too.

As Jesse ran from the barn crying, Matt thought, *Yeah, I understand what you're going through, kid.*

Matt entered the stable.

JENNY PRESSED her forehead against Flora's hide and bit her tongue. She'd tried to get Jesse to ride again only to have it end in tears—again.

They lived in ranching country and always would. It was unthinkable that a boy would grow up on a ranch and not learn how to ride, but she'd run out of patience.

She'd been at this for a year, bashing her head against the wall of Jesse's resistance. She couldn't do it much longer.

"Why doesn't he want to ride?"

Jenny heard Matt's voice behind her and closed her eyes. Did he always have to hear her failing with Jesse? What about all the times they had fun together, all the times he was warm and sweet and fun instead of recalcitrant?

"A kid of yours should have been born in the saddle," Matt said. "He looks fearless on that jungle gym in the backyard."

"He is," she agreed. As much as she still wanted to limit his exposure to Jesse, she might as well just tell him. Maybe he'd think her less of a failure as a mother if he understood. "The first time he got up on the pony, he was only three, but he loved it."

"What happened?"

"A storm blew in. Before the rain hit, I was leading Jesse into the stable when a crack of thunder came out of nowhere."

Jenny lifted the pony's saddle from her back. Jesse wouldn't be riding today. "It startled a mouse out of a pile of straw, who scooted under Flora's hooves and spooked her. She reared and tossed Jesse on the ground."

A quirky lift of one corner of Matt's mouth had her asking, "What?"

"Flora?"

She smiled. "Yes, *Flora.*"

Matt turned serious again. "Too many things happened together, I guess."

Jenny nodded. "Exactly. Now Jesse's afraid of horses and thunder."

"Can I try?" Matt asked.

No freaking way. "No."

"Why not? He's my child, too."

She took a brush and started in on grooming Flora. "I won't have you making friends with him and then running off."

"I'm going to whether you like it or not."

"Run off?" she snapped sarcastically. It was a good thing Flora liked to be brushed hard. "Yeah, I know."

Matt flushed. "I meant that I would get to know him, not that I'd leave."

Jenny stopped brushing and said quietly, "But you will do that, too."

She knew he couldn't deny it. She watched him try to come up with the right words, but they both knew Matt wasn't a guarantee-giving kind of guy.

She wanted guarantees for her child. Angus was a man who could give her those and never back out of them.

Matt's lips twisted and he stared out the door to where Jesse was sitting in the sunlight with his arms and legs crossed and his bottom lip sticking out. "All right, listen. I had the same problem with horses when I was little."

Matt? "You did? I find that hard to believe."

"Yeah. You'd never know it now. I came to like horses."

THIS COWBOY'S SON

"Like" was an understatement. She thought of the joy on his face when he'd ridden past her during their impromptu race yesterday. It had been stunning what that joy had done to her, stirring long-forgotten feelings. They used to have so much fun racing.

It also stirred the urges she'd developed toward him in adolescence.

He'd ruined it minutes later with his insult, though. Thank God. She had no right nurturing those kinds of feelings for Matt.

"Can you remember why you were afraid?"

"My dad. He shoved me on his own horse too early. Dad didn't believe in starting small on ponies. The guy was all about trial by fire."

"How did you get over it?"

"Funny thing. Dad put that fear there, and then forced it out of me. Made me ride every day, rain or shine, fear or not. One day, I finally saw the light when the horse took off across a flat field and wouldn't stop. Somewhere on that ride, the pleasure took hold."

"I'll only use so much force on Jesse," Jenny said. "Then I'll quit." She walked away.

MATT SWORE up and down that he would get to know Jesse whether the boy liked him or not, whether Matt knew how to deal with him or not. He was finished work for the day and found Jesse, in the kitchen with Angela.

"Angela," Matt said. "Is it okay if I take Jesse outside?"

"Sure. He'd like that." Angela smiled. "Jenny won't be back for an hour."

Matt turned to Jesse. "Do you want to learn how to rope a calf?"

"Yeah!" Jesse jumped up from the table where he'd been cutting cookies out of raw dough for the housekeeper. He ran for the door.

"Just a minute." Matt stopped him with a hand on his shoulder. "Wash your hands first."

"I don't got to."

"Have to," Matt corrected.

"No, I don't."

"C'mon, kid." Matt steered him down the hall to the powder room and squirted soap into his hands. "Now, wash."

When he realized Matt was serious, Jesse did what he was told. Matt remembered how the guest kids on the Sheltering Arms had tested limits. Seemed that kind of thing was universal.

Now that he knew he couldn't push Matt around, Jesse was fine. Matt laughed to himself. How long would it last? An hour?

As it turned out, it lasted half that long.

There wasn't a single kid-size rope on the ranch. Jesse wore out real quick trying to use a full-size rope, leaving them both irritated and on edge.

Finally, Matt said, "That's enough for today."

Jesse ran for the house and Matt strode to the bunkhouse and flopped onto his bed.

How was he supposed to get to know his son when they had so much trouble connecting and Matt didn't have a clue why?

He'd *never* had this problem with kids before.

Matt punched his pillow.

He refused to quit.

CHAPTER SEVEN

THE THIRD TIME Matt witnessed Jenny try to get Jesse on a horse, he'd had enough.

She walked from the stable carefully, like someone who was trying to hold on to her temper really hard, leaving Jesse to sulk in a corner.

Enough was enough. That kid had it in him to ride.

By hook or crook, whether Jesse and he got along today or not, Matt was going to teach his son how to ride.

Jenny doesn't want you involved. Too bad. The kid was his, too.

He approached Jesse, leading Flora down the aisle, and squatted in front of him.

"Hey," he said.

"Hey," Jesse mumbled, picking at a scab on his elbow.

"Don't you like horses?"

"I like 'em. I don't want to ride 'em."

"I know what part of the problem is."

Jesse's head popped up. "You do?"

"Sure. It's your pony's name."

"Really?"

"Sure. How can any pony be happy with a name like Flora? It's too old-fashioned and flowery." What a load of crap. That made no sense at all, but Matt didn't know what else to say.

"It is?"

"Yup. We need to rename her. Give her a sense of pride so she won't go tossing kids on their butts. What would be a good name?"

"Buttercup?" Matt almost laughed out loud—another flower name—but Jesse was dead serious. "I got a book. The horse is named Buttercup."

"You like that book?"

Jesse nodded so hard a lock of hair fell onto his forehead. "A lot! Buttercup wears a hat with holes cut out for her ears and she really likes it."

"There's an idea. Maybe if we make Flora—I mean, Buttercup, happier, it'll be easier to ride her. Let's go."

"Where to?"

"To find a hat we can use."

Matt turned and walked away, not giving Jesse a chance to resist. He left Flora in the corral and walked through the gate without looking back. A second later, the boy followed.

Curiosity had won out.

In the bunkhouse, Matt found an ancient brown cowboy hat on a hook and hoped like hell it wasn't somebody's treasure, because he was about to give it to a horse.

Jesse followed him back to the corral, taking Matt's hand along the way. Matt looked down. Jesse's hand looked incredibly small in his, felt impossibly tiny. He couldn't believe his own had ever been that small.

Matt held the hat up to Flora's head and eyeballed the distance between her ears.

He pulled a multi-tool out of his pocket and used the knife to cut into the hat.

"Let me see," Jesse cried.

Matt squatted and Jesse put one hand on his sleeve. Matt felt the heat of it through his shirt and it warmed more than just his skin. That heat traveled through his veins to lodge in his heart for good.

Fruit of my loins. Shit, how corny was that? But Matt couldn't get over that this little guy had started as a seed too small for the eye to see. Molded in Matt's own image.

No, kid, don't become me. Become a better man than me.

What had Jenny said about Angus?

He's the better man.

She might as well have ripped Matt's heart from his chest, but he couldn't deny the truth. Angus was the better man.

But Jesse was *Matt's* son.

Whether Matt could bring himself to stay or not, this was a forever moment. He swallowed hard. Not one thing in his life had ever felt as good as his son's touch.

Jesse left his hand there and watched patiently as Matt finished cutting two holes for ears.

He stood to place it on the pony's head then thought better of it. Instead, he scooped Jesse up into his arms and gave him the hat.

Jesse set it on Flora's head. Matt helped to push her ears through.

"There you go, Buttercup," Jesse said.

Flora shied away and tried to shake off the hat.

Jesse's lower lip jutted out. "She doesn't like it."

"Wait," Matt said. He stroked Flora's nose and crooned to her. "Beautiful girl. Aren't you pretty?"

He felt Jesse staring at him and explained, "That's how you talk to horses when you want them to do something. Try it."

Jesse stuck out his hand and touched Flora's nose. "Pretty girl," he mimicked.

Still Flora tried to shake off the hat.

Matt pulled a caramel out of his pocket. He unwrapped it and handed it to Jesse. "Here. Try this."

Jesse held the candy out and Flora sniffed it. When she lifted it eagerly from Jesse's palm, the boy giggled.

"That tickles. Look! She likes it."

As she rolled the treat on her tongue, Flora settled down and stopped fighting the hat. She butted Matt's breast pocket looking for another caramel.

Jesse laughed.

"Tell her she can have another one after she gives you a ride."

Again, Jesse mimicked Matt's earlier crooning and repeated his words.

"Okay. Let's get you up on Flora's back."

"She's Buttercup!"

"Right. Buttercup. Listen, that's a mouthful. Can we call her Butter? Like a nickname?"

"'Kay. That's a good name."

Matt lifted him, but Jesse pulled up his legs. "Hey," Matt said, "I'm not going to let go."

"Honest?" Jesse whispered.

"Honest."

Jesse lowered his legs and settled into the small saddle.

Matt wrapped his arm around Jesse's waist and Jesse

placed his arm across Matt's shoulders. It didn't quite reach his far shoulder and was light across Matt's back.

They walked around the corral like that, countless times, until Matt felt Jesse's resistance start to give way, felt him relax and enjoy the ride.

He stared at the smile on Jesse's face. Who would have thought walking in circles beside his son on a horse could bring Matt so much pleasure?

"Can I ride by myself now?"

"You sure you want to?"

Jesse nodded.

Matt taught him how to hold the reins properly and how to control his horse.

With Jesse's expression a mixture of fear and excitement, Matt let go. Jesse continued his circuits around the corral with a big grin on his face.

The sense of pride Matt felt nearly knocked him off his feet. In the vastness of the world, Jesse had just accomplished a small feat, but for Jesse it was huge— *huge*—and Matt couldn't hold back his own grin.

Man, his eyes felt damp. How crazy was that? Dad had beaten into him that a man never cries, but at this moment, Matt didn't give a damn.

He wanted to teach Jesse more things, and give him stuff, the kinds of toys he'd always wanted as a child. Not all the new electronic gadgetry like iPods and computers that kids had these days, but simple tools like compasses and binoculars and maybe a telescope.

Hey, a bow and a quiver of arrows would be great. Matt could teach Jesse how to shoot at a target.

Did Angus still have his iron horseshoes? They would probably be too heavy for Jesse to lift. He might be able to toss quoits, though.

Matt's brain wouldn't quit.

JENNY CLOSED HER EYES and leaned her forehead on the living room windowpane.

She'd just watched Matt do what she hadn't been able to do with Jesse in the past year. How? By putting a hat on the pony? What was that about?

Jenny pounded her head a couple of times against the glass. She didn't want this happening.

This was exactly what she had been afraid of.

Jesse was falling for his dad, so much faster than Jenny could have predicted. Maybe she should pack a bag for herself and Jesse and go away until her wedding day, pull one of Matt's own tricks on him. Run away.

That would be cruel, though, to Matt and probably to Jesse.

Angus entered the room. "What are you doing?"

Jenny lifted her face away from the glass. "Matt just taught Jesse how to ride Flora."

"Really? How'd he manage that when the rest of us couldn't?"

"I don't know, but it has something to do with putting a cowboy hat on Flora."

"What?"

"Look."

Angus stood beside her and she leaned into his warmth.

"I'll be damned," Angus said.

"I'm scared," Jenny whispered. She looked up into his sympathetic face. "They're bonding, Angus. What happens when he leaves?"

Angus stared out the window, not appearing to be totally happy.

"How do you feel about Matt getting to know his

son?" she asked. He was involved in this, too. Angus was expecting to be Jesse's dad after they got married.

"It's good. It's the way it should be."

"Oh, Angus, you're always so fair. Doesn't it worry you that Matt might replace you in Jesse's heart?"

Angus didn't answer for a while then said, speaking low, "Maybe."

ANGUS DIDN'T KNOW what to feel. He watched two generations out there—Matt, his surrogate son, and Jesse, his almost son—and missed Kyle and the chance to have his own grandchildren. He could have more children with Jenny and raise brothers and sisters for Jesse, and then have grandchildren many years from now.

But Matt. Where would he fit in?

Angus strode from the house and walked to his car. He needed to sort out his feelings.

When Matt saw him, he called Angus over to the fence, his face alight with the kind of excitement he'd never seen there when Matt was younger.

"Are you heading into town?" Matt asked.

Angus nodded. He couldn't speak to Matt right now, not until he figured out what was wrong, why he couldn't be happy for Matt.

Pulling a hundred bucks out of his wallet, Matt handed it to Angus. It looked as if that cleaned him out. "Can you pick up a pair of binoculars for Jesse? If you can't find any in Ordinary, can you get me a compass instead?"

Angus silently tucked the money into his pocket.

"Hey," Matt said. "Do you still have that telescope of Kyle's?"

Angus nodded.

"Can I borrow it tonight?"

"Sure. It's in Kyle's closet. Help yourself."

He had no intention of going in there and hunting it out for Matt. Angus hadn't entered Kyle's room since his death.

He got into his car, anxious to get away from the heartwarming scene of the burgeoning relationship between Matt and Jesse. Even the reasonable thought that Matt deserved it did nothing to allay Angus's new irrational jealousy.

JENNY AND MATT STARTED cleaning the pile of trash that had accumulated on the far side of the barn beside the workshop door—bald tires, lengths of rusted wire, part of a stove, a dented truck fender and the list went on. It would take more than one afternoon to clear it out.

Since both of the ranch's trucks were out, they tossed the refuse into Matt's pickup to haul to the dump.

The entire time, Jesse followed Matt, imitating everything he did. Matt had already outfitted the boy with a too-big pair of work gloves like his own. When he'd pushed Jesse's tiny hands into them, it had just about melted his heart.

This was good. Too good.

By dinnertime, the truck bed was full to overflowing and they'd made decent progress on the pile. Jesse insisted on following Matt to the bunkhouse while he washed up and changed into clean clothes for dinner.

Matt walked to the house with his hand on Jesse's small shoulder, then, like a real father, sent him upstairs to change and wash his hands.

Later Matt followed Jenny into the kitchen with Kyle's old telescope in his hand.

"I know he would love it," he said. "What kid wouldn't?"

Jenny rinsed the glass she'd been using and set it in the sink. Jesse had hung around with Matt for the rest of the afternoon and evening, following him like a truncated shadow. Now Matt wanted to take him out past his bedtime to lie in the grass and look at the stars.

Things were moving too quickly.

"He's still young. I keep him to a schedule."

"So what? He can break it for one night."

Jenny spun to face him. "Listen, I've been his mother for four years. I know what he needs and what he can do without for a while."

Matt pushed one hand into his pocket and stared at her. "I missed those four years. I want to make up for them now."

Jenny knew she'd robbed him and guilt ate away at her, gnawed its way through her stomach lining. That he'd spoken the words quietly instead of in anger made her feel even worse.

"Okay," she said. "But only for tonight. Tomorrow he goes to bed at his regular time."

"Sure," Matt said too lightly.

"Promise?"

"Promise."

Jenny wondered how much Matt Long's promises were worth these days.

"I'll get you a couple of blankets."

"Blankets? It's May."

"Exactly. The evenings are still cool and Jesse will get cold lying on the ground."

"Fine. Whatever. Can we just get them and go?"

Matt was behaving like an eager boy. This parent-

ing business was all new to him. What would happen
when the novelty wore off? What would happen when
he had to be a real parent, to use discipline when Jesse
acted up, or nurse him when he got sick? When he had
to do the work and not just the play?

Now he was having fun. What about when that fun
stopped? What then, Matthew Long?

UPSTAIRS, MATT TOOK the pair of heavy blankets that
Jenny handed him, then ran downstairs to tell Jesse
what they were going to do.

Jesse squealed and ran for the back door.

Jenny ran to Kyle's old bedroom at the rear of the
house and opened the window in time to hear Jesse say
outside in the yard, "Here, Matt, here's a good spot."

Compelled to watch everything that Matt did with
her son, she left the lights off so there would be no re-
flections on the glass. So she wouldn't miss anything.

Matt spread the blankets and lay down on them.
Jesse lay down beside him, tucking his small hip against
Matt's side.

Don't, Jenny thought, *don't get close to him.*

Matt put his arm under Jesse's head and adjusted
the telescope for him. He held it while Jesse looked
through the lens.

"Wow, look! The moon is real big."

"See all the stars?"

Jesse grabbed the telescope and moved it around
wildly.

"Whoa," Matt said, taking it back. "Let me find some
for you."

He pointed straight up. "Know what those stars are?"

"What?" Jesse asked.

"The Milky Way." Matt focused the telescope, then handed it back to Jesse, holding it steady.

"Can you see stars now?"

"Yeah, but they just look like lights. They don't look like the pointy stars on the Christmas tree."

"No, they don't, do they?"

"Show me more, Matt."

Jenny watched Matt show her son more stars. She wished she was down there with them, but she hadn't been invited, and her guilt had prevented her from asking. She wanted to lie on her son's other side, tuck him against her body instead of Matt's, keep him safe in the world she'd created for him and planned to cement with her marriage to Angus.

She heard Matt say, "I'll teach you about all of the stars."

No! Jenny's blood surged through her veins. She barely held herself back from leaning out the window and yelling at Matt to stop making promises he probably wouldn't keep.

A few minutes later Matt took the telescope from Jesse. Even from up here, Jenny could tell that he'd fallen asleep.

Matt watched him sleep, stared at Jesse's small head tucked against his shoulder. In the light spilling from the kitchen window, Jenny saw Matt touch Jesse's hair, run it through his fingers with reverence.

He stayed there for a long time, watching his son sleep.

Jenny remained at her post at the window, watching a quiet scene that nearly broke her heart. This was the way it should have been all along.

Eventually, Matt picked up Jesse and brought him inside.

Jenny ran to the top of the stairs and waited.

Matt appeared at the bottom with Jesse curled in his arms like a trusting little puppy. When he reached the top Jenny reached out to take him, but Matt shook his head.

"Show me his room."

No. He's mine.

Jenny led the way to the front of the house and opened a door. She'd painted his room light blue and his furniture every color of the rainbow. Matt laid him on the bed and Jenny moved to take off his clothes, but Matt brushed her aside.

"I'll do it."

That's my job. "I'll get his pajamas."

"No, I will. I want to know where his stuff is."

Jenny pointed to the top drawer of his dresser.

Matt undressed their son and looked around for a laundry basket. Jenny gestured to the plastic bucket sitting below the fake basketball net she'd hung on the back of his door. Usually, Jesse threw his clothes through the net and, when he got lucky and actually got one in, it dropped through into the laundry bucket.

Matt smiled and tossed the clothes into the bucket.

He dressed Jesse's tiny body in the pajamas then tucked him under his blankets.

When he leaned over and kissed his forehead, the scene was so sweetly tender that Jenny didn't know whether she wanted to kiss Matt or give him a boot in the rear end.

Those were all *her* jobs, not his. Jesse was *her* son. But that was unfair. He was Matt's son, too.

Jenny turned on a small night-light and closed the door behind them, leaving a gap in case he needed her during the night.

"He didn't brush his teeth." Her tone was faintly censorious.

"Does he brush them every night? And every morning? Is he pretty good at doing it, or do you have to get on his case about it?"

He'd been pestering her with questions all evening and she was tired of it.

"Matt, I'm heading to bed."

She walked down the hall to her room. Just before closing the door, she caught him watching her. He looked…lost.

She hardened her heart and tried not to feel sorry for him. She had her own unruly emotions to sort through.

IN THE DAYS that followed, Jesse trailed Matt everywhere. Jenny felt as though she'd lost her son, or at least had lost some of her control over him.

Jenny had to force him to stay with Angela for a few hours every day so she and Matt could get work done.

They finished clearing out the junk pile and Matt took three loads to the dump.

They delivered salt blocks to the bulls, who craved it and thundered over. This, plus the minerals laid out by the crew all winter, would keep the cattle healthy.

They oiled and greased all of the ranch equipment, including two big Caterpillars used to shovel manure, earth or snow, depending on the weather.

One morning they took over driving out to the fields to feed the cattle while the crew started early on the fencing that needed to be finished.

As ranch foreman, Jenny spent hours on solitary rides on horseback or in a truck, checking up on the crew and the land, and trying to anticipate problems. It was strange to have Matt around so much and it left her feeling distracted and confused.

Angus became broody and spent more time away from the house, sometimes riding his land and sometimes in town, she guessed. She didn't know for sure. Jenny worried about him, and wondered what was going on in his head.

One night, Matt wanted to take Jesse to sleep in the bunkhouse with him.

Jenny fought it, but Jesse begged her to let him and, along with Matt's pressure, it was more than she could resist.

"Okay," she finally said. "I'll pack him a bag."

"Pack him a bag?" Matt's tone was incredulous. "We're only going to the bunkhouse on the other side of the barn."

"I know, but routine is important to children his age. He needs his toothbrush and his bedtime story."

To Jesse, she said, "Go pick one of your books for Matt to read to you before bed."

While Jesse chose a book, rummaging on his bookshelves until he found the one he wanted, she packed a toothbrush, toothpaste, his pajamas and a bathrobe in case he got cold during the night.

"Hey, Matt," Jesse hollered downstairs, "I'm bringing Buttercup's story. 'Kay?"

"Sounds good," Matt called up.

So that was where he'd gotten the new name for Flora. Butter. Part of Buttercup. And the hat. Jenny had forgotten all about that book.

Jesse ran down ahead of her. "I think I packed everything he'll need," she said.

Matt smoothed a frown from her forehead. "Stop worrying."

It was the first time he'd touched her deliberately since he'd come back, and the scrape of his callus felt good. She shivered and pulled away from him, too abruptly, judging by his frown, but she couldn't worry about his feelings. She needed to keep her distance.

"I'm not worried."

"Liar." Matt grinned. He and Jesse were the only two who seemed cheerful these days.

They left the house and Jenny felt lost. Angus was out somewhere again. Her footsteps rang hollow on the hardwood floors.

She turned on the TV, flipped through the channels and switched it back off. Nothing but junk.

She ran a scented bubble bath and tried to read a romance novel. That lasted half an hour.

After she dried off and spread her favorite cream on her skin, she pampered herself with a manicure and pedicure, a rarity. Hank's wife, Amy, had taught her how to take care of her nails properly, but most of the time, this stuff was a luxury.

Finally, all out of things to do, she climbed into bed and turned off the light.

Sleep refused to come.

ANGUS SAT IN HIS CAR across the road from Moira's shop, thinking about what-ifs and should-have-beens.

He watched a shadow he knew to be Moira cross in front of the window above the shop in the only room with a lamp burning. She lived up there. Had when she was young, with her mother.

He'd wanted to try again to talk to her about his crazy, jumbled feelings, but realized as soon as he'd arrived that meeting her up there, in her apartment, would be an enormous mistake.

A warm light shone in the room, filtered through the closed curtains. So she still used the same bedroom she had when she was young.

The light went out.

He tucked his palms under his thighs and listened to the gentle patter of rain on the roof of the car, staring at a dark window that matched the emptiness in his heart.

Moira.

MATT HAD BEEN TRYING for over an hour to get Jesse settled down in the bed beside his, but the other ranch hands were playing cards at the far end of the bunkhouse. He'd already told them Jesse was his son. They'd taken it in stride.

Jesse's head shot up at every remark, every question, every game won or lost.

Jenny had been right. This was a terrible idea. Still, in for a penny...

He read *Buttercup's Favorite Hat* for the tenth time, then turned off the light for the tenth time. The only other lights on were over by the card game, and for Jesse's sake, the boys had turned on just enough to see their hands.

Matt tucked the covers around Jesse and kissed his clean, soap-scented forehead. For the tenth time.

"Now, stay put and go to sleep."

Matt lay down in the semidarkness and stared at the ceiling.

"Matt?" Jesse said. He sounded sleepy. At last.

"Yeah?"

"I love you."

My God. Dear God. Matt had had no idea how this would feel, to hear his child's sweet high voice murmur that he loved his dad. And Matt was that dad, even if Jesse didn't know it yet.

Matt drifted off to sleep on a high.

He was awakened by a massive crack of thunder and Jesse screaming, "Mommy! Mommy!"

"You okay?" one of the ranch hands mumbled to Jesse.

"I got him," Matt answered. He picked up Jesse, hugged him and rubbed his back. "Hey, it's okay, partner. It's just a little thunder."

"It's dark in here." Uncertainty and tears shook Jesse's voice.

"Yeah, that's how the ranch hands like to sleep."

"I want my mo-o-om," Jesse said, sobbing.

"You sure? She's probably asleep."

"I want her."

He sounded so miserable, Matt couldn't deny him. Maybe if Matt could get Jesse to sleep in his own bed, he wouldn't awaken Jenny.

"Something smells stinky in here," Jesse said, calmer now that he knew he'd see his mom.

"One of the guys farted."

"Mine don't smell like that."

"You weren't drinking beer tonight."

"Beer makes farts stinky?"

"It's been known to."

"I'm never gonna drink beer in my whole life."

"Want to bet?"

Matt heard someone chuckle, then roll over.

He pulled Jesse's robe on over his pajamas, slipped his own boots on and covered both their heads with a raincoat from beside the door.

Then he ran out into the night. Rain pounded on the coat as they crossed the yard.

Matt entered the house just as a furry pink thing threw herself at him and Jesse.

Jenny.

"What's wrong?" she cried. "Jesse, are you okay? What happened?"

"Nothing serious," Matt answered. "Thunder woke him."

Jenny grabbed Jesse and squeezed him.

Matt shook the rain off the coat and hung it on a hook by the door.

"Mom," Jesse said, but it came out muffled since Jenny had his face crushed against her chest. Her soft, braless chest. Her very nice chest.

"I can't breathe," Jesse said, and Jenny eased her grip. Cripes, you'd think she'd never had the kid out of her sight before. Did she always worry when Jesse was away from her? Or only when Jesse was with him?

"How'd you know we were coming over here?" Matt asked.

"I heard the bunkhouse door close."

"Really? Over the thunder and the rain?" Mother's ears must be better than normal people's. "Did the thunder wake you, too?"

"I wasn't asleep."

Matt followed them up the stairs and down the hall

to Jesse's room, hoping to tuck Jesse in and kiss him good-night again. He couldn't get enough of the normal stuff that most parents no doubt took for granted.

Another crack of thunder shook the house and Jesse wailed and reached for his mother. "I want to sleep with you."

"Okay, come on, sweetie."

Matt trailed along behind them to Jenny's room, curious. What was her room like? How was it decorated? With cowboy decals and wagon wheels? The thought gave him a chuckle.

When he walked into her bedroom, though, his mouth dropped open. He would never have taken Jenny for a lacy kind of girl, but there it was, on the bedspread and pillows scattered around the room and on the curtains. White lace everywhere.

Jenny set Jesse on the bed.

"I'm thirsty," he said while she wiped his tear-stained cheeks.

She turned to Matt. "Would you mind getting some water from the bathroom? The blue plastic cup is his."

Matt ran the water to get it cold, filled the cup and returned to the bedroom.

Jesse drank it down and Jenny placed it on the bedside table. She'd turned on a night-light plugged into an outlet near the door.

"Matt," Jesse said, "I need a good-night kiss."

Gladly.

Matt leaned over and kissed him, his small lips cool from the water, his breath smelling faintly of the popcorn they'd shared earlier in the bunkhouse.

Matt told him so.

"Don't tell Mom you putted butter on it," he whispered loudly enough for Jenny to hear every word. "She says it's just solid fat and clogs your arthuries."

Matt straightened and looked at her. Her hair was dark, shiny and bed mussed.

"Mommy, come into bed and Matt can kiss you good-night, too."

Jenny blushed. "No, I'll get in after Matt leaves."

Jesse patted the bed beside him. "Come on, it's okay. Matt's really nice. You'll like it."

Lord, so will I, Matt thought.

He watched her cheeks flame and wondered what she would do.

She brushed past him and climbed under the covers. Seemed she'd do just about anything for her son.

Matt put his hands on either side of her head and leaned toward her. She watched him cautiously, the hazel highlights of her irises glinting in the yellow lamplight.

Eyes wide open, he brushed his lips over hers.

Her lips were soft and moist, her skin scented with lilacs. He recognized that scent. He'd smelled it on her before.

It was the closest he'd been to her in five years and he suddenly realized how much he'd missed his friend.

She'd known him better than anyone else on this earth, starting from those times they'd met under the cotoneasters as kids, to talk about everything and anything, big and small.

He pulled away slowly.

"See, Mom?" his son said. "It's nice."

Yeah, so goddamn nice.

Matt stepped to the door and turned off the light, Jenny's eyes tracking his every move.

He left the two most important people in his life wrapped up cozily in her room and walked out of the house into the cold downpour. He'd forgotten the raincoat. Didn't dare go back in. If he did, he wouldn't leave a second time. He'd march back up the stairs and into that bedroom, sit on that flowered armchair in the corner and watch them sleep by the night-light until dawn.

As he entered the bunkhouse, headlights swung into the yard. Angus. Matt glanced at his watch. Three o'clock.

Where the hell had Angus been all night?

CHAPTER EIGHT

ON FRIDAY, Hank and Amy and their two kids came over. Jenny had already mentioned that Matt could take an hour off to visit with them.

Matt shook Hank's hand and kissed Amy's cheek. Man, it felt good to see them again. He was introduced to their children.

Matt watched Amy and Jenny bustle off upstairs with Jenny's wedding dress. He'd forgotten about the wedding.

One more week. Could he stay and watch Jenny and Angus get married and then live on the same ranch with them?

He had no choice. It would be months before he'd worked off all that he owed Angus for those taxes.

Jesse ran up to greet Michael, then they took off together. To Matt, they looked the same age.

Amy's daughter, Cheryl, trailed after her mother and Jenny. She looked to be younger than her brother, Michael. Like her mother, she was going to be a real beauty when she grew up.

Matt and Hank leaned on the veranda's posts and faced the Circle K yard.

"You ever have trouble saying no to that little girl?" Matt asked.

Hank grinned. "All the time. I have to be real careful with her."

Matt turned confused eyes on Hank. "I'm a father, Hank, and I don't know what the hell I'm doing."

"So she told you," Hank said.

Matt nodded.

"We never asked her about it," Hank went on, "but Amy and I always knew it had to be you. She'd started that dumb argument with Amy about you, had run off and you'd chased her. The next morning you left the ranch. Didn't take Einstein to figure out you were the father. Why'd you run, Matt?"

Matt let out a breath. "I'm no good at getting serious with women."

Hank squeezed Matt's shoulder. "I'm glad you're back now."

Matt stared after his son. "It's a big responsibility. Does it ever scare you?"

"Not usually. My kid-raising philosophy is pretty simple."

"Yeah? What is it?"

"Love them like there's no tomorrow," Hank said in his familiar rusty growl.

Matt listened intently, wanting to learn secrets from a man he'd always admired and respected.

"Let them know they are loved," Hank continued, "every minute of every day."

Hank stopped there.

"That's it?" Matt asked. There had to more to it than that.

"Uh-huh," Hank replied. "Any mistakes you make will even out in the end."

Matt nodded. He'd felt loved for the first few years of

his life, before everything had changed with his mother. What if the rest of it hadn't happened? What if Matt had felt loved every day and the only mistakes his parents had made were normal ones. Too strict. Too lax. Love would make up for a lot of mistakes.

He shoved his hands into his pockets. If only he could get rid of this damn yearning.

Hank's son, Michael, ran onto the veranda with Jesse. The boys were almost the same age, but Michael was tall, like his father. Amy must've gotten pregnant pretty soon after she married Hank. Their love for each other looked good, real good.

Matt was glad things had worked out the way they had. For a while, before Amy and Hank had realized how much they loved each other, Matt had been interested in Amy. It would have been a fling, nothing more. He couldn't do more.

Then he'd spent that night with Jenny and realized where his heart belonged and what kind of trouble that would cause. And he'd run.

"Dad, Jesse and me are going to play outside," Michael said. "'Kay?"

"Yeah, have fun." Hank mussed his son's hair.

Jesse stood beside Matt, looking up at him, expectant.

Finally, he said, "We're going outside, okay?"

"Sure," Matt said.

Still, the boy waited for something. Matt reached out his hand, tentative and wondering whether this was what Jesse wanted, and mussed his hair. A great big grin split Jesse's face, then he took off after Michael.

Matt's heart flipped over. Affection and tenderness

oozed through his body along with wonderment. What had he done to deserve this boy?

Matt got beers for himself and Hank and sat on the veranda, watching their sons run in the yard.

Matt told Hank about the calf incident.

"There's been some cattle rustling over in the next county," Hank said. "Everyone's on alert. Let Angus know."

"Sure. There's no shortage of dishonest people in the world, is there?"

"No." Hank took a swig of his beer then said, "I'm putting my hands out riding the perimeter of the ranch all weekend."

"Even on a Sunday?"

"Yep, prime time for them to hit. Sheriff Kavenagh wants everyone vigilant for the next few weeks."

"Damn rustlers," Matt said, but without force. The day was too sunny and the beer too cold to worry about much.

"Angus might want to do the same," Hank said. "He's got the wealthiest ranch around."

"So the ranch hands won't get any days off this week."

"Nope."

Hollering from out behind the barn made them run. Jesse and Michael were screaming like they were being killed.

When Matt rounded the back corner of the barn, he stopped and stared.

Both boys lay on their backs in the manure corral, yelling their lungs out and crying.

Matt hustled to the fence. "Jesse, stand up real slow."

Jesse thrashed in the manure, setting up an aroma that threatened to gag Matt.

"Careful!" he said. "Don't get any more of that stuff on you than you already have."

Both boys stood, slowly, trying not to put their hands down in the decomposing manure, hands that were already covered to the wrists.

Their feet made sucking noises with each step they took toward the fence. Not that they had far to walk.

"What the heck were you two thinking?" Hank growled.

"We were just walking on the fence," Michael said.

"Yeah," Jesse piped up. "Like on a tightrope."

Probably one of them had dared the other to do it and they'd both ended up walking the top railing. One had lost his balance and then thrown off the other's balance. They'd landed in a pile of shit.

Matt remembered being that stupid when he was young. As if whatever *could* happen never would. Not to him, anyway.

He watched Jesse climb over the fence, just like Hank was making Michael do.

They marched the boys to the hose at the side of the house. Hank walked inside and shouted up the stairs, "Amy, Cheryl, it's time to go." He didn't sound the least bit happy. He rejoined Matt outside.

Matt turned the garden hose on low and sprayed Jesse.

"Ow!" Jesse cried. "That's cold."

Matt hardened his heart to his son's cries. "You fall into a manure pile," he said, raising his voice to be heard above the spraying water and his son's caterwauling, "you gotta expect to suffer for it."

"Why can't I just have a bath?" he wailed.

"Because you aren't walking into the house with shit all over you."

"I'm telling Mom on you," Jesse screamed. "You said 'shit.'"

"Yeah, well, at least I'm not wearing it."

"I don't like you," Jesse yelled.

It should have hurt, but somehow it didn't. Matt hid a smile and said, "Calm down."

"Your turn, Michael." Hank took the hose from Matt and turned it on his son, who started to yell.

"It's freezing! It's freezing!"

"What on earth happened?" Amy stood behind them, her hands on her hips. Jenny stood beside her with wide eyes.

"Your son fell in the manure pile," Hank said.

"*My* son?" Amy asked with a dangerous edge to her tone.

Hank turned to her, making sure his son didn't see the grin hovering around the corners of his mouth. "Your son," he repeated.

Amy suddenly looked as if she was trying not to smile, too.

They read each other well. For some reason, that fact intensified Matt's longing.

He turned to Jesse shivering and sobbing in the shade of the house, and said kindly, "Go stand in the sun and peel those clothes off."

"Not out here," he said, sounding more miserable than defiant. Matt caught the shy looks his son was casting toward Cheryl. Matt guessed her to be only a year younger than Jesse.

Did it really start that early? Shyness in front of a girl? He didn't remember.

"All right," he said. "Run around back and take them off. Then get inside for a bath."

Jesse took off.

"Leave those clothes on the grass," Matt called after him. "They're garbage."

Hank ordered Michael into the car. "No sitting. Stand up in the backseat. Don't put your bum anywhere near the upholstery."

Michael dragged his feet over to the car. "What can I hang on to?"

"My headrest."

Cheryl wrinkled her nose. "Do I gotta sit in the backseat with Michael?"

"Have to, honey. Do I have to?" Amy turned to Hank with a helpless little shrug.

"Put Cheryl on your lap," he said quietly. "We'll drive home real slow on the back roads."

Hank waved to Matt and Jenny. "See you two later."

He opened all the car's windows. Michael stood behind his father's seat and gripped the headrest, his face a picture of misery and humiliation. Cheryl and Amy climbed into the front seat. Hank started the car and pulled away at a crawl.

"Guess we'll be cleaning out that manure tomorrow. It's overdue," Jenny mumbled. "I'm going to run Jesse's bath."

Matt nodded, but didn't answer. He should go in to help her, but he didn't. He couldn't handle so domestic an incident with Jesse and Jenny. His emotions were all over the place these days, bad enough already without spending more time with them as if they were a real family.

One big thing relieved him—that he and Jesse were getting along so well. That this fatherhood business wasn't as tough as it looked.

He loved the daylights out of his son, and one day his son would love him in return.

Fatherhood was a breeze and pure, pure pleasure.

IT HAD STORMED badly Saturday night. On Sunday morning, deep puddles riddled the yard. Looked like they wouldn't be cleaning that manure lot today.

Matt watched Jesse and Jenny cross the yard toward the stable.

"Don't forget what I told you," Matt heard her say in a no-nonsense, I'm-telling-you-for-your-own-good kind of way. "No going anywhere near that creek. Do you hear me?"

"Mom, I want to get another frog. You said I could go today. Bucket's lonely."

The corner of Matt's mouth twitched. The frog's name still amused him.

"You can," Jenny said. "Just not today. The water will be running high and fast."

Jesse sighed and Matt chuckled to himself. The kid acted as if it was the end of the world.

When Jenny passed Matt, she said, "Can you help muck out the stalls? The other hands are repairing fences."

Matt followed her and picked up a rake to start working.

Jenny handed a kid's rake to Jesse.

"You do Flora's stall."

"Her name's Butter," Jesse grumbled.

While Jenny and Matt herded horses out into the corral, Jesse halfheartedly raked old straw.

They worked quietly for an hour.

"You want a glass of iced tea?" Jenny asked Matt.

"Yeah. I'd appreciate it," he answered, swiping his sleeve across his forehead. It was a warm morning.

"Jesse," Jenny called, "do you want something cold to drink?"

Matt heard her walk to Flora's stall.

"Jesse?" she called.

No answer, then, "Have you seen Jesse?"

Matt looked up. She was asking him, with a crease of concern wrinkling her forehead.

"No. I thought he was raking the stall."

Jenny ran out of the barn, calling her son's name. Still no answer.

Matt had a bad feeling about this and walked outside.

Jenny rushed into the house, still calling for Jesse. A minute later she ran back out and to the horses in the corral.

"What's happening?" Matt called.

"He snuck away. He's probably at the creek. He wanted another frog so much." Fear permeated her voice. "I shouldn't have told him not to go. That just made him want to go more. It'll be bad down there."

Matt jumped the fence and ran to Masterpiece, hauling himself onto his horse by a fistful of mane.

He rode bareback out to Still Creek, which was anything but still. It roiled from the night's downpour and overflowed its banks in some places.

Matt's heart lodged in his throat, a great lump of

panic that made swallowing hard. A little kid like Jesse wouldn't stand a chance in the writhing current.

Matt raced along the bank. Nothing. What if the boy had come down here and been swept away? Would they be searching for a dead body?

Oh, God, no.

Matt chased the movement of the water downstream. He and Master flew over sodden ground. He stared at the banks, afraid of what he might see, what he might find.

A sound that might have been his name caught his attention and his gaze shot up toward the middle of the creek.

What he saw filled him with icy panic.

Jesse stood on a flat rock, surrounded by rushing water.

Alive! Thank God!

He hadn't drowned, but the stone couldn't have been wider than three feet. Matt's blood ran cold.

Tears streamed down Jesse's face, along with snot and what looked like a bit of vomit on his chin. He was cold and trembling.

He'd been vomiting up water. Lord. Lord.

Matt jumped from Master's back. "Jesse, don't move," he called. "Stay as still as you can."

Jesse didn't respond, just kept crying.

"Did you hear me?" Matt yelled. "Don't move. Nod if you can hear me."

Jesse nodded. His skin was pale and he was trembling, but he stood still as Matt had asked him to.

Jenny's voice carried on the wind as she rode up to the water's edge, her screams blood churning.

Jesse wailed harder and Matt motioned to Jenny to be quiet.

"Jesse," he said, his voice urgent, "don't move."

Matt ran to Jenny and Lacey. She'd saddled Lacey before riding out. She'd also thrown a blanket across her thighs and a rope on top of that.

Smart girl. Even in her fear, she'd been rational enough to bring the right things.

Matt grabbed the rope and tied it around the trunk of a Russian olive. A two-inch thorn pierced his shoulder. He tied the other end of the rope around his waist.

He waded into the stream, buffeted by the insistent current that urged, *Go this way. Follow me.*

Managing to stay his course, Matt stopped five feet away from the rock. The rope was too short.

He let loose a string of curses. Making sure his footing was sound, he untied the rope from his waist.

Holding the last six inches of it, he spread his arms. He still couldn't reach. Damn!

He could tell Jesse to jump, but what if he couldn't jump that far? What if Matt missed?

By some miracle, Jesse had survived falling into this maelstrom once. They wouldn't be so lucky a second time.

Matt let go of the rope altogether.

The current was wicked and strong, but Matt made it to the rock.

He lifted Jesse against his chest and told him to hang on tight.

When he felt sure of his footing again, he set out for the bank of the stream. Water buffeted him and, like a willful child, tried to make him do what it wanted him to. To change course. To rush downstream. To go with the crazy, frothing flow.

His foot slipped on a submerged rock and they went under. Matt's arms clenched around Jesse and he pushed them both to the surface. Jesse coughed up water and more vomit.

Matt gagged on the water he'd swallowed. Jesse's arms were wrapped around his throat tightly enough to choke him.

The stream carried them too far before Matt could grab a handful of weeping-willow branches. One arm still clutched Jesse and the other clung to the tree for all he was worth.

He heard Jenny ride up on Lacey, but Lacey refused to ride into the Russian olives on the other side of the willow. The horse knew that the thorns would tear her hide to pieces.

"I'm tying the rope to Lacey's saddle," Jenny called.

A minute later, she was forcing her way through the thorns of the olive trees with loops of rope curled around one hand.

"Jesse," Matt ordered, "I need you to keep your arms and legs wrapped around me. I have to let go of you for a minute."

"No!" Jesse cried.

"I need you to be a big boy for me now. Okay?"

Jesse nodded, but uncertainly.

"I'll keep you safe," Matt whispered against his ear. "Nothing is going to happen to you while I'm here with you. Understand?"

"Yeah," Jesse whispered back. He was shuddering in Matt's arms from equal parts terror and cold. The water was freezing.

Jesse's teeth chattered.

"When I count to three," Matt told him, "I want you to squeeze me real tight."

He told Jenny what he was doing.

"One…two…three…now!"

She tossed the rope to Matt. Jesse choked him and he held his breath so he wouldn't gag. He snagged the end of the rope.

"Got it," he yelled.

Working quickly, he knotted the rope tightly around his waist. Hand over hand, he pulled on the rope and got himself and Jesse out of the water and onto the muddy bank.

It felt unstable, so he continued to pull until he reached Jenny.

Jesse wailed and reached for his mother. Jenny took him in her arms.

Her son clung to her like a leech.

Jenny turned to go back through the olive trees, but they got caught in her hair. Jesse cried out. One of the thorns must have stuck him.

"Wait," Matt said.

Jenny came back to him.

He peeled off his jacket and then his shirt, and handed the denim shirt to Jenny. "Put this around you. The second layer will protect you."

He told Jesse to hang on to him again, just like he had in the river. Jesse wrapped himself around Matt's bare torso. Matt slipped his arms through the jacket backward so Jesse would be protected.

Pushing the collar up to cover Jesse's head, he dived through the trees, wincing as thorns scored his back.

The jacket and his arms protected Jesse.

Jenny waited on the other side with the blanket and bundled Jesse into it after Matt took off the jacket.

While Jesse cried, Jenny held her son in her arms, squeezing her eyes closed. She whispered his name.

Matt bent over with his hands on his knees, trying to stop shaking, feeling about as substantial as a dried-out leaf tossed about by the wind.

Somehow, Jesse must have been swept up onto the rock. If he hadn't, Matt would have been searching for his body. Or, if he'd hit his head on the rock instead of being tossed onto it, he would have drowned. Still, Matt would have been looking for a tiny dead body.

Jenny said, "Hold Jesse," and handed the child to him while she mounted her horse.

Now that Jesse was safe in his arms and the danger was past, a fear larger and deeper than Matt had ever known swept through him. With it came pure cleansing anger that washed the sharp edges of his shock and panic away.

"Don't you ever, ever go near the stream again without an adult," Matt said from behind tightly clamped teeth. He gave Jesse a shake, not rough, but not gentle either.

"Do you understand?" he asked.

Jesse howled.

This was awful, *awful,* this pain of parenthood, this danger of losing a child. Why did people have children willingly? Why did they *choose* to put themselves through this? Were all parents insane?

Jenny leaned down and took Jesse away from Matt.

Jesse whimpered and pointed at Matt. "I don't like you."

"Shh," Jenny said, her voice shaky. "Matt just saved your life."

She made sure he was snug and safe on her lap, and completely covered by the blanket.

She glanced at Matt and mouthed, *Thank you.* No sound came out, but he read her lips.

"Let's get back to the house," he said, shrugging into his wet jacket.

He whistled for Master, who grazed in a meadow. The horse trotted over and Matt rode home.

He'd lost his temper, badly. Had Jesse deserved what Matt had given him? Or was Matt becoming like his mother—unreasonable and crazy?

The anger he'd felt had come from purely primal fear. Terror. Jesse was lucky to be alive. Had Matt gone overboard? He didn't know.

At the house, Jenny carried Jesse inside while Matt took care of the horses. He finished mucking out the last of the stalls, giving himself time to calm down before he went in to see how Jesse was doing. When he was ready, he changed into dry clothes and headed toward the house.

JENNY SAT on the sofa with a clean, dry child on her lap who was dead to the world. Matt winced. Terrible thing to think at this time.

She feathered her fingers through her son's hair as if she couldn't stop touching him. Matt was sure there must have been a time when his mother had done that to him, when he must have felt as safe and protected as Jesse was now.

He couldn't remember.

Jesse had a couple of bandages on his hands where thorns had gotten him.

Matt sat down next to Jenny, touched one of the bandages and whispered, "Are these the only scratches he got?"

"Yes, thank goodness."

"How is he?"

"Scared. Exhausted. I only managed to get a little soup and hot chocolate into him before he fell asleep. He'll probably be out for a couple of hours."

Matt leaned against the back of the sofa then hissed in a breath and shot forward.

"What's wrong?" Jenny's face showed alarm.

"Olive thorns tore me apart."

"Let me see." She shifted to put Jesse on the sofa, but Matt stopped her with a hand on her arm.

"Don't disturb him."

"I really need to look at your back." She pointed to the spots of blood he'd left on the beige upholstery. His blood had soaked through his clean shirt.

"Come," Jenny ordered.

Matt followed her upstairs to the bathroom. She put down the toilet lid and told him to sit with his back to the sink.

Jenny gasped when she saw his damaged skin. "Why didn't you say something earlier? You're a mess."

She rummaged in the cupboards and found a bunch of bandages. "I'm so sorry this happened."

With a clean washcloth and warm water, she cleansed his wounds.

"You're covered with deep scratches," she said.

Matt flinched when she touched them. "They sting like a bugger."

"Sorry to make them feel worse, but we need them to be clean so you don't get an infection."

She dabbed the scratches with antibiotic cream. Matt tried not to notice how good her hands felt on him, but it was hard.

He tried not to notice, too, how her hands slowed, as though maybe she liked it as much as he did.

Gently, she covered his back with gauze pads, securing them with tape.

Jenny had always been a wild child, impulsive, sometimes defensive, and often crazy, but he remembered how she had also always been tender and gentle with the children they took care of at the Sheltering Arms.

He appreciated that tenderness now, but knew it was nothing more than gratitude on her part. Since he'd come home, she'd been nothing but distant with him.

He had saved their child today, though. He just wished he hadn't been so hard on Jesse. The boy was only four.

"Listen," Matt said when she'd finished. "I'm really sorry I yelled at Jesse. That I got so mad."

"He deserved it. If you hadn't yelled at him, I would have. It's a natural reaction to the fear."

Jenny packed away the first-aid kit. "Today was completely my fault. I should have watched him more closely."

"Hey, remember how some of the kids on the Sheltering Arms could be so unpredictable?"

"Yes, but not one of them ever came this close to drowning."

Her eyes were huge and still held traces of the fear he'd seen in her down by the stream.

He brushed her arm and she hissed and jerked away.

"I'm not going to jump your bones," he said, angry now. "Haven't I shown you that you can trust me?"

Jenny held up a staying hand. "It's just a scratch I haven't tended yet."

Matt's anger changed direction. "Why not? Why did you do mine first? Are there more? Let me see how bad they are."

Jenny shied away. "I can take care of them."

"Did you get any on your back?"

She shrugged. "I might have."

"Let me see." His tone brooked no argument from her. "Now."

She unbuttoned her blouse, turned away from him and slipped it partway down her back. The thorns had gotten her, all right. Four long scratches marred her shoulders.

He picked up a clean facecloth and soaked it in hot water. She stood still while he cleansed her wounds, but he knew they hurt. She'd always been stoic and stronger than anyone he knew.

Jenny held her shirt up over her breasts, so he couldn't tell how bad she was at the front.

Matt got the kit back out of the cupboard and applied the antibiotic cream to the scratches. Her skin and his fingers warmed it quickly. He'd forgotten about her skin, about how soft it was.

He ran his finger down her spine and she shivered.

Maybe she was remembering, too, how good they'd been together that night. But that was then and this was now.

Nothing would happen here between them.

He reined himself in and stepped away from her.

"Can you get the rest yourself?" he asked.

"No problem." Her voice didn't sound as nonchalant as her words did.

"What's going on?" The deep voice from the hallway startled them both. Angus.

Great, Matt thought, this looks bad. Both he and Jenny had their shirts off.

Matt turned his back to Angus and pointed over his shoulder to his bandages. "Russian olive thorns."

Jenny pulled her shirt all the way on and buttoned it. Then she rolled up her sleeves to bare her arms, where the thorns had left livid scratches.

"What on earth were the two of you doing in those trees?"

Jenny bit her lip.

"Jesse nearly drowned today."

Then the woman who'd been so calm and strong throughout the ordeal turned toward the sink and vomited.

CHAPTER NINE

SOMETHING HAD CHANGED between Matt and Jenny since this morning. She'd dropped the hostility, the distance. Maybe because they'd lived through a harrowing experience? Matt didn't know for sure why, but he felt his barriers fall with hers.

"How do people survive having kids?" he asked her after dinner in the stable as they groomed the horses properly. Matt had done only a rough job earlier. "Why do they put themselves through so much?"

Jenny ran her long fingers down Masterpiece's nose. "What do you think of Master?"

Huh? "What do I think of my horse?"

"Yes. Do you care about him? Or is he just a tool you need to get your work done on the ranch? Do you also have affection for him?"

"Me and Master are a team. You know that, Jenny. I love that horse."

"You do know that he won't live forever? That someday you will have to say goodbye to him?"

"What's your point?"

"When Master dies, will you refuse to buy another horse because it hurts too much to lose him?"

"Of course not. I'll need another one and I'll start to like him as much as I like Master."

"Right. Despite being a workhorse, he also enriches

your life just by his existence and by how much pleasure you derive from each other's company and from
your rides across the prairie."

"Okay."

"What if Jesse came to you and asked you for a dog?"
Jenny asked. "Would you tell him he couldn't have one
because someday the dog would die?"

"Of course not."

Jenny scratched Master's neck and the horse closed
his eyes. "Jesse enriches my life."

Matt stood and watched Jenny charm his horse.

"It would be horribly painful to lose him," she continued. "If he died, for a long time afterward, I would
probably believe that life was no longer worth living,
but I would never regret having had him just because
his loss had caused me so much grief and anger."

"But how do you deal with the fear?" Matt asked.
"You know that at any moment, on any given day, something bad could happen to Jesse."

"Yes." Jenny shivered. "Most days I don't think about
it. I just live my life with him as if the bad things won't
happen. After his near drowning, though, it'll be hard
to relax for a few days."

Jenny smiled sadly. She still looked pale but seemed
to have gotten some of her strength back. She left the
stable and went into the house.

She'd apologized many times this morning for vomiting, as if she wasn't allowed to be human, as though
she had to be strong at all times. Why was she so hard
on herself?

Matt got what she had meant about loving and losing, totally understood, but just didn't think he could

live constantly on edge, constantly fearing he would lose his child.

He wasn't strong enough to be a parent.

And yet, he was one.

Jesse ran down the aisle, trailing a long rope behind him. He seemed to have recovered his equilibrium pretty darn quickly.

"Can you show me some roping and riding now?" Jesse said, as happy and eager as if today's near disaster had never happened. "I can ride a horse."

"You can ride a pony," Matt said. Maybe kids were really resilient, but he wasn't.

"Can I learn how to rodeo on Butter?"

"No, you don't start to learn on horseback."

"How do I start?"

Matt didn't want this intimacy, not anymore. Not after the shit-kicking his nerves had taken.

He should tell Jenny to teach her son how to rodeo. He should walk away now with his sanity intact. He should leave, just as Jenny had predicted he would.

Jesse watched him with hero worship in his eyes.

Aw, kid, I'm no hero.

Matt couldn't help himself. He took the rope from Jesse then frowned. "This one's awfully big for you. We need to get you a kid's rope."

"I'm gonna ask for one for Christmas."

"Christmas? That's too far away. You need a little plastic calf's head to stick in the hay. Your mom gonna get you one of those, too?"

Jesse shrugged.

"Let's ride over to Hank's ranch," Matt said. "He's got all that stuff. We can borrow some from him."

They wandered across the yard together and entered the house.

"Jenny?" Matt called.

Angela stepped out of the kitchen, wiping her hands on a dish towel. "She just left to get me something from town.

"Look at you two. Like two peas in a pod." She smiled.

Peas in a pod? Matt looked down at the blond-haired boy beside him. Not quite. While Matt still reeled with this morning's terror, Jesse was ready for the next adventure. "I need to slip over to the Sheltering Arms to talk to Hank about something. I'm taking Jesse with me. Okay?"

"Sure," Angela said. "He'll like that. Right, Jesse?"

"Uh-huh."

"Okay, off with you. I'll tell Jenny where he is."

Matt left the house with Jesse in tow.

They returned an hour later with a small rope of Jesse's own. Jesse clutched it in one fist. He had his other arm wrapped around a plastic calf's head.

They stuck the calf's head in a bale of hay and took it onto the lawn.

Jesse roped for two hours straight. The tip of his tongue stuck out of the side of his mouth and drool ran down his chin. By the end of the afternoon, he was hitting the target more often than he missed. The kid had real staying power.

Matt didn't. He was terrified that he didn't have what it took to nurture a kid and stick around. The outcome could be so damn painful. If Jesse died, Matt knew he wouldn't be able to survive the grief. Yes, he knew most kids grew up just fine, but Jesse had clearly inherited Jenny's stubborn wild streak. He would take risks and Matt knew he wouldn't be able to cope with the consequences.

Best thing to do was to keep his distance.

He felt himself grow cold and withdraw from his son. It broke his heart after all they'd shared.

Jesse was watching him with his head cocked to one side. "Whatsa matter?"

Matt couldn't answer.

Jenny pulled into the yard and waved.

Jesse waved back.

Matt turned and walked away.

Jesse could explain to his mother what they'd been doing. Jenny could take over his rodeo training now.

Matt went to the bunkhouse and threw himself onto his cot.

A few minutes later, Jenny came in. "Thanks for teaching Jesse how to rope."

"No problem." He sounded short. Tense.

"What's going on?"

"I can't— After this morning, I can't be the father Jesse needs." He sat up. "You were right about me. I don't have the guts for the job."

"Until now, you've been doing really well." That admission looked as if it cost Jenny a lot. "You can still get to know him more."

"That's quite a statement coming from you." Matt smiled grimly. "You should be pleased. You've never wanted me here, or anywhere near my son. Now I'm agreeing with you that I'm not good for him and you want me to get to know him even more."

"True."

"Listen, compared to me, you are Mother Teresa.

You're the best damn parent a boy could want. I can't measure up to that."

A look crossed Jenny's face that Matt could only interpret as…self-recrimination.

"What?" he asked.

Jenny sat on the cot across from his. "I'm not so great. I have to tell you something. It's been eating away at me."

"What?"

She stared at her hands, took her time weaving her fingers together. "I did something terrible and I've been ashamed of myself ever since."

"Jenny, spit it out. How bad can it be?"

"Pretty bad. That night in your parents' cabin?"

Matt nodded.

"I planned the whole thing. I pretended to be angry with you for being attracted to Amy. I set up that argument with her so you would be the one to come after me."

"Because you wanted to sleep with me? I figured that out already."

"No, because I wanted to get pregnant and I wanted you to be the father."

Matt sucked in a breath. She had to be kidding.

"Why?" he shouted and the air whooshed out of him, leaving him stunned and empty. "We talked for *hours* about how rotten my parents were. I told you I didn't want kids."

"Yes," Jenny whispered. "But I loved you with all my heart, and I knew I would feel the same way about your children."

"So you always planned to be a single parent?"

Her cheeks reddened. "No, I thought that once I was pregnant, you'd marry me."

"So you wanted to trap me into marriage?" She reached a hand toward him, but he recoiled. "You knew how I felt about marriage."

"I know." She lifted her chin and her tone became defiant. "You were my best friend. I didn't understand how you could believe that anything we had would be wrong."

She jumped up from the cot. "I was tired of waiting for you."

Matt cradled his head in his hands. "And now I have a son without ever deciding I wanted one." His voice came out muffled. "You made that decision for both of us."

"You didn't *have* to sleep with me."

"After I saw you naked in the cabin I wasn't thinking too clearly."

"I was. I plotted the whole thing. I was regular like clockwork and I knew there was a good chance I'd get pregnant." She looked and sounded regretful. "The choice I made for both of us was wrong."

Jenny's words sounded thick and Matt looked up. Her chin trembled.

Oh, Lord, don't cry. I'm not in a forgiving mood.

"I don't regret Jesse," she went on, setting her jaw so it wouldn't shake. "I do regret not being honest with you. You deserved better from me."

She left the bunkhouse before he could respond.

Matt couldn't take it in. Jenny was the most ethical person he knew, but she'd lied to him. Not in a little white-lie kind of way, but in a huge, screwing-with-someone-else's-life kind of way.

He couldn't get his head around it so gave up trying, but for the rest of the day, Matt kept his distance from her.

From Jesse, too.

LATE SUNDAY AFTERNOON, an ominous light hovered over the silent landscape. Not a creature stirred. No birds chirped. A couple of raindrops fell. Looked like it was going to be a bad storm.

Matt rode along the boundary between the Circle K and the Sheltering Arms. Last night, Angus and Jenny had decided to err on the side of safety and get everyone out patrolling the ranch.

A half hour ago, Matt had called Angus on his cell because he hadn't liked what he saw brewing on the horizon.

Angus wanted to patrol until six o'clock. He was certain the storm would hold off until then.

Staring around him, Matt knew Angus was wrong. The storm was almost on top of them and they should all head back. The prairie was no place to be caught in a thunderstorm.

His radio crackled and Hip's voice came over, yelling, "We've got cattle being stolen."

Matt swore.

Angus responded on the radio. "Where?"

"Just past the old quarry," Hip said. "They don't know Will and me are watching them. We can take them by surprise."

"Wait for us," Jenny said. "They could be dangerous."

"Let's catch these bastards." Angus's voice was strong despite the static.

They converged from different directions until they rode abreast, Will and Hip on ATVs and the rest on horseback, their horses' hooves driving a demanding beat.

When they came up over the rise Hip directed them to, they saw five men on horseback below herding about twenty head of Circle K cattle away from Angus's property.

"Hell," Jenny yelled.

"Shit," Matt swore.

"Let's get them," Angus shouted, then spurred his horse.

They took off, but the second the rustlers heard them coming, they abandoned the cattle and rode away, hard and fast, three of them veering off to the left, two of them to the right. Splitting up.

Damn.

"Hip! Will! We'll take the three on the left," Angus yelled, his words blown behind him by a cold wind swirling across the prairie.

He pointed to Matt and Jenny. "You take those two."

Matt cursed, but couldn't think about how he didn't want to be anywhere near this woman. He needed to focus on the chase. They were delayed by having to ride around the herd then pick up the trail farther on. Bastards. He couldn't let them get away. He leaned forward, almost level with Master's neck.

The sky darkened, and the afternoon descended into a gray-green twilight. Fat drops of rain hit Matt square in the face. He brushed them away and rode like a demon. There was no way he was losing those guys. Angus depended on him to catch them.

"Matt," he heard Jenny call through the roar of the wind that had grown steadily worse.

"What?" he called back, not breaking speed.

"Look!" she shouted.

He turned back to her then looked where she pointed. Damn. The howling wind had saplings bent nearly to the ground and was stripping mature trees of leaves and smaller branches. A solid wall of rain was coming right at them. Within seconds, he was drenched to the skin. Jenny looked no better, but she could drown for all he cared, his anger at her sharp and righteous. He slowed Master, then pulled up. Too hard to see the ground in front of him.

The chase was over before it had even begun. They wouldn't catch anyone today. Frustration ate at Matt, but there was no sane choice but to stop. They'd ridden too far to return to the Kinsey house in this rain. They couldn't even head to his old house on the far side of the ranch.

"Where can we go?" he asked, but his words were blown away by the wind.

Jenny and Lacey sidled closer. "What?" she yelled. She looked as frustrated as he felt.

"Where-can-we-go?" He enunciated and she read his lips.

"Back to the ranch."

"Are you crazy? We could get hit by lightning out here."

He saw the uncertainty in her eyes and knew it wasn't about lightning. She didn't want to be alone with him, either.

A shaft of lightning hit the earth a hundred yards in front of them and sent up the scent of scorched earth.

The hair rose on Matt's arms. Master reared on his hind legs to turn away, but Matt held him steady with his thighs.

Lacey skittered away. Jenny forced her back beside Master.

Matt yelled, "What's around here?" He knew Jenny had traveled every inch of this terrain over the years.

She looked around wildly. He knew she was trying to come up with some alternative to being trapped with him.

Her hat flew off and hit him in the chest. He caught it—just—then shoved it inside his shirt. He snuggled his own hat down hard on his head. The wind whipped rain under his brim, stinging his skin. He turned away from it.

He looked at Jenny. "Where?" he shouted. "Hurry."

Jenny said something he couldn't catch, then pointed. She might have said "MacCaffery," but he wasn't sure. When he tried to ask, he got a mouthful of rain. Then he remembered the small cabin the MacCafferys had on the back end of their property, put there for ranch hands who spent nights on the range.

He spurred Master and followed Jenny. She rode hard and fast into the sheeting rain. By the time they finally found the cabin, his breath came out of him in gusts.

Jenny pulled up around the far side of a ramshackle cabin he could barely make out in the downpour and quickly dismounted. She and Matt secured the horses on the leeward side of the small building under a small lean-to, out of the worst of the wind. Thunder cracked overhead, close by. They whipped the saddles off the horses, rubbed the animals down as best they could with their sleeves, then ran for the entrance.

Warped by the elements, the door stuck. Matt put his shoulder against it and shoved it open with a high screech. Jenny shut the door behind them and latched it. They stood in the dark, panting in the stale, musty air.

Damn. This couldn't be happening. Déjà vu all over again and he hated it. He'd rather be anywhere than trapped in a cabin with Jenny Sterling. Judging by the building's small exterior, it was only a one-room cabin.

Matt let his eyes adjust to what little light filtered in through the windows. Lightning flashed, illuminating the room for a split second. In that brief moment, he saw enough to know they were in a rudimentary cabin little better than a shack. It had a fireplace, though, a necessity for stranded ranch hands.

If the storm blew through quickly enough, they could ride home. At any rate, that's what Matt prayed would happen.

Matt tried to raise Angus on the radio, but it was dead. He pulled out his cell phone and managed to get through to tell him where they were.

He shuffled toward the fireplace. He heard Jenny creep along the far wall and rummage around on a table or counter. He heard pots moving. Then she struck a match and lit an oil lantern, illuminating that end of the shack.

"Toss those matches over here," Matt said. He caught them easily when she did. She'd always had a good arm. He knelt beside the fireplace. His soaked jeans stuck to his skin, pulling at the hairs on his legs.

"Cold in here," he said, trying to make normal conversation.

"No fooling," Jenny answered and he heard her teeth chatter.

Matt sorted through a stack of wood, found shreds for kindling and a couple of smaller logs. He set them up in the fireplace then put a match to them.

When he stood, he noticed a pack of cigarettes on the rough-hewn mantel and picked them up. He blew off a layer of dust and sneezed. Must've been here at least a year, he guessed.

He threw the empty pack into the burgeoning fire, where it flared and crinkled, then burned to ash.

The storm raged around the cabin, thunder shaking its walls and wind whistling through its cracks, but inside, the intimacy was broken only by the crackle of the fire and the sound of Jenny rummaging in the cupboards.

"Find anything?" he asked.

She held up a can of coffee and some tinned beans, her mouth set in a thin line and her eyes not quite natural. If he hadn't known Jenny for the fearless creature she was, he would have said she was terrified of being alone with him. Like this.

Her wet shirt clung to her, molded her breasts like a second skin, or a man's hands. Matt shuddered and turned back to the fire.

It was so damn stupid to get trapped like this.

He couldn't repeat what happened five years ago. In his worst nightmares, he hadn't imagined that he would ever be stuck alone with Jenny in a cabin again, in a storm, with no escape. Even his rage didn't feel like enough to keep him away from her. He gripped the edge of the mantel.

"MacCaffery's boys obviously use this place at times." Jenny sounded as strained as he felt. Matt stared at her. She pointed to the tins in the cupboard and the jar of instant coffee.

He said nothing.

A gust of wind rattled the windows and Jenny shivered.

"We need to dry our clothes," she said.

Not this again. Not this.

Jenny walked to the door and claimed a couple of oilskin coats hanging from a hook behind it.

"These are old but they'll have to do."

She dragged two rickety ladder-back chairs from a small table and set them next to the fire.

"You want to build that fire up real high?" she said.

He watched her over his shoulder and willed her to move, to take off her clothes.

Reading the heat in his eyes accurately, Jenny waited for him to look away. He turned away from her slowly, and added a log to the fire.

"Don't look," Jenny said.

Matt stared into the fire. *Don't turn around. For God's sake, don't look.*

He clenched his fists and rested one of them on the hearth, letting the stone dig into his knuckles so the pain in his hand would be stronger than in his heart. And in his loins.

He heard the soft rustle of fabric and knew that half of Jenny's clothes had just fallen to the floor. He kept staring blindly into the flickering flames as though his life depended on it. As angry as he was with Jenny, as much as he hated what she'd done in the past, he still wanted her—and chastised himself for that.

His body didn't know the difference between then and now, the old Jenny and the new, the past betrayal that colored the present. His body knew only what it wanted at this moment. Jenny.

"You can turn around now." She wore one of the coats and draped her clothes over the back of a chair, hanging a skimpy piece of pink lace over one of the arms and a pink lace bra over the other.

Matt clenched his jaw.

She stepped toward the hearth to stoke the fire. Her coat brushed his arm and he jerked away.

She flinched. "Your turn to change," she said, her tone ringing with equal parts defiance and hurt.

Matt untucked his shirt from his pants. Everything stuck to his skin and felt clammy. He peeled his pants down his legs then put on the coat. It was stiff. He wondered how Jenny could stand it against her own soft skin. He remembered that skin—how it felt like satin, but softer; like silk, but warmer.

"Are you hungry?" Jenny asked, her voice tentative. He hated that. He couldn't fight with a hesitant or hurt or vulnerable Jenny, and he really needed to fight with her. Or else he was going to take her in his arms and kiss the daylights out of her, drown himself in her. Why was love so frigging hard?

Love? Déjà vu was right.

JENNY STARED at Matt. This was her worst nightmare. Her absolute worst nightmare. What quirk of fate had them here alone? She didn't care how they got here. She just knew she couldn't let history repeat itself.

Five years ago, she had shaped their night together to come out one way. She could shape this night to turn out very differently.

She turned away from Matt to busy herself along the

wall that could be called a kitchen only by a stretch of the imagination. She found a can opener some cowboy had left behind at one point—as old as the hills and hard to use—and jabbed the sharp end into the top of the tin of beans. It hurt her wrist and took all her strength to cut around the top of the can, but she'd be damned if she'd ask Matt for help.

At the fireplace, she dumped the beans into a pot and placed it on the hearth to warm slowly. She found a couple of plates, chipped around the rims, and set a fork onto each.

Finished with as many chores as she could think of to distract herself, Jenny stood and stared out the window at a dark, angry landscape. The thunder had moved on, but rain still hammered the tin roof of the cabin.

She felt Matt's eyes on her. *Stop. Don't look at me.* She'd already seen the heat of anger, and more. Lust. Passion.

When she turned back to him, she found him a foot away, staring at her. Just staring, his eyes full of anger and confusion. The confusion broke her. She'd hurt him badly. Worse than she would have ever thought.

"I'm sorry," she whispered. "I'm so sorry."

In spite of her righteousness and her fear, she could no longer deny that what she'd done was wrong. That she shouldn't have tried to trap him. That she should have told him the truth as soon as she knew she was pregnant.

It had been a knee-jerk response to the worry that Matt couldn't possibly be any better than his crazy parents. That he wouldn't stick around for her any more than he would have for Elsa. He'd already proved that by running away after that night. Or so she'd believed at the time.

"I'm sorry," she whispered again. She'd known Matt well as a child. On that hill lined with cotoneasters, they'd talked so often, about everything, including his twisted family, trying to make sense of a world that was often senseless.

Matt grabbed her, hauled her against his chest and kissed her with a fierce passion that matched the depth of her remorse. His fingers bit into her upper arms. She struggled against him, not to get away, but to get closer, to crawl into his skin if she could, to comfort him, and to seek his absolution for the terrible things she'd done.

The kiss was rough and hard, not at all the way he'd kissed her five years ago. His tongue probed the corners of her mouth. His arms became steel bands across her back. His erection pushed against her belly and she welcomed it.

She needed this. Wrapping her arms around his neck, she pressed herself against him, absorbing his scent, dizzy with passion. Matt. Oh, Matt.

He broke the kiss, leaving her lips wet and cold. He shoved the fingers of one hand into her hair and cupped the back of her head. His heart hammered against her chest, his breath warmed her temple.

He shook and she trembled with him. Then he was dragging her onto the floor in front of the fire, lying on top of her, heavy and solid and so welcome. He clawed at the buttons on her coat. She clawed at his, touched his hot skin. He pulled her nipple into his mouth and her eyes flew open.

No!

What was she doing? She was going to marry Angus

at the end of the week, and here she was on the floor with Matt again.

She had no sense where Matt was concerned.

He pulled her wrists above her head and she squirmed beneath him. No.

"Matt, no."

He didn't hear her, just sucked on her nipple harder, sending shards of response through her belly. She shuddered then held herself taut. She couldn't do this with Matt while Angus trusted her so deeply.

"Matt." She wriggled one arm free and grabbed his hair. "No!"

MATT OPENED HIS EYES, struggled to understand what Jenny was saying, winced at the pain at his temple. She had hold of a fistful of his hair and pulled it hard enough to keep his head away from her.

"What," he mumbled, trying to break out of the angry, horny daze he was in. "What?"

She repeated what she'd been yelling at him, but quietly now. "No."

"Why not?" he demanded, breathing his frustration into her face.

"Angus." She said the only word she knew would make sense to Matt at this moment.

He rolled off her and away, until he came up hard against the chairs. They screeched across the floor.

He let out a cry of pure, impotent frustration but kept away from her as he brought himself back under control.

Jenny rolled over to face the fire, trembling with her needs and overwhelming emotions. She needed Matt in one way, and Angus in another, but she couldn't have both, and she would never, ever betray Angus.

The stress that had built in her since Matt had returned boiled over and tears threatened, but she fought them. She wasn't a crying kind of girl.

She'd had only two sexual encounters with Matt. One had been better than she'd ever dreamed it would be. Tonight, it was so much less and she mourned her loss.

THE STORM STILL RAGED outside, but Matt's inner storm had calmed.

Staring at the ceiling, Matt realized the truth he'd been hiding from himself. He loved Jenny. He had since that night they'd spent together.

No. He'd loved her for years before that.

He was filled with such an aching, beautiful love for her that it pained him. It was so much more than the lust that had just overwhelmed him.

She'd lied to him, twice, yet still he loved her and always would. He admired her strength and her honesty. She could have never told him that she'd gotten pregnant on purpose and he would have been none the wiser. But as soon as he'd praised her, she'd had to be honest.

She wasn't his. He didn't want her to marry Angus, but he wouldn't marry her himself.

He'd been running scared for a long time. He wasn't afraid for himself, though.

He feared for Jenny. In this moment when he *knew* that if he tried hard enough he could seduce her, he became noble. For this one night, he became more than his father had ever taught him to be, and more than he'd thought he was.

He could do the right thing and leave Jenny to her dreams. She could live a better life without him to screw it up for her the way Long men had been doing for generations.

Matt might have thought that he had grown now that he'd met his son, that the experience might have matured him, but he knew better.

After his reaction to Jesse's near drowning, he realized he still didn't have the courage for long-term, lifetime relationships.

With a concerted effort to overcome his fear, he would stay in his son's life, but watch Jenny from afar.

She stirred beside him and he felt her shoulders shake.

"Are you crying?" Never, not once in his years of knowing her, not even after she'd lost her home, had Matt seen her cry.

"No," she said.

"I don't believe you."

She rolled toward him. "I'm not lying and I'm not crying. I'm trying *not* to cry."

He started to laugh. That was Jenny, defiant and resistant and resilient. He couldn't stand to leave her alone.

"Come here," he whispered, because as much as she'd been wrong and as deeply as she'd hurt him, she needed him. And he needed her.

Jenny went straight into the arms he opened for her, and burrowed against his chest.

"I'm so sorry," she whispered. He heard the truth in the words.

"I know," he said and kissed her temple. "I know." He felt old and tired, but cleansed. Both he and Jenny were safe from his needs tonight.

He closed his eyes and sighed.

Matt lost track of how long they lay together, hearts beating, breaths sighing in and out in unison. The absolute peace of the moment flowed over him like warm maple syrup, melting some of his fears, and his shame.

He'd spent a lot of years living down to his family's reputation. Could he change now?

He didn't know when he'd ever felt so calm. If this wasn't heaven, it was close, lying here in the isolation of the cabin, with rain pounding a steady rhythm on the tin roof and a fire crackling in the hearth, with Jenny in his arms and only two layers of oilcloth and his new-found nobility between them.

He pulled back to look into her eyes, to judge whether she was as affected as he, but they were closed. He nudged her gently, but she didn't move. She'd fallen asleep. He laughed.

After all the drama and tension, she was out like a baby calf without a care in the world. He laughed again and she stirred.

She woke, stared at him with her back to the fire and her face in shadow. He rolled her over and the firelight set the whiskey highlights of her hazel eyes dancing.

He pulled away from her, because to lie this close to her without making sweet, sweet love was hell.

CHAPTER TEN

MATT KISSED HER forehead once then rolled onto his back.

Jenny turned toward him and he felt her staring at him.

"Have you been to the house since you got back?" she asked. The question came out of nowhere and he stiffened.

She must have sensed it, because she turned onto her side and placed her hand on his chest. Even through the coat, he could feel the weight of it like an anchor. He relaxed slightly and sighed.

"Yeah," he said.

"How was it?"

"Tough." He swallowed and it sounded loud in the room. "There was nothing there for me."

"Nothing?" she asked.

He thought of the mail on the table. "There was an envelope. My parents' autopsy report."

"Oh, Matt." Jenny reached her hand toward his face then dropped it to her side. He knew why. They were already playing with fire, just barely skirting trouble.

"Did you read it?" she asked.

"Mom shot Pop and then killed herself." His fingers spasmed on his stomach. "I already know what happened." He made himself relax. "Why would I want to read the report?"

"What if they found something they weren't expecting?"

"How would that change anything?"

"I don't know. I wonder what they found. I just feel... something."

Before they'd slept together five years ago, Matt had always depended on Jenny to see things about his family he sometimes couldn't figure out on his own.

He remembered the sheer helplessness he'd felt when his parents died. Jenny had anchored him, pure and simple.

"HEY, KID." Deputy Ormstead stood on the veranda, holding his hat in his hand. At least it wasn't Sheriff Saunders, who hated Matt. Matt had opened the door to a knock, already apprehensive. No one visited the Longs. No one *ever* knocked on their door.

When he saw the cop, his first thought was, *I didn't do anything.*

"What do you want?" he asked, his tone belligerent.

The deputy didn't bat an eye, didn't rise to the bait, and Matt felt something shift in him. Had Pop done something? Did Matt need to drag the drunken idiot home from town? How? He'd been driving since he was fourteen, was old enough to drive now that he was sixteen, didn't have the money to get a license.

Shit, what now? Where was Mom? The house had been empty when he got home.

The cop twisted his hat in his hand. He looked nervous. What the hell was going on?

"What?" Matt said, his tone still hard. Whatever it was, Matt wanted him to spit it out and get it over with.

Ormstead took a deep breath. "I have some bad news for you, kid."

"I'm not a kid," Matt said, because he really didn't want to acknowledge the bad-news part and clung to the part that didn't matter.

Ormstead opened his mouth again, hesitated then rushed on. "Your parents are dead."

Matt blinked. What? He didn't know what Ormstead meant. Dead, as in gone for good?

When Matt didn't respond, the deputy repeated it. Matt felt his mouth fall open, suddenly understanding. Couldn't be. No way could Pop die. He was too strong, too fast. He would give death one hell of a chase.

"You okay, kid?"

"Yeah," he said, but his voice cracked.

"Mom's dead, too?"

"Uh-huh." The cop looked as though he'd rather be anywhere but here. "You want someone to come stay with you?"

Yes! "No," Matt said, keeping his voice steady. He didn't want the big man standing in front of him to think he was weak. "I'm okay."

Ormstead nodded and turned away. He walked down the stairs.

Matt needed something, but he didn't know what. Just as Ormstead reached his cruiser, Matt called, "Wait a minute."

The deputy turned back, the hat on his head now and his eyes shadowed.

"What happened?" Matt didn't want to know, but some strange need drove him.

"Your mom caught your dad in the motel with Missy Donovan. She shot him."

Matt sucked in a breath. Yeah, Pop could have given death a run for its money, if not for Mom. He always came back to her—sooner or later—before or after whatever trouble he courted.

"Mom?" he asked, his voice rising.

"She turned the rifle on herself, son."

Matt swayed, had to put a hand on the doorjamb to stay on his feet.

"You sure you don't want someone out here with you?" the deputy asked.

Matt shook his head and focused on a detail.

"How's Missy?"

"She's hysterical, but alive. Your ma didn't touch her."

Matt exhaled. Missy was okay. She wasn't too bright, was too peroxide-blonde and big-chested for her own good, but she was always real nice to Matt.

He nodded. Deputy Ormstead got into his cruiser, slowly, watching Matt. Turning the car in the yard, he still watched him. At the end of the driveway, he stopped, checked Matt in his rearview mirror, gave one hard wave of his hand and drove off.

Matt stood alone on the front porch until he realized he was cold. He must have been standing there for a while. It was a bright September day and the sun shone, but his hands were like icicles. He closed the door and stood in the living room, staring at the unfolded laundry on the table and the margarine and peanut butter open on the kitchen counter and the fireplace full of old ashes.

On the other side of the fireplace, he knew he would

find his parents' bedroom a mess. The bathroom would be the same—toothbrushes scattered on the counter, a ring around the toilet bowl, mold between the tiles surrounding the bathtub. Pop's towel on the floor. Matt knew it was there because he'd kicked it out of the way when he got up and had his shower an hour ago. Stupidly, he wondered if that was why Mom shot Pop.

Matt shuddered and fell onto the sofa. This was all his now, every musty bedsheet and all the stale food in the fridge and the ironing board propped in the corner that never, ever got used.

The whole place was his now. The whole kit and caboodle. What did that mean, anyway? Kit? Caboodle? What the hell did it mean? It didn't make sense.

Matt picked up a dirty mug from the scarred coffee table and threw it against the brick fireplace. It shattered into shards of blue and white.

What did it mean?

He picked up another mug and threw it at the fireplace, too. It shattered just like the first.

"What does it mean?" he cried. No one answered— no friend, no family, no God. He dropped to his knees on the floor.

"I don't know what it means," he whispered.

MATT REMEMBERED everything that happened that day— looking out his front window to find Jenny sitting on the big rock in the yard watching the house, with her legs folded under her like a silent guardian angel.

When the reporters came from the larger towns around, Matt pulled her into the house. Jenny sat on the sofa beside him, for hours and hours, listening to the ringing telephone he wouldn't answer, talking quietly to Kyle and Angus at the door, until he felt strong enough to stand up and phone the one and only funeral home in Ordinary. He made arrangements for the visitation and funeral then sat back down beside Jenny. They didn't say a word to each other, didn't touch, but he felt her presence beside him. She'd steadied him.

MATT JUMPED UP to throw another log on the fire.

Jenny smiled, because she knew he was avoiding the conversation. He knew it, too.

She sniffed the air and laughed. "Take the beans away from the fire. It smells like we burned dinner."

Matt moved the pot.

"There might not be anything new in the autopsy report." She shrugged. "I just feel you need to deal with what happened to your parents."

He lay down alongside her and rested his head on his hand. With his other hand, he picked up a piece of her hair and tickled her nose with it.

She grabbed his wrist and held it still, watched him steadily, daring him to be serious.

"What happened to you was huge. Most people never have to experience anything even half as traumatic as that. You need to deal with it then put it to rest. You need closure."

"I don't go for that kind of psychobabble."

"Anyone would need to deal with his emotions after that kind of ordeal."

He shook his head. "I dealt with it years ago."

"Really?"

"Yeah, really. I got them buried, didn't I? I arranged a funeral service most people came to only because they were curious and scandalized."

"I wasn't."

Yeah, he knew that. She'd shown up at the funeral home two nights running and had stayed until he'd left, trailing him to make sure he got home. Then she'd come to the funeral with a bunch of wildflowers in her hand, picked from the fields and wilting in the heat. She'd clung to those until everyone had left but the two of them. She'd handed him that bouquet of dying flowers and then hugged him.

That gutsy little twelve-year-old, unashamed of either her youth or her premature wisdom, had wrapped her thin arms around his big, sixteen-year-old body, around his anger and shame and insecurity, and had held him until he was just this side of tears. By then, she'd already lost her own parents and knew how he felt. He'd walked away and dumped those flowers in the garbage. Matthew Long, the only son of those two nut jobs in the fresh graves, didn't deserve what she was offering.

He came out of his memory slowly. He'd been staring into the flames and had missed whatever Jenny had said. He looked at her, really looked at her, and realized that he still didn't deserve her. Jenny Sterling had changed over the years. Matthew Long hadn't.

"You're too good for me, Jenny."

He'd startled her. "How can you say that after what I did? I tried to *trap* you into marriage."

"Yeah, you did. That was wrong. But in everything else, you are good and strong."

She looked bemused, as if it confused her to hear a compliment from him.

"Why?" he asked. "Why marry Angus?"

"I want my home back, Matt," she said, her voice full of conviction.

"I remember when it happened," he answered. "When they had the auction on your front lawn."

He needed to do something for her—to comfort her. As much as she sounded confident, her eyes told a different story.

He reached for the buttons of her coat and slipped one out of its hole. He slid the tips of his fingers inside until he felt the soft skin of her belly. She gasped and he kept his fingers still, because he would go too far if he touched more of her.

He remembered how bad he'd felt for the skinny, rough-and-tumble cowgirl who wouldn't let herself cry in public.

She'd sat on the hill overlooking her home, the sorrow and anger seething on her face, yet refusing to give in and cry. Not much more than ten years old and already tough.

He thought about growing up in a home you loved, on land you loved, with parents you loved, and then losing it all. He could finally begin to imagine it. He felt a keen sense of loss for something he'd never had, but had always longed for. Jenny had had it all, and then had been taken away. How must that have felt?

"Is it worth marrying Angus for?" he asked.

Jenny stared at him, swallowed hard, and opened and closed the fist lying on the floor between their heads.

"You want your ranch," he said, his breath stirring her hair. "Angus wants kids. Is that it?"

"It's more than that, deeper than that sounds, but I don't know if I could describe it well enough to convince you that I'm doing the right thing."

"Angus can't get Kyle back and you can't get your ranch back. Life doesn't work that way, Jenny. Once a thing is gone, it's gone." Her fist clenched on the floor. "We don't get things back. We move forward."

"This *is* moving forward."

"How do you figure that?" His tone had sharpened. "You're selling your body for a house and a piece of land."

She tried to move away from him, but he reached his whole hand inside her coat to rest on her belly and pressed, forcing her to stay and hear him out.

"How is that any different from selling yourself for money?"

She winced at the harshness of the idea. He wouldn't say the ugly words out loud—words like *whoring* and *prostituting*. He would never have thought to see her in those terms and it rattled him.

Awareness filled her eyes and he knew she'd thought of it all herself.

"Don't do it," he pleaded.

"I need to," she whispered. "It's my home. It's what I've always wanted."

"Don't do it," he repeated.

"I have to." There was no softness in her implacable tone. She was going through with it.

In six days, Jenny was going to marry the closest thing to a father figure Matt had ever had. The two people he loved most in the world were marrying each other and it was all wrong. And there wasn't a damn thing he could do about it.

"I need to do this," she said softly.

He grabbed her to him and nestled her back against his front, settling her head on his arm, facing the warmth of the fire. He couldn't fight with her anymore.

"Tell me about it," she said.

"What?"

"Growing up in that house. Do you have any good memories? Or were they all bad?"

He recoiled and tried to move away from her. She held his arm where it was wrapped around her, keeping him there.

"Tell me," she insisted.

Her voice soothed him. Her body curling against him eased his pain.

"Mom used to make pies." Matt smiled. He'd forgotten about that. "When Pop would come home with another rodeo belt buckle, she'd bake a pie—raspberry for first place and apple for second. Not that it mattered. Pop and I loved both."

"So it wasn't all bad?" Her soft voice enticed more happy memories out of him.

"They used to laugh. A long time ago. Early on. In their bedroom late at night."

His throat constricted.

"Matt?"

He told her about the day everything changed, when his mother started to turn into a stranger.

It floated out, the entire memory, and drifted around the room on the heat rising from the fire, told without anger, but as a matter of fact. *This was my childhood.* It just was what it was.

"Do you think we can ever overcome our childhoods?" she asked. "Do you think people have the ability to change profoundly?"

She sounded sleepy.

"I don't know, Jenny. You're asking the wrong person."

Her eyes were half closed, already starting their slide

into sleep. She fought it—like a child—forcing them to stay open.

"Tell me more about Wyoming."

"There isn't much to tell," he mumbled.

He felt the moment she lost her battle with sleep. Her body went slack.

He held her close and stared into the fire while she slept, disturbing her only to add wood throughout the night. He couldn't sleep. This would never happen again—Jenny sleeping in his arms as if he had a right to hold her. As if he deserved her.

In spite of having forgiven her, there was still a basic truth that held him back. Jenny had said it about being Jesse's father, but Matt knew it also applied to his relationship with her.

Angus was the better man.

"I'll never marry you, Jenny," he whispered.

She stirred beside him.

She'd heard him.

JENNY AND MATT RODE away from the cabin on the heels of a stunning sunrise. Jenny wanted to hold on to the magic of waking up in Matt's arms as long as she could, but knew there was something she had to discuss with him.

She had enjoyed last night too much. It would never happen again, though. She would only touch him again at work, and that was as it should be. Last night should never have happened. They hadn't shared their bodies, but they had been intimate nonetheless.

Angus deserved better than that, but also, so did she. Matt had made it clear that he would never marry her.

"Matt," Jenny said, her tone resolute.

"Yeah?"

"I'm going to have to ask you to leave the ranch."

He spun his head toward her. "What? Why? Last night won't happen again."

She turned to him with her heart in her eyes. "I'm going to marry Angus on Saturday. It's too hard to have you on the ranch."

His lips thinned. "What about the money I owe Angus? What about Jesse?"

"You can come to the ranch every day to work, but I'll ask Angus to give you your orders."

She directed Lacey into the Circle K yard. Her smile felt infinitely sad. "As far as Jesse goes, I won't keep you from him."

"So I can still work here, I can still see my son, but I can't sleep here."

Jenny nodded. "Yes."

"I can't see how that makes a difference or say that I understand completely."

"Neither do I. It's just something I have to do."

"Okay." He dismounted. "I'll go pack my stuff."

"Matt, come in to breakfast. You can still *be* here, you just can't live here."

Jenny stabled Lacey in the stall next to Master's. She and Matt unsaddled their horses, rubbed them down and left them eating their fill.

They walked across the yard not touching. Remembering his hand on her belly, she regretted that. She wanted to hold his hand, to muss his hair and joke with him, but Angus would always come between them.

They met Angus in the dining room. He sat at the head of the table with a cup of coffee and the newspaper. A flash of relief crossed his face.

He stood and held out a chair for Jenny. "How'd you two do? Find a place to stay?"

Jenny found she was able to greet Angus honestly. She had nothing to hide. True, she and Matt had kissed, but they'd restrained themselves from betraying Angus. And never would betray him in the future. "We stayed in the MacCaffreys' old shack. You?"

"We made it to the MacCaffreys' ranch house. They put us up for the night in the bunkhouse." He sipped his coffee. "Gave us a hot meal, too."

Jenny sniffed. "Something smells good. What did Angela make for breakfast?"

"Buckwheat pancakes."

"You want some, Matt?" she asked, walking toward the kitchen.

"Sure," Matt replied as he watched her cross the room. When he brought his glance back he found Angus regarding him steadily.

The only sound in the room was their breathing.

Matt didn't like what Angus and Jenny were about to do—and couldn't stop them—but he needed to make sure Jenny would be okay.

"I'll take care of her," Angus said, as if he'd read Matt's mind. "You know that."

"Yeah, I know," Matt replied, his hands gripping the back of one of the chairs. Angus would take better care of her than he could.

"She deserves it," he said. But Angus deserved her more.

"I know." Angus refilled his coffee cup from a carafe on the table and picked up the newspaper. "She's a keeper."

She was that, all right, Matt thought, just not his.

Jenny came out of the kitchen with two plates piled high with pancakes. She set one down in front of him, then sat at Angus's place and poured syrup over her pancakes. Matt tried not to watch her, or to remember much of last night. An impossible feat. He would remember every look, every touch until the day he died.

A commotion down the hall caught his attention. Jesse bounded into the room, a big grin on his face.

"Mom! You're home."

Jenny smiled widely and opened her arms. Her son jumped into them and she grunted and said, "Oof," and laughed. He laughed, too.

"Hi, baby. Did you go home with Angela?" Jesse twisted himself around in her arms to face the table.

"Uh-huh. She's got kittens. Can we have one?" He picked up her fork.

"Angela said you were okay. She said you're smart. You'd get out of the storm. Can I have some?" He shoveled a big, adult-size piece of pancake into his mouth, and syrup pooled at the corners of his lips.

"Hi, Matt," he mumbled around a mouthful of food.

"Hey," Jenny said, nudging him. "Don't talk with your mouth full."

Jesse waved to Matt while he chewed. Matt smiled back. The boy was a wonder, full of life and energy, and so loved by his mother it was almost painful to see.

Nothing was going the way it was supposed to. He'd arrived here only a week ago, intent on paying off his debt to Angus and then scooting back out of town, out of Montana, maybe heading north to Canada this time.

But today? Today he was so confused he could barely see straight. One minute he was riding high on the relationship with his son, and in the next minute, he hit bottom in his fear of losing him. Life was unpredictable. Matt didn't want to be anywhere near when any of life's shit hit the fan for his son. Jesse would be better off with a father like Angus to see him through it.

SINCE MATT'S ARRIVAL, Jenny had been on a rollercoaster ride. As much as asking him to leave hurt her, she wanted her quiet life back, just her and Angus and Jesse, with the world on its proper course and them working toward a common goal.

They could get on with the business of marrying and moving forward with the rest of their lives.

How would Matt fit into that now? She just didn't know.

Jenny sighed. Jesse was going to be so disappointed when he realized Matt wasn't staying on the ranch anymore. She had less than a week to get everyone calmed down and focused on the future.

Satisfied that her life was back on the right track, Jenny left the table to tell Angus what she'd done. She really, really hoped he wouldn't blow a gasket.

As usual, she found him in his office, his refuge.

She knocked on the open door. "Can we talk?"

He looked up from the accounts he was working on. "Sure. What's up?"

"I don't want to upset you, but I've asked Matt to leave the ranch."

Angus didn't look surprised. Why not? Had he noticed her attraction to Matt?

He put down his pen. She had his complete attention. "Where will he go?"

"I don't know. Probably not far. He'll still work here

during the day and spend time with Jesse, but he won't be living here."

Angus nodded slowly. She wondered why he didn't ask her how she'd come to the decision, but given that she and Matt had spent the night together, she was afraid he would think the worst.

"Angus, nothing happened last night."

"Never occurred to me that it would. You have a strong set of values."

Maybe, except for what she'd done to Matt.

She twisted her fingers together. "I'm just not comfortable with him here."

"Okay," Angus said. "No problem."

Jenny ran her nail along an indent in the doorjamb. "I'm going to take Jesse over to the Sheltering Arms for the day. I'll stay there, too, for a couple of hours."

She didn't want to watch Matt ride away with his bags packed.

ANGUS SPENT the afternoon on horseback, out on his land. He tried hard to rekindle his pride in his ranch, but his senses had been deadened when Kyle died.

If not for Jenny, he probably would have lost the ranch for all the interest he'd felt in it.

Jenny had got rid of Matt, had sent him off to sleep elsewhere at night. To his shame, Angus was relieved. He loved Matt, but envied him his son. Angus couldn't even take solace in Matt's presence as the surrogate son he'd once been. He still missed Kyle too much.

Face it, you thought Matt could replace Kyle. It didn't work that way. Even his love for Jesse couldn't fill the terrible void in Angus's soul.

The only time Angus felt anything was when he was

with Moira. Those feelings were often in turmoil, anger and pleasure intertwined, but in the middle of the confusion, he felt *alive*.

He spun his horse around and headed back to the house.

The day passed in an endless blur of events to which he felt no connection. Simple things like conferring with Jenny about ranch business, eating lunch and dinner with her and Jesse, checking out a problem with one of the horses.

None of it meant anything. And it had been like this since Kyle's death.

When he was on this ranch, his life was unfocused and gray.

Now Moira was back in town and his moments with her were stunning in their intensity. The grayness of his days became more and more depressing as he got more and more uncertain about the decision he'd made.

The thought of marrying Jenny should bring him joy, but he could see no change in his future other than starting to sleep with Jenny.

That idea left him cold. Jenny was a beautiful young woman, but he didn't love her. Would affection be enough?

He used to think it would be. It might have been had Moira not returned.

But Moira *was* here, she was his one and only, and he panicked at the notion of losing her again by marrying someone else.

Finally, after dinner, he could stand his blue funk and worried thoughts no longer.

He might be on the verge of making a terrible mistake. He needed to talk to Moira.

Minutes later, he was in his car on the road to Ordinary.

He parked in the alley behind Moira's shop and walked around to her door.

The overhead light came on when he knocked. The lace curtain in the window moved.

The door opened.

Moira stood in a satiny pink robe. She stared at him, waited for him to say something.

At this moment, he realized what was about to happen, that the moment he'd left the ranch to drive here, he'd made a decision.

He was desperate and needed more than conversation. He needed the physical warmth with Moira that he'd been missing for too many years.

He opened his mouth. "I can't live the rest of my life with a woman I don't love."

Moira flew into his arms and he held her and closed his eyes. Colors flashed behind his eyelids. He took her head and kissed her, more deeply than he ever had before and she returned his kiss in equal measure.

Her body was lush in his arms, mature and full and perfect. She was sensual and, he hoped, still bawdy after all these years. He meant to find out for sure tonight.

She pulled him into the apartment and turned off the light above the door. Holding his hand, she led him upstairs, her hips swaying in front of him.

She took him to the bedroom where a small yellow light burned beside a high bed covered with lace and roses.

She drew off her robe and tossed it onto a chair.

The silk nightgown she wore was soft and supple and hugged her generous curves.

He pulled one thin strap off her shoulder to reveal a breast that was more than enough to fill a man's hand. A large brown areola surrounded a dark pink nipple.

Angus bent forward and took it into his mouth and was rewarded with a sigh from Moira.

Her hands scrabbled for his jacket and pushed it from his shoulders, and then reached for the buttons of his shirt, all while he suckled her and she gasped.

In frustration, she tore his shirt open, sending buttons scattering everywhere.

"Angus," she cried, "take off your clothes."

He laughed and obliged her.

"Look at you," she said, rubbing his chest and curling her pink nails through his thick hair. "You've gained weight and muscle. Oh, Angus. You're a man now."

She let her nightgown fall to the floor and lay back on the bed, with her legs open, her only secrets hidden by copper curls.

Yes, she was still bawdy and Angus loved her for that.

He dropped his pants and stood naked in front of her.

She reached for his erection. "Come here. Look at you, my darling."

Angus lay on top of her and loved her. She loved him back. They used everything at their disposal. Lips and mouths, tongues, fingers and toes.

He'd never thought himself a weak man, never behaved so selfishly, but he needed this night with Moira, to convince himself that giving up his dream of more children was the right thing to do. Judging by how Moira surrendered to temptation, she needed him, too.

She stirred in his arms and released the scent of roses from the rumpled sheets.

He ran his hand over her thigh and around, caressing her full buttock, his fingertips dipping into the crease to fondle the impossibly soft skin where bum meets leg. Running his hand along the back of her thigh, watching her emerald eyes darken, he lifted her leg onto his hip, positioning himself against her.

Her heated aroma rose to greet him, but he stayed where he was, tormenting them both. He knew there was something more she wanted of him than just his body—an answer to the question he read on her face.

When he rested his hand on her chin, his large palm dwarfed her fine jaw. He ran one rough, callused finger across her cheek. "Will you marry me?"

The hope he saw in her eyes turned to joy. "Yes."

She pressed against him.

Her breast overflowed his hand. Yes, this was the right decision.

He suckled her breast, the dark nipple hard on his tongue. She writhed against him.

Dipping lower, he ran his mouth over her round stomach, catching her skin between his teeth, making her gasp, then dipping his tongue into her navel. She moaned and rubbed her generous breast against his shoulder.

He loved every inch of her.

Pulling back, he stared into slumberous eyes and sank into her. He gasped with the sweet ache of her warm welcome.

She was there with him every step of the way. Meeting him thrust for thrust, demand for demand. As if she couldn't get enough of him, of his flesh and his passion, of this union. And he knew how she felt.

He loved her.

Squeezing his eyes shut, he thrust hard and high one last time. Her muscles quivered, draining him dry.

They lay facing each other, sated, and breathed in the heady scent of roses and musk. Moira fell back against the pillow to stare at him.

"In every molecule, I want you. You have all of me. With every particle I will love you."

Angus closed his eyes. His ragged breath fanned copper curls and sent them fluttering around her beautiful face.

He glanced at the clock. Another six hours before he had to return to the ranch and talk to Jenny, to break her heart. He knew what she wanted. And he knew he could no longer give it to her.

CHAPTER ELEVEN

Matt drove to his parents' house.

The closest hotel was too far away to do him any good if he was still going to put in full days on Angus's ranch.

Before he'd left the bunkhouse, he'd stripped the blankets from his bed. He had no idea whether anything in that house was worth sleeping on, or whether it was riddled with bugs or mice.

He stepped onto the veranda and stared at the front door, at the green paint peeling, to reveal old white paint underneath. The doorknob had lost any claim to shine years ago.

He raised his hand to push it open, but didn't touch it. Couldn't.

No. He could not, absolutely *not,* sleep in there.

He turned around and strode back to the truck. From the backseat, he retrieved the sleeping bag that he always kept with him. A cowboy just never knew when he would be somewhere where he would need one.

He spread a couple of tarpaulins in the bed, spread out the sleeping bag on top of them and layered the blankets he'd brought on top of that.

He'd forgotten to bring a pillow.

Fully clothed, he slid into his makeshift bed, pillowing his hands under his head, staring at the light-pricked black blanket above him, picking out the constellations he'd shown his son a few nights ago in the Circle K's yard.

He didn't agree with Jenny's decision that he sleep elsewhere, but he guessed he understood her need to force distance between them.

The wind picked up, whistling through a couple of tall pines behind the house, whispering to him. His loneliness closed around him like a cloak, cooling instead of warming him.

The days of his life stretched before him, with him living a nomadic existence without a home base. He thought of the broken-down house across the clearing. Naw, that could never be home.

Nothing would.

JENNY STEPPED out of the house.

The sun had risen an hour ago and bathed the land with gold.

She breathed deeply of dew-dampened earth and spring grasses.

Angela's yellow crocuses were perky and bright in the sun, her mauve hyacinths fragrant.

Jenny had slept better last night than any night since Matt had returned.

What about those hours in the cabin wrapped in Matt's arms?

Those didn't count. They couldn't mean anything to her. She couldn't let them.

She strode to the bunkhouse and issued the orders for the day. She made a terse statement about Matt sleeping at his own house from now on. There were a few odd looks, but she ignored them. The ranch hands could think whatever they liked. She herself would stay close to the house and spend time with Jesse.

Matt drove into the yard.

She steeled herself to talk to him, to deny the rogue feelings that blinded her when she saw him.

When he climbed out of the truck, he was wearing the same clothes as yesterday. He pulled a bag out of the bed and walked toward her.

"If you don't mind, I still have to shower here."

"Of course, Matt. Do what you need to do."

He looked sullen, but underneath that she sensed real confusion.

"So I can work here and spend time with my son here and eat and shower here, but I can't sleep here. Do I have that right?"

"Matt." A sigh of frustration gusted out of her. "This is just the way it has to be right now. It doesn't make sense to me, either. I just need you to do this for me."

"Fine. Can you ask Angus what my marching orders are for the day? I'll be ready to work in about a quarter hour."

"Eat with the others in the backyard. I'll hunt down Angus and find out what he wants you to do."

Matt headed for the bunkhouse and Jenny to the house to find Angus.

Angela hadn't seen him yet this morning. A pot of coffee sat untouched on the counter. Strange. Angus was usually up long before now and would have consumed a couple of cups.

She checked to make sure he hadn't gone straight to the office.

Turning for the stairs, she tried to remember the last time Angus had slept in past nine.

She checked Jesse. Still asleep.

At the other end of the hall, Angus's bedroom door was open. Strange. He kept it closed when he was sleeping. The bathroom door down the hall was also open. He wasn't in the shower. Jenny stepped inside his bedroom. The bed hadn't been slept in.

Jenny's blood ran cold. Where was he? Where had he spent the night?

She wandered back downstairs. What—?

The sound of a car drew her outside.

Matt stood on the other side of the yard, staring at the approaching vehicle. His face looked flat, neutral, and that in itself was a bad sign. If a friend was driving down the lane, he would be smiling. If an enemy, he'd be angry.

The car pulled into the yard. Angus. But he wasn't alone. The new dressmaker in town, Moira, sat beside him.

Dread started a dance in her chest. No. Please. No.

Moira turned toward her and Jenny saw pity in her eyes. Sadness.

Angus stepped out of the car and stared at her over the roof. His expression of compassion said it all.

There would be no wedding on Saturday, not for Jenny at any rate.

Her head felt as though it would spin off her neck. She grabbed one of the veranda's support columns.

She didn't know where to look. She couldn't stand to face either Moira or Angus. She hated the understanding she felt coming from Matt's eyes.

She badly wanted to run, but didn't know where to go.

The cotoneasters were out of the question. They

were too close to the yard and Angus and Moira. To Matt. They held too many of her hopes, too many of her dreams shattered beyond repair.

The screen door opened and Jesse joined her on the veranda. He put his hand on her leg.

"Mom, can I have breakfast?"

She peered at him. The words weren't registering. She had nothing to give to her son at that moment.

Angus approached the steps and said, "I'll take care of him."

"No!" Jenny snapped. She didn't want him near her son. She searched for Matt. Where had he gone?

She grabbed Jesse in her arms and scooted around Angus. He tried to catch her arm. She wouldn't let him, couldn't stand the thought of him touching her, and ran for the bunkhouse.

Matt stepped out of the stable leading Lacey. He had saddled her. He'd known exactly what Jenny would need.

She handed Jesse to Matt and mounted her horse. "Watch him for me."

When she would have ridden off, Matt put a restraining hand on her thigh.

"Run. Get the anger out of your system, but do it safely. Come back in one piece."

His eyes said so much. He understood. He felt bad for her. He was her friend.

She and Matt had resisted each other the night of the storm. It had been one of the toughest nights of her life. Matt had restrained himself when he could have seduced her so easily.

Angus, on the other hand, had spent last night with

another woman and Jenny knew they'd done a hell of a lot more than talk.

Who was the better man now? Angus? Or Matt?

She flew out of the yard.

Two hours later, she returned. She wouldn't force Lacey to keep up the pace that Jenny needed to burn off the anger and the terrible, terrible sense of betrayal.

An hour ago, she'd slowed down and had taken her time, riding the ranch that would never, ever be hers again.

When she had finished putting Lacey away, she found Angus sitting on a wicker chair on the veranda.

"Why, Angus?" she asked.

"Thirty-five years ago, Moira and I were in love. We didn't act on it then. I couldn't stand for us to ignore a second chance."

"And last night?"

"Last night, I was weak and I'm not proud of it. I should have broken it off with you first before going to Moira."

"Yes, you should have."

She was drained of all feeling, frozen, wishing that her anger was greater than her shock so she could tell Angus what he and his girlfriend could go do to themselves. And it wouldn't be pretty. Good God, she hated cowards.

Angus's gaze slid away from her. "Jenny, I'm more sorry than I can say. You are a good, good woman. I wish I could be what you need."

"Should Jesse and I move to the bunkhouse?"

Angus stared at her. "Why?"

"Are you going to marry that woman?" Jenny couldn't bring herself to speak her name.

"As soon as possible. Until then, I'll stay in town with Moira. You won't have to see me around here."

"And on your wedding night, will you come back here?"

"I don't know yet. I don't think so. We haven't thought that far ahead."

"Too busy doing other things to talk?" That was low and dirty, but she was only human.

Angus's face flared a deep red. "Jenny—"

She didn't wait to find out what he had to say and entered the house.

What now? Her heart was broken, her life was falling apart, she'd lost her home, and she didn't have a clue what to do next.

THAT NIGHT, as she tucked Jesse into bed, he asked, "So Angus isn't going to be my daddy?"

"No, I'm afraid not."

His lower lip trembled. "Who is?"

"I don't know, honey. Right now, you're stuck with just me."

"If you're not gonna marry Angus, then what about the party?"

"There will still be a party, but it might not be on Saturday night and it won't be for Mommy and Angus. It will be for Angus and a different woman."

"But we can still go, right?"

"Do you want to so badly?"

"Yeah. Mikey says there's going to be lots of pop and cake." Jenny laughed mirthlessly. The things she never let him eat at home.

That word tripped her up. This was no longer her home. She didn't have one. Neither did Jesse.

"How about if I ask Hank and Amy if you can go to the party and sleep over with Michael?"

"Yeah." That made Jesse happy enough to let Jenny leave him for the night. She heard him settling in as she walked downstairs.

After she phoned Amy to tell her the change of plans and to ask if Jesse could attend the wedding party, whenever that might be, Jenny took a thick sweater out of the closet by the door, wrapped it around her shoulders and stepped outside.

She sat in the aging wicker rocking chair and rocked. And rocked. And rocked.

Around midnight, she knew she should head in to bed.

She did, wondering why she was bothering, knowing full well that she wouldn't sleep.

Two MORNINGS LATER, with gritty eyes and a sore back from sitting out so long in the chilly air the last couple of nights, Jenny rode the ranch alone.

She didn't know where the ranch hands were or what they were doing. She didn't know where Matt was. She didn't care much about anything today.

Where would she and Jesse go? She'd learned that Angus and Moira were taking a four-day honeymoon after they got married in a couple of days and were then returning to the ranch. Funny, Angus had never offered her a honeymoon.

How could Jenny possibly stay here?

The only good news in a week of bad was that the cattle rustlers had been caught on a ranch on the far side of Ordinary. One less thing to worry about.

The radio crackled. Someone was calling her. It sounded like Matt's voice. She ignored him.

Where would she and Jesse go? The question had rattled around and around her brain for two nights now, and she still had no answer.

The radio crackled again and she turned it off with an impatient flick of her wrist.

Ten minutes later, she heard a horse coming up fast behind her.

Matt rode up. "Something wrong with your radio?"

"Nope."

"Why didn't you answer when I called?"

"Didn't want to."

"We've got a problem along the banks of the creek, in the olive trees."

"You can take care of it."

"I haven't told you yet what the problem is."

"I don't care. Take care of it anyway."

Matt wrapped his fingers around her arm. Where he touched her, he warmed her. She hadn't realized how cold she'd been. Frozen. Dead. His fingers thawed a few square inches of her flesh, but the heat was only skin deep. She wasn't sure what it would take to thaw out her core, but doubted she'd figure it out anytime soon.

"Jenny, you're ranch foreman," Matt said. "Do your job."

She stared out across the fields and felt numb. "Matt, I've worked my ass off for this ranch. When Angus lost his will after Kyle died, I kept it going for him. I cared and cared and cared. For years, I've cared, and it's gotten me nowhere. It got me nothing."

She ambled away. "I don't care anymore."

"Jenny, come with me. Work will help. Come."

He almost sounded as if he was begging. For the first time since he'd ridden up, she looked at him and what she saw would have made her cry if she weren't already so cold and empty.

Dry ice. That's what she was. A big lump of dry ice.

Matt gazed at her with such tenderness, such compassion.

He took Lacey's reins and turned her in the direction he wanted her to go. Then he pressed those reins into Jenny's hand. He laced his fingers through Jenny's other hand and rode along beside her until they reached Still Creek.

MATT DIDN'T LIKE what he saw on Jenny's face, or rather, what he didn't see. She looked dead and that broke his heart. It angered him, but he was afraid to take it out on her.

He wasn't mad at her, but at life. She'd dealt with so much already, and had picked herself up every time, but life had kicked her in the teeth yet again.

"What's the problem?" she asked when they stopped, her voice toneless.

Matt pointed with a coil of rope. "Those steers hiding in the trees. Hip and Kelly moved the herd to another pasture but these guys refused to go. They ran into the trees knowing that neither the men nor their horses would go near those thorns."

"They do that sometimes so they don't have to move. There must be something in these fields that they like to graze on."

Matt dismounted.

Jenny started to ride toward the trees.

"Stop," he yelled and pulled her out of her saddle.

"You know you can't ride in there. Those thorns will tear Lacey's hide apart."

She felt limp in his arms, lifeless, and that worried him.

Her eyes were unfocused. He shook her gently. "Jenny, if you can't care for yourself, at least care for Lacey."

She perked up a little. Maybe he was getting through to her. "Okay." She sounded weary. "What do we have to do?"

Jenny knew better than he did what needed to be done here, but she was clearly lost. Somewhere inside her was the strong Jenny he loved. He just had to coax it out of her.

"I'm going to go in there and wrap the rope around the first steer and then we're going to drag him out. Together. Got it?"

He untied and unrolled his heavy duster from behind his saddle and put it on to protect himself. Those scratches these trees had given him the other day still hurt. He wasn't in the mood for more.

Putting on a pair of sunglasses to protect his eyes, he headed in for the closest steer.

The animal stared at him placidly, chewing on whatever grass or weeds grew under the trees.

He kept chewing while Matt wrapped the rope around his neck. Matt tried to lead him out, but the steer held his ground.

Matt pushed his way backward out of the trees and handed the end of the rope to Jenny. Wrapping his arms around the rope, he said, "Pull."

Nothing happened. "Goddammit, Jenny, pull. I can't do this alone."

She put effort into it this time and they persuaded the steer to come out of the trees.

"One down," Matt said. "Wait here and I'll go back in."

She pulled a little harder with the next and they managed to coax another one out.

Matt dived in four more times and they persuaded every steer but one to come out from among the trees.

The last had a mind of his own. They pulled and pulled until they both let go of the rope at the same time and fell. Matt tried not to land with his full weight on top of Jenny.

He rolled off her as soon as he could.

She started to laugh and laugh. "And people say animals are *dumb*."

"Jenny?" She was hysterical and he didn't know how to help her.

"Jenny," he breathed and held her until her laughter turned to tears. Amazing how sometimes there was so little difference.

"Oh, Matt…" She sobbed against his chest and he thought his heart would break in two.

He held her while the sun beat down on his back. He held her while the steer, still with the rope around his neck, walked out of the trees on its own and started to graze a dozen feet away. He held her until she'd cried herself out.

When she stopped and rolled onto her back, eyes closed, he took off the duster that had turned into an oven while they had lain on the warm earth.

He spread it out then pulled Jenny back into his arms on top of the coat.

She hiccuped. "Matt," she whispered. "What am I going to do?"

She looked at him with such trust, as if he might have all the answers in the world. Him, a screwup. A coward.

He had no answers for her. He couldn't stand the bleakness in her eyes, though. To make her feel better, he kissed her, gently opening her lips with his tongue and slipping inside.

She stroked the side of his face with her palm, her touch light and tender.

He answered in kind, with soft touches on her face, her neck, the vee of her chest exposed by her shirt.

Unbuttoning it, he caressed her more, over her bra, onto her ribs, across her velvet skin.

He pulled the tails of her blouse out of her jeans, spreading it open.

Unclipping the front closure of her bra, he opened her to the sun. He'd always thought her beautiful, but she'd grown lovelier with maturity.

Her breasts were high and firm, her nipples soft and brown. Eyes still closed, she groped for his hand and brought it to her mouth, where she rested her pursed lips against his palm. Then she placed that moist palm on her breast and her nipple beaded beneath his callused skin.

She draped one arm across her eyes and raised the other above her head, resting it on the grass at the edge of the duster.

She needs me. While Jenny lay still and waited, Matt lifted her breast with his hand and took her hard nipple into his mouth.

He played his tongue over her nipple and on the skin

around it, washing her breast with all the comfort he had to give her.

He loved her other breast as well as the first before moving on to her belly.

Lowering the zipper of her jeans, he pulled them down over her hips. A vee of dark hair peeked through the pink lace of her panties. After removing her boots and socks, he slid her jeans off.

Her panties soon joined them in the grass.

She lay in the sun like a goddess. He spread her long, strong legs open and let the sun greet white skin and chestnut hair that had never known its kiss before today.

He ran his lips from the arch of one foot to her ankle, her calf, her knee, her inner thigh, her curls. With his tongue, he parted her and heard her sigh.

He grasped the backs of her thighs and spread her wider, slid his tongue inside her and loved her, gave her all his caring and compassion and tenderness. She poured her response over him, her moisture and her trembling flesh and her need for him.

She whimpered until she came deeply and quietly.

He moved up to lie between her legs and hold her, until her trembling stopped.

"Oh, Matt."

He rose onto his elbows. She moved her arm from across her eyes and the sun turned her hazel flecks to gold. Grasping his head, she kissed him long and fiercely.

His own response was immediate. She reached for his jeans, unzipped them frantically and pulled him out, murmuring, "More."

He pulsed in her hand to the beat of his heart.

He tried to slow her down, sensed her need, gave in and entered her in one stroke.

She was wet and ready and she moved against him like a madwoman. They came together.

He buried his face in her neck, smelled musk and grass.

While she calmed, softened, breathed deeply, he held her, probably for the last time.

He was still the same man he'd always been, not the staying kind that Jenny needed, but while she was here now, his, he would stay and hold her.

Later. He would leave later.

They made love again, with Jenny on top proud and pretty in the sun, whispering nothing more than each other's names. For now, it was enough.

JENNY FELT MATT WITHDRAW, knew the moment he was going to say the things she didn't want to hear.

"Don't," she said.

"Don't what?"

"You know. Don't say whatever it is you have to tell me next. That you can't stay. That you're leaving."

"We both know it's true. We both know it's only a matter of time. Better sooner than later."

She'd known that, but had hoped that in the middle of their magical lovemaking, he had changed.

Her panties lay pink and fragile on the green grass. She pulled them on, then found her bra and covered herself.

Beside her Matt got dressed, too, silently.

When Jenny finished buttoning her blouse, she stood and walked to Lacey, who grazed nearby.

Before she could mount, Matt turned her around and took her into his arms.

It was a goodbye of sorts, and an apology, that he couldn't stay, but that he wasn't yet ready to let her go.

She clung to him. "Thank you," she said softly.

"Don't say that, as if I did you some big favor. You deserve so much more."

He held her face in his hands and whispered fiercely, "You deserve more than me."

She crumpled a bit and then pulled herself together. Matt had given her more than he thought he had. He'd given her strength and comfort for the moment. He'd eased her soul. Had relieved some of the darkness.

"When we get to the house, I'm going to leave. Tell Angus I'll pay him somehow. Take care of our son and love the daylights out of him."

"Matt, don't ever come back. Ever. I can't do this again. I can't keep loving you and losing you."

He nodded.

"If you still want to be Jesse's dad, we'll find a way. But the only reason I ever want to see you again is if you want to marry me. I won't take anything less. Never."

She meant it. Matt wouldn't commit. So she would never see him again.

Tonight, she would mourn. Oh, how she would mourn.

THE FOLLOWING MORNING, after a night of sadness without tears, she mourned hard. The grieving was hell.

Amy had driven over to pick up Jesse for Angus and Moira's wedding. Everyone had decided that, since Hank and Amy had already ordered the food for Angus and Jenny, the wedding would take place that day. Amy knew how awful Jenny would be feeling, so Jenny had the worst time getting her to leave. But she needed to be alone.

The ranch hands had left to attend the celebrations.

The Circle K ranch had never felt so lonely. Well, maybe once, just after her parents had lost it and before Angus and Kyle had moved in.

She couldn't cry, was cried out. She'd gotten rid of her tears yesterday, with Matt's help.

Don't think about Matt and yesterday and the sun on your bare skin.

She knew she would survive. She always did, but she'd lost her anchor.

Loving Jesse would save her. Her love for him would have to be her anchor again, would keep her placing one foot in front of the other every day, would keep her hunting for somewhere else to call home.

MATT CRAWLED out of the sleeping bag and sat up in the bed of his truck, scrubbing his fingers through his hair.

He'd slept badly.

Jenny. Jesse.

He missed them with an intensity that burned. How could he ride out of Ordinary now that he knew about his son? Now that he loved him? How could he leave Montana after what he'd shared with Jenny yesterday?

His heart hurt, ached as if it was going to break in two. Did hearts really break? Could the human heart recover from this kind of loss?

He wanted his woman. He wanted his son. He wanted his family.

The house mocked him in its run-down drunken

glory, as if to say, *What do you know about family? What do you know about love?*

If what he felt wasn't love, he might as well dig his grave now, because he didn't think he could survive this misery.

He thought he'd been lonely after he'd left Jenny five years ago? Ha! This was hell on earth. Why couldn't he learn to stay? Why didn't he deserve what other people had so easily? A normal life.

Enough cowardice.

He jumped from the bed of the truck ready to face down some old demons, his ancient devils.

The front door cried its protest when he pushed it open. He should put a match to it. He should burn down the whole house.

He had only one reason to enter this house for the last time.

He needed answers. He craved whatever might set him free of his legacy. Why couldn't he be his own man, apart from his parents, apart from his past? Apart from the terrified teenager he'd been when he'd gotten Elsa pregnant?

Why couldn't he rise above it all to become a better man? How did he lay his past to rest?

Read the autopsy report, Jenny had said. *You need closure.*

Whatever that meant, he'd give it a shot.

The envelope still lay on the kitchen counter where he'd left it. He picked it up and slit the top open then carried the report to the table.

His hand trembled when he tried to read the first sheet. He couldn't get past his mother's name. He knew how his parents died. Gunshot wounds. Case closed. He dropped the report.

You need closure, Matt. Jenny's voice again—calm and confident. *What if they found something they didn't expect?*

Okay, he'd make himself read the report. He held his breath while he picked up the document.

Then exhaled loudly when he read the findings.

Dear God. What kind of joke had fate played on his family?

His mother had had a brain tumor. His poor mother had lived with an undetected tumor that had slowly driven her mad. Here it was in hard-edged letters on a crisp white sheet. His mother hadn't had crazy genes. She hadn't passed insanity on to him. The loving mother he remembered from before was his real mother. The older woman had no more control over her actions than a two-year-old would. She had slowly, slowly gone mad, and had been helpless to stop it.

Matt was suddenly furious. What the hell had Pop done about it? Nothing. Not a goddamn thing. Matt remembered her complaints of headaches, and of not feeling well. Pop had let the woman he married lose her mind and hadn't lifted a finger to save her.

He needed to put his demons to rest. He needed to know it all.

Before he left, Matt picked up the framed photograph of him and his mother. In her lucid moments, had she studied it and wondered where she had gone? Why she was no longer the woman in the photograph?

He drove into Ordinary, to visit Missy Donovan.

Missy lived in a small, neat bungalow on the far side of town. She'd had a gentleman friend who'd set her up in this house and had furnished it for her. He'd taken care of her until his death five years ago. Matt wondered how she got by now.

Rosebushes lined the path to her front door. A wicker chair sat on the whistle-clean veranda, pure white with a green cushion.

A brass knocker in the shape of a cat gleamed on the front door. Matt rapped it against the wood.

Missy answered, her eyes widening when she saw him. She nodded, then said, "I thought you might show up eventually. C'mon in."

She led him into a small, neat living room. She gestured to the sofa. "Have a seat."

Matt was glad to see Missy no longer dyed her hair. It had changed back to black, streaked with gray. It curled softly around her face, making her look younger than the long, blond stuff had. She'd gained weight in middle age, but she still looked good. She always did have half the men in town panting after her like bloodhounds. Everyone said she was easy. He didn't know about that.

"You want an iced tea?" she asked.

He nodded. "Thanks."

She didn't ask why he was here.

Matt studied the room when she went to the kitchen. The furniture wasn't the best, but neither was it cheap. She'd got herself a cozy little setup out of her last man.

A photo of a stunning young woman caught his eye. She looked familiar. He stood and walked to the mantel, studying the picture with every step. The woman looked out at the world with a sensuality that rivaled Missy's, but with more confidence and in-your-eyes bravado. This was a woman who made dares—and never turned one down.

The black of her hair gleamed with the healthy sheen of youth, and matched the eyebrows above her brilliant blue eyes.

"That's my Angel," Missy said behind him.

"This is little Angel?" He looked at Missy over his shoulder. He vaguely remembered Missy's daughter—a child just passing into adolescence when he'd left town. "She's grown up real well. She's a stunner."

Missy smiled. "She's nineteen and a lot prettier than I ever was."

"That's not true. She got her looks from you."

Missy laughed. "Your father was a charmer, too." She saw Matt's face tighten and said, "He could be kind."

Not likely. Not his father.

She put his glass of tea on the coffee table in front of the sofa then sat in the armchair and reached for her cigarettes. She lit one and her bosom rose and fell as she drew on it.

The cancer society oughta shoot Missy Donovan, Matt thought. She was the only woman he'd ever known who made smoking look sexy. On everyone else, it looked cheap and tough. Missy had a sensuality a man could lose himself in. Was that what Pop had done? Matt felt bad for his mother. How could she fight what Missy had to offer, with half of her brain already eaten by a tumor?

"He loved her, you know." Missy must have been a mind reader. "Your father was crazy about your mother until the day she killed them both."

She sucked on her cigarette again with those beautiful lips then blew smoke through the small perfect circle they made.

"I saw your father off and on for years." When she read the disapproval on Matt's face, Missy continued, "I don't say this to hurt your feelings. I want you to know the man your father really was. I'm pretty sure you didn't see much of the good in him when you were growing up."

She cleared the huskiness out of her throat. "He came to me for sex. That was it. What he and your mom had the last few years was too wild for him, but he couldn't stop going back for more."

This was way too much information. Matt didn't want to know any more about his parents' sexual relationship than he already did.

"He came to me for boring, plain, dull, ordinary sex."

Matt frowned. He couldn't imagine that of Pop, or of the sensual creature sitting across from him.

"Trust me. He gave his passion to Gloria. He brought his physical needs to me." She took a final puff on her cigarette then squashed it in a small crystal ashtray. "And we talked. We'd make love once each night, then we'd talk for the rest of the night—about Gloria and how much he missed the woman he married."

Matt felt the anger rise in him again, that Pop had done nothing to help Mom. "Why didn't he take her to a doctor? Why didn't he help her?"

"He took her to a shrink who gave her medication that made her a vegetable. He couldn't stand it. Neither could she. She threw the pills away."

Matt gripped the arm of the sofa. "Couldn't he have done something else?"

"He didn't have a clue what else to do. He was so mad at her for going crazy, but he could see the hurt and frustration in her eyes. He got so angry whenever he saw her."

"Tell me about it," Matt muttered.

"He had to booze himself up just to go home and then he'd come back to me, crying."

"Pop? *Crying?*" Matt shook his head. "No way."

"Yes," Missy said in her calm, husky voice. "Crying. He missed her, Matt. He missed the real woman inside."

So did Matt. He put his hand over his heart, where it ached for missed opportunities, for what-might-have-beens if his mother had never developed that tumor.

"Your father just wasn't mature enough, or sophisticated enough, to deal with it. It killed him in the end."

"She had a tumor," he said.

"Oh, Lord. Was that what made her crazy?"

Matt told Missy about the autopsy report.

"That's tragic. So sad for all of you."

"Did you know my mother?" he asked, starving for the parts of her he only hazily remembered. He hungered for details about her.

"Your father married her and brought her home from a rodeo in California. He boasted that he came back with two trophies, a belt buckle and your mother."

Matt smiled. He could imagine Pop doing that, showing Mom off in her young prettiness.

"She was a waitress in a bar. Had a lovely smile. Used to sing a bit, too." Missy seemed lost in her memories.

"Keith never came into town without Rose on his arm." Missy's smile was tinged with envy. "They were glued to each other. Madly in love. No wonder. Rose sure was a knockout. Friendly, too."

Matt drank it in, ate up all the details of the woman

he remembered in feelings, inside, if not in actual memory.

"What happened to them later was a real shame," she said.

When she lit another cigarette, a gold wedding band glinted on her finger.

"Hal married me before he died," she said, answering his curious look. "Only time I've ever been married. It lasted twenty-four hours. He died the next day."

"I'm real sorry about that."

She shrugged. "We had two years to prepare for it. We made good use of those years." Her lips curved into a soft smile and Matt was glad she had happy memories.

"What did he die of?" he asked.

"Cancer. I nursed him."

Matt nodded. Yeah, she was the kind of woman who would stick with a man to the end.

When the iced tea and memories were spent, Matt stood to leave.

"There's something else you need to know before you go," Missy said.

"What's that?"

She pointed to her daughter's photograph. "Angel is your half sister."

CHAPTER TWELVE

He had a sister.

Matt couldn't get his head around that. His dad and Missy had made a sibling for him and he'd never known. All those years when he'd felt so alone, he'd had a little sister in town. So close. He could have gotten to know her. Could have cared for her the way older brothers do with baby sisters.

He sat in his pickup truck outside Missy's house, still stunned by her announcement.

Matt needed to see Angel, to talk to her, to find out what she thought about having a brother, but she was away in Bozeman attending Montana State University. Missy was proud of Angel, with good reason. With Missy's poor background, she'd probably never thought a child of hers would continue her education after high school. Thanks to Hal's money and to Missy's nursing him in his last years, Angel had a chance to move ahead in life.

Hal had done better by Angel than her natural father had. Did Angel even know about Keith Long? So many questions needed answering. Missy promised to contact him the next time Angel came home for a visit. He couldn't wait to see her.

Matt thought about his parents.

One lousy, lousy twist of fate had screwed up his

parents and their marriage and, as a consequence, him. Matt wanted to howl at the savage injustice of it.

He would never end up like his mother. If he ever got her symptoms, he would know what was wrong. He'd have them check for a tumor.

He wasn't his father, either. Except for that one mistake with Elsa and the terror of the depth of his love for Jenny, he'd been responsible. Matt had sown a few wild oats, had made a bit a money on the rodeo circuit, but he hadn't spent ninety percent of his life chasing belt buckles, booze and women. He'd also been a hard worker.

He would never die from a shotgun blast.

Was he enough like his father to abandon his son? No!

He refused to be his dad, or to act like him. He was the one Long father who was going to break the mold and raise his child with reliability and a whole *shitload* of love.

Matt had been alone for so many years. He wasn't alone anymore.

A couple of weeks ago he'd had nobody. Now he had a son and a half sister he'd never known about. His heart swelled with the knowledge that it mattered to him. It *all* mattered—having a family. Keeping a family.

Keeping Jenny.

He wanted her with an ache that left him breathless. He wanted her for all eternity. He wanted to make a family with her.

When Angel returned to town, he would get to know her. And he'd get to know his son even more than he already had.

There was no comparison between his relationship

with Jesse and what he'd had with his own father. Already Matt felt he was doing a better job.

He'd go to Jenny and marry her. He'd treat her and Jesse with all the tenderness and love they deserved, because some weird twist of fate could screw it up. He was tired of living a buggered-up, lonely life. He was stronger than his poor, lost man-child of a father.

Whatever problems he encountered, he was capable of dealing with.

He was going to grab hold of his family and hang on tight, and stay through everything.

Matt needed Jenny. Now. Yesterday. Tomorrow. Forever.

He was going to marry her.

Jenny Sterling, my pure, steady guardian angel, I'm coming to get you.

"Thanks for the tea," he called as he waved out the window and drove away from Missy Donovan's house. He needed his family. He needed his son and the woman he loved.

He had no idea where they were going to live, or how they would support themselves, but they were going to be together.

TWENTY MINUTES LATER, Matt arrived at the Circle K. The place was empty. Of course. The wedding was today.

Jenny wouldn't have gone. He ran into the stable. Lacey was in her stall.

He went into the house and called her name. No answer.

Just about ready to check the top of the hill, he had a thought.

Had she slept as badly as he had last night?

He took the stairs two at a time.

She lay on top of her bed in a T-shirt and panties. Her jeans lay on the floor where she'd dropped them when she went to bed.

She'd left her socks on. One of them was half off, making her foot look twelve inches long.

He smiled. Lord, he loved everything about her.

Nudging her, he lay down beside her. She moved in her sleep, rolling halfway over.

Starting with her foot, he touched her, ran his hand up her leg, skirted the apex of her thighs and rested his hand on her stomach.

Her skin felt soft enough to sink into.

He leaned up on one elbow to watch her wake and moved his hand once more, to her breast. No bra.

She came awake gradually, with a tiny purring sound in her throat. He'd always known this about his tomboy—that she was a sensual creature.

Jenny opened her eyes slowly.

"Dreaming?" she whispered.

"No."

She closed her eyes again, and moaned in what sounded like pain. He'd done that to her, to this woman who was too strong to break. He'd wounded her. No more.

Her body reacted to him, her nipple beading against the fingers that played with it.

"I can't say no to you," she said. "I thought I was strong, but I'm not."

He kissed her temple and tasted salt on his lips. "You are strong, the strongest person I know."

His hand roved to her other breast.

"I can't be strong when you're touching me."

"I'm making a commitment," Matt said.

A furrow appeared between Jenny's eyebrows. She didn't understand. Or was afraid to believe him. He was suddenly desperate. If he couldn't explain in words, he'd find another way to show her. Heat smoldered in his body. He needed her. He pulled off his shirt and threw it onto the floor with her jeans. She stared at his chest.

He lay down beside her again, still circling her breast with his fingers. His erection strained against his pants, but he refused to rush. He had all the time in the world. He held her gently but firmly, not wanting to hurt her, but not wanting to let her go either. This, *this,* was heaven, holding Jenny.

She turned around in his arms, color high on her cheeks.

"What did you say?"

"I'm making a commitment. I want to marry you."

She stared at him. "Really?"

"Really. As soon as possible."

"Why— How?" Her warm breath fanned his face.

"Shh. Later. For now, just enjoy."

Matt reined himself in, forced himself to go slowly, to lick her from breasts to navel with a measured intensity that inflamed them both. Jenny writhed beneath him, and let out small moans that heated him with tenderness, made him search harder for the spots that would entice more of those delicious sounds from her.

He needed to see more of her and pulled back.

Jenny watched him silently, solemnly, her hands on his shoulders, her body long and lithe, and bathed in soft light filtered by lace curtains on the window.

He slipped one finger under the fragile thong strap

riding high on her hip and dragged her panties down her legs.

He spread her legs and stared at the treasure there, protected by curls dark against the intimate flesh.

"Jenny." He breathed her name like a benediction, knowing how it would warm her. She shivered and waited for his next move.

He pressed his lips to the soft curls.

Her heat rose to greet him. Her legs widened to welcome him. He explored. Licked. Stroked. Dampened. Tasted. Cradling her tush in his palms, he lifted her to him to delve more deeply into her wet core, getting drunk on her essence.

She writhed and pushed herself against his ravening mouth. He gave everything he had with the sweet hope that it would be enough. She keened high and softly, and he wanted to swallow that sound. She stiffened and wrapped her thighs around him to hold him still.

Her lush scent sent him reeling with need.

She dropped to the bed with a long sigh that sounded like his name. He smiled, saw his future full of endless nights of loving Jenny.

He sat back on his heels and stared at the long, hot vision in front of him, a muscled, sleek cat of a woman who stretched sinuously. Then she opened her eyes, dark with passion and satisfaction.

She rose to sit in front of him, to lean in and kiss him. He closed his eyes, felt the tip of her tongue against his lips, knew that she would taste herself there.

Jenny opened her mouth on his and became bold, holding his face between her hands while she explored him, pulled away with slow luxury before pushing him onto his back. She straddled him, sitting on his erection, which strained for release from his jeans, and moved her hips in circles of exquisite torture.

She threw her head back, leaving her neck long and bare above her gently swaying breasts. Her hips undulated. Her stomach tightened and eased with each luscious circle. The bare flesh of her upper thighs gripped his hips.

Matt groaned. He could watch her for all eternity.

Sweet Jenny.

Devouring him with the eyes of a hungry woman, she leaned forward, raised his arms above his head and pressed them into the bed. Then, with wonderfully slow strokes, explored his biceps and shoulders and chest and his sensitive heaving abdomen with her capable hands, leaving a trail of heat as potent as the Montana sun.

Those hands unzipped the denim and touched his flesh and he gasped. He felt the wonderment in her, in the way she cradled him with tenderness that suddenly changed to conviction to urgency to a wet hot tight Jenny welcome thank you thank you thank you.

He hissed.

She gripped him hard and tight, moved muscles, spectacular flesh, pretty breasts. Yes, love. Yes, Jenny.

He stiffened, held her hips still, came and shivered.

This woman.

Jenny.

He pulled her down onto him, held her against him while their hearts hammered in their chests. He shoved his fingers into her hair and ravished her mouth, pouring himself into her until he fell back, spent, against the lace comforter.

He stroked her skin and held her beautiful behind in his hands.

"I love you, Jenny."

She lifted her head and met his gaze with sleepy eyes.

"I love you, Matt," she whispered, her voice deep and womanly.

He stroked her cheek with one finger then placed his hand back on her behind.

"My beautiful, true Jenny."

She rested her head on his chest. The satin of her hair brushed his sensitized skin.

He sighed.

Matt awoke to a dim room, lit only by the soft grays and purples of dusk, with Jenny still on his chest, asleep, his hands on her bum. He grinned. Life was good.

He wrapped his arms around her and squeezed. He would be true to this woman for the rest of his life. Nothing and no one would come between them.

She stirred and moaned.

"Oh, my legs," she murmured. "Oooh, my thighs."

He tapped her lightly on the rump. "You should be used to it with all the horseback riding you do."

Jenny sat up and looked down at him with sparkling eyes. "I will never, ever get enough of this."

He grinned. "We're going to try, darling. We're going to spend the rest of our lives trying."

He lifted her off him and threw her onto the bed on her back. She laughed and he got high on the sound.

He kissed her stiff thighs to make them better.

She laughed again, lighting the room with her joy.

God, he loved her.

He jumped off the bed and hooted, loud and long. He drew her off the bed and into his arms.

"If I wasn't so hungry, I'd stay here and love the daylights out of you. Let's go downstairs before I give in."

Jenny took a plaid shirt out of her closet.

Matt rummaged through the bedsheets for her panties.

He searched the covers and the floor, then got down on his knees and found them under the bed.

"How the hell did they get under there?" He threw them to her.

She grinned and pulled them up her long, long legs. Matt nearly lost it, nearly dragged her back to bed. He turned around, got himself dressed and ran out of the room.

"I'll see you in the kitchen," he called as he hustled down the stairs. "Hurry! I'm an impatient man. I need to eat and then get right back up here."

"Why here?" she asked. "There's a great fireplace in the living room."

He smiled then sauntered to the kitchen. He was going to enjoy being married to Jenny.

The world was finally irrevocably right.

THEY ATE LEFTOVER lasagna beside the fire that Jenny had built.

"You make a good fire," Matt said. "In more ways than one."

He leaned toward her and kissed her.

With his eyes so close, so blue, Jenny asked, "Is this real, Matt?"

"More real than anything I've ever done."

"When you left this last time I thought I'd never see you again. What happened?"

"I've been sleeping in the bed of my pickup. When I—"

Jenny cut him off. "In your truck?"

"Yeah. I couldn't sleep in that house."

"I just assumed you would. If it's any consolation now, I'm sorry. I know I was being irrational." She kissed him before continuing. "I was terrified that I wouldn't be able to resist you, that I would haul you out of your bed one night and drag you into mine."

"For the record, I don't believe you would have done that. You are so strong, Jenny."

When she would have argued, he said, "Moving on, I woke up miserable this morning. I felt like my life was over. I couldn't stand the pain of losing you and Jesse."

Matt stared into the flames. Jenny waited for him to continue. She knew that *he* thought he was sure of his change of heart, but *she* had to hear it herself.

"I kept asking myself why I couldn't have you and Jesse, why I didn't deserve to live a normal, happy life. So I went into the house and read the autopsy report."

That startled Jenny. "Matt, that was brave of you."

"I was shaking the whole time. Imagine that, a grown man shaking because of a few scraps of paper."

When he looked at her, there was wonder in his eyes. "She wasn't insane, Jenny. Mom had a brain tumor."

Jenny covered her mouth with her hands. "A tumor?" All those years lost because of that. Three lives ruined by a mass of deadly tissue.

"Yeah," Matt said. "No weird genetics. No crazy DNA. I'll never end up like her." He wrapped his hand around the back of her neck and urged her forward. He kissed her lips. "And Pop was just a weak man. I won't be that weak again, Jenny. I promise."

She could see in his face his absolute belief that he would never again be his father, he would never be the young man who ran away when the heat became too much.

He had grown. In his eyes, she saw conviction and a new maturity.

Jenny suddenly felt weepy. So many tears in the past had been hidden or buried because of pride or the fear that she might never stop crying, but these? These were happy tears burning the backs of her eyelids.

"This is real, isn't it?"

"You'd better believe it, Jenny. We're getting married and we'll stay that way forever."

Oh, oh, the sweetness.

Jenny took Matt's plate and set it aside on top of her own, then pushed Matt onto his back. This time she was the aggressor.

Too much happiness and love roiled inside of her to put into words, so she put it all into action, telling him exactly how she felt.

THE FOLLOWING MORNING, Jenny woke up sprawled with Matt in front of a cold fireplace. Sometime during the night they'd decided to sleep here.

She'd spread blankets on the floor and had brought down her lace comforter from her bedroom.

Snuggling under it against Matt's side, she counted her blessings. Jesse. Matt. They had no place to live, but that was okay.

Before falling asleep in Matt's arms, Jenny had realized that home wasn't a piece of land or a ranch house. Her home had a pair of names—Jesse and Matt.

They could live anywhere and her love for them

would be as powerful as the love she'd shared with her parents in this house, and would be more potent than her love for this land.

The fire had gone out hours ago. No matter. They'd made good use of the fire throughout the night.

They seemed to have a penchant for making love in front of fires. Jenny vowed to make sure it happened often throughout their lives.

Matt stirred beside her.

She heard his morning-husky voice say, "Good morning," and felt it rumble through the hard chest under her ear.

"Good morning." She looked up at Matt and smiled. "The best morning ever."

"It's chilly in here."

Jenny stated the obvious. "The fire died."

While he unfolded his beautiful body and shoved aside the screen, he said, "I'll build it back up."

"We don't need it. It's time for breakfast."

Matt squatted in front of the grate with kindling in his hand and peered at her.

"Yes, Jenny, we *do* need a fire."

The banked fire in his eyes set parts of her body tingling. She saw his desire for her, but it was different than it had ever been before, uncomplicated and clean.

His love for her was unmarred by the past or someone else's sins. Matt was his own man now.

Under his talented fingers, the fire leaped to life.

Flickering flames lovingly kissed the hills and valleys of Matt's strong body. Lean and muscular, Matt was Jenny's perfect man.

She had a right to touch this body from now on, without fear or shame. Matt was hers.

He watched her over his shoulder. If she had the right to stare at Matt's beautiful body, he had the same right with hers.

She pulled the comforter away from her body and let him look his fill.

Too quickly, her body cooled and she shivered.

Matt covered her from head to toe with his solid heavy body and she'd never felt so warm or so safe.

They loved each other with a thoroughness that left them trembling.

Afterward they lay boneless. Everything in the world was so right.

Jenny's happiness threatened to overwhelm her, so she said, "Let's go get Jesse and tell him about his daddy. He's at the Sheltering Arms. Let's share our news with Hank and Amy, too."

They ran upstairs to shower, but that took a while. Matt didn't think Jenny was quite clean enough and had to wash her pretty thoroughly after she'd already finished scrubbing herself.

Her giggles rang around the bathroom, echoing against the tiles in the shower stall and punctuated by Matt's deep laughter.

Eventually, finally, they finished and dressed, but Jenny wanted tonight to be here *now*.

They rode over to the Sheltering Arms because it would take longer than driving and held hands all the way, while Lacey and Master bumped up against each other. The horses also grazed every time Matt stopped to kiss Jenny, or she stopped to kiss him.

Jenny smiled because she thought she could almost hear their thoughts.

Enough already.

Nope. Jenny sighed. The rest of her life would not be enough. She planned to love Matt well and often.

They rode into the Sheltering Arms Ranch and heard children's laughter floating from the stable. They dismounted and left the horses tied to the corral fence.

Hand in hand, they followed the sounds of that laughter. Jenny's heart raced. Wait until Jesse heard.

She saw Hank first.

"How was the party?" she asked.

Hank stared at them as if he'd never met them before. Most particularly, he stared at their joined hands.

Jenny grinned. "We have good news."

Hank didn't wait to hear what it was because it had to be so clearly written on her face. He hauled Jenny up into an embrace that could rival an Angus Kinsey hug. A split second after he dropped her to her feet, he grabbed Matt and hugged him, slapped his back, shook his hand.

Since marrying Amy, Hank loved anything to do with marriages and happily-ever-afters.

Jenny couldn't wipe the grin from her face. Her muscles refused to obey.

"Where's Jesse?"

"Jess!" Hank hollered.

Jesse came down the aisle, jumping over beams of sunlight where they fell through small cracks in the wall.

When he saw Matt and Jenny he squealed, "Mom! Matt!" and he threw himself against their legs.

"Michael, Cheryl," Hank called. "We're heading inside." To Matt and Jenny, he said, "Let's go share this with Amy."

Amy shrieked when she heard and hugged Jenny and kissed Matt soundly on the mouth.

"Where is the wedding?" she asked.

"We haven't even talked about that." Jenny had no idea where their future lay, whether they could find a place near Ordinary for themselves.

When she mentioned this, Hank asked, "The Long land?"

Matt shook his head. Knowing the reasons for his past unhappiness didn't erase the bad memories.

"How about here?" he asked. "We can find someplace for you to settle in."

"Hank, thank you, but we need a place of our own." She didn't know whether Matt agreed until he caught her eye and nodded.

Two hours later, they left the Sheltering Arms on horseback. Jesse rode on Matt's lap. The picture they made warmed Jenny to the tips of her toes.

CHAPTER THIRTEEN

ANGUS AND MOIRA returned Thursday from their mini-honeymoon. As they drove down the laneway to the house, Angus was nervous. He didn't know what to expect. How was Jenny going to feel about him? About Moira?

Would she even still be here?

He stepped onto the veranda just as Jenny came to the front door.

A soft smile lit her face, untainted by anger. Why?

"What happened?" he asked. "The last time I saw you, you were furious with me. You looked like you never wanted to see me again."

"I was, yes. I can't agree with your methods, Angus, but you were right. We didn't love each other. Getting married would have been a mistake."

Angus's fear evaporated. "Thank God. I thought I'd lost your friendship."

Jenny's expression sobered. "You have lost some of my respect, but I'd like to find that again. You were always good to me, Angus."

He opened his arms and Jenny walked into his hug.

"I'll miss your Angus Kinsey hugs," she said.

"Hey, I'll make sure Moira understands that they're available to you whenever you need one."

"I'd like that, Angus." She seemed to turn shy. "I might not need them, though."

That saddened him. He had deep affection and respect for Jenny.

"I have good news of my own."

He smiled. "What's that?"

"Matt and I are getting married."

Angus let out a shout of laughter. "That's wonderful! How did this come about?"

"Come," Jenny said. "Let's sit over here."

"I'll tell Moira to join us. She was too worried to get out of the car."

"Wait, Angus. I'd like to talk to you alone first. It'll be hard for me to accept her. What you two did was pretty rotten."

Angus's collar suddenly seemed too tight. "Jenny, I'll regret what I did to you for the rest of my life. I should have handled the situation better."

"Yes, you should have. I care for you, Angus. Because of the good times we've shared, it's easier for me to forgive you than Moira. She knew we were engaged and she slept with you anyway. The least she could have done was to send you home to break things off with me first."

Jenny brushed a lock of hair from her face and held it while the breeze tried to move it again. "I have no relationship with this woman, no happy past, but I will try to like her and to forgive her. For your sake, if nothing else. No guarantees, though."

"I understand." Angus covered her hand with his and squeezed. "If you're willing to try, that's enough for me."

He turned and gestured for Moira to join them.

Angus couldn't watch Moira step out of the car and mount the veranda steps without feeling his heart swell. He'd been given a second chance at love and was holding on to it with both hands.

Moira stood in front of Jenny hesitantly. Strange for her to hesitate about anything. Then Angus realized that she wanted Jenny to like her and his heart swelled even more.

"You two have never officially met," he said. "Moira, this is my special friend, Jenny."

Moira smiled and extended her hand. "Jenny, I want to apologize for my behavior. I wronged you and I'm sorry."

Jenny's expression was cool, but she unbent enough to shake Moira's hand.

"Jenny and Matt are getting married," Angus said and Moira smiled.

"I'm so glad," she said.

Angus directed them all to the wicker chairs. "Tell me," he said to Jenny.

She related what had happened while he and Moira had been gone.

Angus laughed. "Where's Matt? I want to congratulate him."

"He's out looking for a place for us to live."

That surprised Angus. "But why not here?"

Jenny leaned forward. "I don't think that would work, Angus."

"Why not? You could stay on as foreman. Matt could continue to work here."

"Where would Jesse and I sleep? In the bunkhouse with Matt?"

"You could stay in the house. It's large enough."

"Not for two sets of newlyweds."

"She's right, Angus," Moira said, laying a gentle hand on his knee. "We all need our privacy. Jenny will have a family. She should have a place of her own."

"Has Matt had any luck?" Angus asked.

Jenny shook her head. "There's nothing available these days."

Angus knew what the answer would be but asked the question anyway. "Matt's house?"

Jenny shook her head harder. "Too many bad memories. He'd just as soon burn the place down."

"I can't say I would feel differently if I was him."

"Apparently, when he first came back, Matt put the ranch up for sale. He only changed his mind after I told him about Jesse. Then he decided the land could be Jesse's legacy. But the house? No. Matt doesn't want Jesse in there. Ever."

The breeze kicked up the scent of lilacs.

"Matt's going to try to sell it again. Paula Leger and her father are searching for properties, but it looks like we may have to move a fair distance away to get something we can afford."

Angus's heart dropped into his boots. He knew that Matt could never replace Kyle, but he sure felt like a son to Angus anyway. He wanted Matt nearby.

His affection for Jenny was genuine and strong. He would love to start thinking of her as a daughter, which meant he didn't want to see her leave, either.

And Jesse? Jesse made him feel alive. It was good to have someone young in the house after so many years without children around. And now Angus might lose them all.

"Where's Jesse?" He rose out of his seat. He needed to see the little guy.

"In the kitchen with Angela," Jenny said.

Angus moved to the door and called into the house, "Jesse."

He heard a scream of delight and then Jesse was running down the hall and jumping into his open arms.

Angus clasped him to his chest. The small bundle smelled like vanilla and chocolate.

"You been baking?" he asked.

Jesse nodded so hard flour drifted from his hair onto his shirt. Onto Angus's, too.

Oh, Lord, he would miss this child.

"Come out here." He carried Jesse to the women and sat down, settling Jesse onto his lap. "I want you to meet someone."

Angus took Moira's hand in his. "This is my new wife. Her name is Moira."

"I meeted Mora already."

Angus pushed his eyebrows up high for Jesse's benefit. "You did? I didn't see you at the wedding."

"I was there! Mommy couldn't come so I went and stayed with Mikey. Mommy stayed here. Matt did, too."

Angus's brows rose for real this time. "Really?"

He glanced at Jenny and her cheeks flushed. He started to laugh.

"Well, well, well," Angus said. "So *that's* how the engagement came about."

Jenny shrugged and looked away, but those cheeks stayed pink.

Angus was grateful that Jenny was still his friend.

Angela stepped out of the house with coffee and warm cookies.

Jesse took one and bit into it. He twisted around in Angus's lap to look at him and told him about what he'd done since Saturday.

Angus's heart melted at the normalcy of the scene. He loved this boy dearly. He wanted him close. And Jenny. And Matt.

Later, after he'd carried his luggage up to his room and he and Moira had sorted out where her clothes would go, Angus looked around and said, "This isn't half as pretty as your room is."

"Can I change it?"

"Yes."

"Are you sure you wouldn't mind?"

Angus grinned. "Not at all. I've grown fond of flowery sheets and the scent of roses."

He kissed his wife and their tongues danced.

Angus wrapped his arms around her and sighed. "I love you. I'm so glad you're here."

Moira pulled back to look at him. "You'll miss Matt and Jenny and Jesse, won't you?" Her eyes held an understanding he didn't expect to see there. They'd been apart for so many years yet she knew him well.

"I will. They mean a lot to me."

Angus stepped away. While he'd been unpacking, a wild idea had been running through his head. "Would you mind taking a drive with me?"

"Of course not."

Minutes later, they were out on the small highway that led to Ordinary.

Angus turned off at a narrow road and drove through a tunnel of overgrown lilacs.

"Those need to be pruned," Moira said. "They don't have as many blossoms as yours do."

"You noticed that already?"

"I noticed a lot of things about your ranch while I was waiting for you to talk to Jenny."

She shifted to watch him navigate the rough dirt road. "You did well for yourself over the years, Angus."

Her pride in him felt good.

"I want you to keep an open mind about this place until I can explain some things to you. Okay?"

"Okay."

The road opened into a clearing where the most run-down house this side of Billings listed in the sun and seemed about to fold in on itself.

"What is this place?" Moira asked.

"This is where Matt grew up." Angus told her as much as he knew about Matt's upbringing as well as the stuff he'd suspected. "I'm pretty sure Matt never wants to set foot here again."

He leaned across her to get a better look at the property.

"I want you to ignore the house and just look at the land."

They stepped out of the car. Moira turned full circle.

"Those lilacs would be beautiful if they were in bloom. And those pines around the back are stunning."

She touched the big rock in the centre of the clearing in the front yard. "I would plant perennials around this and surround those with a lawn."

She peered around. "This is a lovely, lovely piece of land. I see a lot of potential here."

She met his gaze. "I could certainly live here, but not—" she pointed to the old house and finished emphatically "—in *that*."

Angus smiled. Oh, yeah, she understood him well. "Are you thinking what I'm thinking?"

"Yes."

"Good. Let's go tell the kids."

MATT SAT at the kitchen table, so damn discouraged. There were plenty of foreclosures in northern Montana, but all big ranches, nothing that they could afford even at those bargain prices.

He'd checked out one cheaper place, but it had made his parents' house look good.

Jenny sat across from him, picking at her lunch desultorily.

"There's no way around it," he said. "I have to get a job and save up a down payment on a little house. I'll hire on elsewhere. I can't ask Angus to pay me a wage when I owe him money for those taxes. I'll see if he can wait a while for me to pay him back. You can live here for a year or two then we'll find a house in a small town somewhere. We just can't afford a ranch of our own."

"I don't want to live in a town," Jenny protested, but Matt cut her off.

"We'll see how much I can get for my land and add whatever I can save to it. Maybe then we can buy a small ranch."

There was a commotion at the front door followed by the hammer of little feet running down the hallway.

A second later, he burst into the kitchen. "Angus and Mora want to talk to you."

"Her name is Moira," Jenny said.

"That's what I said, Mora." Jesse ran back out of the room.

Matt stood and stared down at Jenny. "Don't move,"

he said, drinking his fill of her. Her hair was loose and it curled in long waves across her shoulders, echoing all the curves of her body. Matt was looking forward to spending the rest of his life learning all her nooks and crannies.

Moira and Angus sat in the living room. Matt greeted them both with a bear hug for Angus and a gentle hug for the pretty woman with him.

They suited each other, felt right together.

Jesse lay on the floor turning the pages of a new book that Angus must have brought home for him.

"Sit down," Angus said. "I have a proposition for both of you."

He was speaking to Matt and Jenny, but Jesse piped up. "Me, too?"

"Of course for you, too," Angus answered. "I wouldn't leave you out."

Angus took Moira's hand in his and smiled down at her. "Matt, we want to make you an offer on your land."

"What?" Matt felt his mouth fall open, but he couldn't seem to comprehend what Angus had just said.

"I'm serious, Matt." Angus named a figure that curled Matt's toes.

"It can't possibly be worth that much."

"Matt, because of everything that went wrong in that house, you haven't been able to see it clearly, but the land is real pretty."

"Really?"

"Yes," Moira answered. "It's beautiful."

"Still Creek runs through it," Angus said, as though that explained everything.

"But how can you possibly move all your cattle there? The property isn't large enough."

"Well," Angus said, "I'd like to sell the cattle to you when you buy this ranch."

Matt left his armchair. "What?" He paced to the window. "You're joking, right?"

Angus was dead serious. "What I'll pay for your land will make a solid down payment for this place. You'll have no trouble getting a mortgage for the rest."

"You're *not* joking?" Matt turned to look at Jenny. A wide grin graced her face. Her eyes glistened suspiciously.

Matt couldn't believe it yet. "You're a rancher, Angus. How can you give this up?"

"I lost my drive after I lost Kyle. The ranch just doesn't mean as much to me anymore. I thought I could get that back by marrying Jenny and having more children, but that was unreasonable."

He glanced at Moira and smiled. "We want to raise bison. Your land is perfect. We want it. We want to sell you this ranch. I'd say that makes life pretty well perfect for all of us."

Matt noticed Jesse smiling, but looking bewildered. He picked him up. "Jesse, remember your mom and I said we would have to move away from this ranch?"

Jesse bobbed his head.

"We won't have to anymore," Matt said. Lord, he felt his own eyes get damp. "We're going to live here forever."

Jesse fought to get out of Matt's arms then started to dance in the middle of the room. To Matt, he was goofy and wound up and perfect.

Jenny joined Matt and wrapped her arms around his waist. She rested her head on his chest and he gripped her hard.

How had all of this come out of that awful house he grew up in and his sorrow-filled childhood?

Angus stood and laid one hand on Matt's shoulder. He cleared his throat.

"There is a catch."

Matt should have known it couldn't possibly be as perfect as it sounded. Then he saw the twinkle in Angus's eyes.

"We want to tear down that old house and build our own."

Okay, Angus's already perfect offer just became even more so. Matt was no longer angry about the things that had happened in that house. Now he felt deep sorrow.

Getting rid of the house would close the last chapter of his childhood.

He shook Angus's hand. "It's a deal."

Out of the blue, Angus looked unsure of himself. "There is one more stipulation."

"What?" Matt asked warily.

"I would like to be honorary grandfather to your children."

"Cripes, Angus, of course!" Then Matt was hugging both Angus and Jenny, his two best friends in the world.

Jenny pulled out of his arms and knelt in front of their son.

"Would you like Angus to be your grandfather?"

"Yeah!" Jesse pointed to Moira. "Is she my grandma?"

Jenny turned to the older woman. "I don't know. Give me time."

Moira said, "I understand."

"Jesse," Jenny said. "There's even more good news. Matt is your daddy."

"You mean like Angus was gonna be my daddy after you married him? Now Matt is instead?"

"Matt isn't going to be your father because I'm marrying him. Matt *is* your daddy, your really, truly, forever-after father."

Jesse started dancing again.

Matt wasn't sure how much happiness one body could hold, but he did know that the more he held, the bigger he felt. He was learning that there was no limit to how much a man could grow, or how much he could become.

EPILOGUE

ROSE SQUIRMED in Matt's arms as he stepped out of the church and into the bright frosty sunshine. He sheltered her with his chest, provided shade with his shoulder and she settled.

Jenny and Jesse walked on either side of him, just as they had when Matt and Jenny had gotten married last June. They'd conceived little Rose soon after.

Rose's godparents, Angus and Moira, followed.

Reverend Wright had performed a beautiful baptism ceremony.

Many of Ordinary's citizens who were now his friends gathered around.

Angel Donovan stood in the crowd and smiled at Matt. They'd gotten to know each other over the holidays. Missy and Angel had joined Matt, Jenny and Jesse for Christmas dinner, along with Angus and Moira, just like a real family. Angel hadn't known who her real father was, as Missy had always refused to tell her. Angel was having trouble dealing with Missy's omission, but she was working on it. One thing she had told Matt was that she liked having a brother.

Like her mother, Angel was a knockout. Matt saw the way some of the younger men were looking at his sister, and scowled at a couple of them, feeling very much like a big brother. But he knew that Angel was a grown woman who would make her own choices.

Their footsteps crunched on dry late-February snow.

Hank and Amy wanted pictures. Matt stopped on the steps, pulled his wife against his side and kissed her, long enough and passionately enough that the crowd hooted.

When he finished, Jenny's cheeks were rosy. She smiled and picked up Jesse.

Angus and Moira stood behind them.

Camera shutters clicked.

Matt thought back to the first time he'd ever made love to Jenny. He remembered sitting in his truck and staring at his parents' house. Lightning had lit the place up like a photographic flash, catching a freeze-frame image of a sad history.

That image had defined his life for too many years. No longer.

The house was gone now. Angus and Moira had built a pretty Victorian home in its place and Matt and Jenny and Jesse visited often.

That clearing held good memories now.

Hank said, "One more," and took a last shot.

Matt knew what these images would show—a happy couple with their two children, in front of another happy couple, the honorary grandparents, all of them surrounded by brilliant white snow.

While the photos were being shot, Jesse pointed to each member of his family and named them. In the second-to-last photo, he pointed to Rose and said, "That's my sister, Rose."

In the last photo that Hank shot, Jesse pointed to Matt and said, "That's my dad."

Matt ruffled Jesse's hair and then kissed Rose's tiny pink forehead.

Yeah. Matt was a dad. And he was here to stay.

* * * * *

We hope you enjoyed reading

HOME ON THE RANCH: MONTANA.

If you liked these stories, then you're in luck—Harlequin has a Western romance for every mood!

Whether you're feeling a little suspenseful or need a heartwarming pick-me-up, you will find a delectable cowboy who will sweep you off your feet.

Just look for cowboys on the covers of Harlequin Series books.

Available wherever books and ebooks are sold.

HTHMS0814-3

"You had my son's DNA tested, why?" Jessa demanded. But that was as far as she got. Her chest started pumping as if starved for air, and she dropped back and let the now closed door support her.

The dark circles under her eyes let him know she hadn't been sleeping.

Neither had he.

It'd taken every ounce of willpower for him not to rush back to the hospital to get a better look at the little boy.

"How's Liam?" he asked.

She glared at him for so long that Cooper wasn't sure she'd answer. "He's better, but you already know that. You've called at least a dozen times checking on his condition."

He had. Cooper also knew Liam was doing so well that he'd probably be released from the hospital tomorrow.

"He'll make a full recovery?" Cooper asked.

Again, she glared. "Yes. In fact, he already wants to get up and run around. Now, why?" she added without pausing.

Cooper pulled in a long breath that he would need and sank down on the edge of his desk. "Because of the blood type match. And because we never found my son's body."

Even though she'd no doubt already come up with that

answer, Jessa huffed and threw her hands in the air. "And what? You think I found him on the riverbank and pretended to adopt him? Well, I didn't, and Liam's not your son. I want you to put a stop to that DNA test."

Cooper shook his head. "If you're sure he's not my son, then the test will come back as no match."

Her glare got worse. "You're doing this to get back at me." Her breath broke, and the tears came.

Oh, man.

He didn't want this. Not with both of them already emotional wrecks. They were both powder kegs right now, and the flames were shooting all around them. Still, he went closer, and because all those emotions had apparently made him dumber than dirt, Cooper slipped his arm around her.

She fought him. Of course. Jessa clearly didn't want his comfort, sympathy or anything else other than an assurance to put a stop to that test. Still, he held on despite her fists pushing against his chest. One more ragged sob, however, and she sagged against him.

There it was again. That tug deep down in his body. Yeah, dumber than dirt, all right. His body just didn't seem to understand that an attractive woman in his arms could mean nothing.

Even when Jessa looked up at him.

That tug tugged a little harder. Because, yeah, she was attractive, and if the investigation and accusations hadn't cropped up, he might have considered asking her out.

So much for that plan.

Find out what happens next in
MAVERICK SHERIFF
by USA TODAY *bestselling author Delores Fossen,*
available September 2014, only from
Harlequin® Intrigue®.

American Romance®

You Can't Hide in Forever

The minute he lays eyes on Forever's new doctor, Brett Murphy knows the town—and he—won't be the same. Alisha Cordell is raising the temperature of every male within miles. But the big-city blonde isn't looking to put down roots. The saloon owner and rancher will just have to change the reticent lady doc's mind.

A week after she caught her fiancé cheating, Alisha was on a train headed for a Texas town that was barely a blip on the map. So she's stunned at how fast the place is growing on her. That includes the sexy cowboy with the sassy smile and easygoing charm. Brett's also been burned by love, but he's eager for a second chance…with Alisha. Is she ready to make Brett—and Forever—part of her long-term plans?

Look for
Her Forever Cowboy
by *USA TODAY* bestselling author
MARIE FERRARELLA

from the *Forever, Texas* miniseries from
Harlequin® American Romance®.

Available September 2014
wherever books and ebooks are sold.

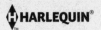

Harlequin® American Romance®

A Little Bit Country…

Emma Donovan ran off to Nashville when she was young and full of dreams. Now she's back home in Colorado with a little more common sense. And that sense is telling her not to count on Jamie Westland. He won't be around long—not with his big-time career in New York City.

Jamie's never felt at home, not with his adopted family, not with himself. Now, on his grandfather's ranch, the pieces of his life are coming together in a way that feels right. And Emma has so much to do with it. But when an opportunity comes along back in New York, he has to decide between his old life and the promise of a new one…with Emma.

Cowboy in the Making
by JULIE BENSON

Available September 2014
wherever books and ebooks are sold.

NOT JUST A COWBOY

Don't miss the first story in the
TEXAS RESCUE miniseries
by **Caro Carson**

Texan oil heiress Patricia Cargill is particular when
it comes to her men, but there's just something
about Luke Waterson she can't resist. Maybe it's
that he's a drop-dead gorgeous rescue fireman
and ranch hand! Luke, who lights long-dormant
fires in Patricia, has also got his fair share of secrets.
Can the cowboy charm the socialite into a
happily-ever-after?

Available September 2014
wherever books and ebooks are sold.